Other books of the *In Her Name* series by Michael R. Hicks:

Book 1: *Empire*

Book 2: *Confederation*

Book 3: *Final Battle*

In Her Name (Omnibus Edition)

IN HER NAME

FIRST CONTACT

ISBN: 978-0692005866

IN HER NAME: FIRST CONTACT

Published by Imperial Guard Publishing
www.kreelanwarrior.com

Michael R. Hicks

In Her Name
First Contact

*For all the men and women
whose service and sacrifice keep us free.*

FORWARD

I can sympathize with how George Lucas must have felt when he produced the *Star Wars* saga. While most of us didn't realize it when the original *Star Wars* movie first came out, Lucas was really starting at the mid-point of the story, and took us through the end of the tale with *The Empire Strikes Back* and *Return of the Jedi*. Then, after an agonizing wait, he told us the beginning of the story with the second trilogy.

Likewise, although I make no claim to being in the same league as Lucas, I unwittingly did something similar with the *In Her Name* novels. When I first wrote the story back in the mid-1990s, I really told the end of it first like Lucas did, with the first trilogy - *In Her Name: Empire*, followed by *Confederation*, and *Final Battle* - telling the tale through a young hero's eyes of how the Human-Kreelan war was finally resolved.

Taking place a hundred years before the events described in *Empire* and its companion novels, *In Her Name: First Contact* describes how that devastating war began, starting with the initial encounter between humans and the Kreelan Empire. Many stories have been written about first contact situations, of course, but I hope you'll find that this one has enough of a different twist on a well-worn theme to be both entertaining and even a bit thought-provoking.

For those readers who have enjoyed the previously published trilogy (or the omnibus edition - *In Her Name* - which contains all three under one cover), you'll get to learn a bit more about the Kreelan culture and even get reacquainted with one of the main supporting characters from the original trilogy. As you've come to expect, there will be plenty of gritty action - this is war, after all! - and lots of characters to follow and, hopefully, empathize with.

So, get reading and see how the saga begins!

Acknowledgements

I find myself in the happy situation of having a number of people to thank for the five months of hectic writing and editing "fun" that led to the publication of this book.

First and foremost, I'd like to thank the readers who enjoyed the original trilogy (and the omnibus edition) and encouraged me to pick up writing again after a hiatus of many years. In particular, my friends at KindleBoards - you know who you are! - deserve a lot of credit for getting me back in the writing game, as well as for making the original novel(s) a success.

For Stephanie Hansen, my "alpha reader," I owe a debt of thanks for taking the time to read through the original drafts - straight from the keyboard, as it were - to dig out bloopers and make suggestions about the story. She claims she enjoyed the process, but it's hard to believe she doesn't have a masochistic streak a mile wide.

Mindy Schwartz, my primary "beta reader," did an extraordinary job of helping me polish the text even more with a ton of editing suggestions. She was really tough on me, and I sometimes cringed and sometimes laughed at what she found. It was an enjoyable, if sometimes humbling, process, and she really helped make this a better story and made me a better writer. That she enjoyed the book was simply icing on the cake.

Finally, to Jan, the boys, and Mom and Dad: thank you, as always, for the love and support you've given me. I couldn't succeed at anything without you.

ONE

Captain Owen McClaren was extremely tense, although a casual observer would never have thought so. Commanding the survey vessel *TNS Aurora*, he was one of the best officers in the fleet, and to his crew he had never appeared as anything but calm and in control. Even when one of the ship's newly refitted reactors had suffered a breach during their last run into drydock, McClaren's deep voice had never wavered, his fatherly face had never betrayed a hint of fear or apprehension as he personally directed the engineering watch to contain the breach. A man of unusual physical and moral courage, he was the perfect captain for the exploratory missions the *Aurora* and her sister ships mounted into distant space, seeking new homes for humanity.

McClaren had made thousands of jumps in his twenty-year career, but every one was like the very first: an adrenaline joyride. As the transpace sequence wound down to zero, his heart would begin to pound and his muscles tensed like spring steel. It wasn't fear that made him react that way, although there were enough things that could go wrong with a jump to make fear a natural enough reaction.

No, what made the forty-three-year-old former middleweight boxing champion of the Terran Naval Academy hold the arms of his command chair in a white-knuckle grip wasn't fear. It was anticipation. To *Aurora's* captain, every jump - particularly out here in uncharted space - was a potential winning lottery ticket, the discovery of a lifetime. No matter where the *Aurora* wound up, as long as she arrived safely, there was bound to be a wealth of astrogational information to help human starships travel ever farther from Man's birthplace: Earth.

On rare occasions, precious jewels - habitable planets - were to be found. Finding such systems was the primary goal of the survey ships. McClaren was currently the fleet's leading "ace," with twelve habitable planets to his credit in return for nearly fifteen years of ship-time, sailing through uncharted space.

"Stand by for transpace sequence," the pilot announced, her words echoing through every passageway and compartment in the *Aurora's* five hundred meter length.

McClaren tensed even more, his strong arm and back muscles flexing instinctively as if he were back in the ring, preparing to land a solid upper cut to the chin of an imaginary opponent. But his calm expression never wavered. "Very well," he answered, his dark brown eyes drinking in the growing torrent of information on the navigation display.

"Computer auto-lock engaged," interjected a faux female voice reassuringly. McClaren always had to suppress a grimace: the one thing he had never liked about *Aurora* was the computer's voice. It reminded him too much of his first wife.

For the next few seconds, the crew was little more than excess baggage as the ship's computer guided the transition from hyperspace back into the Einsteinian universe with a precision measured in quadrillionths of a second. While the bridge, which was buried deep in the *Aurora's* core habitation section, had no direct observation windows, the wraparound display depicted the eerie streams of light that swirled around the ship in complete detail. But what the human eye saw in the maelstrom of quantum physics beyond the ship's hyperdrive field was an illusion. It was real in one sense, but in another it wasn't. Space and time as humans commonly understood it did not exist in this realm. As the captain of a starship, McClaren had to understand both the theory and the practical application of hyperspace and the means to travel through it. But he was content in the knowledge that he never could have come up with the breakthroughs that allowed this miracle to happen: he stood on the shoulders of the scientific giants who had made the first test jump into hyperspace long before he was born.

While in hyperspace, the display would normally show the computer's assessment of the relative location of stars and other known celestial waypoints as the ship moved along its straight-line (relatively speaking) course. But McClaren always cleared the display to show what was really outside the ship just before they dropped back into normal space. It was a sight he never tired of.

"Ten seconds..." the computer's voice began counting down to the transition. "Five...four...three...two...one....sequence initiated. Hyperspace Engines disengaged."

The display suddenly shifted, the swirling light streams condensing into a bright yellow sun against a background of stars. McClaren knew that the system had several planets; gravitational perturbations observed from their last jump point had confirmed that much. The question was whether there were any orbiting at a distance from the star where water could exist as a liquid. For where there was liquid water, there was the possibility of carbon-based life. The trick now was to find them. Planets were huge close up, but in the vast expanse of a star system they seemed incredibly small.

"Engineering confirms hyperspace engines are secure, sir," the executive officer, Lieutenant Commander Rajesh Kumar, reported. "Engineering is ready to answer all bells, and the ship is secured for normal space."

Nodding his thanks to his exec, McClaren turned to the most important person currently on the bridge: the navigator. "Raisa, what's the word?"

The navigator looked like she would have given McClaren a run for his money in the boxing ring. Big-boned and heavily muscled, Lieutenant Raisa Marisova had in fact been a champion wrestler in her college years. But it was her genius at stellar astrogation that had won her a place on the *Aurora's* all-volunteer crew.

"Well..." she murmured as she rechecked her readings for what McClaren knew was probably the fifth time in the few moments the ship had dropped back into normal space. Raisa was always able to confirm the ship's emergence point so quickly because her calculations for pointing the various telescopes and other sensors at known stars to make a positional fix were always so precise. "It seems we are...right where we are supposed to be," she said as she turned and smiled at her captain, "give or take a few meters. We're above the ecliptic plane based on our pre-jump survey information. Now it's up to the survey team to find your next habitable planet, captain."

McClaren grinned, then opened a channel to the entire ship. "Well, crew, it looks like we've made another successful jump, and emerged right on target. The bad news is that we're even farther out in the Middle of Nowhere. But that's what they pay us for. Great job, everyone." The last few words were more than just a token verbal pat on the back: he truly meant it. Unlike most transits that took regular ships into hyperspace for a few days or even a week or two, the *Aurora* routinely made jumps that lasted for weeks or months. While McClaren's crew made it look easy, he knew quite well that an amazing amount of planning and preparation went into every jump, and his crew followed it up with painstaking diligence every moment they were in hyperspace. It wasn't just that they didn't want to wind up somewhere other than where they had planned, or because their captain expected perfection. It was because they had no intention of settling for second best. Period. "Everybody gets an extra round on me when we get back to the barn. Carry on."

The bridge crew grinned at one another: the captain ran up a huge bar tab on every mission, but he never failed to deliver when the ship made port.

They had no way of knowing that all but one of them would be dead in a few short hours.

***

The stranger's arrival was no surprise to the Imperial warships that orbited the Settlements on the third and fourth planets from the star. While even the greatly advanced technology of the Empire could not track ships while in hyperspace, they could easily detect the gravity spikes of vessels about to emerge in normal space. The stranger had been detected many hours before, as measured in the time of humans.

While this system was at the distant edge of the Empire, far from the Homeworld and the Empress, its defenses were not lacking: of the dozens of starships in orbit around the two settled worlds and the hundreds plying the asteroid belt, four were battlecruisers built within the last century. Humans might have considered them old, until they understood that the warriors of the Empire had sailed among the stars for over one hundred thousand of Earth's years. Even the most ancient of Her warships still plying the void between the stars was tens of thousands of years more advanced than the arriving stranger. Humans would barely have recognized them as starships.

But the warriors charged with protecting this far-flung system had no way of knowing the primitive nature of the incoming stranger. Nor would they have cared. The Empire had encountered other sentient races over the millennia, and the first contact protocol was no different now than it had been in ages past: the stranger would be greeted with overwhelming force.

In unison, the four enormous battlecruisers left orbit for the gravity anomaly at maximum velocity, safe behind shields that could protect them from titanic energy discharges and made them all but invisible to anything but direct visual observation.

Behind them, smaller warships and the planetary defense systems prepared to welcome the new arrival should it prove more than a match for the great warships sent to greet it.

***

"Bridge, this is Survey..."

Captain McClaren frowned despite himself. He knew that Lieutenant Amundsen's survey team worked fast, but they had been in-system less than fifteen minutes. It often took days for them to identify the orbits of any planets in the temperate zone unless they had extensive perturbation data on the star or stars in the system. And that they rarely had: humanity's rapid expansion to the stars didn't allow for years-long observations of any given star. His frown deepened as he took in the expression on Amundsen's face in the comms display. The normally very reserved man was uncharacteristically excited. And just as frightened. "What is it, Jens?"

"Sir..." Amundsen began, his pale blue eyes darting away momentarily to another display. "Captain...we've confirmed not just one, but *two* planets in the temperate zone..."

"Hot damn!" McClaren couldn't help himself. One planet that might have liquid water was miracle enough. Their pre-jump analysis had suggested there was one, but two had been too much to hope for. "That's fantastic!"

"Sir...they're both inhabited," Amundsen said in hoarse whisper. Normally a quiet man, often more at home with the stars and planets than his fellow human beings, the volume of his voice dropped with every word. "We didn't have to find their orbits. We found them from their neutrino and infrared readings." He paused. "I've...I've never seen anything like this. Even Sol system doesn't have this level of activity. The two planets in the temperate zone are highly industrialized. There are other points of activity throughout the asteroid belt, and on several moons orbiting a solitary gas giant. We have also observed ships through the primary telescope. Hundreds of them. They are...nothing like ours."

The captain sat back, stunned. *First contact*, he thought. Humans had explored thousands of star systems and endless volumes of space, but had never once encountered another sentient species. They had found life aplenty on the hundred-odd discovered worlds that would support human life or could be terraformed. From humble bacteria to massive predators that would have been at home with Earth's dinosaurs, life in the Universe was as expansive as it was diverse if you looked long and far enough. But no one had discovered a single sign of sentient life beyond the mark *homo sapiens* had left behind in his celestial travels.

Until now.

"Jesus," the captain breathed, conscious now of the entire bridge crew staring at him. They hadn't heard Amundsen's words, but they immediately picked up on the captain's reaction. "XO," he ordered, pulling his mind back to the here and now, "let's have the first contact protocols." He looked pointedly at Kumar. "I want to make damn sure these folks understand we're harmless."

"Aye, sir," Kumar replied crisply as his fingers flew over his terminal. "Coming up on display one." A segment of the bridge wraparound screen darkened as the standing orders for first contact appeared.

"Lieutenant Amundsen," McClaren ordered, "let's see some of these ships of yours on display two."

"Sir." Amundsen's face bobbed about slightly in the captain's comms terminal as he patched the telescope feed to another segment of the main bridge display.

"Lord of All," someone whispered. The *Aurora's* primary telescope was nearly ten meters across, and dominated the phalanx of survey instruments mounted in the massive spherical section that made up the ship's bow. Normally used to search for and map stellar and planetary bodies, it could also be pressed into service to provide high magnification visuals of virtually anything, even moving objects that were relatively close, such as nearby (in terms of a stellar system) ships.

But what it showed now was as unlike the *Aurora* as she herself was unlike a wooden sailing ship. While the *Aurora* was largely a collection of cylindrical sections attached to a sturdy keel that ran from the engineering section at the stern to the instrumentation cluster at the bow, the alien ship displayed on the bridge display was insectile in appearance, her hull made up of sleek curves that gave McClaren the impression of a gigantic wasp.

"Why does the focus keep shifting?" Marisova asked into the sudden silence that had descended on the bridge. The alien vessel shimmered in the display as if a child were twisting an imaginary focus knob for the primary telescope back and forth, taking the image in and out of focus.

"That's what I was about to say," Amundsen answered, McClaren now having shifted the survey team leader's image onto yet a third segment of the bridge display. Before he had seemed both excited and frightened. Now it was clear that fear was crowding out his excitement. "That is one of at least four ships that is heading directly toward us from the outer habitable planet. The reason you are seeing the focusing anomaly is because the ships are moving at an incredible velocity, and the telescope cannot hold the image in alignment. Even what you see here has been enhanced with post-processing." He visibly gulped. "Captain, they knew we were coming, hours - possibly even a few days - before we arrived. They knew right where we were going to be, and they must have left orbit before we arrived. They *must* have. It's theoretically possible to predict a hyperspace emergence, but...we now know that it's not just a theory." He looked again at one of his off-screen displays, then back to the monitor. "I don't know exactly what their initial acceleration rate was, but they're now moving so fast that the light we're seeing reflected from their hulls is noticeably blue-shifted. I estimate their current velocity is roughly five percent of C."

Five percent of the speed of light, McClaren thought, incredulous. *Nearly fifteen thousand kilometers per second. And they didn't take much time to reach it.*

"I'm trying to estimate their acceleration rate, but it must be-"

"A lot higher than we could ever achieve," McClaren cut him off, looking closely at the wavering image of the alien vessel. "Any idea how big she is?"

"I have no data to estimate her length," Amundsen replied, "but I estimate the beam of this ship to be roughly five hundred meters. I can only assume that her length is considerably more, but we won't know until we get a more oblique view."

"That ship is five hundred meters *wide*?" Kumar asked, incredulous. *Aurora* herself was barely that long from stem to stern. While she was by no means the largest starship built by human hands, she was usually the largest vessel in whatever port she put into.

"Yes," Amundsen told him. "And the other three ships are roughly the same size."

"Christ," someone whispered.

"Raj," McClaren said, turning to his exec. "Thoughts?"

"Communications is running the initial first contact sequence now." He turned to face the captain. "Our signals will take roughly thirty minutes to reach the inner planets, but those ships..." He shook his head. "They're close enough now that they should have already received our transmissions. If they're listening." He looked distinctly uncomfortable. "If I were a betting man, I would say those were warships."

McClaren nodded grimly. "Comms," he looked over at Ensign John Waverly, "keep stepping through the first contact communications sequence. Just make sure that we're listening, too."

"I'm on it, sir," the young man replied. Waverly seemed incredibly young, but like the rest of *Aurora's* crew, he did his job exceptionally well. "I'm well versed in the FCP procedures, sir. So far, though, I haven't come across any emissions anywhere in the standard spectrum, other than what Lieutenant Amundsen's team have already reported. If they use anything anywhere in the radio frequency band, we're sure not seeing it. And I haven't identified any coherent light sources, either."

So, no radio and no communications lasers, McClaren thought uneasily. Even though the aliens knew that company was coming, they had remained silent. Or if they were talking, they were using some form of transmission that was beyond what *Aurora* was capable of seeing or hearing. Maybe the aliens were beyond such mundane things as radio- and light-based communications?

"How long until those ships get here?" McClaren asked Amundsen, whose worried face still stared out from the bridge display screen. *Aurora* herself was motionless relative to her emergence point: McClaren never moved in-system on a survey until they knew much more about their environment than they did now. And it made for a much more convenient reference point for a rapid jump-out.

"At their current velocity, they would overshoot us in just under three hours. But, of course, they will need to decelerate to meet us..."

"That depends on their intentions," Kumar interjected. "They could attack as they pass by..."

"Or they could simply stop," Marisova observed quietly. Everyone turned to gape at her. "We know nothing about their drive systems," she explained. "Nothing about those ships registers on our sensors other than direct visuals. What if they achieved their current velocity nearly instantaneously when they decided to head out to meet us?"

"Preposterous," Amundsen exclaimed. "That's simply not possible!"

"But-"

"Enough, people," McClaren said quietly. "Beyond the obviously impressive capabilities of the aliens, it all boils down to this: do we stay or do we go?" He looked around at his bridge crew, then opened a channel to the entire ship. "Crew, this is the captain. As I'm sure most of you are now aware, the system we've entered is inhabited. We're in a first contact situation. The *only* first contact situation anyone has ever faced. So what we do now is going to become part of The Book that will tell others either how to do it right, or how not to do it if we royally screw things up. I'll be completely honest with you: I'm not happy with the situation. We've got four big ships heading toward us in an awful hurry. They could be warships. I don't blame whoever these folks are for sending out an armed welcoming committee. If it were my home, I'd send some warships out to take a look, too.

"But I'd also make sure to send some diplomats along: people who want to talk with their new neighbors. What bothers me is that we haven't seen anything - from the ships or the two inhabited planets - that looks like any sort of communication. Maybe they're just using something we can't pick up. Maybe the ships coming our way are packed with scientists and ambassadors and they want to make it a big surprise. I just don't know.

"What I do know is that we've got about three hours to make a decision and take action. My inclination is to stay. Not to try and score the first handshake with an alien, but because...it's our first opportunity to say hello to another sentient race. We've been preparing for this moment since before the very first starship left Earth. It's a risk, but it's also the greatest opportunity humanity has ever had.

"So here's what we're going to do. We've got a little bit of time to discuss our options before our new friends reach us. Department heads, talk to your people. Get a feel for what they're thinking. Then all department heads and the senior chiefs are to meet in my ready room in exactly one hour. I'll make the final decision on whether we stay or go, but I want to hear what you all have to say. That is all." He punched the button on the touchpad, closing the circuit.

"In the meantime," he told Kumar and Marisova, "get an emergency jump sequence lined up. Pick a destination other than our inbound vector. If these ships come in with guns blazing, the last thing I want to do is point them back the way we came, toward home."

On the display screen, the alien ship and her sisters continued toward them.

***

The four battlecruisers sailed quickly to meet the alien vessel, but they hardly revealed their true capabilities. While it was now clear that the alien ship was extremely primitive, those who guarded the Empire took nothing for granted. They would reveal no more about themselves than absolutely necessary until they were sure the new arrival posed no threat. The Empire had not lasted through the ages by leaving anything to chance.

Aboard the lead ship, a group of warriors prepared for battle with the unknown, while healers and other castes made ready to learn all there was to know about the strangers.

They did not have much longer to wait.

***

There was standing room only in the captain's ready room an hour later. At the table sat the six department heads, responsible for the primary functional areas of the ship, the *Aurora's* senior chief, and the captain. Along the walls of the now-cramped compartment stood the senior enlisted member of each department and the ship's two midshipmen. The XO and the bridge crew remained at their stations, although they were tied in through a video feed on the bridge wraparound display.

The emotional tension ran high among the people in the room, McClaren could easily see. But from the body language and the expressions on their faces it wasn't from fear, but excited anticipation. It was an emotion he fully shared.

"I'm not going to waste any time on preliminaries," he began. "You all know what's going on and what's at stake. According to the Survey Department," he nodded at Amundsen, who was the only one around the table who looked distinctly unhappy, "the ships haven't changed course or velocity. So it looks like they're either going to blow by us - which I think would probably be bad news - or their technology is so radically advanced that they can stop on a proverbial dime."

At that, the survey leader's frown grew more pronounced, turning his normally pale face into a grimace.

"Amundsen?" McClaren asked. "You've got something to say. Spit it out."

"I think Lieutenant Marisova was right," he said grudgingly, nodding toward the video pickup that showed the meeting to the bridge crew. But McClaren knew that it wasn't because Marisova had said it. It was because he was afraid to believe that what she said could possibly be true, or even close to the truth. "I don't believe they could accelerate to their current velocity instantaneously, but even assuming several days' warning - even weeks! - the acceleration they must have achieved would have to have been...unbelievable." He shook his head. "No. I believe those ships will not simply pass by us. They will slow down and rendezvous with us sometime in the next two hours, decelerating at a minimum of two hundred gees. Probably much more."

A chill ran down McClaren's spine. *Aurora* had the most efficient reactionless drives in service by any of the many worlds colonized by Mankind, and was one of the few to be fitted with artificial gravity - a recent innovation - and acceleration dampers. She wasn't nearly as fast as a courier ship, certainly, but for a military survey vessel she was no slouch. But two hundred gees? Not even close.

"Robotic ships?" Aubrey Hannan, the chief of the Engineering Section suggested. "They could certainly handle that sort of acceleration."

"It doesn't matter," McClaren interjected, gently but firmly steering the conversation from interesting - but essentially useless - speculation back to the issue at hand. "From my perspective, it doesn't matter how fast the aliens can maneuver. We're not a warship, and I have no intention of masquerading as one. It's clear they have radically advanced technology. That's not necessarily a surprise; we could have just as easily stumbled upon a world in the pre-atomic era, and we would be the high-tech aliens. Our options remain the same: stay and say hello, or jump out with what I hope is a fat safety margin before they get here." He glanced around and his gaze landed on the junior midshipman. "Midshipman Sato, what's your call?"

Ichiro Sato, already standing ramrod straight against the bulkhead, stiffened even further. All of nineteen years old, he was the youngest member of the crew. Extremely courteous, conscientious, and intelligent, he was well respected by the other members of the crew, although his rigid outer shell was a magnet for good-natured ribbing. Exceptionally competent and a fast learner, he kept quietly to himself. He was one of a select few from the Terran Naval Academy who were chosen to spend one or more of their academy years aboard ship as advanced training as junior officers. It was a great opportunity, but came with a hefty commitment: deployed midshipmen had to continue their academy studies while also performing their duties aboard ship.

"Sir..." Sato momentarily gulped for air, McClaren's question having caught him completely off-guard.

The captain felt momentarily guilty for putting Sato on the spot first, but he had a reason. "Relax, Ichiro," McClaren told him. "I called this meeting for ideas. The senior officers - including myself - and the chiefs have years of preconceived notions drilled into our heads. We've got years of experience, yes, but this situation calls for a fresh perspective. If you were in my shoes, what would your decision be? There's no right or wrong answer to this one."

While Ichiro's features didn't betray it, the captain's last comment caused him even more consternation. He had been brought up in a traditional Japanese family on Nagano, where - according to his father - everything was either *right* or it was *wrong*; there was no in-between. And more often than not, anything Ichiro did was *wrong*. That was the main reason Ichiro had decided to apply for service in the Terran Navy when he was sixteen: to spite his father and escape the tyranny of his house, and to avoid the stifling life of a salaryman trapped in the web of a hegemonic corporate world. Earth's global military services accepted applicants from all but a few rogue worlds, and Ichiro's test scores and academic record had opened the door for him to enter the Terran Naval Academy. There, too, most everything was either right or wrong. The difference between the academy and his home was that in the academy, Ichiro was nearly always *right*. His unfailing determination to succeed had given him a sense of confidence he had never known before, putting him at the head of his class and earning him a position aboard the *Aurora*.

That realization, and his desperate desire not to lose face in front of the captain and ship's officers, gave him back his voice. "Sir. I believe we should stay and greet the ships."

McClaren nodded, wondering what had just been going on in the young man's mind. "Okay, you picked door number one. The question now is why?"

"Because, sir, that is why we are here, isn't it?" Loosening up slightly from his steel-rod pose, he turned to look at the other faces around the room, his voice suddenly filled with a passion that none of his fellow crew members would have ever thought possible. "While our primary mission is to find new habitable worlds, we really are explorers - discoverers - of whatever deep space may hold. With every jump we search for the unknown, things that no one else has ever seen. Maybe we will not find what we hope. Perhaps these aliens are friendly, perhaps not. There is great risk in everything we do. But, having found the first sentient race other than humankind, can we in good conscience simply leave without doing all we can to establish contact, even at the risk of our own destruction?"

The captain nodded, impressed more by the young man's unexpected burst of emotion than his words. But his words held their own merit: they precisely echoed McClaren's own feelings. That was exactly why he had spent so much of his career in survey.

"Well said, Ichiro," he told the young man. The two midshipmen on either side of Sato grinned and nudged him as if to say, *Good job.* Most of those seated at the table nodded or murmured their agreement. "So, there's an argument - and I believe a good one - for staying. Who's got one for bailing out right now?"

"I'll take that one, sir," Raj Kumar spoke up from the bridge, his image appearing on the primary screen in the ready room. "I myself agree with Midshipman Sato that we should stay. But one compelling argument for leaving now is to make sure that the news of this discovery gets back home. If the aliens should turn out to be hostile and this ship is taken, or even if we should suffer some unexpected mishap, Earth and the rest of human space may never know until they're attacked. And we have no way to let anyone know of our discovery without jumping back to the nearest communications relay."

That produced a lot of frowns on the faces around the table. Most of them had thought of this already, of course, but having it voiced directly gave it more substance.

Kumar went on, "That's also a specification in the first contact protocols, that one of the top priorities is to get word back home. But the bottom line is that any actions taken are at the captain's discretion based on the situation as he or she sees it."

"Right," McClaren told everyone. "Getting word back home is the only real reason I've been able to come up with myself for leaving now that isn't tied to fear of the unknown. And since all of us signed up to get paid to go find the unknown, as the good midshipman pointed out, those reasons don't count." He turned to the woman sitting to his left. "Chief, what's your take?"

Master Chief Brenda Harkness was the senior enlisted member of the crew, and her word carried a great deal of weight with McClaren. Completely at odds with the stereotype of someone of her rank, she was a tall, slim, and extremely attractive woman in her late thirties. But no one who had ever worked with her for more than five minutes ever took her for granted: she was a hard-core Navy lifer who never dished out bullshit and refused to tolerate it from anyone else. She would move mountains to help anyone who needed it, but her beautiful deep hazel eyes could just as easily burn holes in the skin of anyone foolish enough to cross her.

"I think we should stay, captain," she said, a light Texas drawl flavoring her smooth voice. "I completely agree with the XO's concerns about getting word of this back home, but with the alien ships so close now..." She shook her head. "I can't imagine that they'd be anything but insulted if we just up and disappeared on them."

"And the crew?" McClaren asked.

"Everyone I had a chance to talk to - and that was most of them - wanted to stay. A lot of them are uneasy about those ships, but as you said, we just happen to be the 'primitives' in this situation. We'd be stupid to not be afraid, sir. But I think we'd be even more stupid to just pack up and go home."

All of the other department heads nodded their agreement. Each had talked to their people, too, and almost without exception the crew had wanted to stay and meet with the aliens.

It was what McClaren expected. He would have been shocked had they come to any other conclusion. "Okay, that settles it. We stay." That brought a round of bright, excited smiles to everyone but Amundsen, whose face was locked in an unhappy grimace. "But here's the deal: the XO and navigator have worked out an emergency jump sequence, just in case. We'll spool up the jump engines to the pre-interlock stage and hold them there until we feel more confident of the aliens' intentions. We can keep the engines spooled like that for several hours without running any risks in engineering. If those ships are friendly, we get to play galactic tourist and buy them the first round at the bar.

"But if they're not," he looked pointedly at Amundsen, "we engage the jump interlock and the navigation computer will have us out of here in two minutes." That made the survey leader slightly less unhappy, but only slightly. "Okay, does anybody have anything else they want to add before we set up the reception line?"

"Sir..." Sato said formally, again at a position of attention.

"Go ahead, son."

"Captain, I know this may sound foolish," he glanced at Amundsen, who was at the table with his back to Sato, "but should we not also take steps to secure the navigation computer in case the ships prove hostile? If they took the ship, there is probably little they would learn of our technology that would be of value to them. But the navigation charts..."

"It's already taken care of, midshipman," Kumar reassured him from the bridge with an approving smile. Second year midshipmen like Sato weren't expected to know anything about the first contact protocols, but the boy was clearly thinking on his feet. Kumar's already high respect for him rose yet another notch. "That's on the very short list of 'non-discretionary' actions on first contact. We've already prepared a soft wipe of the data, and a team from engineering is setting charges around the primary core." He held up both hands, then simulated pushing buttons down with his thumbs. "If we get into trouble, *Aurora's* hull is all they'll walk away with."

And us, Amundsen thought worriedly.

***

The alien ship had activated its jump drive. While primitive, it was clearly based on the same principles used by Imperial starships. Such technology was an impressive accomplishment for any species, and gave the warriors hope that once again they had found worthy adversaries among the stars.

But the aliens would not - could not - be allowed to leave. Together, the battlecruisers moved in...

***

"Jump engines are spooled up, captain," Kumar reported from his console. The jump coordinates were locked in. All they had to do was engage the computer interlock and *Aurora* would disappear into hyperspace inside of two minutes.

"Very well, XO," McClaren replied, his eyes fixed intently on the four titanic ships, all of which were now shown clearly in the main bridge display.

Suddenly the ships leaped forward, closing the remaining ten million kilometers in an instant.

"What the devil..." McClaren exclaimed in surprise, watching as the alien vessels just as suddenly slowed down to take up positions around his ship.

"Sir," Kumar exclaimed, "they must've picked up the jump engines activating! I recommend we jump-"

"Execute!" McClaren barked, a cold sliver of ice sliding into his gut. Then he jabbed the button on his command console to open a channel to the crew. "General quarters! Man your battle stations and prepare for emergency jump!"

"Interlock engaged," came the unhurried and unconcerned voice of *Aurora's* navigation computer. "Transpace countdown commencing. Primary energy buffer building. Two minutes remaining."

McClaren looked at his command console, willing the countdown to run faster. But it was a hard-coded safety lock. There was no way to override it.

"Navigation lock confirmed-"

"*Captain!*" someone shouted.

McClaren looked up at the screen as a stream of interwoven lightning arced from the bow of the alien ship that had taken up position in front of them, hitting *Aurora's* spherical sensor section. Its effect was instantaneous.

"*Jesus!*" someone screamed as what looked like St. Elmo's fire suddenly exploded from every control console and electrical system on the ship. The dancing display of electric fury went on to cover everything, even the clothing of the crew. The entire ship was suddenly awash in electrical discharges.

But it clearly wasn't simple electricity. There was no smoke or heat from overloaded circuits, and no one was injured by whatever energy washed through the ship and their own bodies. Surprised and frightened, yes. But hurt, no.

Then every single electrical system on the ship died, plunging *Aurora's* crew into silent, terrifying darkness.

***

Having subdued the alien ship's simple electronic systems, the lead warship made ready the boarding party that had been awaiting this moment. While the great warship's crew now knew the layout of the alien ship and all it contained - including the aliens themselves - down to the last atom, the boarding party would be sent without this knowledge. They would give themselves no advantage over the aliens other than the surprise they had already achieved; even that, they would have given up if they could. They wished as even a field as possible, to prove their own mettle and to test that of the strangers. In this way, as through ages past, they sought to honor their Empress.

As one, the thirty warriors who had bested their peers in fierce ritual combat for the right to "greet" the strangers leaped into space toward the alien vessel. Thirty warriors pitted against seven times as many aliens. They hoped the odds would challenge their skills.

***

"*Calm down!*" Chief Harkness's voice cut through the sudden panic like a razor. At her assigned jump station in the survey module inside the spherical bow section, Harkness had immediately clamped down on her own fear in the aftermath of the terrifying electrical surge that apparently had killed her ship. She had people to take care of, and she was too much of a professional to panic. "Listen to me," she told the seven others in the cramped compartment. There were still a couple of them moaning in fear. "Listen, goddammit!" she snarled. That finally got their attention. Of all the things in the ship they might be afraid of, she would be the first and foremost if that helped them hold it together. "Get your heads screwed on straight. The ship's hull hasn't been ruptured. We've still got air. That's priority number one. All the electrical systems must've been knocked out, which is why the artificial gravity is gone, along with the lights." The darkness was disorienting enough, but being weightless on top of it was a cast iron bitch. She was actually more worried that the emergency lighting hadn't come on. Those weren't powered by the main electrical system, and their failure meant that something far worse had happened to her ship than a simple - if major - electrical blowout. "You've all experienced this before in training. So relax and start acting like the best sailors in the Navy. That's why you were picked to serve on this ship." She paused to listen, relieved to hear that the sniveling had stopped, and everyone's breathing had slowed down a bit.

"Now, feel around for the emergency lockers," she told them. "There should be three in here. Grab the flashlights and see if the damn things work." While they could survive for some time on the available oxygen, the total darkness was going to give way to fear again if they didn't get some light.

"Found one, chief," someone said off to her left. There was a moment of scrabbling around, the sound of a panel opening, then a bit of rummaging.

Click.

Nothing.

"Fuck," someone else whispered.

"Try another one," Harkness grated.

"Okay-"

Suddenly she could see something. But it wasn't the ship's lighting or one of the emergency flashlights. It was like the walls themselves had begun to glow, throwing a subdued dark blue radiance into the compartment.

"Chief, what is this stuff?" one of the ratings asked quietly, her eyes - visible now in the ghostly light - bulging wide as she looked at the glowing bulkheads around her.

"I don't know," Harkness admitted. "But whatever it is, we can see now." The compartment was now clearly, if softly lit. "So let's use it and find out what the hell's happened to the ship."

Then something else unexpected happened: the gravity returned. Instantly. All eight of them slammed down on the deck in a mass of flailing limbs and passionate curses. Fortunately, they all had been oriented more or less upright, and no one was hurt.

"Shit," Harkness gasped as she levered herself back onto her feet. "What the *hell* is going on..."

That's when she heard the screaming.

***

The warriors plunged toward the alien ship. They wore their ceremonial armor for this ritual battle, eschewing any more powerful protection. They soared across the distance between the ships with arms and legs outstretched, enjoying the sight of the universe afforded by the energy shields that invisibly surrounded them and protected them from hard vacuum. They needed no devices to assist in maneuvering toward their target: theirs was a race that had been plying the stars for ages, and their space-borne heritage led them to a fearless precision that humans could only dream of.

They were not concerned about any pathogenic organisms the aliens carried, as the healers who would be sent once the ship had been subdued would take care of such matters. The scan of the alien vessel had revealed an atmosphere that, while not optimal, was certainly breathable.

There was no warrior priestess in this system to bear the honor of leading them in this first encounter, but no matter. The senior warriors were well experienced and had the blessing of the Empress: they could sense Her will in their very blood, as She could sense what they felt. It was more a form of empathic bonding than telepathy, but its true essence was beyond intellectual understanding.

As they neared the ship, the warriors curled into a fetal position, preparing to make contact with the alien hull. The energy shields altered their configuration, warping into a spherical shape to both absorb the force of the impact and force an entry point through the simple metal rushing up to meet them.

The first warrior reached the hull, and the energy shield seared through the primitive alien metal, instantly opening a portal to the interior. The warrior smoothly rolled through to land on her feet inside, quickly readjusting to the gravity that the crew of the warship had restored for benefit of the aliens. The energy shield remained in place behind the warrior, sealing the hole it had created in the hull plating and containing the ship's atmosphere.

In only a few seconds more, all the other warriors had forced themselves aboard the hapless vessel.

***

The screaming Chief Harkness heard was from Ensign Mary Withgott. Her battle station was at a damage control point where the spherical bow section connected to the main keel and the passageway that led to the rest of the ship. The damage control point was on the sphere's side of a blast proof door that was now locked shut. She could open it manually, but wouldn't consider it unless she got direct orders from the captain.

"Ensign!" one of the two ratings with her shouted as a shower of burning sparks exploded from the bulkhead above them. The two crewmen stared, dumbstruck, as someone - some alien *thing* - somersaulted through a huge hole that had been burned through the hull and into the damage control compartment.

A blue-skinned nightmare clad in gleaming black armor, the alien smoothly pirouetted toward the two crewmen, exposing fangs between dark red lips. Its eyes were like those of a cat, flecked with silver, below a ridge of bone or horn. The creature's black hair was long and tightly braided, the coils wrapped around its upper shoulders. The armored breastplate had two smoothly contoured projections over what must be the alien equivalent of breasts. While Withgott had no idea what the alien's true gender (if any) might be, the creature's appearance was such that Withgott had the inescapable impression that it was female, a *she*.

The alien stood there for a moment, meeting Withgott's frightened gaze with her own inscrutable expression. Then the sword the alien held in her right hand hissed through the air, cleanly severing the head from the nearest crewman. His body spasmed as his head rolled from his neck, a gout of crimson spurting across the bulkhead behind him.

Withgott screamed, and kept on screaming as the alien turned to the second crewman with the ferocious grace of a hunting tigress and thrust the sword through the man's chest.

Then the fanged nightmare came for Withgott.

TWO

Amundsen knew that he would probably receive a court-martial for abandoning his post in the face of the enemy. But he had few doubts that any of the crew, particularly himself, would survive long enough to have to worry about such technicalities.

While he was the survey section leader, his assigned jump - and battle - station wasn't in the survey module itself, but in the main damage control point just forward of and two decks below the bridge. Amundsen was a "plank owner" of the *Aurora*, having been with the ship since she was launched, and in addition to being a first-rate astronomer, he was also an engineer who had intimate knowledge of the ship's systems. His job was to help the XO manage the ship's damage control parties during any sort of emergency, and to act as something of an insurance policy for the ship during its many hyperspace jumps.

The compartment they were in, which in everyday use served as the lower crew galley, had one peculiarity that was shared by only a few other compartments in the ship: it had a real viewport, a window to the universe outside the ship, and not just a video display.

After the inexplicable electrical hurricane had swept through the ship, killing all the electrical systems and leaving *Aurora's* crew in darkness without gravity, Amundsen had pushed himself over to the viewport to look outside. He could see the huge alien warship off of *Aurora's* bow. His eyes, which reflected more anger now than fear, took in the thing's smoothly curving flank, which was adorned with great runes that stretched from the pointed prow toward the slim-waisted stern. He guessed that the ship must be at least four, if not five, kilometers long. It would have been a beautiful marvel of engineering if its purpose had not been so openly malevolent.

That's when he saw them: roughly two dozen tiny forms that launched themselves from a bay that had opened like a biological sphincter. Sailing across the few hundred meters that now separated the two ships, he had no doubt as to their purpose.

"Commander Kumar!" he called out to the XO, who had been trying to locate an emergency locker in hopes of finding a light that worked. "Sir, you need to look at this!"

"What is it, Jens?" he replied quickly, making his way over to the viewport.

"Look..." Amundsen pointed at the figures who drew rapidly closer. Over a dozen were going to land on the main habitation section, with the others spreading out to cover the rest of the ship. "Boarders."

Kumar stared, openmouthed, at the approaching aliens. He didn't want to believe it, but there could be no other explanation after what had just happened to the ship. "Bloody hell," he whispered. He turned and leaped away across the compartment, back toward the still-dead damage control console, just as the walls, floor, and ceiling began to glow.

"What the devil?" Amundsen gasped as he pushed himself back from the bulkhead, wondering at this latest horrific display of alien technology. Outside the viewport, the boarding party rapidly approached.

Then the gravity came back on. Amundsen heard a loud thump and a brief cry of pain from Kumar as the man slammed down on the deck. Amundsen fell awkwardly, but managed to roll on his back to absorb most of the impact as he landed. He looked across the compartment and saw the XO sprawled next to one of the tables, his right leg twisted under him. A gleaming white sliver of bone protruded from his left calf muscle: a compound fracture.

He quickly made his way to Kumar's side.

"Commander..." It was then that he saw the pool of blood spreading from beneath Kumar's head. He felt for the man's pulse and was rewarded with a faint but steady beat: he was still alive, but clearly badly injured and in need of immediate medical attention.

Kumar's condition left Amundsen in a very difficult situation. In a battle, which this clearly had become, his duty was to stay at his post until or unless relieved: if engineering could get the electrical system back up, he needed to be here to help the damage control parties get to where they were most needed. Or do what he could to help repel boarders.

He was normally the only one posted here during a jump sequence, to act as a partial backup to the bridge and engineering in case something went wrong with a jump. Kumar had only been here because the captain had wanted a bit of extra human redundancy for this particular jump contingency. But none of the half dozen ratings who had their battle stations here had arrived after the captain had hurriedly sounded general quarters. Amundsen figured they had either become lost when the lights and gravity went off-line, had been trapped by the sealed compartment doors, or had been injured like Kumar.

For now, at least, Amundsen was on his own.

He knew that he should first try to get help for Kumar, but he also desperately wanted to get in contact with the captain. Despite the mysterious blue glow that provided enough light to see by, and the convenience the return of artificial gravity afforded, there was no doubt that these were engineered somehow by the aliens. There was absolutely no question that they were now *Aurora's* masters.

The thought suddenly made him uncharacteristically angry. No, more than that: he was enraged. Amundsen had never been an excitable man, nor had he ever been prone to anger, even in the most provocative situation. But these aliens had attacked *his* ship, the ship he had been with since her keel had been laid. The ship they were playing with like a toy and treating her crew - men and women who, while not really his friends, he had come to deeply respect - like rats. And now they had the balls to send over a boarding party...

Something in him suddenly melted and flowed away like white-hot steel. He hated to leave Kumar and knew that he was doing what The Book clearly said he shouldn't. He knew he could be shot if a court-martial found him guilty of abandoning his post in the face of the enemy.

But when he heard the shouts that suddenly rang out down the passageway that led to the rest of the ship, he knew that he had no more time to consider. The boarders had arrived.

Moving quickly, he left the galley compartment and headed down the passageway in the direction opposite from where he heard the shouting. He knew exactly where he needed to go.

The ship's armory.

***

"Damage report!" McClaren's voice cut through the sudden darkness and eerie sensation of weightlessness. He didn't shout, nor did his voice contain any trace of fear. He had always been a problem solver. This was a problem, albeit an incredible one, and he focused himself on finding a way to solve it.

"Everything's off-line, captain," Raisa Marisova reported quickly from somewhere in the absolute darkness. With Kumar down in damage control, she was the acting first officer on the bridge. Her voice expressed her nervousness, but she was on top of it. "All systems - including the battery-powered backups - are dead." She paused. "No communications, nothing. As far as I can guess, the hull hasn't been ruptured. I can't hear any air escaping."

Despite himself, McClaren smiled. *Here we are*, he thought, *in a ship that's a marvel of modern technology, and in the blink of an eye we've been reduced to relying on some of Mankind's oldest sensors.* He knew that engineering would be working on trying to get the ship's power back up, but he had to reestablish contact with the crew. And find out what the devil the aliens were up to.

"Captain!" the yeoman at the communications station yelped. Her console, followed by every surface of the bridge, began to radiate a deep blue glow.

It gave McClaren the creeps, but at least it peeled back the darkness as he floated next to his command chair. "Take it easy," he soothed. "Maybe the aliens are just giving us a hand-"

The return of gravity came as an unwelcome surprise. Some of the crew had been strapped into their positions, some hadn't. There were several meaty thumps as those like McClaren, who hadn't been strapped in, unceremoniously fell to the deck. Fortunately, no one had any injuries more serious than bruised dignity.

"Let's get the door open," he ordered gruffly as he stood up with as much grace as he could manage, "and find out what's going on in the rest of the ship."

Marisova led two of the other bridge crew to the door and directed them in removing the manual access panel on the wall near the floor. It was a cumbersome, if straightforward process of first unlocking the door (all the major compartments of the ship automatically sealed themselves when the hyperspace jump interlock had been engaged), and then turning a crank to open it.

The door was open almost enough to squeeze through when McClaren heard angry shouts and screams of fear coming from both directions down the passageway that led fore and aft. He shoved himself sideways into the still-widening gap in the doorway, determined to find out what was happening. Looking down the passageway toward the bow, he couldn't see anyone - they'd be in the compartments, not running around in the passageways - but that's where most of the screaming was coming from.

Suddenly he felt what could only be Marisova's powerful grip around his arm, yanking him bodily from the doorway, back into the bridge.

"What the devil-" was all he had time to say as the blade of a sword cleaved the air where he had just been.

"Close the door!" Marisova barked at the two stunned crewmen who were still cranking the door open. *"Shut it now!"* She had seen the alien rush up behind the captain as he struggled in the doorway, and hadn't paused to think. She had just reacted, grabbing her skipper and using her considerable strength to pull him back just as the creature attacked.

McClaren faced the thing that stood on the other side of the doorway, baring its fangs at him. It pointed its sword at his chest, and he noticed the black rapier claws on its hands flexing just as the door slid closed.

***

Ichiro Sato fought to control his fear. It was an oily, slippery sensation that coiled and uncoiled in his gut. It wasn't because of whatever had happened to the ship that had cast them into darkness and shut down the artificial gravity. It wasn't the fear that the aliens might be hostile.

It was the dark. It was always the dark. His roommates at the academy had always thought him strange for keeping a tiny flashlight by his bedside. He claimed that it was simply in case of emergency, a prudent preparation for the unknown. He rarely used it anymore, but even at the age of nineteen the fear would sometimes come back. He would wake up in a cold sweat, panic welling in his chest until his hand found the comforting shape of the light, itself no bigger than his thumb. Just touching it would usually reassure him enough that he could control his raging fear, but sometimes he had to turn it on. Just to peel away the darkness.

When he was a young boy and his father was particularly displeased with him - which was often - he would lock Ichiro in a tiny closet in their apartment. His father had gone to great trouble to ensure that there was enough air, but that absolutely no light penetrated his son's prison. And there Ichiro would have to sit, silently, until his father chose to release him. If the boy made so much as a whimper, his father would drag him out and beat him and then throw him in for even longer. Breaking the unwritten law of female submission that was typical for many families on Nagano, his mother had tried to stop her husband once. He had beaten her savagely, and she had been greatly shamed when she had to go out in public. Until the bruises healed. After that...

Ichiro shook himself. *The past is gone*, he told himself. *Focus on now.* Reaching into his tunic with a shaking hand, he removed the tiny flashlight he always kept with him. He squeezed it to turn it on, but nothing happened. Like everything else electrical in the ship, it was dead.

He felt a wave of panic rise like bile in his throat.

"Ichiro, are you okay?" a disembodied voice asked quietly from the darkness. He suddenly found a comforting hand on his arm. It was Anna

Zalenski, the senior of the three midshipmen. Ichiro was a second year at the academy, she was a fourth year. He felt her hand move down to take his. Ashamed that he needed such comfort, he nonetheless returned the reassuring squeeze she gave him. He also silently thanked her for not bombarding him with any reassuring *it'll be all right* platitudes.

He got his breathing under control. He told himself firmly that it would indeed be all right. The captain would know what to do.

A burst of what was no doubt a very poetic curse in Chinese filled the compartment as Petty Officer Yao struggled in the dark to get the hatch from auxiliary engineering open. While China and Japan on Earth had never exactly gotten along famously, Ichiro had taken an immediate liking to Yao Ming. It was a feeling that was echoed by the older enlisted man toward the young midshipman, although Yao would never have publicly admitted it. A human encyclopedia of curses (in Mandarin, of course, with happily provided translations into standard English, which had come to be known simply as "Standard") who always wore a smile, Yao was also a genius with computers. He had been offered the chance to go to officer candidate school numerous times, but had politely declined. "If I did that," he had said in his very formal Standard grammar, "I can no longer do that at which I am best." The logic was irrefutable. He had no higher ambitions than to be just what he was.

Not surprisingly, his post was in the computer operations center, which itself was separate from the physical computer core, down toward the engineering section. And since Ichiro and Zalenski had demonstrated very high aptitudes for applied computing, it had only made sense for the captain to assign them to Yao as a mentor. "Just don't repeat anything he teaches you in Mandarin in a bar," the captain had warned them with a smile, "or you'll wind up with somebody swinging a chair at your head."

Yao had taken on the youngsters eagerly, teaching them all he could and enjoying their company immensely. Over the six months they had been together, the three had become close friends (although Ichiro still hid his feelings). The midshipmen reminded Yao of his own children, whom he missed terribly.

The compartment suddenly began to glow as if it were radioactive, and Yao uttered another passionate stream of expletives.

Ichiro could see him now, crouched down by the door. The access panel was open, and he carefully cranked the handle a few times, opening the door just a hair.

"I wished to verify that the passageway was still holding atmosphere," he told them, almost as an aside. "I had not heard any sounds of decompression, but one may never be too careful."

He began to vigorously crank the handle, and the hatch began to smoothly open.

Ichiro made to get out of his chair (Yao always insisted that both midshipmen strap in for every jump) when the older petty officer admonished him, "Remain in your seat, please, young sir." It was as if he had eyes in the back of his head.

"Right, Ming," Ichiro said sheepishly, calling Yao by his given name as he relaxed back into his combat chair. He noticed Anna smiling at him, and a hot flush of embarrassment crept up his neck as he realized they were still holding hands. With a shy smile, he squeezed her hand once more and then released it. He saw her smile back.

"Ah!" Yao exclaimed suddenly as the gravity returned. He was already in a semi-crouch next to the panel, holding himself in place with one hand braced against the access panel while he cranked the door open with the other. His feet flexed as they took up his weight, almost as if he had been somehow prepared for it.

Ichiro felt his weight return, of course, but because Yao had kept them strapped in, he hadn't been at any risk of injury. Yao looked after his midshipmen like a mother, and of all the duties the man had, it was the one he took most seriously.

"Perhaps our illustrious engineers have managed to partially repair the ship's systems," he said with a big grin as he stood up and turned toward them, the door now fully open. "Now let us seek out the rest of the crew-"

"*Yao!*" Anna screamed in warning, pointing past him into the passageway.

Ichiro, who had momentarily been preoccupied with unfastening his combat harness (even though Yao hadn't yet given his permission to do so), snapped his head up in time to see a humanoid apparition smoothly step into the compartment. It - *she*, from the shape of the breastplate - looked much like one of the pictures of Samurai warriors his grandfather had been fond of showing him. And this warrior, for she could be nothing else in any civilization, was as frightening to Ichiro as fully armored Samurai must have been to simple peasants in long-ago Japan. Clad in shimmering black armor with a sword clutched in her right hand, she fixed the two young midshipmen with the predatory gaze of a big cat.

Suddenly realizing that Yao was standing right beside her, she spun with unbelievable speed, bringing her sword up to slash at his neck.

Ichiro watched in awe as Yao, standing still with a serene expression on his face, suddenly *moved*. Stepping fluidly toward the alien like fast-flowing and deadly water, he blocked her sword arm with his own left arm, breaking her attack. At the same time, he pushed out with his right hand against her upper left arm and chest, momentarily pinning her arm, neutralizing it, before sweeping his hand up to hammer the elbow of her sword arm, causing her to lose her grip on the weapon. His left hand smashed into the side of her face in a brutal open-handed attack that stunned her, followed by an open-palm strike by his right hand straight into her face that snapped her head back. Then Yao grabbed her sword arm with both hands and yanked her down along his right side, exposing the base of her skull to a savage strike from his left forearm.

The alien crashed to the floor, unconscious or dead, her sword clattering to a stop at Yao's feet. The fight had lasted little more than a second.

Anna and Ichiro gaped at Yao, completely stunned. "Ming..." Ichiro managed, "...how?"

The little man, his face still bearing a serene expression, ignored him for a moment as he knelt down to pick up the alien's sword. Standing up, he assumed a fighting pose, then swung it through the air with professional interest. "Magnificent," he conceded quietly, impressed by the weapon's balance and - in truth - its beauty. The craftsmanship that went into making the weapon was astonishing.

"Ming?" Anna urged, now free of her combat harness. She and Ichiro moved next to the older man, who held the alien's sword carefully down by his side.

"It is what I have been teaching you, of course," he chided gently as he searched the alien for any other useable weapons. She had a long knife and what looked like some sort of *shuriken*, commonly known as throwing stars. But these alien weapons were different, something that clearly required considerable skill to use. Ignoring them, he took the knife. "Not all the forms of *t'ai chi ch'uan* are slow and gentle," he explained as he gracefully stood up. Yao had taken to instructing them in *t'ai chi* as a way to help them stay in good shape, and as something enjoyable to do together. But he had never let slip the fact that he was, and had been for quite some time, a *t'ai chi* master whose close-quarter combat skills were lethal.

Without hesitation, Yao handed the alien's knife to Zalenski. She was senior to Ichiro, and also had some limited close-combat training.

While he felt a momentary flush of shame, having grown up in a very male-dominated society, Ichiro knew that Yao had made the right choice. It was one of the many ironies of his own youth that he had grown up on a world where ancient martial arts were nearly worshipped. But his father had never bothered to teach his "worthless offspring" any of what he knew, and Ichiro purposefully showed no interest. While he would have treasured having such skills now, he doubted he would have survived his father's methods of instruction. His grandfather had tried to pass on what he could, but what Ichiro remembered from those days was little more than pleasant memories.

"Come," Yao said, leading them out into the main passageway that wound its way through the ship. He turned left, heading toward the bridge, then stopped.

Three alien warriors, swords drawn, blocked their path.

Yao, his face serious now, turned to the young midshipmen. "Run, children," he said quietly, before turning his attention back to the enemy.

***

The screaming suddenly stopped.

A few moments later, Harkness could see the alien moving toward them up the passageway from the damage control point, the strange blue glow that illuminated the ship's interior glinting from the thing's black armor. Harkness saw the sword and knew that the dark streaks running its length must have been from blood. Human blood.

Like most of the other members of the crew, Harkness had never had any formal close-combat training. The closest thing she'd ever had to that was brawling in seedy bars. When she was new to the Navy she had started her share of fights. As she'd risen in the enlisted ranks, she'd broken up her share. But her style of fighting was limited to in-your-face punches and smashing beer bottles over the head. And the last thing anyone had ever worried about in the list of potential situations *Aurora* might encounter was a hostile boarding. But here they were. Aliens. On her ship. Killing her crew.

"Fuckers," Harkness hissed, her fury boiling away any trace of fear she might have had.

"Chief," Seaman First Class Gene Kilmer asked, "what do we do?" A big man who'd done his share of brawling and more, Kilmer's ham-sized fists were clenched tight, his eyes fixed on the approaching apparition.

"We take back our fucking ship," she replied. Turning to the others, she said, "Grab anything you can use for a weapon. There's seven of us and one of them. Some of us are going to get tagged," she watched the alien raise its sword as it approached, "but we can take this one easy."

The rest murmured agreement and quickly scattered through the module, grabbing whatever they could to throw at or strike the alien.

Harkness had a sudden inspiration. She reached under one of the consoles and grabbed a miniature fire extinguisher. It was small, about the size of a beer bottle, and didn't have anything harmful in it. But it might give them just a second of surprise.

"Let it come in here," she told the others, spreading them around the module away from the doorway.

Without hesitation the alien stepped into the module, surveying her planned victims with what Harkness was sure could only be boredom.

Keep thinking that, you bitch, Harkness thought as she stepped toward the alien. Three meters. Two. The alien began to raise her sword. Then Harkness darted in just a bit closer and triggered the fire extinguisher in the creature's face.

The alien closed her eyes and whirled away, trying to avoid the white spray.

"Now!" Harkness yelled, and the six other crewmen, led by Kilmer, leaped at the alien, swinging or thrusting whatever they had chosen as a weapon.

The alien blindly lashed out and caught Seaman Second Class Troy Fontino across the ribs with her sword, slicing muscle and bone as if it were paper. He collapsed to the deck, howling in agony.

But that was the only chance the alien got. Kilmer slammed into her, knocking her to the deck, and the others dog-piled on top of them. Kilmer was holding a heavy lead-lined isotope container, and started slamming it into the alien's head, over and over, while the others kept the alien's arms and legs pinned. He kept hammering at her, reducing the left side of her face to pulp, until he heard Harkness call out to him.

"Kilmer," she said in an oddly subdued voice, "that's enough."

He smashed the container into his lifeless opponent one last time, then turned to look up at Harkness, his face spattered with alien blood.

Three more aliens had suddenly appeared, and one of them held a wicked looking knife at Harkness's throat.

***

At first the warriors found nothing but hapless creatures that were as meat animals before their swords and claws, crying piteously for what must be mercy. But it was a mercy they would not be shown. The warriors understood the concept, but no mercy would be shown to those who would not fight.

Moving through the alien ship, they sought not to simply slaughter these beasts that largely mimicked their own form, but to bring them to battle, to see if they were worthy of the honor of the arena. Other species in millennia past had proven worthy opponents for Her Children, and it would be a great blessing to find another.

Such encounters were momentous events in the history of the Empire, and the Empress had decided to send a warrior high priestess to act as Her eyes and ears, Her sword and shield. This priestess was the Empire's greatest warrior.

She had not come by ship, but had simply materialized on the command deck of the lead warship, transported from the far side of the Empire in what was purely an act of will by the Empress. Such were the least of Her powers.

Standing quietly aboard the great vessel, the warrior priestess cast her mind outward to the alien ship, noting with quiet satisfaction that the aliens were beginning to pose a challenge to the warriors. They were starting to fight back.

Perhaps they would be worthy opponents, after all.

***

McClaren still stood staring at the closed door, trying to believe what he had just seen. *Alien boarders with swords,* he thought. *What the devil?*

"So much for first contact," he muttered hoarsely.

"Captain," Marisova said quietly, "what do we do?"

For the first time in his career, McClaren didn't have an answer to that. Marisova's question really got to the heart of what being a captain was all about: showing or telling people what needed to be done. Letting them use their brains to figure out things as much as possible, but when all hell broke loose, it all came down to that one question, and the captain was always expected to have an answer. He had to have the answer, because the captain was one step down from God.

For all that, McClaren was first and foremost an honest man. He was lousy at poker and couldn't tell even the smallest white lie without giving himself away. Besides, the people he worked for, his crew, deserved only his best.

"I don't know, Raisa," he told her, loud enough for the others on the bridge to hear. He swept his gaze over them in the strange blue light the aliens had somehow provided. "But here's what I *do* know," he told them firmly. "Yes, we're in a bloody pickle," that was as close as he ever got to cursing, "but we're not going to panic. We've lost control of the ship, and our first priority is to try and regain control, at least long enough to make sure the computer is destroyed and our navigation records are kept out of enemy hands." He didn't bother calling them *aliens* any longer. "To do that, we've got to somehow reestablish contact with the rest of the crew to make sure someone else does the job, or somehow get past those...things out there," he gestured toward the closed door, "so we can make sure it's done ourselves." He paused. "Without power, that's the only option I can think of, unless someone else has some bright ideas?"

The others were silent. The bridge only had one exit. As for weapons, unlike some of the other compartments that had some items handy that could be pressed into service as weapons, there was really nothing on the bridge they could use but their own bodies.

"Okay, then," he said quietly. "Let's get the door open. There won't be any finesse to what we do after that, because we don't have a lot of options. Just-"

He saw the pilot's eyes go wide, looking past him, and McClaren whirled around just as the door - hardened alloy that was ten centimeters thick - suddenly glowed white and then just disintegrated into a pile of coarse black powder on the deck.

Beyond stood the alien that had tried to attack him earlier, and one of its companions, wearing nearly identical armor. The first one darted forward, raising its sword to strike.

McClaren didn't even pause to think. He had grown up in a tough neighborhood in a gray-hearted city on the world of Bainbridge, and had managed to channel his violence into boxing. He probably could have made it as a professional on the Bainbridge circuit, but that wasn't where he wanted to take his life. He had always been captivated by the stars, by all the worlds that humanity had found and colonized, and by the new ones that appeared in the news reports. He wanted to be an explorer. As it turned out, he managed to get accepted to the Terran Naval Academy because of his "sports" abilities. He wasn't the most promising of the plebes that year, but he graduated second in his class four years later, with the additional title of world college middleweight champion. Not bad for a kid with skinned knuckles who'd grown up fighting his way out of the slums.

Those instincts and the many hours he had devoted since then to keeping in top shape served him well now. As the alien's sword reached the top of its deadly arc, he danced forward - *fast* - and faked a left hook that drew the alien's attention, just as he'd hoped. It dropped its sword arm - the right arm - to try and block his strike, and lashed out with the claws of its left hand just as McClaren twisted his body, throwing all his power into his trademark right cross. His fist slammed into the alien's jaw, rocking its head back. He could hear and feel the *crunch* as the creature's jawbone broke under his knuckles, but he didn't stop there. The alien's armor limited the options he had for punches, but when it lost its balance, reeling backward, its right arm - still clutching the sword - windmilled upward, exposing the armpit. McClaren had no idea if the alien's physiology was anything like a human's, but he wanted to take the sword out of the equation and it was a target of opportunity. His left arm swept up in a powerful jab that landed squarely under the alien's arm where there was no metal armor to protect the bundle of nerves that served the arm, only what looked like smooth leather.

With a grunt of agony, the alien dropped its sword and slammed against the bulkhead next to the door. McClaren was going to move in and finish it off, but suddenly Marisova was there. She grabbed the warrior's right arm, paralyzed from McClaren's left hook, and snatched it up in a fireman's carry. McClaren watched, wide-eyed, as his navigation officer tossed the alien over one shoulder, then smoothly dropped to a kneeling position on the same side. Marisova had one arm still wrapped around the alien's neck, guiding its spine down to the navigator's bent knee. McClaren clearly heard a wet *crack* as the alien slammed down, its head bent back at an extreme angle over Marisova's leg.

He was no surgeon, but to him that sounded like a broken neck. *Score one for the home team,* he thought grimly, turning to the other alien behind him.

The creature simply stood there, its outstretched sword keeping the other members of the bridge crew at bay for the few seconds he and Marisova had taken to finish off its partner. While he couldn't read the alien's body language or expressions, if he had to guess, he'd say it looked satisfied.

"Your turn," he growled as he moved toward it, fists raised in their ready position, with Marisova moving off to one side to flank the creature.

But he never got a chance for a second round. The alien casually brought its free hand to the collar around its neck, from which hung a dozen or so glittering pendants, and touched it in a peculiar fashion.

McClaren's vision exploded in a white flash before darkness took him.

***

Ichiro sprinted down the passageway, Anna right behind him. His gut boiled with fear and self-loathing, feeling like a coward for abandoning Yao Ming. But his friend's quiet order to run had left no room for doubt or argument.

And so the two of them ran. At first, Ichiro had no idea where they were going, except to get away from the three aliens who had confronted Yao Ming. The ring of sword against sword still echoed in his head, and tears threatened to burn his eyes at the thought of Ming being killed. But Ichiro's subconscious was guiding him with a purpose, even if it was one he didn't understand or recognize.

He and Anna, breathing hard with the exertion of running and fear of what must be somewhere behind them, suddenly found themselves standing in front of the doors to his quarters. These doors weren't designed to be airtight, nor were they normally locked. Taking the alien knife from Anna's hand, he shoved it into the center slot of the door and pried it open enough to get a grip with his fingers. Then he simply shoved it open enough for them to enter.

"In here," he breathed, grabbing her arm and leading her inside.

"We can't hide here, Ichiro," she gasped, trying to catch her breath as he handed the knife back to her. He could run like a greyhound, and she'd had trouble keeping up. "The door..."

"We didn't come here to hide," he told her as he quickly rummaged around in the closet at the end of his bed. *Aurora* was a naval vessel, but her accommodations were far more luxurious than any warship designed strictly for combat: even the midshipmen had their own tiny cabins, and plenty of storage space. It was a small tradeoff for deployments that could last a year or more.

"Ichiro..." Anna said worriedly, keeping her eyes on the door.

"Ah..." he said finally. She watched as he pulled something out of the closet that was over a meter in length, and that at first glance looked like a shiny black tube several centimeters across, slightly curved...

"Is that a *sword*?" she asked, incredulous. Personal weapons like that were not normally allowed aboard ship.

"Yes," he told her as he held the *katana* by its handle, then reverently drew the gleaming blade from the polished black scabbard. He had been tempted to show it to Yao Ming once, but had chastised himself for wanting to show off. He had no idea how impressed his friend would have been with the quality of the weapon. "It belonged to my grandfather." He glanced at her as if reading her mind. "The captain gave me a waiver for it. It is the only thing I have to remember my family by."

He had no time to tell her about the old man, and about how much he'd loved him. His grandfather had been the only thing to keep Ichiro's father in check, at least until he was paralyzed from the neck down in a freak transportation accident when Ichiro was only five years old. After that, bedridden in a closet-sized room at the back of his family's apartment, the father of Ichiro's mother endured his own special form of hell. But it was a hell he and Ichiro shared, and the old man was the boy's childhood hero. His grandfather had been a great swordsman, his mother had told him, and the old man had told his grandson what he could of his former life, and showed him pictures from books and the information network - when his father was not around - of what it meant to be a warrior. He couldn't train the boy in the way of the sword, but he could teach him what it meant to have a sense of honor.

"He never had a chance to teach me to use it," Ichiro explained softly. "But he always told me that it was the spirit of the warrior that mattered most." He looked at her, fierce determination lighting up his eyes even as tears streaked down his face. "I accept that I will die here. But I will *not* dishonor him. Nor will I dishonor my shipmates."

She leaned forward and gently kissed him on the lips. Anna had entertained fantasies about being more than friends with Ichiro, but she realized now they would never have the chance. "Let's go," she said quietly.

They left his quarters and moved quicky down the main passageway that would eventually lead them toward the bridge, Anna still clutching the alien knife, Ichiro holding his grandfather's *katana* at his side.

Turning a corner that would lead them to a set of stairs that would take them up to the level the bridge was on, they nearly collided with two aliens coming in the opposite direction.

Ichiro, simply reacting on instinct, brought his sword up over his head for an overhand slashing attack, while Anna backed away slightly: her knife had no business in this particular fight.

The alien easily parried his amateurish attack with her own sword, then casually moved in close to slam her opposite elbow into his jaw.

Dazed, Ichiro was sent flying to the deck. The only thing he was conscious of was that he had managed not to drop his grandfather's sword. Anna moved to a position between him and the two aliens, holding her knife in an underhand grip.

"Come on," she hissed at them. "*Come on!*"

As one of the aliens made to step forward, an ear-splitting roar filled the passageway, and her head disappeared in a spray of bone and gore.

Quick as a cat, the other alien went for something on her shoulder that looked like some sort of throwing weapon, with several wicked blades attached to a central hub, but she never reached it.

There was another roar, and the second alien pitched forward, a hole the size of a dinner plate in her chest.

Her ears ringing, Anna looked around to see what - *who* - had done this, when Lieutenant Amundsen stepped around the corner from the direction the aliens had come, smoke streaming from the muzzle of the M-22 Close-In Assault Rifle he was holding. Pausing just long enough to give each of the aliens a spiteful kick, Amundsen quickly made his way to Ichiro and helped him up.

"Lieutenant..." Anna said, so grateful to see him that she nearly burst into tears.

"Are we ever glad to see you!" Ichiro finished for her, his jaw aching fiercely.

"You're the only two I've found so far who are alive," he told them grimly. "The rest..." He shook his head slowly.

After leaving Kumar behind - an act that threatened to crush him with guilt, particularly once he saw what had happened to most of the rest of the crew - he had gone to the ship's small armory. Amundsen couldn't fight worth a damn with his hands, but he knew how to handle a rifle. He wasn't an Olympic marksman by any stretch, but at the ranges afforded by the ship's passageways and compartments, he didn't have to be.

The main problem had been getting into the armory, which was no more than a small locked closet inside one of the ship's storage holds that held a few "just in case" weapons and ammunition that the ship's designers had put in as an afterthought. But he didn't have to use his knowledge of astronomy, physics, or engineering to open the armory. Some problems yield themselves quite satisfactorily to the judicious application of a crowbar and hammer.

After that, moving through the ship had been a nightmare. He hadn't gone through all the compartments, of course, but from what he'd found so far, *Aurora* had become an abattoir. He had vomited after stumbling across the first butchered bodies, and periodically had been beset by dry heaves ever since. He had never seen a dead body before, let alone one of someone he'd known and worked with. Some bodies had been decapitated. The heads were strewn about the deck, expressions of terror forever fixed to their faces. Some bodies had arms or legs hacked off...

He shuddered, then went down to one knee as he felt his gorge rise again.

"Lieutenant?" Anna asked worriedly, putting a hand on Amundsen's shoulder.

"I'll be all right," he said hoarsely, trying to regain his composure. A genius in many ways and aware of the fact, he had never claimed to be a leader of men. But he realized that he had a responsibility now to these two younger almost-officers. While his rage at what the aliens had done was as fierce as ever, he wasn't on a quest for vengeance anymore. He had to try and look after these two. And find the captain. "It's just..." he shook his head and chuckled mirthlessly. "Never mind." He forced himself to stand up. "Come on, let's see if we can get to the bridge and find the captain."

They made their way back to the stairs leading up to the next level, only to find another pair of aliens standing halfway up the steps, as if they had been expecting the humans.

Amundsen reacted instantly, bringing the rifle to his shoulder and sighting down its length at one of the alien horrors, but he never had a chance to pull the trigger.

One of the aliens already had her hand on her collar, touching it *just so* as Amundsen raised his weapon to fire.

The last thing he saw was a blinding flash of white. He hit the floor, unconscious, the two midshipmen collapsing beside him.

THREE

"Sir? Captain, are you all right?"

McClaren heard the voice as if from far away, through a dull ringing in his ears. He tried to open his eyes, and was rewarded with a thousand hot needles lancing into his optic nerve. He hissed with the pain.

"It'll pass in a minute, captain," the voice said again, closer this time. Chief Harkness. "You must've gotten a big jolt," she went on quietly, her hand on his shoulder. Her touch felt very warm. "Fucking alien bitches," she suddenly spat.

He smiled grimly. Whatever had happened to the ship, he was glad Harkness had made it. This far, at least.

"How many," he asked her, squinting up into her worried face. "Do you know how many of the crew...are okay?"

For a moment she didn't answer, but looked up at someone else. His eyes followed her and found Amundsen, kneeling at his other side.

"Twenty-three survivors, sir," he said quietly. "Including yourself."

McClaren couldn't hide his shock. "*Twenty-three?* Out of a crew of two hundred eight?" They helped him sit up. The aliens had gathered the human survivors in *Aurora's* main galley.

Amundsen was only grateful that it hadn't been the lower galley where he had been forced to abandon Raj Kumar. The ship's XO was not among the survivors, and Amundsen had seen enough in the rest of the ship to know what must have happened to him. "Yes, sir," he said. "That's all. Everyone else is..." He shook his head slowly.

McClaren didn't have to hear the word to know that all the other men and women of his crew were gone. Dead. Amundsen's haunted eyes told him that they hadn't gone down easily. He remembered the swords that the aliens who attacked the bridge had been armed with, and imagined the havoc that such weapons could cause in the close quarters of a ship. *Fucking alien bitches*, Harkness had said. He couldn't have agreed more. "Get me up," he ordered. Harkness and Amundsen helped the captain to his feet, where he stood, swaying. His inner ears were playing tricks with his balance, and he smelled the sharp scent of ozone. But his vision was clearing, and he took a look around the galley.

The members of his crew - what was left of it - all stood to attention. Marisova and the rest of the bridge crew. Yao and two of the midshipmen. The half dozen sailors from the forward survey module. Another half dozen from the engineering section. Harkness. Amundsen. And himself.

Then he saw the blood. The left side of the galley was covered in it, with pools of it among the tables. He stared at the streaks and sprays of crimson that stained the dark gray deck tiles and the white walls. Even the ceiling. So much blood. He couldn't tear his eyes away.

"They allowed us to move the bodies, captain," Amundsen explained, nodding toward the four aliens who stood wary guard at the galley's entrance. "Six crewmen were cornered in here. We...moved the remains into the storage closet in the back and covered them."

McClaren turned back to Amundsen. That was when he noticed the blood on Amundsen's uniform. On his hands and arms. On his face. McClaren imagined - *knew* - that this is what the entire ship was like. It had become a slaughterhouse. His stomach suddenly dropped away into a bottomless abyss, and he felt his sanity starting to follow down after it. *No,* he told himself desperately, trying to reassert control of himself. *No! The crew needs you. You're not taking the easy way out. You can't.*

Forcing his eyes shut, he blocked out the horror for a moment. He took a deep breath to calm himself, but the smell of blood suddenly poured through the stench of ozone he had been smelling. The coppery scent threatened to overwhelm him, and he started to lean over, about to vomit.

He suddenly felt a steadying hand on his shoulder again, squeezing tightly. Chief Harkness. He covered her hand with his, squeezed it tight in return. He willed away the tears as anger began to replace despair.

At last regaining his composure, he let go of the chief's hand and turned back to his crew. *Back to business*, he told himself. "Does anyone know if the engineering crew was able to destroy the navigation computer core?"

"No soft wipe was performed, captain," Petty Officer Yao told him immediately, his eyes downcast. That would have been his responsibility had the order been given. He knew intellectually that there was no way he could have wiped the core after the aliens overwhelmed the electrical system, even had he been given orders to do so. The order had never come, but he felt a sense of shame nonetheless.

Beyond that, Yao was not even sure how he had survived to be here. After he had told the two midshipmen to run, he had turned back to fight the aliens confronting them. They surprised him by refusing to fight him as a group, only singly. But after he had managed to kill two in a set of fierce sword fights, the last one had somehow paralyzed him and rendered him unconscious. He remembered nothing else until waking up here, maybe fifteen minutes ago.

"There was nothing you could have done about that, Yao," McClaren reassured him. "If anyone is to blame, it's our blue-skinned hosts."

"Captain," Amundsen interjected, "I went through the computer core compartment before I met up with the midshipmen," he nodded to Anna and Ichiro, who stood next to Yao. "The engineers weren't able to set off any charges because of whatever the aliens did to our power systems. They opened the core manually and tried to destroy the primary crystals. Some of them were destroyed, but..."

"There would have been far too many to destroy in such a fashion in the moments they had before the enemy arrived," Yao finished for him. He had spent more time in and around the primary computer core than anyone else in the ship, and he knew better than most the futility of trying what the engineers had done. But he gave them great credit for making the attempt, and said a silent prayer for their spirits. He and Amundsen had talked briefly before the captain woke up from the stun he had received, and the computer core had been their first topic of conversation. The younger officer had described the carnage he had found in the compartment, where three young engineers armed only with basic tools had fought against some of the alien warriors. The engineers had died, but they had taken one of the aliens with them, a long screwdriver shoved through her neck. The alien's killer, a young woman Amundsen had barely recognized, lay dead beside her, the alien's knife still buried in her chest. "They will have destroyed some information," Yao went on, "but the chances are great that most of the navigation data remains intact. The system is holographic and redundant. Critical data is stored and phased across multiple crystals."

"People," McClaren told them through gritted teeth, "the aliens *must not* be allowed to retrieve our navigation data. We cannot allow these...*things* to discover where we came from." He swept his gaze over the blood stains left on the galley walls and floor. "We can't allow this to happen to our home planets-"

"Captain," Harkness interrupted softly, "look."

McClaren turned to see half a dozen warriors enter the galley, taking up positions next to the four already standing guard. They were accompanied by four more aliens who wore no armor, but simple white robes and collars around their necks. Aside from their mode of dress, they looked identical to the warriors. Looking more closely, he noticed that these aliens didn't seem to have claws on their hands. Then he took a close look at what each of them was holding.

"What the hell is *that*?" one of the crewmen behind him said, a thread of fear twisting through his voice as he saw the same thing that McClaren had noticed.

Each of the robed aliens held an amoebic mass of what could only be living tissue. Roughly the mass of a grapefruit, each of the gelatinous blobs was dark green and purple, slowly writhing in their bearer's hands.

McClaren felt an immediate visceral revulsion toward the things, and almost in unison the humans stepped back, away from their captors.

The warriors took that as a cue to move forward, spreading out with their swords held at the ready to deter their captives from doing anything rash. Two moved over to one of the young female ratings from engineering, roughly grabbing her arms and dragging her toward the waiting robed figures and their undulating pets. She screamed and struggled, kicking fiercely at the warriors' legs. One of them raised her sword hand to smash her in the face-

"Stop!" McClaren boomed. The aliens may not have understood the word, but they certainly seemed to understand a command voice when they heard it. The warrior about to strike the woman paused, turning to look at him, as did the others of her kind. McClaren calmly walked over to them. "Let her go," he said quietly, gesturing at the young woman the two warriors held. "Take me instead." He pointed at himself.

The warriors paused, still holding the woman, when one of the other warriors standing near the robed aliens spoke. "*Ka'ana te lath.*" The young woman was immediately released, and her captors looked expectantly at McClaren.

"Go on, Ramirez," he told the woman, "get back with the others."

"But captain..." she whispered hoarsely, her frightened eyes darting to the robed aliens and what they held waiting for him.

"It's okay," he reassured her with a confidence he didn't feel. He glanced at Amundsen, and the younger man nodded sadly. *You're in charge now, lieutenant,* he told himself. But he didn't trust his voice to speak the words aloud.

With that, he turned and walked toward the galley table the four robed aliens had gathered around. One of the warriors stopped him, then in a few swift motions with an incredibly sharp knife cut off his uniform, even his boots. The robed aliens gestured for him to lay on the table, and he did so, the cold metal burning against the skin of his naked body. Then the four robed aliens gathered around him and one of them began to knead the mass of pulsating tissue she held.

The crew watched in horrified fascination as the alien worked the strange tissue like it was pizza dough, expertly kneading, pressing, and twirling it until it was no thicker than a piece of paper, but large enough to cover McClaren's entire body. With one last twirl, she let go of the thing, and it settled through the air to land on him.

As the hideous shroud touched him, McClaren suppressed a scream. It wasn't because the thing was causing him pain, because it wasn't. But he felt such a primal *wrongness* as it touched his flesh. It was cool and slimy against his skin, covering him from head to toe, and he desperately held his breath, because the thought of that thing falling into his mouth was a nightmare come to life.

Then he felt it start to move. It began to wrap itself tighter about him. It wasn't constricting him, but seemed to be making a better fit for itself, like a self-shaping glove. He even felt it somehow working its way under him, insinuating itself between his body and the table. The sensation of being completely encased in oozing, living slime was hideously unpleasant even before it began to probe his nostrils and ears. Then it started on his eyes, forcing itself between his tightly shut eyelids. Nothing being sacred to this alien horror, it pressed against his anus, even the opening of his penis.

Between that and his burning lungs, McClaren had had enough. He tried to move his arms to clear the thing from his mouth and nose, but any movement he made was futile: this thing seemed slimy and malleable, but when he tried to move it hardened like concrete. He was totally immobilized.

He willed himself to hold his breath until he was unconscious, but his body betrayed him. With a soundless scream on his lips, he opened his mouth wide as his body forced him into a last-ditch attempt to gather in some air. As if it had been waiting for this, the thing rushed into his mouth, then down his throat as the tendrils invading his nostrils suddenly pulsed through his sinuses, then expanded down his trachea into his lungs.

On the verge now of blacking out, McClaren was sure he was going to die. Absolutely, positively sure.

But as the slime entered his lungs, the strangest thing happened: the urge to suck in huge breaths abated, and the stars that were forming in his vision as his brain ran out of oxygen disappeared. He wasn't breathing, but he was clearly getting oxygen now. The slime was somehow doing it.

Then he felt a sensation of pleasant warmth. It wasn't localized to one spot, but was throughout his body. He'd never felt anything like it before. It was as if someone had taken a magical heating pad that didn't just lay on a part of his body, but actually became a part of it, warming and massaging every cell. He was afraid to admit it, but aside from a brief flare of hot pain in his lower back, this part of this bizarre experience was actually pleasant.

Suddenly he became aware that he could move his arms again. Not only that, but his eyes seemed clear. He blinked them open to see the four robed aliens looking at him attentively. He held up one of his hands to look at it, and saw the last traces of slime as it sank into his flesh, as if it had melded with him on a cellular level. He ran his hands over his chest, his upper thighs: the slime had disappeared. *Right into his skin.*

He lay there for a few more moments before he felt a tremor in his chest. The terror suddenly returned, with visions of some nightmarish apparition bursting from his rib cage, but - fortunately - he was disappointed. Another moment of increasing discomfort passed, and then suddenly the entire mass of slime forced itself back out of his lungs, oozing out of his mouth.

"Agghhh!" he gagged as the thing's keeper retrieved it. He had no idea how the whole thing had managed to get into his lungs. It was as if it had somehow penetrated his body like some sort of biological scanning device, then gathered in his lungs for convenient extraction.

The robed alien, who seemed distinctly more pleasant than the warriors, gestured for him to get up. He made to return to the others, but she gently stopped him. Standing behind him, she ran her hands professionally (he had no other word for it) along his lower spine. Then she gripped one of his hips and put her opposite hand on a shoulder, gently pushing him forward, apparently trying to get him to bend forward at the waist. He did so, and after she ran her fingers over a few of his lumbar vertebrae, she gestured for him to straighten up, which he did. She exchanged a few quiet words with the warrior who had spoken earlier, and then gestured for him to return to the others.

As McClaren rejoined his elated crew, who pointedly ignored his nakedness, something struck him as odd: his lower back, where he had felt the surge of painful heat earlier, now felt fine. Better than fine. It felt perfect. And he knew that it shouldn't, because he had a very mild case of arthritis in his lumbar region that the ship's surgeon had warned him would ground him at the end of this deployment. It didn't interfere with his duties, and consistent exercise helped keep it at bay, but it was a constant source of mild discomfort. Now it was gone. And the robed alien had known it would be; that's why she examined that particular area. Somehow, that blob of slime had communicated to her whatever it had done, or seen, in his body.

The fucking alien bitches, as Harkness had called them earlier, had completely cured him.

***

The warriors looked on as the animal who was dominant convinced the others to come to the healers without further struggle. One by one, and then in groups of four, they came to be tended. The healing gel was the only instrument used by the healers other than some specialized potions; it was the only instrument needed. A product of forced evolution millennia long past, the gel was at once an organism unto itself, yet also a part of the healer to which it was bonded. It had no intelligence of its own, yet could perform the most complex tasks to heal or repair another organism, even a completely alien species.

Through this unique symbiont, the healers could "see" the bodies of the aliens down to the sub-cellular level. While the purpose of the healers here was primarily to learn all there was to know about the aliens' physiognomy, they also employed the gel to seek out any pathogenic organisms and compounds that could be harmful to Her Children. At the same time, the gel immunized the aliens against potentially harmful pathogens carried by the denizens of the Empire, and also did for them what it was normally meant to do: heal disease and repair injury.

Once the healers had finished their task with the living humans, they communed with another group that had studied the remains the warriors had left behind. Pooling the gel together, each symbiont exchanged its information with the others. The healers, their minds conditioned to assimilating such information, now understood the human body and its inner workings far better than all of humanity's physicians combined.

In the human sphere, such information would have to be communicated elsewhere by technology. But an outside observer would have seen no technology in evidence here: once the symbionts had digested the information about the aliens and been merged together, other symbionts throughout the Empire began to spontaneously mutate, reflecting this new knowledge.

The final task of the healers was to transfer the genetic knowledge from the symbionts to the members of their own race to immunize them. This was accomplished for the warriors and other castes simply by placing a small piece of the symbiont on any convenient patch of skin: it merged into the flesh of the patient and made any necessary alterations. The symbiont regenerated itself by merging with its parent healer, whose body provided the necessary nutrients for recovery. This immunization was accomplished quickly throughout the Empire, not just to those here in this system.

For while the final test of the aliens had yet to be performed, the Empress had sensed enough through the blood of Her Children here to know what lay ahead: war.

FOUR

"Lord of All," McClaren breathed as the alien gently shoved his naked body through the perfectly circular hole, about three meters across, that they'd cut in the side of his ship. He had thought at first that they were going to push him into hard vacuum through some sort of invisible barrier, for there was nothing visible between the *Aurora's* hull and that of the enemy vessel that now stood very close alongside. But he had seen that there were warriors at a few spots along the invisible gangway that somehow linked the ships, and that had held his fear in check. Barely.

But my God, the view, he thought as he crossed over the threshold from the metal deck into the void. Suddenly leaving the ship's artificial gravity behind, his stomach momentarily dropped away as he became weightless. He could see down the *Aurora's* flank, noting the holes where the enemy warriors had burned through the hull to board his ship.

Then there was the enemy ship - *huge!* - that didn't look a thing like any spacecraft ever made by humankind. The smooth metal (he assumed it was metal) of the hull gleamed a deep but brilliant green, with contoured dark gunmetal-colored ports and blisters where he assumed some sort of hatches or weapons were mounted. Unlike a human ship, which was a patchwork of plates, the surface of the alien ship's hull was as smooth as a still pond: he couldn't see any joints or welds, rivets, screws or other fastenings as he got closer. It was as if the hull was one gigantic sheet of...whatever it was made of. The craft was all graceful curves, as if it were designed to fly in an atmosphere, with none of the boxy fittings and other angular projections typical of human ships. Looking forward, he saw that giant runes were inscribed along its raked prow, perhaps proclaiming the ship's name, whatever it might be.

And all around him: the stars. As if his hand had a will of its own, he reached out to touch them. He knew they were billions of miles away, but they seemed so close. The alien sun burned brightly mere millions of miles away, and a point of light far brighter than the other stars proclaimed itself the planet from which the four warships had come. He had been on plenty of spacewalks, but this wasn't the same. Maybe it was the emotional exhaustion of the last few hours since the alien ships had been spotted. So little time on the scale of his life, but an eternity for those who had lived through it.

The stars. Part of him knew that this would be the last time he would ever see them. He looked outward, and the unfeeling Universe returned his gaze.

He felt one of the warriors take his arm, amazingly gently, he thought, to propel him onward to his destination. With one last heartbroken look at *Aurora*, he turned toward the open maw of the alien ship that awaited him.

Behind McClaren, the other survivors of the *Aurora* were ferried along, naked and still dazed from the emotional and physical trauma of the healing gel. Even though a number of them had performed spacewalks countless times, they gawked in awe at the great Void around them, and felt a deep tremor of fear at the huge alien warship that seemed in their eyes as big as a planet.

As McClaren approached the "hatch" of the alien ship, he looked closely at the smooth petals of the material (he was less and less convinced that anything on this ship was metal as he understood it) that had irised open. He had no doubt that when this aperture was closed, it would be totally invisible against the hull. Or maybe the aliens could open an aperture like this anywhere, if needed.

His professional curiosity warred with the fear of what would happen to humanity if these creatures were able to trace the path *Aurora* had taken here. His failure to ensure the navigation computer core had been destroyed ate at him like a bitter acid in his gut. And with his crew now removed from the ship, any opportunity - *Not that there really had been any,* he thought bitterly - to somehow break free of the warriors and destroy the core had been lost. His only hope now was that the *Aurora's* computer technology was sufficiently alien that they couldn't figure it out. But after seeing what the aliens with the goo did with his body, and the heart-stopping technology he saw in this ship, he knew that hope was truly a vain one. It was a disaster of literally stellar proportions, and he knew his name would go down in history as the man who had unwittingly opened the human sphere to invasion. The thought was a crushing blow to his soul.

He floated across the threshold into the alien ship, and a gentle artificial gravity gradient allowed him to land gracefully on his feet. There was a phalanx of warriors waiting for the humans to arrive, and a pair escorted McClaren down the connecting passageway that, like everything else on this ship, was huge: it could have easily accommodated a pair of elephants walking side-by-side, with room to spare.

As on the *Aurora* after the aliens had attacked, the walls themselves gave off a soft light. Unlike the dark blue glow on the *Aurora*, however, this was near the color humans viewed as normal sunlight, although tinged with magenta. It gave him the impression of an everlasting sunrise, a thought that struck him as supremely ironic given the very questionable nature of his fate.

The deck felt soft and warm to his bare feet, its dark gray surface pebbled to provide a superior grip. Like the rest of the hull, he had the impression that this wasn't any sort of metal, and he was struck by the thought that perhaps the ship was semi-organic. The thought of such radically advanced technology chilled McClaren to the bone.

By contrast, the walls and ceiling appeared to be nothing more sophisticated or high-tech than stone, perhaps a type of granite that was a very pale rose color. He thought for a moment of the ancient burial places like the Pyramids on Earth, where the walls and rooms of the dead were decorated with ancient writing. For that's exactly the way these walls appeared: there was writing everywhere in the form of alien runes, as if the walls and even the ceiling were part of a giant book that someone had written. Chancing that his guards wouldn't notice or perhaps care, he drifted to one side of the passageway and stretched out a hand to touch the wall's surface. While it could certainly be artificial, to his touch it felt like nothing more sophisticated than very finely polished granite. But how the aliens made it give off light to illuminate the passageway - and why they would have something like stone for the interior of a starship - he couldn't even guess.

Making sure he kept pace with the warriors, who seemed content not to harass him, he glanced back to check on the other members of his crew. Like him, each of them had a pair of warriors as escort, except for Yao Ming, who was surrounded by four warriors. McClaren's people were spaced out evenly behind him at five meter intervals. Those who saw him looking nodded back, fear written plainly on their faces. After the slaughter on the *Aurora*, there was no reason to think anything pleasant awaited them here.

***

Like the rest of the crew, Yao Ming had been appalled at the wanton murders of the rest of the crew. But unlike the other survivors, he had seen such horrors before. The colony world on Keran where he had been born and raised had been settled by an unlikely mix largely made up of ethnic Chinese and Arabs. The two communities, while maintaining distinct cultural identities, interacted peacefully and had rapidly expanded from the original towns they established on landing to intertwining cities and villages. While not a rich world compared to many, it was prosperous and generally peaceful.

But when Yao Ming was eleven years old, an ethnic Chinese gang that had been brutalizing the local Arabs and that local authorities in his town had been unable to control finally went too far: they kidnapped, gang-raped and murdered three young Arab girls. What turned out to be the final insult that made a violent confrontation inevitable was that they stuffed the girls' mouths with pork before they killed them.

Citizens of both communities were shocked and horrified. A local mullah wasn't satisfied with the claims by the police that the gang would be brought to justice, since they never had before. He led the grief-stricken worshippers in his mosque - nearly two thousand of them, including the parents of the murdered girls - on a rampage through the adjacent Chinese district.

While the violence was localized and didn't affect the overall population, Yao Ming's neighborhood became a killing ground as the frenzied mob surged through the narrow streets. Armed with everything from fists and knives to assault rifles (authorities later determined that more than a few of the perpetrators had gone to the mosque bearing concealed firearms), they grabbed, mutilated, and killed anyone in their path who couldn't run away fast enough. They surged into shops, homes, and apartments, leaving a trail of bloody carnage: nowhere was safe. Some of the Chinese tried to stand and fight, but they were simply overwhelmed by numbers.

Yao Ming's parents were among the victims, caught in the local marketplace as they did their daily shopping. Both of them were masters of t'ai chi, a skill they had been passing on to their only son, but even that couldn't save them from the mob. As Yao himself had told the midshipmen to run when he turned to face the aliens who had boarded *Aurora*, his parents had said the same to him that day before plunging into the seething mob, fists and feet flying. His escape had been a harrowing flight through blood-filled streets that still haunted his dreams. He never saw his parents again, for they were among the hundreds who died that day.

Now, walking through this alien ship, he had the honor of having not just two, but four warriors as escort. Unlike those escorting the others, these had their swords drawn and were exceptionally alert. Having killed three of them in close combat earlier, the first with his hands and the other two with the sword from the first one, Yao took some measure of grim satisfaction that they felt he was more of a threat than the others. But he had no illusions about what probably awaited them. Just like McClaren, he had taken a last longing look at *Aurora* before stepping aboard the alien warship, because he knew in his heart that he would never see her again.

After moving through what Yao estimated to be nearly half a kilometer of twisting and turning passageways, they came to a huge door. Like most of the other doors they had passed, this one was deep black in color, polished to a reflective shine, with runes similar to those carved in the stone-like material of the passageway walls. However, these runes were much larger, and inlaid with a material similar in appearance to lapis lazuli.

The door stood partway open, and Yao's guards ushered him in, following the remaining human survivors. Inside, there were more aliens of what he assumed was another caste. Like the ones who had applied the healing gel earlier, these wore robes - black, this time - and also lacked the lethal claws of the warriors.

This group, numbering perhaps fifty individuals, wasted no time carrying out their task. Two quickly approached each human and began to take measurements with what Yao realized was nothing more ominous than a tailor's cloth measuring tape. While these had no numbers or other markings that he could discern, the way the two aliens stretched it along various parts of his body left no doubt. After his parents had been killed, he had gone to live with his uncle - his father's only brother - who worked as a tailor and taught young Yao Ming his craft, along with continuing his education in *t'ai chi*.

"Mister Yao..." he heard young Sato call to him quietly from off to one side.

"*Kazh!*" one of the boy's escorting warriors hissed. The aliens hadn't harassed the humans coming here, but they had refused to allow them to speak to one another.

Yao met the young midshipman's gaze and nodded, adding a wry smile as a small gesture of reassurance. Whatever was to come, at least they would not have to die naked.

***

The armorers worked quickly, as was their custom. While their caste was known for its great skill in handling the living steel from which their weapons were forged, they also created the other clothing and accessories in which their race was attired. Ignoring the strange coloring and pungent scent of the strangers, but welcoming the fact that they were amazingly similar to Her Children in form, they measured their bodies in the time-honored fashion. Like their sisters throughout the Empire, in all the castes, perfection was the goal toward which they strived from birth until beyond death, and they allowed themselves no room for error. Measuring several times, they left the main hall for a series of anterooms where their materials waited. The strangers would not receive any armor, for the priestess had determined that they did not wear such things, and thus would not be accustomed to it.

Instead, the aliens were given only the undergarments worn by all the castes, be it beneath armor or robes. Like virtually all things made by the hands of their race, it was the essence of perfection and would last indefinitely if given a small amount of care. The armorers fashioned close-fitting long sleeve shirts and long pants of a black gauzy material that was perfectly smooth against the skin. It would keep the wearer cool in the heat, and warm when it was cold, and this batch of the material had been specially prepared to accommodate the strangers' unique thermal requirements. Each piece would fit the individual wearer perfectly, tailored only for them. It would stretch effortlessly, but would never bind or lose its shape. Since it had been created to be worn under armor, it never interfered with a warrior's movements when in combat.

Once the armorers finished covering the aliens' pale bodies, they shod their feet in traditional black sandals, open-toed with wraps that secured them above the wearer's ankles.

***

Amundsen wasn't sure what bothered him more, the overt advanced technology such as the ship, or the almost supernatural craftsmanship of everything the aliens made. The clothing in which he now found himself, as the humans were once again herded down the labyrinthine passageways, fit - literally - like a custom-made glove. He had owned tailored clothes, but they were nothing like this. The material itself would be worth a fortune for its clearly advanced properties, and the fit was astonishing. The footwear, in particular, felt like part of his body. This was no small achievement, for Amundsen had a slight deformity in his left foot that required custom-made shoes. But, like his tailored clothes, they were nothing compared to this.

The reason it bothered him was that these aliens seemed to do what they did, be it healing or making clothes, almost by instinct. They did it perfectly, every time, apparently without the assistance of anything he could recognize as technology as he understood it: there were no machines, no computers; only simple tools like the cloth measuring tape. From the looks he had exchanged with the other members of the crew, particularly the captain, it was clear that everyone else was equally awed by the clothes they now wore. Most of them even wore smiles at the incredibly pleasant feel of the garments, at least until they remembered how they had come to be here.

The warriors, certainly, had more advanced technology available to them, such as whatever device they used to stun a number of *Aurora's* crew. Yet their preferred weapons would have been at home on any battlefield on Earth before the widespread use of gunpowder weapons.

That and the lack of claws among the robed castes - which appeared to be natural, and not a surgical modification, as best he could tell - made him think that this species was likely far older than humanity. Yet how much older, and how much more advanced, he couldn't hazard a guess.

But the biggest puzzle was that they had seen no males. He didn't want to make any assumptions about why that might be - they knew almost nothing about this species, except for their predilection for violence - but he found it extremely curious. Since he and his shipmates hadn't exactly had a chance to do a full physiological examination of the aliens, perhaps they were hermaphrodites. But something in his gut told him otherwise: even though their paths of evolution had followed somewhat different courses, his own race and the aliens shared far more similarities than differences. He was convinced that all of the aliens they had seen so far were biologically female.

His internal analysis was interrupted when the humans were herded through yet another massive door, far larger than the others they had passed. Inside was a gigantic compartment - hundreds of meters across - that reminded him of an amphitheater, with concentric rows of steps for spectators to stand on so all could clearly see what transpired on the "stage" below.

The humans were positioned in the last row, behind two other rows of perhaps three dozen aliens. Spaced wide apart in a semicircle around the stage, these aliens also wore robes, but of a dark blue color. The aliens stood erect, staring at the stage, holding their hands out in front of them as if they were pushing something away. While he couldn't read their body language, it was clear that they were concentrating intently on the stage below.

As he looked down at the dark surface, he discovered that it was more akin to a huge liquid pool whose surface had been completely still when they first walked in, with whatever it contained merely mimicking a solid surface.

Suddenly the material in the pool below began to morph, and he watched with growing horror as it took shape.

***

"That's impossible," McClaren breathed as he watched the apparition begin to rise and take shape in the alien cauldron that lay below. He tore his gaze from the thing and looked first at Amundsen, then Yao. Both of them were staring back at him, eyes wide with shocked disbelief.

McClaren, in what was a major act of will, turned back to look at what was taking form, somehow being created - cloned - using the black material in the pool: the *Aurora's* central computer core. Next to it the navigation core began to take shape. Just like with the healing goo, the black material in the pool was being used as a matrix to create whatever the blue-robed controllers willed. The components were still taking shape, with the various assemblies supported by tendrils of the shimmering black material. McClaren had no idea how the aliens did it, but they must have made an incredibly detailed scan of his ship, probably as part of whatever happened to the electrical system. And now, as humans could model a three-dimensional object in a computer and have a machine produce an exact physical replica, the aliens were recreating the computer systems here. He realized with a sinking feeling that it wouldn't have mattered if they had blown the computer hardware to bits. The aliens already had what they needed. And he no longer entertained any hopes that they would have difficulty interpreting the computer data. They would get whatever they wanted, and there wasn't a bloody thing he could do to stop them.

Before his eyes, the computer systems continued to take shape. While he only saw the exterior of the components, he knew with cold certainty that the memory crystals, which were custom grown in a zero gee environment, were forming inside, and that the data held in their matrices would be completely intact. Threads of the black substance connected to the extruded human technology where optical links and power conduits entered the system, providing power and input/output streams that the human design could interact with.

He chanced another glance at Yao. The brilliant petty officer's face was ashen. Yao would know better than anyone, even Amundsen, the implications of what they were seeing. None of them were good.

In a few minutes, the entire array of hardware and necessary peripheral systems had been created. McClaren heard a series of soft clicks, and then the telltale lights on the core casings flashed on: the system was booting up.

***

The priestess watched silently from the shadows, invisible to the aliens, as the builders performed their work recreating the alien ship's control system. While primitive, she nonetheless granted them respect for the achievement of creating systems that took them to the stars, and courage for relying on such simple machinery to take them there.

The matrix in the formation pool below was an analog of the symbiont used by the healers. Advanced as it no doubt appeared to the aliens before her, it was a feat achieved in what were now very ancient times, and was one of the many examples where the lines between technology and biology had become blurred. The builders - those who created that which the Empress required, from tiny things invisible to the naked eye, to entire worlds - no longer used the interfaces that were once required to control the matrix material. Their evolution was shaped by the Empress over the ages, and the power to control the creation of inanimate objects was now an effort of will, guided by the mental vision of what was desired. Like the healers, the minds of the builders could grasp the totality of a thing, see its construction on a subatomic level. Her race did not use computational devices - computers - as the aliens might understand them, for her people had no need. The use of such things had long ago faded into the Books of Time.

But that did not prevent the builders from understanding and creating what was needed. The alien machines quickly took form, and the matrix was guided into providing the necessary electrical input and other connectivity. The major challenge the builders faced was to recreate it exactly as they had memorized it when the alien vessel had been scanned, and not to improve upon it. Otherwise they would have finished much more quickly.

The system activated, and they monitored its initiation sequence. In their perception, time was variable: they could slow down events relative to the actual timescale. In this way they analyzed each function undertaken by the machine. They did not learn the language the machine used, exactly, but they understood on a fundamental level how it worked, much as the healers understood the aliens' bodies after they had been treated with the healing gel. Following the machine's primitive processing routines was a laborious, excruciatingly painstaking experience, but the builders excelled at such things. And with the priestess looking on, her Bloodsong echoing strongly in their veins, the builders' usual obsession with perfection was taken ever higher.

At last they understood what they needed to know about the machine and the data it contained. Others would be required to interpret most of it, but one thing they could show the priestess now...

***

"Oh, *fuck*."

McClaren heard the words, but didn't know or care who said them. He wasn't a man who used foul language, but in this case the words exactly fit his feelings.

Above the pool, where the clones of the ship's computer systems hummed with unnatural life, a stellar chart began to form. It was hologram

- incredibly realistic - that spread across the entire breadth of the huge theater. It displayed the series of waypoints tracing *Aurora's* path to reach this system, and after a moment additional data began to appear for each waypoint. Much of it was visual, with realistic representations of the system stars and planets, but some of it was also being translated from Standard into the aliens' language, judging by the runes that began to appear next to a number of the systems and waypoints.

He thought his sense of horror couldn't get any worse until he saw the first colony world on the Rim, the last friendly port of call before *Aurora* had jumped into the unknown, appear in the rapidly expanding course the ship had taken. Much more data in the aliens' language suddenly appeared next to it, suspended in the darkness above the renegade computers. Then onward to the next, and the next.

Finally, there was Earth itself, the home port from where they'd sortied months ago. The home of Mankind.

And then came the final insult: the navigation trace shifted to show Earth at the center, and outward from there every single human colony and settlement was displayed. The aliens might not have everything sorted out yet, for a great deal of information was stored away in files that they would have to learn Standard to interpret, but McClaren had no doubt they would: among its other wonders, the computer contained a complete educational library. And then every single human being would be at the mercy of these monsters.

He turned again to look at Amundsen and Yao, but instead caught a fleeting glimpse of a towering figure detaching itself from the shadows along the wall at the rear of the theater. Clearly a warrior, and the largest he had seen by far, she silently disappeared into the passageway, her black cloak swirling behind her.

FIVE

Ichiro marched along between his two guards as the humans were once more paraded through the ship. He had been trying to keep careful track of the turns and distances, and he guessed that they must be somewhere close to the center of the great vessel. He had been shocked by what he'd seen in the theater they'd just come from, his fear hammered deep by the ashen looks on the faces of the officers and Yao Ming.

Beside him, one of his guards carried his grandfather's sword. It was clear that she was handling it very carefully, as if it were her own treasured heirloom. She wore a weapon that bore more than a passing resemblance to the *katana*: a gently curved blade, somewhat longer than his grandfather's weapon, that ended in an elaborate but functional guard plated in what appeared to be gold, and an equally elaborate grip. That, of course, wasn't the only weapon she carried: there were three of the throwing-style weapons clinging to her left shoulder, and a wicked-looking long knife with a crystal - *Diamond?* he wondered - handle strapped to her side. Most of the other warriors were similarly equipped, although every single weapon except for the throwing stars - for lack of a better term - appeared to be custom-made. While sometimes similar, no two were exactly alike.

His reverie ended quickly as they passed through a portal that was even larger than the one to the theater. As the humans were escorted in, a chill ran down Ichiro's spine. This, too, was a sort of theater, but not one he wanted to be in: it reminded him all too clearly of the Colosseum of ancient Rome that they had studied as part of their military history lessons. In fact, had Roman gladiators been snatched through time and dropped onto the sandy arena that must have been nearly a hundred meters in diameter, he had no doubt that they would have felt completely at home. It was built from tan-colored stone, the finely set blocks polished to a smooth finish. While it wasn't dilapidated like the Colosseum, Ichiro couldn't shake the uneasy feeling that this alien version was terribly old, perhaps older than Rome itself.

The seating was arranged in two dozen or more rising tiers, and Ichiro wondered at the size of the crew this vessel must carry: if this was designed purely for those aboard this ship, there must be thousands of aliens aboard, yet they had seen so few. There were arched portals arranged around the sand of the circular arena, and above...

He paused, another wave of awe momentarily suppressing his fear. Above him was a blue sky, slightly tinged with magenta, and a bright sun. It didn't just look like it was outdoors, as if it were a good projection or hologram, it felt like it, too: the radiant warmth on his face from an alien star, just the touch of a breeze, and faint odors from what must be some type of alien flora, and not the scents they had noticed thus far on the ship, which had mostly reminded him of cinnamon. There was a palpable sense of scale that he had only ever felt planetside, almost as if they'd been teleported off the ship and onto an alien world.

But when he turned around to look behind him, the passageway and the portal through which they'd entered were still there.

After a moment of allowing the humans to gawk freely, their guards again ushered them onward. Descending through a set of wide, curved steps, Ichiro followed the others into a large anteroom that let onto the sands of the arena through one of the portals that he'd seen earlier. He half expected there to be torches on the walls and gladiators preparing themselves for combat.

When robed aliens - wearing black - entered the room, he realized that while the light was coming from the walls and not ancient torches, there were indeed gladiators here: he and his shipmates.

The warriors took up positions along the walls as the robed ones brought in a veritable arsenal of weapons, from daggers and throwing knives to spears and pikes, and swords of a bewildering variety. They arrayed them carefully on several low benches clearly tailored for the purpose, then stood off to one side.

***

The ritual had its origins in time before legend, and the aliens were not expected to understand. As with many things in the lives of those who served Her, tradition and ritual reminded the living of the past, and were a mark of the personal discipline and obedience of Her Children.

These aliens, the survivors of the original crew, would fight for the honor of their race. They likely would not comprehend why they were about to die, and win or lose, it would not avert the fires of war that would soon descend on their worlds. It was for the sake of honor, and honor alone. The outcome was inevitable, for in this ritual there were no survivors, save one: the Messenger, who would be spared to tell the tale of what had happened here. And to tell of what was soon to come.

After the armorers had laid out a suitable assortment of weapons the aliens could arm themselves with, should they choose, the bearers of water brought food and drink. The builders had replicated samples of the food and liquids aboard the ship, based on what the healers had told them would be appropriate. Fearing a trick, no doubt - one thing they need not have feared from their hosts - some of the aliens refused the refreshments; others consumed what they would.

The priestess watched them with her second sight, content to let the aliens eat in peace. When they had finished, she nodded to her First, who commanded that the warriors and clawless ones enter the arena and take their seats, spectators to the ritual combat that was soon to begin.

As they quickly filed into the arena's stands, the priestess decided that it was time to greet the aliens herself, and guide them in what must be done.

***

McClaren had forced himself to eat and drink something, not so much because he was hungry or thirsty, but because he suspected he would need the energy soon. He was also trying to lead by example, as some of the crew feared that the food or drinks - which included water, coffee, and beer, of all things - might be poisoned. But McClaren figured that the aliens could kill them a million different ways, and poisoning didn't seem to be their style. Their preferred methods of mayhem and murder seemed a bit more direct.

The other officers had joined him in taking at least a token bite to eat of some of the fruit and other food the aliens had offered. At first he had thought the food must have been taken from the *Aurora's* galley, but on further inspection he decided that the aliens had probably replicated it, just as they had the ship's computer systems. As much as anything, he was curious about the taste, and wasn't disappointed when he sampled one of the apples. It was delicious, and he quickly ate it down to the core, then drank some water.

He noticed Yao moving slowly along the tables holding the weapons, looking at them carefully, and walked over to join him. He knew more about Yao's background than anyone, except possibly Harkness, and he wanted his insights. "What do you think, Yao?" he asked quietly. Since they had arrived in this room, the aliens had relaxed their ban on the humans speaking to one another. He was keeping his voice down because he didn't want the other members of the crew to hear.

Yao paused and looked up at him with troubled eyes. "You realize what is coming, do you not, captain?" He glanced at the others, most of whom stood huddled in a fearful group near the center of the room, watching the warriors along the walls. "The crew...there is no way to prepare them."

McClaren's mind had been grasping at possibilities, at outcomes that would at least give them a chance of survival. "I can't accept that they're just going to kill us," he grated, "not after all this. What would be the point?"

"The point may be irrelevant, captain," Yao replied. "I believe we are to face a test of character," Yao told him. "We will never know the reason behind it, for the aliens cannot communicate it to us, even if they wanted to, and we must accept that. But I do not believe that any of us are destined to leave this place alive." His gaze hardened, revealing the warrior who dwelled within. "The best we may do is to earn their respect."

"I agree," Amundsen said softly from behind them, having quietly moved over to join the discussion. Marisova, Harkness, and the two midshipmen stood with him. "I don't see a positive end-game in this, captain. I realize that I'm usually considered a pessimist, and often enough that's true. But this," he gestured around them, at the weapons, at the portal that led onto the sands of the arena, then shook his head. "I see nothing here that gives me any hope. We're sacrificial lambs."

"Kuildar mekh!" one of the warriors suddenly barked, startling the human survivors. As one, the other warriors lowered their heads and brought their left arms up to place an armored fist over their right breasts in some sort of salute. The clawless ones did the same.

McClaren looked up toward the warrior who had spoken, wondering what was going on, when behind her a huge warrior *walked right through the wall into the room.* Had he not seen it with his own eyes, he would never have believed it.

"Jesus fucking Christ!" someone cried, and the group of crew members clustered toward the center of the room darted away from the apparition like a school of terrified fish.

McClaren realized that it was the same warrior he had caught a glimpse of leaving the theater where they had reconstructed the ship's computers. She was something different from the others, over and above however she had managed to walk through a solid wall. She was easily the tallest being in the room, standing a full head taller than McClaren, with the most impressive physique he had ever seen on a female (if inhuman) form. While her armor was a gleaming black just like the others, hers had some sort of rune of blazing cyan in the center of her breastplate. Her collar was also different, holding some sort of ornamentation - he had no other word for it - at her throat that bore the same marking as her breastplate, and a dozen or more rows of the strange jeweled pendants that the other aliens, including the robed ones, wore from their collars. Only this warrior had far more than any of the others. The claws that protruded from her armored gauntlets reminded him of the talons of an eagle, and were the longest he'd seen by far. Her hair was also much longer than that of the others, but like theirs was carefully braided, with the long coils looped around her upper arms. Her face struck him as regal, with deep blue skin that was as smooth as porcelain. Had her features been translated into the form of a human woman, she would have been a thing of beauty. But here, now...

Ignoring the other humans, she walked straight toward him, bearing a staff in one hand that he knew he would have had difficulty lifting off the ground with one arm.

Mustering his courage, he stepped forward to meet her, gesturing for Yao and the others to get behind him.

She stopped an arm's length away, appraising him with silver-flecked feline eyes that pierced his soul, and he felt as if he was staring into the eyes of a hungry tiger.

In a way, he was not far wrong, for she was the ultimate predator among a race of predators.

***

Tesh-Dar, high warrior priestess of the Desh-Ka order and blood sister of the Empress, looked upon the alien in silence. She was the Empire's greatest living warrior, a legend among her fellow warriors, her peers, and had been sent by the Empress to observe these beings. Aside from the Empress Herself, Tesh-Dar was also the most sensitive to the song of the spirit - the Bloodsong - that bound her people together, and to the Empress herself. She had studied the aliens closely in this short time, and while she could sense their minds and their churning emotions, she could hear nothing of the spiritual chorus that might reveal their souls to her questing senses. Without the Bloodsong, they were but animals in Her eyes, beyond Her grace and love. Yet they could still serve the needs of the Empire.

For the way of their race, the *Kreela*, was forged in the fires of battle, and Tesh-Dar knew that they had at last found another worthy foe among the stars. The last such enemy had been defeated and its flame extinguished from the galaxy many generations before she was born. It had been a worthy race that had fought well for hundreds of great cycles until, exhausted at last, their civilization had collapsed in defeat. Unwilling to fight on, no longer able to challenge Her Children in battle, the Empress had swept their race from the stars. All that remained to prove they had existed were the accounts of the war collected in the Books of Time, and samples of stone and flora taken from their worlds, which had long since been reduced to molten rock and ash.

The Bloodsong. It was an ethereal thing, unmeasurable by any instrument or technology, but was as real as the ten thousand suns of the Empire. If the aliens' blood could be made to sing, they would be spared, for they would be one with Her. But if not...

Tesh-Dar nodded to one of the warriors and held out her staff. The warrior took it reverently, and another warrior handed her a small urn whose mouth was large enough for an alien hand to reach inside. Turning to the dominant alien, she offered the urn to it. After a moment of deliberation, the creature took it, holding it in unsteady hands. It peered inside to find it empty.

One of the armorers, a clawless one robed in black as were all her sisters, stepped forward. She held a small disk in each hand: one was black, the other cyan. Tesh-Dar first took the black one in her ebony talons, holding it up to the alien. She gestured with her free hand at the disk, then at the alien, then the weapons, then the sands of the arena beyond. The creature's face began to turn pale, and she could sense its heart beating faster. It suppressed its fear from the others of its kind, but it could not do so against her heightened senses.

She dropped the black disk into the urn, and the armorer produced twenty-one more, dropping them in slowly so that the creature could count them.

Then she handed Tesh-Dar the cyan disk. Tesh-Dar again gestured at the disk, then at the alien, and then she projected an image of the alien ship in the air around them, and pointed to it; the image morphed to show the ship returning to its point of origin, which the priestess now knew was where this species had first been born. As tradition demanded, whichever alien chose the cyan disk would be the Messenger. She dropped the disk into the urn, held in the alien's unsteady hands.

Twenty-three disks.

Twenty-three aliens. Twenty-two would die, and one would live to bring the tidings of war to its people.

She did not have to know their language or read their thoughts to know that the dominant animal and its companions understood.

***

"It's a fucking lottery," someone choked in the shocked silence that followed the innocent sounding *clink* made by the last disk - the one McClaren thought of as *the ticket home* - as it fell into the urn he was holding.

"Throw the goddamn things back at them!" Gene Kilmer, the brawny rating who'd been with Harkness when the aliens attacked, shouted angrily. "No," one of the enlisted men said quietly, his eyes wild. "I'm not going to die here. *I'm not going to die here, do you hear me!*" he shrieked, his eyes a mask of undiluted fear as he backed away from the tall alien woman who now speared him with a rapacious gaze. In a blind panic, he tried to bolt toward the entrance they'd come through earlier, oblivious to everyone and everything around him.

Before the warriors could react, Marisova darted sideways and deftly grabbed the younger man in a full nelson hold, her arms wrapped under his armpits and locked behind his neck, totally immobilizing him.

Harkness was there an instant later, her hands clamped to either side of his face, her nose a centimeter from his. "Listen to me, Lederman!" she shouted, but he continued to struggle, trying to kick her and drive Marisova off balance. Harkness let go of him with her right hand and slapped him hard enough to snap his head back before turning his dazed face toward hers again, her eyes boring into his. "Listen, damn you!" she hissed. "You are not going to panic, you bastard. You are *not!*" She shook him, her hands in his crew cut hair now, holding on so hard her knuckles were white. "Do you hear me? *Do you?*"

Lederman's eyes slowly focused on hers and his struggles eased, then stopped. He sagged in Marisova's grip, and she suddenly found herself not having to restrain him, but to keep him from collapsing to the deck. He suddenly burst into tears. "I don't want to die, chief," he said miserably. "Not like this." He shook his head. "Not like this..."

"We all die, Lederman," Harkness told him, her voice softening as she released her death grip on his hair, her hands moving now to his shoulders, giving a gentle squeeze of comfort. "And most times we don't get to pick how we go. But listen," she told him, leaning to touch her forehead against his, "if we have to die, I don't want to give these fuckers the satisfaction of seeing us afraid. They attacked our ship. They murdered our friends and shipmates in cold blood, Lederman. I don't know about you, but I want some goddamn payback. If they kill me, fine. But I plan on kicking some of their blue-skinned asses before I go down." She lifted his chin with one hand so their eyes met again. "What do you say?"

With an obvious effort, she could see that Lederman was getting it together. He was still terrified, but she could see the spark of anger she'd planted growing in his eyes. "You're right, chief," he rasped, nodding. "Shit, I'm sorry."

"Just use it, Lederman," she told him as she stepped away. "Get pissed at what these bitches did and use it."

He nodded, and Marisova released him. "I'm sorry, captain," he told McClaren. "I...lost it-"

"It's okay, son," McClaren said, nodding his thanks to Marisova and Harkness. "You just said and did what most of us would like to." He looked around at the others. "Petty Officer Yao told me a theory, that this is a test of character, and an opportunity to gain the respect of the aliens. Now that we know what's in store," he gestured to the urn, "I think he's right."

"Captain," one of the others asked, "what if we just refuse?"

Glancing at the tall warrior who stood watching them intently, he said, "We'd be slaughtered where we stand," he said bluntly, "just like the rest of the crew." He paused, thinking of what Harkness had said, and suddenly he felt the fear start to slip away from him. Part of the fear of death lay in uncertainty, the fear of when, or where, or how you would die. But that was gone now. He knew that he was going to die here, in a time probably measured in minutes from now, at the hands of one of these alien warriors. In that moment, he accepted death's inevitability as something more than an intellectual understanding. He looked over to see Yao looking at him, a knowing look on his face. "No," McClaren went on firmly. "We're going to stand and fight. Aside from Yao, most of us don't have extensive martial arts training, so we're at a big disadvantage. But our goal here isn't to win. Our goal is to do what we can to make them pay for what they've done." He could see that his resolution was beginning to take root in the others. Most of them were still clearly afraid, and he didn't blame them a bit. But they were good men and women. The best. And he could think of worse ways to die. "Are you with me?" he asked them quietly.

Each of them met his gaze as he looked around the room, nodding their agreement.

"Okay, then," he said with a grim smile. "So much for the tough breaks. Now for the lucky sod who gets to go home." He gave the urn a good shake, mixing the disks it contained. Then he went to the lowest ranking survivor of the crew, a young African woman who had been plucked right out of advanced training to serve on the *Aurora*. It was to be her first and only deployment. "Subira," he said softly, calling her by her first name, "you get first shot at the golden ticket."

Subira, whose skin was nearly as black as the armor the aliens wore, slowly shook her head. "I'm not leaving, captain," she told him firmly, her face proud and defiant, not toward him, but their hosts. "Let someone else pick first."

He nodded, not trusting his voice as tears began to form in his eyes. He was so proud of her. So proud of them all. One by one, they refused to reach into the urn.

Finally, Ichiro, the youngest among them, spoke. "Captain," he said formally, drawing himself to attention. "Sir, none of us are leaving. We are your crew, and we are staying together. Staying with you."

"Is that what you all say?" McClaren asked them softly. "As honored as I am to have you here, one of us has the chance to get home and tell them what happened here."

"If they want, I'm sure they have the means to send the ship back with the bodies of the crew," Amundsen said darkly. "That should tell the story close enough, sir."

The rest of them nodded agreement. They were staying. All of them.

McClaren turned back to the tall warrior and stepped up to her, his fear gone now. The die was cast. He pointed at himself, then the others, then at the weapons and the sands of the arena where he could see what must be thousands of aliens now. He held out the urn to her, and she took it. Her expression was unreadable, but if he had to guess, he would have said she was pleasantly surprised.

***

As she took the urn back from the dominant alien, Tesh-Dar was indeed pleased. These creatures had demonstrated resilience and a will to survive that would challenge Her Children in the war-to-be, and she eagerly awaited the coming combat.

While the aliens had declined the lottery, a Messenger would still be chosen. A Messenger was always chosen, for that was the way of things since ages long past. She did not know yet which one to choose, but she was content in the certainty that she would when the moment came.

In the meantime, the aliens began to choose their weapons from among those the armorers had provided. And beyond the wide portal to the arena, the peers continued to gather.

SIX

Reduced from the captain of one of humanity's most advanced starships to a gladiator with only modest skills, Captain McClaren stood in the center of the line formed by *Aurora's* survivors in the sands of this strange arena. The stands were packed with alien spectators, thousands of them, who murmured amongst themselves in their own language. As he and a number of the others in the crew had noted earlier, every single one of them appeared to be female: armored warriors or those that wore robes of a bewildering variety of colors, there was not a single male among them that he could see. He realized this would no doubt be important to the xenobiologists back home, but it was purely academic to a man about to die.

Unlike most of the rest of his crew, he had chosen to forego any of the many weapons they had been offered. He was trained as a boxer and knew how to use his fists as weapons. He wasn't as young or as strong as he once was, but he felt better than he had in a long time. He couldn't say that his soul was at peace, exactly, but he was determined to send a clear message to the aliens that, despite their advanced technology and the massacre aboard the *Aurora*, humans weren't going to let them have a free ride. He only hoped that the aliens would meet him and the others on roughly equal terms, or the coming bloodbath would be an extremely brief affair.

He had already said his goodbyes to the others just before they'd been herded out here and formed into a line facing the far side of the arena. He had shaken everyone's hand and told them that it had been an honor to serve with them, and he meant it down to the bottom of his heart. It had taken all his willpower not to break down and cry, not in fear, but in pride at their courage and resolution. If the aliens wanted a showing of the best humanity had to offer, they would find it here among his crew, his comrades.

When the alien warriors gestured for them to move out to the arena, Harkness called the crew to attention, and the men and women of the *Aurora* fell into formation as if they were in a fleet inspection. After a glance at the warriors to make sure they didn't plan to interfere, she turned her attention back to the crew. She cast a critical eye over them to make sure their formation was nothing less than perfect. Then she did an about face, waiting for her captain to take charge.

As McClaren stepped to the head of the formation, he came to attention and she rendered a sharp salute. "Ship's company ready for..." she paused, her face hardening, "...ready for battle, sir."

McClaren returned her salute, snapping his arm up, fingers at his brow. "Post, chief," he ordered her quietly before snapping his arm down to his side.

Her eyes held his for a long moment before she replied, "Aye, aye, sir!" in her best deck formation voice, her words echoing off the stone walls. Then she pivoted on her heel and took up position at the rear of their little formation.

With one last look over the men and women of his command, McClaren marched them out in single file onto the waiting sands of the arena.

***

Ichiro stood to his captain's right, holding his grandfather's *katana*. After the captain had given in to the crew's desire to stay, everyone had begun choosing weapons. Ichiro had started toward one of the tables when the alien warrior who had taken his grandfather's sword stopped him. She held it up before him in both hands, arms outstretched, and bowed her head to him as he took it from her, grasping the black lacquered scabbard in shaking hands. She held his gaze, and for just a moment he thought he detected a trace of empathy in her inhuman eyes. She murmured something to him in her language, her long ivory canines flashing behind her dark ruby lips, and then she turned away to join her fellow warriors.

He had left the scabbard behind in the weapons room, for he knew he would never need it again. The weapon felt good in his hands, the carefully wound leather of the handle easy to grip, despite the sweat pouring from his palms. Because he had never had any training in swordsmanship, he knew that he would only last a matter of seconds against any of the alien warriors, who were clearly trained from childhood in combat. But the *katana* represented his heritage, and as his grandfather had often told him, the true nature of the warrior rested in his spirit, not in his knowledge of technique or the weapon he held. He would die, but he would die a man, and with honor.

He hadn't completely mastered his fear, but as the captain himself had discovered, removing the unknowns had allowed him to control it. He hoped it would be quick, but he also hoped that he would give a good accounting of himself before he died, that he would make his grandfather's spirit proud.

***

Standing at the far right of the human line, Amundsen had chosen an alien version of the quarterstaff. He had no experience with any of the other types of weapons, but as a child he and his brother had often engaged in sparring with poles not unlike this. He would have been much more comfortable with a rifle, but that wasn't one of the options they had been given, and he was completely useless at unarmed combat.

Like the captain, he had noticed the complete lack of males among the gathered spectators. It was indeed an academic question at this point, but those were the types of things he had spent his life exploring. If he lived only a few more minutes, then it was worth spending them analyzing the aliens. To satisfy his own curiosity, if nothing else. He just wished that he would have been able to pass on the information to someone who could have put it to use.

He guessed there were probably upward of twenty thousand of them packed into the arena to see the coming slaughter. The warriors, so far as he could see, appeared to be a completely homogenous group: all wore gleaming black armor, all wore a black collar around the neck with some number of the gleaming pendants (this adornment appeared to be common to all of the aliens), and all were armed to the teeth with completely customized weapons. The only exception had been the huge alien who had faced off with McClaren in the strange lottery business. She was clearly a warrior, but was not one of the rank and file: aside from her size, she wore that strange adornment on her throat that echoed the rune on her breastplate, carried that huge staff that looked like it probably weighed twenty kilos, and wore a black cloak. Unlike the other warriors, she only carried a single weapon, a short sword, although he suspected that she was more dangerous than a dozen of the others, particularly in light of that walking-through-walls stunt she had pulled earlier. The other crewmen were sure that it had been some sort of illusion using holographic projection. Amundsen hadn't argued, but he was completely convinced that what they had seen had been real: she had somehow walked right through a stone wall that was probably a full meter thick. How she had done it, he couldn't even guess. He didn't believe in magic, but the level of technology this civilization had achieved was so far beyond humanity's that it may as well have been a form of sorcery.

As for the other aliens, they had two common features that were distinct from the warriors: they wore robes and they didn't have any claws on their fingers. It was clear to him now, having seen several of them in action in the last couple of hours, that the color of the robe identified the functional caste (for lack of a better term) of the wearer. What he took to be physicians wore white; the ones who worked on weapons and personal garments and armor wore black; then there was the dark blue of the ones who recreated the *Aurora's* computer systems. All of them were highly specialized, and in some cases - particularly with the physicians and the ones who recreated the computer systems - they apparently were able to interface with other "systems" (if one could consider such things as the healing goo and the black matrix in the tank of the theater as systems) without any visible intervening technology.

Looking through the crowd, he identified at least two dozen different colors of robes being worn. On the surface that seemed like a lot of specialized castes, but on the scale of human technical specialization it was nothing: everything from fixing a toilet to designing a starship required some sort of specialized skills, and it often took years to learn them. Surely the aliens still had need of a similar variety of skills, far more than the two dozen or so castes here represented. But perhaps their people didn't need nearly as long to learn such skills, or maybe each caste could do many things in a given area. The physicians, for example, replaced in a single caste hundreds of different types of specialists among their human counterparts. They also did a far better job, even having known nothing about their human guinea pigs prior to a few hours ago.

While the others were more concerned about the next few moments, Amundsen's reflections on the nature of the aliens chilled him in more abstract terms: if what he thought was even close to being correct, the aliens would have an incalculable advantage against humanity in a conflict. With warriors like these, backed up by legions of their robed sisters who could create or do virtually anything, they would be unstoppable.

Gripping the quarterstaff in his hands so tightly that his knuckles were bled white, Amundsen for the thousandth time cursed the fate that had brought them to this system.

***

Yao Ming stood to the right of young Sato, with Midshipman Zalenski on his own right. By tacit understanding with the captain that was made with no more than a quick look and a nod, he had positioned himself between the two young cadets - with Marisova on the other side of Zalenski - in what he knew was the vain hope of providing them some protection in the coming ordeal. No one doubted the outcome of this alien duel, but Yao was determined that the two youngsters would not be among the first to die.

While Yao had considered one of the finely crafted alien swords, like the captain and a few of the others he had decided that his most trusty weapons were those provided by his own body. He was an outstanding swordsman, but he was even better with his bare hands and feet. And those were the weapons he would use.

While the others stood upon the sands and tensely watched the alien crowd, wondering what would happen next, Yao was thinking of...nothing. Having assumed the standing meditation, or *Wu Ji*, posture, he stood with his feet shoulder width apart, toes pointed forward, and a slight bend in his knees. His hands dangled loosely at his sides, all the tension having been drained away from his shoulders and upper body. Head held suspended as if by a string, his eyes were closed, and he was perfectly relaxed. He focused on the union of his feet to the alien sand, imagining that it was the Earth, and drew power from it as he slowly inhaled its energy, then exhaled the tension from his body. He imagined the energy flowing upward from his feet, filling his entire body as he swept everything else away.

His companions, looking at him, might have thought he was in a trance. Nothing would have been further from the truth: he was totally alert. In fact, he was far more alert than the others, for he had eliminated all distractions, all fear, all doubt.

With a contented sigh, he continued his meditation, only opening his eyes when the alien challengers stepped into the arena.

***

Harkness gritted her teeth as a stream of warriors emerged from one of the portals on the opposite side of the arena. She counted them, noting with no surprise that there were twenty-three. One for one.

On her right stood the captain; on her left stood Kilmer. He had muscled over one of the other ratings who had taken the spot first, insisting he be next to her.

"Chief," he said awkwardly as the aliens formed up into a line and began to slowly advance toward them, "it's...it's been an honor."

Harkness turned to stare at him. He had always been a monumental pain in the ass and she'd always put up with him only because he was so damn good at his job. When it came right down to it - pain in the ass aside - he'd been a good sailor and a good shipmate. She smiled at him, brushing away a tear that threatened to race down her cheek. She never in a million years would have expected him to say something so sentimental. "Fuck you, you big ape," she said hoarsely.

He gave her a huge smile in return, and quipped, "You know chief, I'd love to take you up on that offer, but your timing really sucks."

She made a very un-ladylike snort as she suppressed a laugh. Then, seriously, she told him, "Good luck, sailor boy."

He nodded, his roughly chiseled face grinning eagerly as he casually slammed a fist into his open palm. "You, too, chief," he told her. "Let's kick some fucking alien ass."

As she turned her attention back to the approaching aliens, she saw that they had removed their armor and were now dressed identically to the humans, wearing only the black garment and sandals, plus their collars. *Evening the odds a bit for us,* she thought. They bore weapons similar to what each of *Aurora's* crew members had chosen, with each warrior squaring off opposite her human counterpart.

Harkness studied the woman - the enemy - who came to stand in front of her, looking at how she carried the weapons Harkness herself had chosen: two sticks made of something that was like wood (but probably wasn't, Harkness thought), each a bit less than a meter in length and maybe as big around as her thumb. A practitioner of *Eskrima*, a Filipino martial art, would have been quite comfortable using them, but Harkness had never heard of *Eskrima*. She knew nothing about martial arts except the hopped-up sequences she'd seen in the holo-vids, and figured she'd probably only last two seconds with a bladed weapon in her hands. But the two sticks were at least easy for her to hold and swing, and having one in each hand gave her a small illusion of being able to defend herself. She might even be able to give her opponent a whack or two.

She spared a glance at Kilmer's opposite number: a husky warrior who held no weapons. Kilmer had fondled just about every sword and other killing contraption they'd had to choose from, but in the end had decided - like the captain and Yao - that he was most comfortable fighting with his fists. He was a brawler, and a good one: Harkness could attest to that from the times she'd seen him wallop landlubbers in planetside bars, just before she'd had to drag him and any others out before the modern day shore police arrived.

She looked toward the captain, wondering what was supposed to happen next. He only shook his head and shrugged.

The tall warrior chose that moment to enter the arena, and the babble of the thousands of aliens gathered in the stands of the arena stilled.

***

Tesh-Dar strode through the portal the other warriors had used to enter the arena. Unlike them, her sandals made no imprint upon the sand as her long and powerful legs carried her to the stone dais set at one end of the arena. Last of the great warrior priestesses of the Desh-Ka, the oldest order that had ever served the Empress since a time before legend, Tesh-Dar was as much spirit as she was flesh. Her powers were beyond the understanding of most of her own race, let alone the wide-eyed strangers who now watched her with a mixture of awe and fear. She no longer wore her short sword, an ancient weapon many generations-old, or her cloak, but was armed for combat: she wore a wicked longsword in a scabbard sheathed at her back; another sword, not unlike the one brought by one of the young aliens, hung from her left waist; and her favorite weapon, the *grakh'ta* - a seven-stranded barbed whip - was coiled at her right waist. Three of the lethal throwing weapons, known as the *shrekka*, were clipped to the armor of her left shoulder in the traditional position.

As she entered, the gathered peers stood and saluted, left fists over their right breasts and heads bowed, the crash of the warriors' armored gauntlets against their breastplates echoing as though from a single giant hammer. This was the way of things throughout the Empire wherever Tesh-Dar went, for she had no living equals: she stood upon the first step below the Throne itself, upon the great pyramid of steps that defined the status of each and every one of Her Children. Even the few remaining great warrior priestesses of the other orders climbed no higher than the third step from the Empress. Only the Empress held a higher place in the hierarchy of their people. Had Tesh-Dar not been who and what she was, no doubt the Empress would have come Herself to oversee this Challenge, such was the importance of what was to take place here. But She was closely linked to Her blood sister, and instinctively trusted Tesh-Dar's judgement and feelings. For with Tesh-Dar here, the Empress could concentrate fully on the changes even now sweeping many parts of the Empire to prepare for war with the strangers. Such trust was a singular privilege and honor for the great priestess, but her towering status among the peers made for a lonely aerie, even for one whose soul was bound to countless billions of others.

Standing upon the dais, the stone of which had been quarried from the Homeworld thousands of human years before, she gestured to the gathered peers, the crews of the squadron of ships that still hung in space around the alien vessel, and they silently took their seats. She looked upon the two lines of warriors: one of her own kin, whose blood sang clearly with want of battle; and the strangers of pale flesh who were silent, soulless creatures to her spiritual ears. She knew that they would not understand any of what was to come, or why it was so important to Tesh-Dar's people. Few even among Her Children truly understood the importance of these rare encounters with other civilizations. For they did not realize that their own race had been slowly dying for over a hundred thousand years as marked in the time of the orbit of the aliens' homeworld around its parent star. With every encounter with another race that Tesh-Dar's people had experienced in past millennia, the Empress and those who knew the heart-wrenching truth behind some of their ancient legends built up their hopes that they would find among the strangers that which they had sought for tens of thousands of great cycles: one not of Her Own kind whose blood would sing, one who could save Tesh-Dar's people from eventual extinction.

But their hopes had thus far been in vain. The dozen spacefaring species encountered in past ages had been given every chance for the blood of even a single one among them to sing, but none had. Truly, they had served in glorifying the Empress through battle, but in the end the defeat of the strangers of old had left nothing but more pages in the Books of Time. And Tesh-Dar knew as well as the Empress that there were few enough pages left before Her Children would be no more. Centuries, perhaps, but no longer.

Such were Tesh-Dar's thoughts when she began to speak. "Long has it been, my sisters, since we have encountered strangers among the stars," she told the gathered thousands in the New Tongue, her powerful contralto voice echoing across the arena. While her words carried no farther than the stone walls around her, her Bloodsong cast her emotions and sensations in a wave that swept through the Empire. As she spoke, the toil and labor of the billions of Her Children across ten thousand star systems came to a halt as they rode the emotional tide experienced by Tesh-Dar and the peers gathered here as witness. "Coming to us of their own purpose, of their own accord, they do not know the Way of Her Children, for their blood does not sing. Soulless they may be, but as in ages past, in the time since the First Empress left us, they will be given the right of Challenge, to give them every chance for their blood to sing.

"For as the warriors of Her Blood well know, the Bloodsong echoes in our veins the strongest when in battle, just as it sings most clearly from the hearts of the clawless mistresses when achieving perfection in form. For this is our Way. So has it been-"

"-so shall it forever be," the crowd replied as one.

"The warriors chosen to fight this day I have carefully matched to the strangers," Tesh-Dar went on. "For while it is a battle to the death, we seek no advantage, for that brings Her no glory, no honor. For the Way of Her Children is not a path easily traveled, and honor is not given, but must be earned." She paused to look closely at the strangers who stared at her, uncomprehending. "None of the strangers may leave, save the Messenger, whom I shall choose." Looking at each of the warriors arrayed against the aliens, she added, "Should all of our sisters fall at the hands of the strangers, I shall complete what they began with my own hand." She raised her staff a hand's breadth and then hammered it down onto the dais, the sound reverberating like a gunshot. "In Her name," she called to the warriors standing ready in the arena, "let it begin."

SEVEN

Captain McClaren listened to the speech made by the commanding warrior, although of course he couldn't understand her. It infuriated him, because his crew had been murdered - the few of them here were walking dead now, he knew - and he couldn't even ask her why.

When she rapped her staff on the stone dais, he knew it must be time for the fun to begin. For with the last few words she spoke, the warriors facing his crew went from simply being wary and alert while they listened to their leader to being as tense as spring steel under a heavy load.

The warrior opposite him was just a bit shorter than he was and probably weighed less by a good ten or more kilos, but he had no intention of underestimating her. It was abundantly clear that her people trained their entire lives for whatever skill they would have as adults. That was okay by him, because many humans did, too.

He assumed the classic boxer's stance, hands raised up to guard his face with his arms protecting his upper body, with one leg forward, knees bent. He felt light on his feet as he began to move toward his opponent to test her skills and see what he was really up against. Adrenaline surged through his arteries, now that the fight was upon them. He almost hated to admit it to himself, but he felt oddly ready for this. He felt *good*.

As captain, he wanted to be the one to land the first blow (or take the first hit); this was part of the "first in, last out" philosophy that had been one of the guiding principles of his style of leadership. But he refused to let himself rush in like a fool: he was too experienced for that, and while he knew he would die on these sands, he wanted to take out at least one of the enemy - one of Harkness's "fucking alien bitches" - with him.

But the first blow wasn't to be his: he suddenly saw Ichiro Sato rush toward his opponent, his bellow echoing across the arena as their swords crashed together.

***

Ichiro had stood silently, eyeing his opponent as the big warrior spoke. Unlike the other alien warriors, who were roughly similar in size (and presumably age, although that was impossible to tell) to their human counterparts, Ichiro's was clearly smaller than himself. If he had to guess, had she been a human girl she might have been twelve or thirteen, if that. She held a sword similar to his - it seemed that the *katana's* form was a universal constant in bladed weapons - and he had no doubt she knew how to use it far better than he did.

Nonetheless, it was a maddening insult. He had reconciled himself to dying, but had imagined he would be cut down by a warrior like the one who had handed back his grandfather's sword: he clearly would have been no match for someone like her, and he would have been content with that.

But this was simply too much. In the brief moment of uncertainty that took hold in the arena after the big warrior had spoken her final words, Ichiro's indignity overrode any pretense of logic or sense.

Whipping the gleaming *katana* above his head, holding it high with both hands, he charged his opponent, roaring his undiluted rage.

***

Tesh-Dar watched intently with both her physical and spiritual senses as the battle was joined. The rash young alien was the first to strike. Tesh-Dar noted with satisfaction that Li'an-Kumer, the young warrior chosen to face the human, did not kill him right away, as she easily could. Instead, she parried his spirited but foolish attack, then twirled in closer to deliver a cut that left only a minor flesh wound. The alien animal howled - more in indignation than in pain, Tesh-Dar thought - and slashed ineffectively at Li'an-Kumer with his sword.

Content that the young warrior had this creature well in hand, she swept her gaze over the other combats that were developing. Some of the combatants had not yet actually closed with their opponents in these first few seconds, but were still sizing up their opposition.

And then, as if a secret signal had been given, they all crashed together in a mass of snarling fury.

Tesh-Dar focused her attention on the one about whom she was most curious, one of the older animals whose inner strength radiated like a beacon...

***

For a fleeting instant as Sato charged forward, Yao Ming prepared to save the young man from his impetuosity. But there was something about the stance of the alien girl opposite him that told Yao that he need not intervene - yet. As Yao stood, no longer in the *Wu Ji* posture, but simply standing calmly, he watched Sato's attack in slow motion, and was content with the young alien's reaction. She seemed happy to play with Sato for now, and that would allow Yao some time to deal with his own opponent.

The warrior facing him wore many more of the pendants around her collar than the other aliens, which Yao assumed meant she was far more accomplished. She also had silver claws, which perhaps a third of the others had, as well; the remainder had black claws. He had no idea if this was an adornment of some sort, or if it was physiological. He had also recognized her fluid grace in step and posture as she had strode forward into the arena. All of the warriors possessed a sort of feline grace, but this one was different, more like the great warrior who now stood watching the proceedings. For in her he had seen a grace and power, quite apart from her size, like he had never seen before.

His opponent calmly stared at him, her form a mirror image of his own, radiating confident strength. Yao had considered going on the attack, and would have if he had perceived an immediate major threat to either of the midshipmen. But Sato appeared to be all right for the moment, and on Yao's other side, Midshipman Zalenski was sparring confidently with her own opponent, armed with the alien equivalent of a saber. This gave Yao the choice of going on the offense or letting the alien do so. While *t'ai chi* could certainly be used in the attack, its roots were in defense, and he lost nothing by ceding the initiative to her. In fact, that gave him a certain advantage in his own fighting style, allowing him to use her own energy against her.

So he stood there, relaxed, staring into the alien's eyes as the battle was joined around him in a frenzied cacophony of curses and cries of pain, of metal striking metal, striking flesh. One second passed, then two.

And then she attacked.

***

Harkness reeled from the agonizing pain in her left thigh and right breast. The simple sticks were not as glamorous - or gory, perhaps - as a sword, and not as swiftly lethal, but she had never felt such agony as she was feeling now: it felt like her flesh had been seared by white-hot metal.

She had managed to stave off most of the blows the alien had rained down upon her since the match began, at least until the bitch had grown tired of playing around and decided to systematically attack Harkness's right hand, breaking three of her fingers in a savage strike. Then the alien smashed both of her sticks against Harkness's right breast, and whirled around to do the same to her left thigh as Harkness reflexively brought both hands up to try and protect her chest from another attack.

Her left leg collapsed under her, effectively paralyzed from the pain. As Harkness went down, the alien slammed her sticks down in a brutal one-two strike on the chief's exposed shoulders. Harkness screamed as she fell face-first into the sand, her body quaking from the pain. She tried to roll over and free her left hand, which still clung desperately to one of the sticks, to defend herself, but she couldn't. It felt as if the muscles in her shoulders had been severed with a knife, and she couldn't move her arms. The best she could manage was to turn her head enough to spit out the sand from her mouth.

She suddenly felt the alien slip a foot under her belly and lift, flipping her over onto her back like a turtle. The alien stared down at her impassively as she brought her weapons up to deliver the *coup de grâce*.

"Fuck you, you bitch," Harkness spat, staring the alien in the eye.

Suddenly a hulking figure swept across Harkness's vision, and with a surprised grunt the alien warrior was literally carried away. Harkness watched in wonder as Kilmer, his face already a tattered mess, slammed her tormentor into the sands of the arena and straddled her chest. Grabbing her by the neck with one hand, he began to rhythmically pound her in the face with his other bloodied fist. The warrior frantically beat at him with the sticks, hitting him in the head, in the side of the ribs, in the legs, but he seemed impervious to what Harkness knew must have been blinding pain.

Then the warrior abandoned the sticks and used the weapons she was naturally equipped with. Snarling in fury and pain, one of her fangs snapped off by one of Kilmer's hammer-blows, she stabbed him in the throat with the talons of her right hand, while using the left to claw at his face.

He contemptuously swatted away the hand she tried to claw him with and simply ignored the fact that he'd been stabbed. With blood streaming from his torn throat, the alien's hand still desperately slashing and tearing, his right fist became a jackhammer against the alien's face, battering her down to the bone.

After a few more seconds, her hand fell away from his throat, and she stopped struggling. Whether he had strangled her or had fractured her skull - or both - it was clear that she was done. Dead.

Kilmer turned to Harkness and gave her a smile through his bloody lips. Then he slowly sank down on top of the second warrior he'd killed.

Harkness managed to crawl over to him, her own injuries seeming like trifles in comparison. "Kilmer," she rasped, tears flowing freely down her cheeks, "you didn't have to do that, you damn fool."

"Couldn't stand...to see...my chief scream," he whispered, the sound more of a wet whistle as it passed through what was left of his throat, "except at me."

Harkness cradled his head gently against her chest. Turning to where Kilmer's original opponent lay still in the sand, Harkness saw that the warrior's jaw was misshapen, no doubt smashed to splinters by one of his fists, and her face was a patchwork of bloody flesh. He must have fought like a lion to defeat her so quickly so he could help defend Harkness.

She held him tenderly the few remaining moments until he died. Then, grasping one of the sticks with her good hand, she struggled to her feet. If she was going to die, she wasn't going to do it whimpering in the sand.

***

McClaren was holding his own, but that was about as much credit as he could give himself. The alien was simply a better fighter, although not by much. But in a battle to the death, it didn't necessarily take much. He had seen Kilmer and Harkness go down, but they weren't the first. About half a dozen others had died already, and the battle had become one of exhausted attrition.

Most people who had never engaged in a real fight didn't realize just how much physical stamina it required. While most of his crew, including himself, were in good shape, only a handful had the athletic conditioning for combat that the aliens clearly had. Even those who had close-combat training were simply being worn down.

McClaren dodged another open-handed strike from his opponent. Her fighting style would have been interesting if he wasn't in a fight for his life. It was similar to boxing, but instead of using clenched fists, she struck with her hands open, using the heels of her hands instead of her knuckles. It made sense, since it would be difficult for her to clench her hands like he did: her claws would cut right into her palms.

Regardless, her style was quite effective: the blows she'd landed felt like he'd been hit with a small sledge hammer. He had managed to give her some satisfaction in return, but she was faster than he was, and equally tough. He had snapped her head back a few times and gotten solid hits on her torso, but it felt like he was hitting a leather punching bag packed with sand and solid as a rock.

She dropped low and made a quick jab for his midsection, and he twisted his torso slightly to deflect part of the blow while lashing out with a right hook. Luck was with him this time, and he made a solid connection with her jaw. She spun away from him, blood spraying from her mouth, but it was only a momentary victory. Stepping back from him, not letting him pursue the advantage, she shook her head vigorously, regaining her bearings as she warded off his jabs.

Then, baring her fangs in anger, she bored into him with those feline eyes and moved back into the attack, driving him back with a blinding flurry of open-handed strikes.

***

While Yao was anything but a sociologist, he was able to tell a great deal about the aliens' culture from the way his opponent fought. As with many human martial arts that emphasized hand and foot strikes in the attack, the alien's style of fighting clearly was based on the offense, at expressing aggression. Considering the humans' experience with their hostesses thus far, that came as no surprise.

But she was clearly surprised, and growing increasingly frustrated, at Yao's employment of a variety of moves based on the fundamental *t'ai chi* principle known as *pushing hands*. Her arts had certainly endowed her with great skill in a variety of attack and defense techniques, but she simply could not get through Yao's fluid deflection and absorption of her attacks. In a civilization like that of the aliens where combat was the centerpiece of the society's existence and aggression was the rule, Yao suspected that it would be very unlikely for martial art forms like *t'ai chi* to evolve, for it was fundamentally based on the ideals of self-defense and compassion toward one's enemy. And thus his opponent had no effective counter but frustration. And frustration inevitably leads to mistakes.

She suddenly lashed out with a high roundhouse kick aimed at his head, and Yao decided he had learned enough. He sank back on his legs, easily avoiding the kick, and suddenly surged forward while her leg was still following through, leaving her lower body dangerously exposed and her balance fixed on only one leg. While *t'ai chi* had its foundations in quiet strength, certain offensive variations that Yao had been taught long ago were quite lethal: he landed a crippling strike with his right closed fist against her lower abdomen, then followed it up with a brutal attack with his right shoulder, concentrating all of his internal energy into a thrust against her lower ribs. He grimaced inwardly at the *crunch* several ribs made as they shattered, the splintered ends spearing several of her internal organs as his attack lifted her from the ground and sent her flying backward. Her part in this battle was finished.

Without further thought of his vanquished foe, Yao quickly moved to help the others.

***

Sato knew he should have been dead a dozen times over. The alien imp who faced him was toying with him, humiliating him. He hadn't managed to make a single blow against her: all he had for his efforts was a dozen flesh wounds and at least as many gouges along the razor sharp blade of his grandfather's *katana* where it had slammed ineffectively against the alien's sword. He was shaking with exhaustion and pain, gasping for breath, and wished that the young fiend would finish him off and be done with it.

He had tried to keep track of Yao Ming and Anna, but if he let his attention wander at all, he was brought back to reality by yet another bloodletting from his tormentor.

She darted forward again in what he knew must be a feint, but he didn't know enough to counter it effectively. She jabbed her sword at his left leg, goading him into defending it with his own sword, then she twirled and slashed at his shoulder.

Ichiro braced himself for the pain, but it never came. As on the *Aurora* when the aliens first boarded, Yao was suddenly *there*. In a brief flurry of powerful blows from his hands, the alien girl fell to the sand, unconscious or dead.

Collapsing to the ground himself, Ichiro gasped, "Thanks, Ming...I don't think I could've lasted-"

His words were cut off by a scream from only a few feet away. He looked up in horror to see Anna Zalenski clutching an expanding red spot on her stomach where her opponent had stabbed her. Her face growing pale as blood flooded out of the severed abdominal aorta, the major artery that carried blood to her lower body, she slowly sank to her knees.

Her opponent raised her sword to take off Anna's head, but never got the chance. Yao snatched up the weapon Ichiro's tormentor had been using and hurled it like a spear, the blade stabbing clean through the neck of Anna's killer.

"*Anna!*" Ichiro screamed as he ran to her side, catching her in his arms as she collapsed.

"Ichiro..." was all she said as she reached up to caress his face. He held it tightly, bringing it to his lips to kiss her fingers.

But she was already dead.

***

McClaren staggered backward, putting some distance between himself and his opponent. He had evened up the odds slightly with a few lucky blows to her head and what he hoped had been an extremely painful punch to the kidneys (assuming she had kidneys), but he was exhausted. He had gone a full twelve rounds a couple of times in unofficial fights, and knew just how grueling it could be. But that was when he had been a young man in prime shape. Even with whatever the alien healers had done to fix him up, he still wasn't young anymore. Even their miraculous powers couldn't turn back time.

Looking around through his one good eye - his right, since his left had swollen shut after the warrior had gotten through his defenses and clobbered him good - he saw that the battle was almost over. He had no idea how long they'd been fighting; it was probably only a matter of minutes, but it felt like hours. Everyone who had been off to his left, except Harkness, was down, and she was barely able to move, limping badly on her left leg as she slowly made her way toward him. On his right, Yao and Sato were still up and moving, and he noted with an amused grin from his bloodied lips that Amundsen was still alive, too. He wondered how the brilliant pessimist was dealing with that turn of events. But the others, including Midshipman Zalenski and Lieutenant Marisova, were gone.

They hadn't gone down without a fight, though. At least half of the aliens were either dead or crippled, and the only ones still actively fighting were his own sparring partner and the alien Amundsen was fending off. The other warriors, after finishing off their victims, had backed away from the action and taken up position in front of the dais where the huge warrior still stood watching. McClaren didn't think they were going to get out of this alive, but it was nice to see that they were at least playing fair. Sort of.

He glanced at Yao as he fended off another flurry of punches from his personal alien training assistant, and shook his head slightly. While he hadn't won every match he'd fought, he'd never been carried out of the ring, and he didn't intend to start now. He knew Yao could make short work of his opponent, but that wasn't how McClaren wanted it.

With one last surge of adrenaline, buoyed up by the fact the others were still alive, he moved in on his lighter opponent. He was done trading blows with her: they were going to finish it now, one way or another.

The warrior had come to the same conclusion. They crashed together, and McClaren used his weight advantage to push against her, keeping her slightly off balance as he sent a series of right uppercuts into her abdomen. She slammed the heels of her hands into the side of his head, sending him to the verge of unconsciousness before he put everything he had left into a punch to the side of her ribcage that actually lifted her from the sand. With a grunt of agony, the fight suddenly went out of her, and she collapsed to her knees, clutching her left side.

McClaren staggered for a moment, ready to collapse himself, but he wasn't going to let the job go undone. He took a shaky step toward her, grabbed her hair with his right hand, and smashed the bloody knuckles of his left fist into her temple as hard as he could. Once. Twice. Three times, until he could tell that he was just holding her up by the hair. He let go, and her body flopped limply to the ground.

He managed to turn toward where Amundsen was still fighting and took two wavering steps before falling unconscious into Yao's arms.

***

No one was more surprised than Amundsen that he was still alive. He could only assume that the aliens had made a mistake in choosing his challenger, because from what little he'd been able to see of the other fights around the arena, the others were fairly evenly matched. He had no other explanation for how he had lasted this long. He had even managed to deal some damage to his opponent, landing a completely accidental hit that broke some of her fingers early on, denying her the use of that hand. He hated to admit it to himself, but he was even holding out some hope that he might actually beat her.

The alien made another jab at him with her quarterstaff. Only able to use one hand now, her movements were very awkward, and Amundsen easily fended off her attack, sweeping her quarterstaff to the side. He hated to get fancy, but he decided to take a risk and spun around, dropping low as he swung the quarterstaff like a baseball bat, hoping to hit the warrior's legs.

To his amazement, he did. She wasn't able to get her weapon around in time to stop his attack, and his staff was too high to jump over and too low to drop under. Amundsen had put all the power he could into the blow, and it hit her right in mid-thigh, sending her tumbling into the sand with a yelp of pain.

He lunged after her, raining down a series of frenzied blows on her exposed back and head before she could get back up. He kept hitting her, over and over, his quarterstaff hammering her body.

Suddenly, Harkness was next to him, her hand on his shoulder. "Lieutenant," she said shakily, "you can stop now. You won."

Amundsen felt like he'd just snapped out of a trance. He blinked at her, then got a look at the quarterstaff he held. The end of it was covered in blood. He looked down at the warrior he'd been fighting. He must have hit her dozens of times. Her head looked like a smashed melon, and her torso was misshapen from the bones he'd broken.

"Lord of All," he whispered as he tossed the quarterstaff aside. Falling to his knees, he vomited into the sand.

Harkness knelt beside him, rubbing his back gently as she might to soothe a child. "It's okay," she murmured. "It's okay, lieutenant."

***

The culling is complete, Tesh-Dar thought as she surveyed the carnage of the arena. Of the twenty-three aliens who had begun, only five remained. Of the warriors who had fought them, eight had died, and another seven had been badly wounded. The aliens had displayed great spirit in their fighting, and she knew they would be worthy opponents in the coming war.

But the end of this first battle had come. Tesh-Dar left the dais and strode toward the remaining humans.

***

Yao watched as the huge warrior approached the battered human survivors. Amundsen, recovered now, and Sato stood on either side, with Harkness on the ground behind them, the captain's head propped up on her knees. He had not yet regained consciousness, and Yao feared he never would.

The alien stopped a few paces away and looked them over for a moment. Then she held out her left hand. In her palm lay the cyan disc. The ticket home.

"Take it."

Yao turned to see the captain staring at him with one eye that looked like a bloody cue ball from the burst capillaries.

"Take it, Yao," McClaren rasped. He had regained consciousness, but was clearly fighting to remain awake. "We've made our stand. One of us...one of us has to get back. To tell what happened here."

"I cannot take it, captain," Yao told him. "I-"

"Give it to Ichiro," Harkness suggested, and McClaren nodded weakly.

"Captain, no!" Ichiro begged him. "I'm not going to be the one to leave. I couldn't fight, I couldn't do anything to help anyone. Please don't send me home in shame-"

"It is not dishonorable or shameful to live, Ichiro," Yao told him softly.

McClaren nodded. "Listen, son," he said, struggling to get out the words, "you're young and deserve a chance to really live, if you can get out of here. You've also paid attention to everything you've seen: the people back home need to know what they're up against." He paused, drawing in a painful breath. "If they don't, all of this - the deaths of your shipmates - will have been for nothing. And our worlds will burn."

"Why not Lieutenant Amundsen?" Ichiro countered, turning to look hopefully at the lieutenant. Ichiro never would have thought that he would do everything he could to avoid having to go on living. "Why not send him?"

"Because those are the captain's orders, Midshipman Sato," Amundsen replied. Managing a tired grin that looked more like a grimace, he went on, "I wouldn't mind living another day. But I joined the service late, Ichiro;

I'm nearly as old as Yao. And you're at least as observant as I am. I wish I had time to tell you my thoughts," he glanced at the warrior, sensing her patience was coming to an end, "but you'll come to your own conclusions."

"I'm not going," Ichiro said resolutely, standing up and coming to attention. "I refuse those orders, sir."

"Yao..."

Ichiro didn't even feel the blow that knocked him unconscious a moment after the captain had uttered the petty officer's name. Yao carefully laid his young friend down on the sand beside the captain.

"Now get the goddamn disc," McClaren ordered, "while we still have time."

Yao saluted, did a smart about-face, and stepped up to the huge alien, who still held the cyan disc in her outstretched palm. He took it, then knelt next to Ichiro. Holding it up for the warrior to see, he placed it inside the young man's alien-made shirt, carefully sealing it closed.

***

Tesh-Dar watched as one of the aliens slide the Sign of the Messenger inside the upper garment of the youngest among them. She did not understand their methods, but was in agreement with the one they had chosen. Had she been forced to choose among them, she would have made the same choice, although likely for different reasons. The young animal's spirit burned brightly in her mind's eye, his aura brighter than the others. He would do.

As for the others, it was time...

***

Ichiro's eyes fluttered open. Laying on his back, staring straight up into the sky, he didn't realize where he was until he noticed the color wasn't quite the right tint of blue, but was tinged with magenta.

With an electric surge, he suddenly remembered where he was. He rolled over onto one side, his neck pounding with pain - had Yao hit him? - only to see the captain staring at him with one bloodshot eye. He was dead. Harkness lay on top of him, having tried to protect him with her own body. Her back had been opened up like she'd been hit with a giant meat cleaver. Her beautiful face hung slack and pale in death.

Next to them lay Amundsen. He was on his back, as Ichiro had been, his face turned up to the alien sky above. One might have thought him sleeping, except for the pillar of gleaming alien metal sprouting from his chest: the great warrior's longsword.

"Ichiro..." a voice rasped from his other side.

He turned to find Yao, clutching the shimmering blade of the alien's other sword, the one that looked like a *katana*, that had speared through him, just below the heart.

"*Yao!*" Ichiro cried as he scrambled over to his friend and mentor. "No! No, you can't die...you can't-"

"Remember what I told you," Yao whispered, gripping Ichiro's hand tightly. "There is no dishonor...in living." With a final squeeze of his powerful but gentle hand, Yao Ming was gone.

The big warrior stood a pace or two away, her hands at her sides, intently watching Ichiro.

"Why?" he screamed at her. "*Why?* Goddamn you! *Goddamn you to hell!*" Without thinking, he reached back and picked up his *katana*, a weapon he'd never learned how to use, a weapon that had gone unblooded while his friends and shipmates had died around him. The blade of his grandfather's sword held before him, he charged the alien in his last great act of defiance.

***

Tesh-Dar did not have to understand his words, for she was beginning to sense the emotions of the aliens, and to understand them. Her comprehension was far from perfect, but what this young creature was feeling now, she understood all too well. This one gift she could give him.

As the alien charged, she made no move to step aside. Instead, as he came within range she reached out - faster than the eye could see - and guided the tip of the human's blade toward a weak spot in her armor, just under the breastplate and to one side. The sword pierced the underlying leatherite armor and stabbed through her abdomen. Carried by the young alien's momentum, the tip emerged out her back.

She hissed at the pain, but it was not a new sensation for her: she had endured far worse many times in her long life.

***

For a moment, Ichiro simply stood there, frozen in time as he held the handle of the *katana*. His eyes were wide in shock, fixed on where the blade had entered the alien warrior's body. His momentum had run the sword all the way through her, the warrior's blood running in a dark crimson stream from the wound. He looked up to meet her eyes, sure that she must be about to kill him. But she met his gaze with what he knew must be understanding, and perhaps even a trace of empathy. He wasn't sure how he knew that, for he couldn't read her facial expressions. But he knew that's what she felt. He had absolutely no doubt.

She brushed his hands away from the sword's handle, and then in a single smooth motion pulled it free of her body. It was slick with her blood, and he could see blood running down the armor on her legs from the wound. But if she felt any pain, she certainly wasn't showing it. With a practiced twist of her wrist, she flicked off most of the blood from the blade onto the sand. One of the other warriors stepped forward with the scabbard, and the big warrior slid the sword's blade home. Then she held it out to Ichiro.

He reached out and took it with shaking hands, still unable to believe that she was going to let him live. Blinking away the tears that came to his eyes - tears of shame that he had lived while the others had died, tears of joy that he might be able to go on living - he looked up at her once more.

But there was nothing for him to see but the contemplative faces of the thousands of aliens still crowding the arena. The huge warrior had simply vanished.

EIGHT

Kneeling in the sand, flanked by a pair of alien warriors, Ichiro watched silently as the funeral pyres consumed the remains of his friends and shipmates. After the huge warrior had mysteriously disappeared, a procession of warriors had poured through the portals into the arena bearing kindling wood. Where it had come from, Ichiro couldn't guess, even had he been of a mind to try. They built a pyre for each of the victims of the bloody fight, alien and human alike, using practiced ritual motions that made it appear as if he were watching a well-rehearsed play. Part of his dead heart warmed as he saw a group of healers enter, and carefully - reverently, even - prepare his dead shipmates for their final voyage. Wrapping each of them in a pure white shroud that didn't allow any of the blood to show through, they carried the bodies to their individual pyres and placed them carefully on top, all at once.

In what Ichiro thought was an odd thing for the aliens to do, they removed the dog tags from his dead shipmates. After washing the tags in a clay bowl, carefully cleaning off any blood and then drying them, one of the warriors stepped up to him and bowed, then handed the plastic tags to him. All twenty-two sets. He noticed absently that the same ritual was being performed using the collars from the dead warriors.

His gut churning in a mix of anger, shame, fear, and uncertainty, Ichiro forced himself to read every one of the tags, burning the names into his memory. The alien garment he wore had no pockets, so he simply slid them inside his shirt with the cyan disk, trusting that the elastic material would hold it all in place.

When all the bodies were prepared, one of the warriors barked an order, and the assembled thousands stood up as one. After a moment, Ichiro did, too: he came to attention and saluted. Flames suddenly sparked to life under all of the pyres, and the wood - if that's really what it was - began to burn bright and hot. Watching the smoke from the flames rise high into the sky above, it was hard for him to believe he was on a starship.

In only a few minutes of fierce burning, the fires generating so much heat that Ichiro felt like he was in an oven himself, the pyres collapsed into flickering coals. The bodies that had been upon them were nothing more than ash and smoke. Ichiro, his right arm trembling from holding it up the entire time, dropped his salute.

As the aliens in the seats began to file out, his two guards - one of whom was the same warrior who had handed him his sword before the fight - gestured for him to head toward the portal through which he'd entered a lifetime ago. It was time to leave.

With one last look at the charred remains of the *Aurora's* captain and crew, he turned and followed them out of the arena.

***

The two warriors led him down a different set of passageways than before, although they were as big. The main difference now was that they were filled with aliens bustling to and fro. Their reactions to seeing him were universal: a slight bow of the head, as if he were someone of at least modest importance.

Despite the leaden weight of the survivor's guilt that had settled onto his shoulders and the crushing physical and emotional exhaustion he felt, Ichiro automatically absorbed everything he saw, everything he smelled, everything he heard and could touch. He wanted to catalog every sensation so that he could recall it when he returned home - if that truly came to pass - and help humanity mount a defense against these monsters. Any and every detail might be vital.

But most importantly, focusing on what was around him took his mind away from his battered soul. He was only nineteen, but he had aged decades in the few hours since they'd first seen the enemy ships. Only a few hours. It had been an eternity.

His escorts made no detours this time, showed him no rooms pulsing with mysterious technology. They took him straight back to the semi-organic airlock through which he and the others had originally been brought into the ship.

The huge warrior was waiting for him. He glanced at her side, expecting to still see the wound made by his sword and traces of the blood she had lost, but there was nothing: the leather-like armor was like new, and so was the gleaming metal armor. It was as if his stabbing her had never happened.

Feeling no fear, for that had been burned out of him, he approached the towering warrior who stared at him with her silver-flecked eyes.

***

Tesh-Dar watched as the youngling was brought before her. He had proven to be a hardy creature, for which she was thankful: the task of the

Messenger was a difficult one, and while she knew little yet of his species, she suspected his worst trials were yet to come.

In her right hand she held out a sphere that was roughly the same size as the young animal's head. It was the physical image of one of the worlds of his race, captured and held in an energy capsule. She held it forth for him to see, and it was evident he immediately understood what it represented. The image was of a planet that she had chosen for the first large-scale battle between their civilizations. After her warriors and the builders had studied the records of the primitive alien computing machines, they identified all the worlds the animals had colonized. After a great deal of consideration, they had presented Tesh-Dar with several choices, and she had picked this one. It was not so important that its loss would shatter their will, nor was it so small that it would pose no challenge. It was heavily industrialized, yet not located too near their primary core systems. It had a large population, but not so large that its loss would strike a crippling blow to their ability to repopulate.

"What do they call themselves in their own tongue?" Tesh-Dar had earlier asked those who now worked to understand the language of the aliens.

"They have many tongues, my priestess," one of the builders, a senior mistress, had replied, "although one is dominant. In that tongue, the animals refer to themselves as *human*."

"And this world," Tesh-Dar asked, staring at the image of the planet that she had chosen, "what is its name?"

"They call it *Keran*, priestess."

Now, standing before this young human, Tesh-Dar saw that he recognized the planet, for his lips made the sound of the word the builder had spoken to her.

***

"Keran?" Ichiro said out loud as he looked at the incredibly lifelike globe the warrior held in her huge hand. It was as if the planet had been shrunken down to the size of a bowling ball. He recognized it, because that was Yao's home planet, and the older man had spent many hours regaling Ichiro and Anna with exceedingly unlikely tales of his youth, usually to explain the origins of one of his poetic expletives. Ichiro felt his eyes burn again, but willed the tears away. "Is that where I'm to be sent?" He didn't expect the alien to understand him, but he had to ask the question.

She seemed to understand, or perhaps just guessed. She reached forward and put the palm of her free hand on his chest, right where the cyan disk was, then gestured out the circular hatch toward where the

Aurora waited for him. Then an image of the Earth, as lifelike as the globe of Keran she held in one hand, appeared over one of her shoulders, and she pointed to that.

Then she held up the globe and drew her palm across the face of it, as if her hand was the curtain of a play, and he watched in horror as the bright blue and comforting browns of the seas and land were suddenly stricken with what could only be the smoke and ruin of burning cities, with ships overhead, blasting at the surface and at one another.

She was telling him what planet they were going to invade first. "No," he murmured, shaking his head. "No. You can't..."

Taking her hand away, the replica of Keran returned to the way it had been before, the land, seas, and sky at peace.

With trembling fingers, he reached out to put his hand on the sphere, but he couldn't feel anything. It wasn't solid; it was simply as if his hand was being repelled. He'd never felt anything like it. But the flames of war didn't ignite under his touch as it had hers.

"When?" he asked her. "How long do we have?"

She only looked at him, her eyes narrowed. After a moment of consideration, she moved her hand over the globe in a different fashion, her hand flat as if she were pressing down on something. Starting at the north pole of the globe, her hand held just beside it, she slowly moved her hand toward the equator, then the south pole. As her hand moved, the planet's image took on the ravages of war.

Suddenly, he understood. *The globe is a countdown timer.* The alien couldn't - or wouldn't - tell him how long they had in any measure of time he would understand. But he knew now that when the globe she held had fully transformed into a world at war, the aliens would come. The invasion would begin.

***

Tesh-Dar could tell from his emotional reaction that the alien - the *human* - understood the meaning of the sphere. Their people would be given some time to prepare, although if the legends of past encounters in the Books of Time were to be believed, they likely would not use it wisely. The Messenger was never believed - at first. In the meantime, the preparations now beginning in the Empire for waging war against this new race would be at their peak. The human could not know it, but the sphere was attuned to the will of the Empress, and was not a mere mechanical timer in a sophisticated case.

She handed it to him, and he took it with obvious care, no doubt concerned that it might break. She smiled inwardly, knowing that little could disturb the device short of a release of energy on a scale that would sear half a planet.

For the last time, she looked in the young human's eyes. "Far must you travel, young one," she said to him, "and much have you to do. Go now..." she paused, nodding to him, "...in Her name."

***

Ichiro took the globe of Keran from the warrior's hand as if he were a timid god holding the planet itself. He looked at the globe, amazed at the clouds that slowly swirled across the surface, their shadows passing across the land and seas.

Looking up at her once more, she spoke to him in her language for a moment, then paused. Nodding to him, she then said "...*uhr Kreela'an.*"

He had no idea what any of it meant, but he knew he had heard that particular phrase several times before in the arena. Was it important? He had no way of knowing.

The two warriors who had come this far with him gently took his arms and launched themselves into the invisible energy bridge between the two ships. Looking at the *Aurora*, Ichiro saw with some amazement that the holes the enemy boarders had made were gone. The one in the side of the hull that was their destination was still there, but the rest of the ship somehow looked newer. He thought it was only an illusion, but then it struck him: just like some of his comrades whose physical ailments had been cured by the healing goo, the aliens had done something to the *Aurora*. The pitting left by small particle impacts that had dulled the gloss of her hull over time was gone. It was as if she had just been launched from the yards.

His two escorts expertly landed him in the hatchway burned into the ship's flank, but he hung back, unwilling to step farther into the ship. What lay before him was suddenly striking home: a months-long voyage alone in a death ship. He began to shiver, remembering the blood and gore strewn about the galley where they had been herded together after the boarding. And Lieutenant Amundsen's gruesome description of what had happened to the rest of the crew. He didn't want to be trapped in here with *Aurora*'s rotting bodies, with her ghosts.

The aliens weren't concerned with his fears. Taking him gently, but firmly, by the arms, they led him down the passageways that led to the bridge.

Soon, he began to relax. The interior of the ship was just like the outside: pristine. The lights were on as they normally would be, and the strange blue glow of the walls after the aliens had killed the ship's power was gone. There was no sign of struggle, no traces left of the homicidal mayhem that had taken place only a few hours before. No smell of blood and death. Except for what he remembered, the ship was like new.

They led him to the bridge, where one of the aliens in the dark blue robes, one of the ones who had recreated the ship's computer systems, stood waiting. She gestured at him, and then the primary command console, then made pushing motions with her hands toward him, as if warding him off.

"Don't touch, I assume," he said aloud. The alien made no reply, but simply repeated her gestures. Then she bowed her head to him, and the warriors turned him about and led him off the bridge.

They walked him through the whole ship, although he wasn't really sure why. Possibly to see that they cleaned up all the mess. Not only was everything clean, but even a few minor imperfections, like some dents that had been made in one of the bulkheads from an accident two years before with some heavy repair equipment, were gone. He wondered how deep this "fixing" went, and if some of the ship's systems hadn't been improved.

Finally, the warriors led him back to the hole cut in the hull. The alien in blue robes hovered in open space outside the hull as if she were pinned in place. Turning to him, the two warriors bowed their heads, and then stepped outside the hull, taking up position next to the blue-robed woman. He wasn't sure how they managed that, because their momentum should have kept them moving once out of the hull's gravity distortion field. But apparently the basic laws of physics didn't apply to these people. Humanity's enemy.

The alien in the blue robes closed her eyes and raised her hands, palms out, toward the edges of the hole. Ichiro watched in wonder as what looked like dust motes from the hull of the alien vessel suddenly began to flake off and float toward the *Aurora*. Soon it was like a blizzard of tiny particles heading toward the robed alien, and they swirled around her before coming to rest on the edges of the hole.

He suddenly realized that he was seeing a form of the black matrix material they had used to recreate the ship's computers, and this woman was taking mass from the hull of the gigantic warship and converting it for use to patch this hole in the *Aurora*. But it wasn't just a patch: she was actually recreating the missing section of the hull, all the way through. The outer metal alloy, the insulation layers, the cabling and conduits: all of the bits and pieces of technology that was buried in this segment of *Aurora's* hide was being remade.

In only a few minutes it was done. He stood gaping at a solid bulkhead and the lettering on a small hatch that read, *Pressure Valve 87.* There was absolutely no trace of there ever having been a hull breach here. No seams. No marks. Nothing.

He was suddenly startled by a familiar voice.

"Interlock engaged," *Aurora's* navigation computer suddenly announced. "Transpace countdown commencing. Primary energy buffer building. Two minutes remaining."

Still clutching the tiny effigy of Keran, Ichiro ran for the bridge. He made it in plenty of time. "Bridge display, full," he ordered the computer. The wraparound display sprang to life, showing the alien ships now moving off to give the *Aurora* a wider berth.

"Primary energy buffer threshold achieved," the navigation computer told him. In a way it reminded him of Chief Harkness's voice, from the times when she had sat down with Anna and himself to teach them the finer points of being leaders. "Transpace sequence in ten...nine..."

He clutched the globe of Keran tighter as the sequence wound down.

"...three...two...one. Transpace sequence initiated." Pause. "Jump."

On the bridge display, the alien ships and the bright stars that were the planets that originally drew his captain here suddenly swirled into nonexistence as *Aurora* disappeared into hyperspace, headed for home.

NINE

Terran Navy Commander Pavel Leonidovich Sidorov had a splitting headache. The shift commander for coordinating customs inspections for starships inbound to Earth, he was responsible for orchestrating the actions of over three dozen cutters that shuttled dozens of inspection parties from one merchantman to another, looking for contraband. Even with that many inspection parties, it was a daunting task: Earth had more ships to handle than any two other planets, with hundreds of ships arriving and departing every day. Customs control had several gateways at different orbital nodes spread around the equator, but all the inspection operations were run from this one command center, located at the primary Earth-orbit transfer node located over Africa. Attached to the "bottom" of Africa Station's massive docking and embarkation facility, Sidorov and his crewmen were located in an expansive enclosure of clearsteel that gave them an unrestricted view of the space around them: Earth below, and dozens of starships spread out in orderly rows pointing toward the station.

While this type of duty was normally performed planetside by civilian customs officers or the wet-fleet Coast Guard, outside the atmosphere it was a Terran Navy show. Funded by the Terran Government, which was loosely based on the ancient United Nations but with funding and executive authorities that never would have been conceived for the UN, the Terran Navy had exclusive purview for security matters beyond the atmosphere. Ironically, that had come to include customs inspections after a few nasty incidents of incoming "merchantmen" turning out to be armed raiders. So rather than form a new bureaucracy, the Terran Government simply expanded on the existing one. As a general rule, it had turned out to be a good compromise: the customs inspections were run with Navy efficiency, and there was only one major tax burden to be maintained for exo-atmospheric defense.

But Sidorov wouldn't have minded shoving the job onto someone else on occasion, like right now. "Negative," he grated, his Russian accent barely creeping into his otherwise excellent Standard as he spoke into his microphone to the captain of the bulk cargo transport *Manzanar*, "you are not cleared to maneuver beyond customs until you have been cleared by one of the inspection teams. This has already been explained to you, captain." *About fifty times already*, Sidorov added to himself.

"This is outrageous!" the captain of the other vessel sputtered. "We have been waiting here for two days, and have precious cargo that must be delivered immediately! You have no idea what an inconvenience this is for us, commander."

Sidorov put his face in his hands and shook his head, eliciting grins from the other members of the inspection control crew and the civilian harbor masters who directed the ships in and out of Earth space. The *Manzanar's* captain had been ranting at customs control every two hours on the dot since the ship had arrived two days before, with the man cursing the Navy and customs through both shifts. *The man must never sleep*, Sidorov lamented. And according to the ship's manifest, the cargo that had to be delivered "immediately" was a load of old-growth lumber that had been harvested on Kelsey's World and had been in transit for a month. Chances are it could wait a few more hours. With a sigh, Sidorov said, "Captain, as you have been told repeatedly, you *will* stay in queue, you *will-*"

"*Holy shit!*" one of the senior harbor masters shouted as he and several others suddenly stumbled back away from the massive viewports around the cylindrical command hub.

Outside, not more than one hundred meters away from where Sidorov stood gaping in shock, a ship had emerged from hyperspace almost directly below Africa Station. Such a navigational feat was unheard of - overlooking the stupidity of even trying it - but coming out of hyperspace this close to a planetary gravity well was not only suicidal, but it should have been mathematically impossible.

After the slightest pause where everyone was in utter shock, total pandemonium broke out. The comm panels were suddenly flooded with frightened or angry calls from the ships in queue, a hundred - and quickly far more - calls from passengers in the station who'd seen the ship appear, and the station commander, who had a dedicated channel.

"*Chyort vozmi!*" Sidorov cursed in his native Russian. "Get cutters 12 and 17 over to that ship, and I want her captain on the comm *right now!*"

"Aye, sir!" one of the controllers replied, still in shock.

"Sidorov," the station commander, Captain Rhonda Burke, demanded from his primary video console, "what the hell is going on?"

"You know exactly as much as I do, captain," Sidorov told her. "I've got two cutters on the way and am trying to raise her captain. I'll let you know as soon as I have something."

"Understood. Out." With a brusque nod, Burke signed off so he could get to work.

"Harbor masters," he shouted above the din, "make sure those merchant ships understand that if they break out of line they'll be fined until doomsday and if we catch them I'll throw their captains into the brig!"

"Commander," another controller called, "her telemetry's active. It's the *Aurora*, sir."

Sidorov didn't need the telemetry to tell him what ship it was. He could see the house-sized letters of her name from where he stood: *TNS Aurora*. "That's Captain McClaren's ship, isn't it?" he asked. The controller who was monitoring the ship's signals nodded. "What the devil is she-"

A face suddenly appeared on the central video monitor. It belonged to a young man, but his eyes had the distant look Sidorov had once seen on the faces of the old veterans of the war twenty years before on the Russian colony of Saint Petersburg. Those eyes, set in a gaunt face that wore a haunted expression, gave him a bone-deep chill. His hair was far too long for a man serving in the Navy; while it was clean and brushed out, it looked like it had been growing wild for months.

"Africa Station," the young man said, "this is...I am Midshipman Ichiro Sato of the *TNS Aurora*...commanding. I..."

"What do you mean, 'commanding,' Midshipman Sato?" Sidorov demanded. "Where is Captain McClaren?"

"Captain McClaren is dead. As is the entire crew. All but me. Sir." He struggled a moment for control of his emotions.

"Midshipman, if this is some sort of joke, you'll wish you were never-"

"Sir," Sato interrupted, his voice choked with emotion, "I wish to report that *Aurora* made first contact with a sentient race..." He paused again, his face assuming a cold mask of hatred before continuing, "and that human space is about to be invaded."

There was total and utter silence on the control deck as everyone suddenly tuned in to what Sato was saying. Not just there in customs control, but throughout the station and among the waiting merchantmen, for Sato was communicating on an open channel.

For a second time in as many minutes, pandemonium erupted.

***

Stephanie Guillaume was standing in line with all the other human geese who were waiting for the next orbital transfer shuttle to take them down to the surface when the call came through on her vidphone.

"Stephanie!" her editor and boss at TransCom News, Simon Whyte, shouted at her from the tiny high definition screen. She always went by Steph. He never called her Stephanie unless she was about to get a bonus or a major ass-chewing. "Where are you?"

"What do you mean?" she asked sarcastically. "I'm still stuck on Africa Station because the Transit Authority boneheads can't make the shuttles run on time."

"Thank God," Simon breathed, practically in tears.

"Simon," she said, suddenly concerned, "what the hell's going on?" She had never particularly liked the man, but he'd given her a chance when she'd been stiffed by most of the other news organizations she'd tried for. An attractive, if not quite beautiful, brunette with inquisitive brown eyes and a personality to match, she knew she was good enough - both in terms of looks and brains - for a spot on one of the major news-zines. The only real challenge was getting the break she needed to get into the big leagues. Simon was a pushy jackass, but she knew she could do a lot worse. At least he had never tried to push her toward his bed or pulled any other crap on her. As jackasses went, he really wasn't so bad. *Maybe one of his fifty thousand relatives has died or something*, she thought, trying to come up with a reasonable facsimile of sympathy. It was hard.

"Listen," he went on in a rush, completely ignoring her, "something's happened. Something big. *Right there on the station.* We got a tip - shit, a pile of tips now - that a mystery ship suddenly appeared and there's talk of an alien invasion."

"*What?*" Steph exclaimed. "Oh, come on! How many times have we been sent on wild goose-"

"It's the *Aurora*," he said, cutting her off. "The research guys say it's one of the newest survey ships that went out almost a year ago. Go find her. Find out what happened."

Fuming, Steph grabbed her bags and stepped out of line, tossing them angrily against a nearby wall. That's when she noticed that a lot of people were on their vidphones. More people than usual. Listening closely, she made out phrases that sounded an awful lot like what Simon had told her: "ghost ship" and "alien attack" among them. She saw a growing number of perplexed, amused, and even frightened expressions.

"Listen, Simon-"

"Just do it, dammit! This could be the biggest story since Christ got nailed to the cross-"

Her vidphone suddenly went blank. Then her vid screen filled with an unfamiliar message: "Network connectivity lost."

Around her, everyone else who was using their phones must have experienced the same "connectivity problem," because she heard a lot of cursing and people just staring into their blank vidphones.

"Network problem, my ass," she muttered. Their connection had been cut off intentionally.

"Information," she demanded of the console embedded in the wall. It still was working. "What can you tell me about an inbound ship called *Aurora?*"

"I'm sorry," the disgustingly deferential female voice replied, "that information is restricted."

Steph felt her pulse quicken with excitement. *There might really be something to this!* "Okay, who do I need to talk to for information on inbound ships?"

That information apparently *wasn't* restricted. After she got what she needed, she bolted down the corridor toward the central elevators as fast as her high heels could carry her. She left her bags behind, completely forgotten.

***

"Cutters 12 and 17 are in position, sir," one of the harbor masters reported through the din of frantic pleas and threats being made by the other controllers to keep the merchantmen from scattering in the wake of *Aurora's* spectacular arrival and Sato's equally spectacular claims of invading aliens. The two small vessels, looking like remoras alongside the much larger survey ship, had approached the main port and starboard gangway airlocks.

"Commander..."

Sidorov shifted his attention from updating the station commander back to the face of the midshipman who appeared to be *Aurora's* only survivor.

"Sir," Sato told him, "I strongly recommend that you consider first contact safety protocols before boarding. I don't believe the aliens left any contamination - that wouldn't fit with what I saw of how they do things - but..."

"Don't worry, Sato," Sidorov told him, "the boarding parties will be wearing full vacuum gear." *And weapons*, he added silently. He didn't know whether to believe the young man or not. He had said little - and Sidorov had gotten him switched over to a secure circuit - but first contact? Alien invasion? He sounded delusional, and Sidorov half expected the boarding parties to find some sort of massacre that would wind up being made into a holo vid show for lunatic teens.

On the other hand, Sidorov couldn't take any chances. If the midshipman's wild story did seem to check out, things were going to get dicey very quickly. The station commander had already put through a call to the customs fleet commander, who wanted verification before he woke up the Chief of Naval Staff half a world away. Everyone was thus far taking the story with a big grain of salt, but one thing was indisputable: *Aurora's* reappearance simply should not have happened the way it did, and they wanted an explanation. Fast. "I hate to say it, but you'll probably be in quarantine for a while if this story of yours checks out."

"Understood, sir," the young man replied. "Sir, I have opened the outer gangway hatches and the inner hatches are unlocked. The cutters may send in their boarding parties."

Sidorov noticed the change in Sato's speech as he said *boarding parties*, almost as if he were gritting his teeth.

"Thank you, midshipman," Sidorov told him. He glanced at the tactical controller who sat before a wide-screen console, who nodded in return: he had contact with the boarding parties, and both teams reported they were aboard and moving quickly to secure the bridge and engineering.

After a few minutes the team leader from Cutter 12 reported in. "Sir, so far as we've seen, there's nobody here. Not a soul. No sign of a struggle, no bodies, no nothing. Just a spanking new-looking ship." His video feed confirmed it. Empty passageways. Empty cabins. Empty work spaces. Nothing.

"Same here, commander," the leader of Cutter 17's team reported as he reached engineering. "There's nobody home but the kid on the bridge."

Sidorov could hear the stress in their voices. There were always people aboard a ship in orbit. The passageways might not be teeming with people, but a Navy ship returning from a long cruise would have half her crew at the airlocks, chomping at the bit to get off to shore leave. And there was *always* someone on the engineering watch, even if a ship was in space dock. Always. But this ship had just completed a hyperlight journey of who knew how long with no one but a midshipman aboard. It gave Sidorov the creeps.

"We're at the bridge, sir," the leader from Cutter 12 said quietly. There was Sato in the man's video display, standing rigidly at attention. Sato saluted the ensign who stood before him. "Midshipman," the ensign told him as he saluted, "you stand relieved."

"Aye, aye, sir," Sato replied hoarsely, tears suddenly welling from his eyes. "I stand relieved. The *Aurora* is yours."

With that, Sato collapsed to his knees and wept.

***

Steph stood at the back of the command deck near the access portal from the central elevator shafts, staring in disbelief at the drama playing out on the video monitors around her. Dressed in a tight red dress that didn't leave all that much to the imagination - she was damned if she'd look like a frump while traveling first class on the company's dime - she stood out like a collision beacon among the starched khaki uniforms of the Navy crewmen. But that dress and her press ID had gotten her past some tough gatekeepers before, and certainly hadn't failed her this time: the Navy security people she had to get past to get in here had both been men, and had been easily manipulated into believing that she'd been summoned there by the commanding officer, but she was to keep a low profile until he had a free moment to speak with her. She figured it wasn't *too* far from the truth. The dress and her curves distracted them, while the ID and a sharp tongue gave her credibility. She looked harmless enough, so they let her through.

She watched as the young man on the main screen - the sole survivor of the ship's crew - broke down in tears after the space-suited figure of a member of one of the boarding teams officially assumed control of *Aurora*. For a while she simply stood against the back wall of the command center, about a dozen paces behind where the person in charge - Commander Sidorov, one of the guards had said - stood watching the main monitor. She could see and hear everything, and so could the mini vid-cam array that was clipped to her ear, the video array and microphone on a wire-thin boom that extended forward next to her cheek. With the network shut down she couldn't get her data off the station, but an idea was churning in her brain to not only get around the little problem of censorship, but to make it work to her advantage. She added audio notes quietly, whispering so as not to draw attention to herself too soon.

***

A part of Sato was ashamed for breaking down and crying like a child in front of everyone who might be watching him, but the greater part of him pushed it away. It was an emotional release from the burden he had borne alone for the last few months. He hated to admit it to himself, but it was the first time since the slaughter of the ship's crew that he had felt a positive emotion of any kind. In this case, it was simply relief. Relief that he was back among his own kind. Relief that he was no longer alone on a ghost ship with the nightmares that plagued his sleep each and every time he laid down.

The voyage back had been entirely uneventful and mind-numbingly boring. As he had suspected, the aliens had made more than simply cosmetic changes to the ship: they had modified some of her systems to allow her to function entirely on her own. The things the crew normally had to do to keep her systems in good working order were no longer required, at least for the months it had taken to get back to Earth. *Aurora* had sailed for six months from her last port of call on the Rim to reach the alien system, but had taken about four months to return to Earth. It should have been impossible for the ship to go that far in only four months, even taking a direct transit. So the aliens must also have altered the ship's engines in some way, making her faster in hyperspace than should have been possible. He had tried to learn about the course settings and what the ship was doing, but while the blue-robed alien had warned him away from the command console, the warning appeared to have been unnecessary: he could get no navigation information from the ship's computer at all, no matter what he tried. He couldn't retrieve any information that could even corroborate his story of where the *Aurora* had been since she left the Rim: all evidence of the aliens had apparently been stripped from the ship's records. And the aliens had locked him out of everything that had to do with the ship's drives, navigation, sensors, everything. About the only thing he had free access to were the educational and entertainment sections.

And their sense of navigation...Sato had cried out in surprise when the ship had emerged from hyperspace, literally right next to Africa Station. It was impossible for at least half a dozen reasons. Not just the accuracy - how could they have known that *Aurora* wouldn't intersect another ship when she emerged? - but because of how close they were to the Earth's gravity well. The formulas were complex and handled directly by the navigation computer, and of course varied depending on the gravity index of a planetary or stellar body, but the nearest safe jump radius for Earth was well beyond the orbit of the moon. But the aliens had somehow brought the ship right *here*, matching the orbit with a moving object from an unimaginable distance. It wasn't just a coincidence. It wasn't luck. They had done it intentionally.

At the start of the lonely months aboard the ship, after he realized that he had been locked out of everything he wanted so desperately to know, he became listless, falling into a dark depression. Had there been liquor aboard, he had no doubt he would have spent most of the trip in a drunken stupor, even though he didn't normally drink alcohol.

What shocked him out of it was his obsession with watching the replica of Keran. Three months after leaving the alien system, he noticed that the northern pole had turned from its previous pristine white to a dirty gray as it had when the big warrior had shown him how the globe would change as the time for war drew closer. That's when it struck him that he had only four pieces of evidence to prove what had happened: the alien clothes he'd worn back aboard; the changes the aliens had made to the ship; the cyan-colored disk that had been his "ticket home"; and the replica of Keran. There appeared to be nothing in the ship's computer memory, and certainly no trace that aliens had been aboard the ship.

That meant that everything else - *everything* - was in his head. Everything to show how his shipmates had died. And that was when he finally got a grip on himself again and started acting like the young Navy officer he wanted to become. He started to log all his impressions, everything he could remember, down to the tiniest detail. Then he broke it down into sections, organizing the information into logical categories and cross-checking it for accuracy and consistency. He drew diagrams of what he could remember of the alien ships, outside and inside; of what the warriors and the robed aliens looked like, and how many different kinds of robed aliens there were. Sights, smells, sounds, the taste of the food they'd been given, the texture of things he had touched. Everything. In the end, it was not only a vital exercise in giving humanity some intelligence information on the foe they would soon face, but helped him deal with the crushing survivor's guilt he felt, and the penetrating sense of loneliness and isolation.

But that horrible voyage was finally over. His tears expended now, he stood up and faced the ensign who led the forward boarding party. "My apologies, sir," he said, gathering himself again to the position of attention. "It has been a...difficult trip home."

***

Steph watched as several Navy officers suddenly burst into the room, led by a stern-faced female officer who was all business. Steph frowned to herself, because women like this one were almost impossible to manipulate. She sometimes felt guilty about pulling strings on people, but it wasn't a question of morality, it was a question of getting the job done. It was a part of her job that she wished she didn't have to do, but that's not the way life was. Not hers, at least.

She directed the microphone pickup toward the woman and waited to see what would happen next.

***

"I'm not sure how to handle this, captain," Sidorov told Captain Rhonda Burke quietly as the boarding teams quickly finished scouting through the rest of the ship. He had muted the audio channel with *Aurora* so they could speak in relative privacy in the hubbub of the harbor masters working around them.

"I don't see the problem," Burke replied sharply. "You've implemented the first contact quarantine protocols, and fleet is up to speed on the situation for now."

Sidorov didn't take offense, because he knew that she wasn't impugning his judgement, just making a direct observation. She was direct about everything. But sometimes she didn't see problems that came at her from an oblique angle. "I'm not worried about that part, ma'am," he told her. "I'm worried about containment of any sensitive information. I don't want to speculate, but if news of some sort of 'alien invasion' gets out, there could be some ugly repercussions."

"I'm sure there's a perfectly logical explanation to what's happened that doesn't involve aliens," Burke said, shaking her head and rolling her eyes. "We've had stranger things than this happen over the years. There's not going to be any alien invasion. That's ridiculous."

"Excuse me, but how can you possibly assume that?"

Burke and Sidorov turned to see a civilian woman in an eye-popping red dress stalk forward as if she wore the stars of an admiral.

"And who the bloody hell are you?" Burke demanded hotly. "Security! Get this civilian out of here!"

"Captain," Steph said quickly, recognizing the woman's rank and knowing she only had seconds before she would be bodily thrown out of the command center, "I'm a journalist," she quickly flashed her press ID, "and I can tell you that the secret's already out of your hands. The best you can do is control it and spin it the way you want. And I can help you do that."

"Bullshit!" Burke spat, motioning to the same two guards who had let the mystery woman into the command center. The captain's expression left no doubt that they would get the ass-chewing of their lives later.

"I was up in one of the transit lounges when *Aurora* came in," Steph rushed her words out as the two men gently but firmly took her by the arms and started hauling her out, "and there were dozens of people on their vidphones a minute later talking about it, with their noses pressed up to the observation windows, *looking at the fucking ship and talking about an alien invasion!*"

Burke glanced at Sidorov and saw the indecision on his face. Again, if she was anything, she was direct. "Commander?"

"Ma'am, she may have a point," he said as the guards continued to haul the woman out. "If she's a legit journalist..."

"Hold it!" Burke suddenly ordered the guards. "Take her in there." Burke pointed toward a small briefing room at the rear of the command center. "We'll join you in a moment."

***

Steph's heart was hammering, not with fear but with excitement. She didn't have a "yes" from the captain, but she had at least put off being tossed out on her ass.

The guards led her into the conference room and left her there for a few minutes before the captain - Burke was her name, according to the name placard embedded in her khaki uniform - and Commander Sidorov came in. The guards closed the door and waited outside.

"You've got precisely one minute to convince me why I shouldn't put you under arrest," Burke ordered brusquely.

A minute, Steph thought. *Please.* "Captain, *Aurora's* arrival is news already. Look at any of the info channels and I'm sure you'll see it. And somebody heard something to make them worry about an alien invasion. I don't know where that angle came from, but that's why my bloody editor called me: because he'd gotten wind of it from someone else!" She leaned closer. "And even if the invasion bit isn't true, people are thinking and talking about it. The cat was already out of the bag before you took the station data networks down."

That elicited a stage-perfect "I-told-you-so" look from Sidorov to the captain.

Her frown deepened. "Thirty seconds."

Thirty seconds, my ass, Steph thought. *You know I'm right.* "Listen. I'm a legitimate journalist," she flashed her ID again, holding it right under the captain's nose, "not some idiotic independent blogger. I can help you spin this the way you want, tell the story the way you want it told. Otherwise," she nodded her head back toward the station core where thousands of people were still gawking at the *Aurora* and murmuring angrily about their lost network connectivity, "those idiots out there are going to fuck it up royally for you. I'll bet there are a hundred journalists and five thousand bloggers who just bought tickets to come up and visit Africa Station to see for themselves."

"Give me a break, lady," Burke growled, not impressed. "No news hound is going to give us a free ride. What's in it for you?"

"All I want," Steph said in a rare moment of total and absolute truth, "is exclusive access. I'll agree to any conditions you want, as long as they're legal, but I get access to the ship, your personnel, the survivor," her mind conjured up the image of the haunted-looking young man, wondering at the tale he had to tell, "and whatever else I may need to tell the story that wouldn't normally be classified. Your way. In exchange, you keep all the other newsies out."

"And why shouldn't we just hold the usual press conferences and not tell any of you anything?" Burke countered.

"Because you won't have control of shit," Steph replied bluntly. "People are going to talk, and you can either make it look like the Navy is being up front and honest, or we can play the usual stupid government cover-up game. And you know how those end up."

Burke looked at Sidorov, who only nodded. The captain suddenly leaned down and slapped the controls of a nearby comms terminal.

"Yes, ma'am?" a young navy rating answered.

"Get me Admiral Schiller," Burke told her, directing the call to the commanding officer for public relations at Terran Navy Headquarters. "He's expecting my call." She turned toward Steph, her lips twitching upward in what might loosely be called a smile.

Steph's eyes widened as she realized that Burke had played her. The bottom line hadn't changed: Steph would still get the exclusive access that she had wanted. But instead of negotiating from a position of strength and possibly getting out from under a pile of restrictions that Burke would probably slap on her story, she had practically begged for it. She felt a flush of anger and embarrassment at being manipulated so easily by the captain. It was a sensation she wasn't used to, and definitely didn't like.

"Schiller." A middle-aged man with an olive complexion and a hawk nose appeared on the screen. "Has she agreed?"

"Yes, sir." Burke glanced at Steph again. "We've got what we need."

"Then get moving, captain," Schiller ordered. "We've got to get on top of this situation before we have an interstellar panic." He leaned closer, his eyes narrowing. "We need to know exactly what happened out there. And fast."

TEN

Once over the initial shock, the Navy moved quickly. Burke decided to keep Sato on board *Aurora* for now, both to contain any further revelations and to quarantine him physically until they could make sure the ship hadn't brought back any pathogens or other alien oddities that could pose a direct threat. Two tugs arrived and quickly maneuvered the big ship to a berth in a space dock that had been hurriedly emptied. Several compartments in the dockway were quickly converted over to sterile rooms to accommodate a team of military medical and hazardous materials specialists. And a small team of psychiatrists and physicians had been assembled to debrief and examine Sato.

As all this was going on, Burke, Sidorov - who had passed the command of the watch on to his relief officer - and Steph sat around the table in *Aurora's* main briefing room. It was uncomfortable wearing full vacuum gear, but until the biohazard team arrived with more appropriate suits, it would have to do. Admiral Patrick Tiernan, Chief of the Terran Navy Staff, had given Burke direct orders to start debriefing Sato immediately and determine if the whole thing was some sort of bizarre hoax, or if his claims of possible alien invaders were real. They didn't have time to waste.

No one else was present as Sato told his story for the first time. Burke and Sidorov knew that he'd be telling it a hundred more times to the debriefing team and others later on. But for now it was a closed first-time session.

Steph listened, enraptured as the young midshipman told his tale in a briefing that he'd carefully prepared during the long months he'd been alone on the ship. Burke had ordered that they all hold their questions until Sato had gone through his briefing the first time. As he spoke, Steph noticed that the expressions of both Navy officers grew more and more intense. Despite their initial incredulity, Sato's briefing was extremely convincing. Despite her own natural skepticism, Steph found she believed him, especially when he brought out the dog tags of the captain and crewmen who had died in the arena. She could see him fighting for emotional control as he detailed the ordeal that left him as the sole survivor.

And then he showed them the artifacts, which he'd intentionally saved for last.

"This is the disk," he told them, taking the shimmering cyan disk, his "ticket home," from a pocket in his uniform and passing it to Captain Burke. He had kept it with him the entire trip, and he only gave it to the captain with the greatest act of will.

Burke took it gingerly, finding it difficult to hold while wearing the bulky gloves. "Did you run any tests on it?" she asked him as she handed it to Sidorov.

"Yes, ma'am," Sato told her. He tapped a few buttons on the briefing console and a close-up of the disk appeared on the main screen. "I ran a full battery of basic tests, using everything I either knew how to do or could learn in the time I had, and came up with almost nothing." He nodded at Burke's frown. "I realize that such testing isn't my specialty, ma'am, but basic spectrographic analysis - which is one of the first tests I ran - with the equipment we have aboard is something I was taught early on by Lieutenant Amundsen. But look at the results."

A chart appeared on the display. Most materials were made up of a variety of basic elements, each of which would appear as a line of data showing each element and the amount of that element as a percentage of the whole. But in this case, there were only two lines. The first indicated *Fe*, or iron, with a composition of 0.05183%. The remainder of the material was lumped under the ominous heading of *Unknown*.

"That doesn't make sense," Burke told him as she passed the disk to Sidorov. After turning it over gingerly in his hands, he passed it to Steph, who stared at it, fascinated.

"I know, ma'am," he replied. "But I assure you, it's accurate. I ran it a dozen times, using different equipment, calibrating everything carefully. I also performed as many other tests as I could think of that were non-destructive, all with the same results." He shook his head. "I know someone here will conduct many more tests, but I will be surprised if the results differ. This," he retrieved the disk from Steph, who parted with it only reluctantly after becoming transfixed by the shimmering cyan surface, "is a completely new material to our science."

Steph noticed that he automatically put the disk back in the pocket of his uniform tunic. *He's going to have a tough time parting with that little souvenir*, she thought.

"But it's nothing compared to *this*." An insulated box that was big enough to hold a basketball had been on the table the entire time. He removed the lid, setting it aside on the table. Then he reached in with both hands and pulled out the globe of the planet Keran.

His audience gasped.

"This is what is most important now," he told them, holding it up so they could look at it closely. "I believe this represents the planet Keran, and is some sort of countdown timer to an invasion there." He handed it to Burke.

"Goddamn suits," she grumbled, having difficulty holding it. "I can't seem to get a grip on it."

"It's not the suit, captain," Sato told her. "It's what the globe is made of. Or, perhaps, what it is *not*."

"What do you mean?" Steph asked, fascinated by the incredibly sharp detail of everything shown on the globe, from the lights of the larger cities showing on the planet's dark side, to the deltas of the major rivers emptying into the seas.

"I don't believe that it is a physical object," he explained. "It is more like an...energy capsule of some sort. That is why it's so difficult to hold. It seems to have mass, but I haven't been able to measure it accurately. And you can't actually touch it: it's almost like trying to handle some sort of self-contained repeller field." He shook his head. "I've tried everything from pressing against it with my hand to a low-intensity laser to try and get an accurate measurement of its size. But the results are all inconsistent. The harder you press against it, the harder it presses back. I don't have the necessary physics knowledge to explain, but I believe that what we're seeing here *is* Keran, perhaps reflected in some sort of space-time bubble, and we are seeing it in real-time."

"Impossible," Sidorov breathed, gingerly taking the object.

"What do you mean, 'we're seeing it in real-time'?" Steph asked.

"I believe that the cloud formations and other phenomena you see here on this object - at least the parts that aren't reflections of what the aliens want us to see of the invasion - are actually happening, now, on Keran," he replied, taking the globe back from her. He set it on a ring on the table that acted as a stand. "I have actually studied the cloud patterns, and in the months it has taken me to return home they haven't repeated. I don't think this is some sort of replica that the aliens produced from the ship's navigational records. It is real."

"How can you be sure?" Burke asked.

"It should be simple," Sato told her. "I have made three-dimensional recordings of the object, and the files have been dated. If we can get meteorological data from Keran for those times, comparing them should be a trivial matter." He tapped a few buttons on the console, bringing up the information on the files.

The thought sent a chill snaking down Burke's spine. "If what you're saying is true, the bastards must have a ship in the Keran system, spying on us and relaying this somehow."

Reluctantly, Sato shook his head. "That is a possibility, captain, but..."

"Spit it out, midshipman," she told him. "Now isn't the time to hold back any ideas."

"As I said, ma'am, I think this is more than some sort of transmitted image from a ship or sensor platform in the system. I think what we are seeing here really *is* Keran, as if it was contained in a separate bit of space-time."

"You're not making me feel any better, Ichiro," she said in a softer voice, the implications suddenly striking home. *If the aliens had technology that was that advanced*, she thought, *what chance would we have against them?*

"I want confirmation of this right now," Burke ordered Sidorov. "Get Sato's data to *Hecate* and have her jump for Keran immediately." Direct communications between the far-flung star systems occupied by humanity was, as yet, impossible. Instead, a fleet of courier ships spent their operational lives jumping between systems, gathering up data from special communications buoys that buffered outgoing information. In turn, the incoming couriers dumped their communications files into the buoys for distribution into the local system, or to be held for couriers heading to systems further on. It was a cumbersome and slow way to communicate, but until some of the highly experimental - and incredibly expensive - direct communications systems long in development had been perfected, it was all humanity had.

In the unusual case of *Aurora's* return, the Navy had anticipated the need for priority interstellar communications and had pulled several Navy courier ships off of their regular runs and put them at Burke's disposal. They were small and unarmed, but with their massive engines, they were the fastest ships in human space.

Sidorov spoke for a few moments on a private channel, his voice muted in his helmet. "Done," he told Burke. "We won't have anything back for nearly two weeks, though."

Burke shrugged, the gesture nearly lost in the bulk of the vacuum suit. "We're stuck with what we've got," she said stoically as she eyed the blue globe that sat on the table. "And this thing is going to start changing the closer we get to the time the aliens will arrive?"

Sato noted that Burke's original skepticism, which he had certainly expected, had fled. She believed him. In one way, it was a huge relief that at least someone believed his tale. But it also frightened him: it confirmed that this was a nightmare from which he would never awaken. "Yes, captain." He brought up a view of the globe that he had taken soon after *Aurora* had left alien space that showed it in pristine condition. "This is what it originally looked like. But if you look here," he pointed toward the northern pole, which was a sooty gray, "you can see that it has already changed significantly. It will continue to alter its appearance from the northern to the southern pole as time runs out, sort of like an hour glass. In the four months it took me to return here, this much has run out." He leveled his hand, much as the huge warrior had, at what was roughly fifty degrees northern latitude, which was the northern boundary of where the larger towns and cities began. While the more spectacular visions of war were not yet apparent, the clouds of smoke from burning cities were already swirling into the air of the northern pole. "Again, I have studied its progression, and it seems to be constant. If my projections are correct, we have roughly eighteen months to prepare."

Burke and Sidorov exchanged a look. *Eighteen months.*

"Shit," was all Burke could think of to say.

"But Ichiro," Steph asked, "what of the aliens themselves? We have these two bits of their technology," she nodded toward the globe and implied the disk in his pocket, as well, "but there's nothing about them. No physical evidence-"

"But there is," he said, bowing his head to her. He reached under the table and withdrew a long curved black tube that was carefully sealed in plastic.

"Jesus," Steph breathed. "That's your grandfather's sword, isn't it? The one you stabbed the alien with?"

"The same," he told her. "After I realized its value," he made an apologetic nod toward Captain Burke, "I hermetically sealed it in plastic. The aliens may have erased all traces of what happened from the ship's computers, but I assure you that there is physical evidence here." He slowly slipped the blade from the scabbard to reveal some dried blood along the blade's edge. "I ran some basic DNA testing on it as well as I was able with some of the bio-survey team equipment. Not surprisingly, it is not human." He carefully slid the blade back in the scabbard and set down the sword.

"Midshipman Sato," Burke began, then paused. "*Lieutenant* Sato, I can't express to you the value of what you've done, not just in surviving, but in having the presence of mind to do all the work you did on the trip back to give us a jump start on this thing. You're going to have a rough time for a while answering endless questions from the debriefing team, and you'll also have to sit for a formal inquiry. I apologize for that, but I'll be straight with you: a lot of people in high places aren't going to want to believe any of this, and the inquiry might help with that. It's going to be hell, but not nearly as bad as the hell you've already survived. And if there's anything I can do for you - anything - just ask, and I'll go straight to the bloody Chief of Naval Staff to get it if I have to."

"Thank you ma'am," Ichiro told her, bowing his head in respect. She had just spot promoted him up three grades. "I do have one request..."

"Name it," she told him.

"When the defense plan for Keran - whatever it might be - is put into operation, I want to be there," he told her, his eyes burning with a cold fury as he remembered Chief Harkness's words. "I want to welcome those fucking alien bitches to human space."

***

Steph was deep in thought as she watched Ichiro eat. Burke and Sidorov had left the ship. After going through the strict decontamination procedures in a temporary airlock set up outside the entrance to the space dock, they had been able to get out of their vacuum suits and get back to Africa Station. Burke had put Sidorov in overall command while she went planetside to confer with the brass. Steph already had most of her initial story put together, and had already run it by Sidorov. With a few minor changes, he had loved it.

But one thing was missing: their enemy didn't have a name. Ichiro had tried to make sketches of what the aliens looked like, and no doubt one of the members of the growing debriefing team who waited impatiently in the space dock compartments set aside for the purpose would be a profile artist to help refine Sato's rough vision. But no one had really come to grips with what to call them; they were simply "the aliens."

That just wouldn't do, and she wanted to be the one to set the standard, not some egghead on the debriefing team who'd come up with some idiotic appellation.

The problem was that she couldn't just make up something. Well, she could, she reflected, but the Navy probably wouldn't approve it if she didn't have some basis for it. And it had to have a decent ring to it. She knew that she just needed a bit more time, and had pleaded with Sidorov to give her a while alone with Sato. He had finally agreed, knowing that Burke already had the most critical information, and all the debriefing team was really going to do was polish and further substantiate what Sato had already told them. But they still needed to get a story out, and fast.

Something tickled her mind, some small bit of information, but she couldn't latch onto it. So she let her mind wander as she scrolled through the text and video files that Ichiro had put together.

The next file that came up was a video of Ichiro recounting those things he could recall from the aliens' speech, from what little they had spoken.

"...one of the things that was repeated during the ceremony in the arena, and that the lead warrior said to me before I was put back aboard *Aurora*, was what sounded like *uhr kreelan*," his image said, trying to carefully pronounce it. "I believe there were a couple of other variations, but what sounded like *kreelan* was a common ending of some of what was clearly ceremonial speech. It sounded similar to what you might hear in some religious services, with the congregation answering the clergyman..."

Kreelans, she thought, mulling over the term in her head. Humans might never know what they were really called, but at least this was something that had a basis in fact, and was certainly better than what some of the idiots waiting their turn at Ichiro were going to come up with.

"Ichiro," she asked, leaning forward on her elbows in the increasingly uncomfortable vacuum suit, "we really need a name for these...creatures, other than the 'sword-wielding, blue-skinned bitches from hell.'"

He almost choked on his dinner as he burst out laughing, the first time since before first contact. He had rarely exposed that much emotion to others, but there was something about this woman that made him want to open up to her. He knew that it was probably just the fact that she was a very attractive woman and he was a young man who hadn't seen a human female for months. *Hormones*, he counseled himself. But it was more than that. From the moment he'd met her, he'd felt a strange kinship with her that he was at a loss to explain. "Well," he told her after he'd managed to bring his laughter under control, "that would certainly get some headlines, wouldn't it?"

She smiled at him, genuinely warmed by the fact that she'd been able to inject a little humor back into his life. Feelings like that didn't come often to her as part of her work: she was usually a cause of angst to others in the course of her job, and this was a nice change. It didn't hurt that he was attractive and extremely intelligent, if a little on the young side. She frowned inwardly. Definitely not her type, to judge by her previous history with boyfriends. But this wasn't a social call. She had a story to write, and she set that train of thought aside.

"Okay, so that might make the tabloids happy, but for something serious, how about we call the aliens 'Kreelans'? It's not quite as sexy, I know, but it's something the average Joe can pronounce and remember in between beers, and is something you remember them saying-"

"Yes," he said, interrupting her. The light of humor had left his face, and his eyes were dark pools of thought. "We have no idea what that term means, of course. But yes, I think that would fit the bill." He shrugged. "Not that I really have anything to say about it."

Steph shook her head. "Listen to me, Ichiro," she told him. "You've already made history, no matter how anybody looks at this whole thing, no matter what else happens. And you're going to make more before it's over. You're the only expert we really have, and that counts for a lot." She leaned back, making some more notes on her comp-pad. "Okay, so we'll go with that. For all I know, it might mean 'moron' in their language..." - that elicited another uncontrolled guffaw from Ichiro - "...but it'll work. The next question, though, is what the hell are they? Their civilization, I mean."

"The first thing that I thought of when we walked into the arena," Ichiro said after a moment of thought, "was that it reminded me of Earth's Roman Empire. We studied that a bit at the academy. I know it doesn't necessarily fit, but that's how it felt to me, like we'd been transported back in time to an alien version of Rome." He shrugged. "We don't know anything about their government, of course, unless some of the wizards on the debriefing team can puzzle something out. So the analogy is probably completely wrong. But that's how I felt," he finished quietly, trying to turn away from the memories of the slaughter that arose unbidden in his mind.

Steph saw him involuntarily shiver, and reached a hand across the table to take hold of his. He tried bravely to smile. "Well, we're not really trying to get all the details straight at this point," she told him. "We're just trying to come up with something that we can use to help tell people the story."

The Kreelan Empire, she thought. *Perfect.*

***

Four hours after *Aurora* flashed into existence above Earth, the senior civilian and military members of the Terran Planetary Government were gathered in the main briefing room of the Presidential Complex in New York. They had just seen the first report that Stephanie Guillaume had prepared and that the Navy had approved. The woman had effectively summarized not only the facts - such as they were at this point - of *Aurora's* voyage, but had also turned it into an expertly crafted propaganda piece that gave "the enemy" a face and a name.

Admiral Tiernan, the Terran Navy Chief of Staff, nodded to an assistant to bring the lights back up. With fiery red hair long since faded to gray and piercing green eyes that missed nothing, Tiernan was a sailor's sailor who had started his career as an enlisted man and worked his way up to the highest uniformed position in the Terran Navy over the course of his forty year career. While he could play the political game as well as anyone, his heart and mind were always focused on the ships of his fleet, and the men and women who served on them. "That's what we plan to let TransCom News run through the newswire, Madam President." Tiernan had been briefed personally by Captain Burke, and despite his misgivings - who would want to believe such a story? - she had been extremely convincing. He also knew her reputation as a hard-nosed no-nonsense officer, and if the young man who was the sole survivor on *Aurora* had convinced her, Tiernan felt compelled to believe the story. But he knew he wouldn't be in the majority.

President Natalie McKenna was still staring at the now-blank screen. She was leaning forward in her chair, with her elbows on the table. Her hands covered the lower half of her face as if she were trying to hide her expression. Tiernan knew that wasn't the case; it was simply one of her habits when she was concentrating hard.

"Josh," Vladimir Penkovsky, the head of the Terran Intelligence Service asked Joshua Sabine, the civilian Defense Minister, "Do you really believe this?"

Sighing, Sabine nodded. He'd been present when Burke gave her briefing. He had asked some hard, hard questions, and she'd had straight answers for him. And none of them were encouraging. "Yes, Vladimir," he said, almost grudgingly. "I believe it." He raised a hand as Penkovsky opened his mouth to interrupt him. "I know that it's not ironclad until Sato is debriefed and the engineering team goes over the ship with a fine tooth comb. But I think we've got enough solid evidence to feel confident that *Aurora* did indeed have a first contact encounter, and that this so-called 'Kreelan Empire' poses a clear and present danger to the human sphere."

Several other members of the council - the president had gathered all the members of her cabinet and the senior military staff - began to talk at once.

"Enough," President McKenna said quietly, immediately stilling the babble. A tall black woman from what had once been the state of Mississippi in the United States, she never had to raise her voice. Born in poverty, orphaned at an early age, and raised in a series of foster homes, no one would have ever thought she would make it to the highest leadership position on the face of planet Earth. But her resolution was as solid as her intellect was keen, and she had overcome every obstacle that life had ever placed before her. This one, while potentially greater by unknown orders of magnitude, was no different in her mind. "Like most of the others in this room and elsewhere," she went on, "I don't want to believe this. But we've always known that there might come a day when we encountered another sentient race. Everyone has always hoped that such a civilization would be a peaceful one." She glanced at Tiernan. "But we also knew that it might not be. And we can't afford to ignore what Sato brought back. Not with only eighteen months to prepare for an invasion."

"Our options are limited, Madam President," the Secretary of State, Hamilton Barca, rumbled. Looking more like a professional football linebacker than a top graduate of New Harvard's law school, Barca's appearance often put his counterparts off-balance in negotiations, while his endless patience in diplomatic discussions could wear down even the most difficult negotiator. "Earth has a trade relationship with Keran, of course, and full diplomatic ties, but no military treaties," he explained. "Even if they believe this," he nodded at the screen where they had just seen the proposed press report, "we don't have any mutual support agreements with them, and they don't even have a real spacegoing navy. It's going to take a lot of time to-"

"Hamilton," McKenna interrupted, something she almost never did to anyone, "I'm aware of what you're going to be facing on the diplomatic front. But if we believe the information we have - and I do, based on what Admiral Tiernan has presented today - we simply don't have time for normal negotiations. And if we don't act, and act decisively, the invasion won't stop at Keran. They showed us with *Aurora* that they could as easily attack Earth."

"It's a deception," Penkovsky interjected. "What if they want us to do exactly that? They can lead us into pouring our resources into defending a second-string colony world, and then just appear here and gut one of the core worlds."

The room once again descended into a babble of arguing.

"We need to dust off the Human Sphere Defense Agreement," Barca's voice boomed out.

His remark not only silenced the argument, but elicited a series of groans from around the table. The Human Sphere Defense Agreement - or HSDA - had been proposed years before after a similar scare that had turned out to be a false alarm. While the details of the proposal were complex, it basically would put all the spacegoing navies of the human sphere under unified military control and create an independent force of marines. The main sticking point, of course, was who would then be in control of the new joint military structure. Just like the countries of Earth had been a few centuries before, not all human-settled worlds were democracies, and not all of the world-states got along well (even many of the democracies did not get along well). The HSDA would never come about unless a unified political structure to control it was formed. None of the world-states - including Earth - wanted to give up any of their sovereignty to an inter-system government, and many planets had weak or nonexistent planetary governments, as well. The only reason Earth's Terran Planetary Government functioned as well as it did was that the nation-states that had guided Earth's destiny for so many years were greatly weakened in the series of wars before the Diaspora, when much of Earth's population fled the turmoil to found new colonies. Earth's surviving governments realized that the only hope of long-term survival and renewed prosperity lay in forming a strong global government. It was not an easy or bloodless process, but eventually had put Earth diplomatically and economically far ahead of the colonies whose governments remained decentralized.

"I agree," President McKenna said, much to the chagrin of most of the members of the cabinet. "This is what the HSDA was meant for, but before there wasn't a real threat to make it stick. This time there is."

"If anyone else buys this story," Penkovsky said under his breath.

McKenna fixed him with a burning glare. "I don't care if anyone else believes it," she grated. "If half of what Admiral Tiernan said was true, if the aliens - these Kreelans - have technology that advanced, our entire species is at risk. We will spare no effort - *none* - to protect both ourselves and other human-settled worlds to the best of our ability."

"And that, Madam President," Defense Minister Sabine said, "is the next big question. We've only got about one hundred warships with jump capability, ranging from corvettes on up to light cruisers and a handful of troop transports. Most of them are engaged in anti-piracy patrols in systems that don't have their own navies, with three dozen or so in Earth space at any given time on home patrol or in refit." Admiral Tiernan nodded in agreement. While the Terran Navy sported a big league title, it wasn't nearly as large as any of the old major wet-fleet navies had been. Earth had never really had to fight anyone since the Diaspora, and so had never allocated a huge budget for defense.

"We have quite a few ground troops," General Jaswant Singh, Chief of the Terran Army Staff said. "We could easily deploy several divisions without seriously affecting our own defenses."

"It's the same with us," General Sharine Metz, commander of the Terran Aerospace Defense Force, said. "We could deploy at least six squadrons of interceptors for near-space defense, and cover the gap in Earth's defenses by activating some reserve units to fill in."

Tiernan frowned. "The main obstacle is going to be lining up enough transport capacity to get our forces there and then keep them supplied," he said. "We've only got a few assault carriers, enough to hold two full heavy divisions. The interceptors," he glanced at Metz, "we'd have to take in on civilian freighters, so we'd have to get prior approval from Keran to get the squadrons on the ground and prepare them for combat."

McKenna nodded. None of this was a surprise to her. Everyone was still just trying to get used to the idea that there was another intelligent species out there that had decided to wage war on humanity for no apparent reason, and all they had right now were problems without solutions. She could listen to those who wanted to wait for more information, to see if this would just go away, but she wasn't about to waste any time. Thinking about the strange "hourglass" of the planet Keran and the millions of people there, she knew they had precious little as it was. "Here are my orders," she said formally, "and they are not subject to debate." Everyone nodded. They'd heard that tone of voice before during the major economic crisis that McKenna's first administration had faced, when the global economy was in deep peril and she had redefined the meaning of personal leadership. "First," she said, turning to Tiernan, "I want you to run the story your pet journalist has put together. We'll have a certain amount of apprehension among the populace, but I want to let our people know what we're up against. I'll hold a press conference immediately after the first story runs, and I want periodic updates as we learn more.

"Second, we will make all of our findings from the survivor's debriefing public once the next of kin of the *Aurora's* crew have been notified, and we will honor any reasonable requests by other governments to send observers for independent study of whatever the ship brought back." That raised a few eyebrows, but no one said anything.

"Third, we will offer any and all assistance that we can to Keran. And even if they won't accept direct military assistance, I want an expeditionary force prepared for a rapid insertion into the system if things go south and they need help. If we can help stop the Kreelans there, so much the better.

"Fourth, we will call a special session of the Interstellar Forum and refloat the HSDA. I don't expect it's going to be adopted, but I want it out there again, fresh in everyone's mind. Because if Keran falls, everyone's going to be worried about who will be next and how they can defend themselves, and HSDA will at least give us something to start with.

"Fifth, I want a plan to get our economy on a wartime footing. The red tape and all the rest of the *bullshit* goes out the door." Several members of the cabinet flinched at the expletive. McKenna rarely cursed. "We need ships, weapons, and manpower, and we need them fast. We also need public support for this, both financially and politically." She paused, her face turning grim. "And when we have the plan together, I'm going to go before the Terran Congress and petition for a draft."

Defense Minister Sabine whistled through his teeth. "That's going to be an awfully tough sell, Madam President," he said quietly. The president had complete authority to do everything she'd said except for instituting a draft for obligatory military service. For that, congressional approval was required in the form of a two-thirds majority vote. *And that was tough to get on the* easy *legislation*, Sabine thought sourly. "And if we get into a massive arms buildup, a lot of our neighbors are going to wonder if we're not thinking of doing a little empire-building ourselves."

"Good," McKenna said. "If we can leverage their fear of us, then so be it. But I want us to be transparent about what we're doing. I want other governments to know why we're doing it, and we'll offer to help them do the same. But I don't care if they build ships and weapons for the wrong reason; it will still help our collective defense when the enemy comes. As for Congress, that's up to me." She looked around the room. "Let me be perfectly clear, my friends," she told them in a voice laced with steel. "This is not a time for half-measures. I'll accept the resignation now from anyone who feels they can't get behind this one hundred percent from the start. Because as of today, after learning of the unprovoked attack on *Aurora*, the systematic murder of her crew, and the direct threat made to a human world - even if not our own - I plan to ask the Terran Congress for an official declaration of war against the Kreelan Empire."

ELEVEN

Among the countless planets that orbited the ten thousand suns of the Empire, many were such as this: great barren rocks that were host to gigantic seas of the matrix material controlled by the builders. From this they created the smallest to the greatest of the Empire's physical constructs, even entire worlds. For if the Empress willed it, it would be done.

A great task had She given the builders here and on other worlds, even as the strangers, the *humans*, were fighting and dying before Tesh-Dar's eyes. A new fleet would be created for Her warriors, to carry them forth into battle with their new enemy among the stars.

But this fleet was not meant to seek out and expunge the human animals from the Universe, for even a small task force of Her modern warships could accomplish that menial task. Instead, the builders had to reach back into the Books of Time, far back, to recall the designs created by their ancestors over one hundred thousand human years before. They sought designs that predated even the founding of the First Empire, for that was the level of technology that they sought to match. The bulk of the Imperial Fleet would remain as it was, the physical sword and shield of the Empire, but the new fleet would be roughly equal to the human ships they expected to face. And if the humans brought more advanced technology to bear in the coming encounter, so much the better for the added challenge Her Children would face.

Standing on the crest of a low mountain that held a great underground city, Tesh-Dar looked out across a giant lake of the black matrix. Above her the sky was bright with the artificial sun created aeons ago to light and warm this barren planet. It was a sterile wasteland of a world, useless for colonization, but ideal for the purposes to which it had been put. Much of its surface mass had been converted to the black matrix millennia before, and had been used as She required. A jarring landscape of violently upthrust rocks and ancient impact craters, the builders and the others of Her Children who labored here found solace and beauty in the monumental city beneath Tesh-Dar's feet, where the graceful domes and spires of buildings and dwellings lay under open skies and were surrounded by forests as if they were still on the Homeworld.

While Tesh-Dar's own powers were beyond the comprehension of any builder ever born, their powers left her with a keen sense of respect and awe. She watched as thousands of them stood in a rough oval nearly a human kilometer in length and half as wide, their arms out with palms turned inward to the center of the oval. She could sense the buildup of energy as the builder mistresses - those oldest and most powerful among the builders here - harnessed and guided the power of the acolytes. Other such groups of builders stood in similar ovals farther out; some groups were larger and some smaller, depending on the type of ship they had been called upon to build, with all of them near the shore of the matrix lake.

Tesh-Dar gasped as the power of the nearest group surged, and the surface of the nearby matrix lake began to stir. Its black, featureless surface suddenly began to ripple, and then the first particles began to separate from the depths of infinite black and float into the air. Moving faster and faster, the particles flew toward the center of the oval, the stream of airborne matrix becoming thicker until it blocked her view of the other groups of builders who worked beyond.

After momentarily hanging in the air in a nebulous cloud, the particles began to coalesce, and Tesh-Dar saw the first translucent shapes appear in mid-air where the ship's internal systems would be. At first only as thick as a single matrix particle, the primitive internal components of the ship gradually took form, even as more particles began to form some of the outer hull segments.

The great priestess marveled at the sleekness of the emerging design. Even with primitive spacecraft as ancient as this Her Children had fused the beauty of form with function, so unlike the designs of human ships she had seen from the extracted logs of the human craft. Unlike the boxy and cylindrical utilitarian shapes of the human vessels, this craft was formed with elegant curves and shapely proportions pleasing to the eye, as well as deadly to its foes. Kreelan engineering was as much art as it was science in all that they did, and warships were no exception.

"In Her name," breathed Tesh-Dar's First, a fiery young warrior named Kamal-Utai. This was her first visit to such a place, and Tesh-Dar smiled inwardly at the fascination felt by her apprentice, for she found it no less enthralling after seeing similar scenes countless times before. "Even before the days of the First Empress were we masters of the stars."

Tesh-Dar knew that it would take the builders weeks of painstaking labor to finish the ship that was now taking form, and even more time to complete the others being built for the new fleet, but she was satisfied with their interpretation of the Empress's will. It would take yet more preparation to train the warriors who would crew the ships, for they would have to learn everything anew. She did not envy the task of the ship mistresses who now studied the Books of Time translating from the Old Tongue the information on how to operate these primitive vessels. But she herself would be among the many to receive their tutelage, for Tesh-Dar was to lead this first campaign. Piloting the ships, operating the weapons, learning appropriate battle tactics: there was so very much to learn, and she looked forward to every moment of it.

In the coming war with the human horde, Her warriors would be evenly matched against the enemy. It would be a glorious opportunity to bring honor to the Empress for the warriors chosen to fight. Even now, countless arenas around the Empire were filled with cries of fury and the clash of steel as warriors fought in ritual combat for the right to slay - or be slain by - the human animals. Such combats would continue for many weeks, for many tens of thousands of warriors would be involved in the invasion of the human world, *Keran*, and many more - millions - would fight in the cycles to come. The attack on this first world had no particular strategic value, but was merely to provoke the humans into a fierce response. For this was not a battle or a war to be won or lost: it was simply to be fought for the honor and glory it brought to Her, to the Empress. And Her warriors would keep on fighting through the remaining centuries left to their dying race, should that be the will of the Empress.

With the Bloodsong burning in her veins and her body tingling with the energy unleashed by the builders, Tesh-Dar watched in silent wonder the birth of the fleet that would soon be hers to command.

***

Seated behind a lavish teak desk in his main office at the Keran Embassy, Ambassador Faisul bin Sultan, Keran's diplomatic representative to Earth, listened quietly as Secretary of State Hamilton Barca explained the situation as it was viewed by the Terran Government. Less than twenty-four hours had elapsed since *Aurora* flashed into existence next to Africa Station, and the shock waves of Stephanie Guillaume's news report and the president's press conference were spreading through human space with every successive jump of the communications couriers that carried the broadcasts. Ambassador bin Sultan had, of course, seen both the news release and the president's press statements: Barca had called him beforehand to make sure the news did not catch him by surprise, and to schedule a meeting as quickly as possible at the Keran Embassy.

"...and so, Mr. Ambassador," Barca concluded, "we would like to offer our unconditional support in the defense of your world, including direct military assistance should you so desire. The president made it very clear to me that there were absolutely no strings attached, no *quid pro quo*."

Bin Sultan's eyebrows shot up in surprise. *There were always strings, always conditions,* he thought, *even though they were often invisible.*

"When the enemy invades," Barca told him, "we want to try to stop them cold."

Leaning back in his chair, bin Sultan regarded Barca for a moment before he spoke. "Mr. Secretary," he said finally, his mellifluous voice carrying only the hint of an accent of his native Arabic through his Standard English, "I do not wish to appear ungrateful, because the offer made by your president is truly generous. I also wish to express condolences - on behalf of my government and myself - for the loss of your ship's company, among which was a citizen of our world, as I am sure you know. As with ships that sail upon the seas, the loss of a crew or a vessel on such a long and perilous journey is always a terrible tragedy. All that aside, Mr. Secretary, I will of course convey your government's kind offer immediately to my government." He paused for a moment, clearly grappling with what he was to say next. "But I also cannot help but feel that President McKenna may be reacting with - if you will forgive me - some small haste in the matter. It has barely been a full day, and complete analysis of the information has barely begun. I feel very strongly for the young man who returned alone from this ill-fated expedition, but asking us to go to a war footing based solely upon his account and some interesting artifacts is...precipitous, let us say."

Barca grimaced inwardly at the diplomat's choice of words. In diplo-speak, it was the rough equivalent of bin Sultan shouting that he thought the president was fucking crazy. But Barca couldn't help but agree to some extent with what bin Sultan was saying: the president had been incredibly quick off the mark on this one, and two cabinet members had already resigned after her little in-house pep talk. But to Barca, she was still The Boss, and if she wanted to go balls to the wall to prepare for an alien invasion, he would do everything in his power to help her. Because, God forbid, she just might be right.

"I completely understand, Mr. Ambassador, believe me," Barca said. "We fully realize how much of a shock this must be, and how...well, how incredible it all seems. But the president is fully convinced by the available evidence and is committed to having Earth do whatever we can, as quickly as we can, to prepare for whatever may come. Eighteen months leaves us very little time."

"Thank you, Mr. Secretary. And please rest assured that I will contact you personally the moment I have a response from my government." The ambassador smiled and stood up smoothly, signaling an end to the meeting, and Barca did the same. Shaking the bigger man's hand, bin Sultan told him, "I appreciate your coming here, Mr. Secretary. Please keep us apprised of your findings, and I will contact you soon."

"Always a pleasure, Mr. Ambassador," Barca replied formally.

A few minutes later, Barca settled into the limousine that would take him on to the next of half a dozen visits to other embassies to try and drum up support for the war effort against an enemy that only one man had encountered and survived. Sighing, he put a call through to the president to give her an update. He expected one of her executive assistants, but his call was answered immediately. It was the president herself.

"How did it go, Ham?" she asked him expectantly.

"He said - in a most dignified manner, of course - that he thinks you're a loon and that we're making a mountain out of a molehill," he told her bluntly. "He's going to pass the offer along to his government, of course, but..." He sighed and shook his head.

She puffed out her cheeks and rubbed her temples. "I know," she said, trying to rein in her frustration, "and I don't blame him. And the others will be the same, I'm sure, at least right now. There are huge questions that we can't answer, and precious little evidence-"

Barca snorted. "Ma'am, a five hundred meter ship with a missing crew is plenty of evidence of *something*. It's just that people don't want to believe Sato's story about the aliens. Not so much that there *are* aliens - although there are a lot of folks who won't believe that, either - but that they don't even know us and yet they're coming to look for a fight. If the ship's records had been intact and had shown some reflection of the attack, anything to support Sato's story other than the physical artifacts, it might be different. *Might* be. But even at that," he shrugged, "people have an incredibly powerful sense of denial."

"I know," she said, a trace of strain in her voice, "I know. But I feel this in my gut, Ham. We can't afford to be wrong. We've somehow got to make them see that there's a threat. And get them to do something about it."

He paused before he answered. He had known Natalie McKenna for over twenty years, and had found her to be one of the most noble, intelligent, sensible, and downright tough human beings he had ever encountered. He also remembered that she'd had quite a few "gut feelings" in the time he'd known her, and she had never once been wrong. Not one single time. Call it intuition, call it blind luck, call it whatever you want - it all boiled down to the same thing. If something inside her was telling her that this was the real deal, something beyond the incontrovertible evidence embodied in what the *Aurora* had brought back, then he believed it. And it was starting to scare him to death.

"I'll do my very best, Madam President," he told her solemnly as he flexed his massive arms, stressing the seams of his suit. "Even if I have to pound it into their thick heads."

That won him a tentative smile from his commander-in-chief. "I know you will, Ham," she replied. "And thanks..."

***

Three weeks later, Ichiro Sato was finally released from medical quarantine aboard the *Aurora*. He had stoically endured the endless poking and prodding for blood samples and biopsies, provided urine and stool samples every few hours, had a variety of two- and three-dimensional scans done every week, and suffered even more intrusive and humiliating tests to satisfy the army of doctors and nurses in biological warfare suits. He knew it was in a good cause, both for himself and for his fellow humans, but being released from quarantine was almost as emotional an experience as had been his return to Africa Station.

With the scientists and engineers finally losing interest in him or - in the case of the doctors - having no excuses to continue holding him, Sato had finally been freed from quarantine aboard the ship. But as soon as he stepped out the airlock, he first had to sit through some very tough questioning from the board of inquiry about what had happened to the ship and her missing crew. After surviving that, he was plunged into an endless series of meetings planetside with senior officers and civilians who demanded his story in person. As he was shuttled from venue to venue, he discovered that his image was plastered everywhere. He was an overnight celebrity across the planet, and that was spreading rapidly to the other planets of the human sphere. Some pundits considered him a heroic survivor, but some weren't so kind. A few even went so far as to accuse him of somehow engineering the deaths of the crew so he could return home, overlooking the fact that Earth wasn't his home, and the navigational feat of *Aurora* appearing right next to Africa Station was simply impossible with available human technology. Others were convinced that his body secretly harbored some sort of alien parasite that would suddenly burst forth and begin the process of eliminating his fellow humans.

The only saving grace in his time planetside was Steph. She and her network, which had shot to the top of the ratings charts, had an exclusive, and no other reporters were allowed access to Ichiro unless her network agreed to it. They had made some exceptions, but for the most part Steph had kept them out of his now properly cut hair. She went with him to all of the sessions with the senior brass, and made it all look good in the public eye. While she was doing it for obvious professional reasons and Sato essentially had no choice, they found each other to be pleasant company and had become good friends. In a way, Sato wished it might become something more, but he found that there was a deep emotional emptiness inside him that concealed a sense of guilt that the psychologists and psychiatrists had been unable to expunge. On balance, he was happy enough just having a friend who seemed to understand him.

Today, though, was something special: the courier had finally returned from Keran with the meteorological data he had requested to compare with the images he had taken of the cloud formations circling the alien replica of the planet. That information was what the powers that be had been waiting for before holding the final review of what had come to be called the "*Aurora* Incident."

Sitting at the front of the main briefing complex at Terran Naval Headquarters with the other presenters, Sato listened as Admiral Tiernan, Chief of the Terran Naval Staff, delivered short opening remarks before a battery of experts - including Sato - was called upon to deliver their findings to a joint council that included everybody who was anybody in the Terran military. The meeting was chaired by Tiernan, but representatives from every service were present, as were Defense Minister Joshua Sabine and several other key cabinet members. The president had decided to wait for the executive summary version from her cabinet representatives: in the meantime, she had more battles to fight with congress.

"Because we have a lot of ground to cover," Tiernan told the attendees, "I'd like to ask that you hold your questions until the breakout sessions after the main presentation. And with that, I'll turn it over to Dr. Novikov to begin."

Dr. Anton Novikov was the director of the medical staff that had examined Sato. "After the most exhaustive test battery we've ever run," Novikov explained, "our findings on examining Lieutenant Sato were completely negative in terms of any identifiable pathogens." On the main screen in the expansive conference room, a bewildering list of tests, dates, results, and other information scrolled from bottom to top. But no one paid it any attention: everyone's eyes were riveted on Sato.

"However," Novikov went on, "we did find clear evidence of physiological manipulation." On the screen, the blinding list of tests disappeared, replaced by side-by-side bioscans of Sato's jaw line. "In this case," Novikov went on, "the cracks that Lieutenant Sato had in two of his lower teeth, sustained during his first year at the academy-" the hairline fractures were highlighted in the bioscan on the left, "-have disappeared, as you can see in the bioscan on the right." The audience murmured as they examined the two images. While the cracks were subtle in the "before" image, they were nonetheless clear. And they were plainly gone in the "after" image. "We examined them extremely closely, and they are definitely the original teeth, not replacements. But there are no indications of any type of repair: no fusing or any other technique. It's as though they were never damaged in the first place."

A new set of bioscans flashed onto the screen, this time of Sato's left ankle. "Lieutenant Sato had mild scarring of his left achilles tendon from a childhood accident," the doctor continued. An easily visible mass of tissue at the base of his achilles tendon was highlighted in red. "Again, the evidence of this injury is completely gone in the bioscans we made after his return." The image on the right showed Sato's achilles tendon again, but this time in pristine condition. "Ladies and gentlemen, there is no medical application or science we have available to us today that would repair these injuries and leave absolutely no trace behind. There are also other, more subtle, differences that we detected in Lieutenant Sato's physiology that indicate some sort of medical intervention." He paused, looking across the audience. "Without a sample, we obviously cannot corroborate Lieutenant Sato's report of an alien 'healing gel.' However, based on our findings, we can certainly say that *something* happened to him that is beyond our ability to satisfactorily explain. And that, ladies and gentlemen, concludes the medical portion of this briefing."

"Thank you, Dr. Novikov," Admiral Tiernan told him. "And now I'd like to move on to-"

"What about psychological aberrations?" someone interrupted.

Tiernan frowned - someone always didn't get the message about what "hold your questions" meant - but let the question stand. Novikov hadn't touched on the psychological aspects, and Tiernan himself was curious.

Novikov shook his head. "We ran an extremely intensive series of psychological tests," he said. "The reason I did not include the results here is that, aside from some understandable emotional trauma, we could detect no unexpected or unreasonable variations from normal."

There were some sidelong glances around the room, Sato noticed. More than a few people were concerned that he might have been psychologically influenced or brainwashed by the aliens and made into a spy or assassin. He didn't really blame them: it was a lot easier to believe that than face the truth.

"Any other questions?" Tiernan asked, the tone of his voice making it clear that there had better not be. Heads shook around the room. "Very well. Captain Bennett, if you please."

The woman sitting next to Sato rose and took up a position behind the podium. Captain Leona Bennett was the chief engineer that had led the team that had taken *Aurora* apart from stem to stern. When she looked at the audience, she didn't smile. She had not liked what her team had found.

"As Dr. Novikov's team did with Lieutenant Sato himself," she nodded at him from the podium, "we conducted extended forensics tests of the *Aurora*, including her hull, interior, and all ship's systems.

"We found that *Aurora* herself was completely free of any suspicious microorganisms, particles, or devices. However," she went on, "as Dr. Novikov found with his patient, there were a number of oddities about the ship that we are at a complete loss to explain.

"The first," she said as a projection of the ship appeared on the screen, the camera panning from the bow toward the stern, "is that there was no evidence at all of any holes having been cut anywhere in the hull. Even microscopic examination of several specific areas that Lieutenant Sato pointed out to us revealed nothing.

"However," she went on, "the microscopic scans revealed something completely unexpected, and led to a detailed metallurgical sampling of the hull and interior components." She flashed a chart up on the display screen. "These are spectrographs of samples of the ship's outer hull plating during her last refit. As you can see, there are tiny variations in the composition of the alloy. This is normal from slight imperfections in the production processes. *This*, however," she said as she changed the display to a new chart, "is not." Where the previous chart showed slight differences among the samples, the samples in the new chart were eerily identical. "These samples were taken from the same plates in the hull as those in the chart you just saw. Not only are they all identical, but they're all slightly different than the samples taken during *Aurora's* last refit." She paused, her face taking on a grim expression. "Ladies and gentlemen, this is flat-out impossible unless someone completely remade - on a molecular level and with a precision that we cannot match - the entire ship."

That sparked an uproar until Tiernan ordered everyone to silence so Captain Bennett could continue.

"That's not all," she told them. "More perplexing to us were the findings from the analysis of the ship's engines. As most of you know, certain components have a limited operational life because of heat, friction, or a variety of other factors and must be periodically replaced.

"But everything in *Aurora's* sublight and hyperdrive systems looked brand new," she explained. "And I have to emphasize that some of the components are normally extremely difficult to get to, and require very special tools. It took my engineers a full week working around the clock to pull the hyperdrive core. And it was clear from the part identification markings and three-dimensional scans that they weren't replacements: *they were the very same parts as installed on the ship's last refit.* But somehow made new."

Looking directly at Admiral Tiernan, she summed up her findings and her fears. "Sir, I can't confirm Lieutenant Sato's story from what we found on the ship. But I can definitely confirm that something incredibly strange happened to that ship, something that's well beyond - centuries, at least - our current engineering capability."

Those around the room fell silent. Bennett had a reputation for being an engineering genius, and many had long thought her talents wasted in the Navy. Her last words sent a haunting chill through the senior military officers and civilian officials who sat around the table at the center of the room.

"Thank you, captain," Tiernan said into the resounding silence. He had already read the summary and most of the details of Bennett's findings, but was nonetheless disturbed. While she made it clear that there was no indication that the ship itself posed any danger, whoever had manipulated the vessel was clearly in a league of their own in terms of technology.

"Dr. Larsen will now present the results of the study of the substance - believed to be blood - found on Lieutenant Sato's sword," Tiernan said, nodding toward a tall, thin man with thinning blonde hair who sat on the other side of Sato. "Doctor, if you would, please."

Larsen was nervous as he took the stage. Unlike many academics who had a lot of experience in front of people, even if just students in a classroom, Larsen had very little: his life was spent in the laboratory. He was widely published, but had generally avoided giving public talks himself. Instead, he almost always trusted it to one of his understudies.

Sato grimaced inwardly, expecting a droning catalog of esoteric genetic technobabble, but he - along with most of the rest of the audience - was surprised as Larsen's stage fright was overcome by enthusiasm for his topic.

"You have already seen many incredible things in the various reports from the analyses of *Aurora* and young Lieutenant Sato," Larsen began, reading from his notes after clearing his throat several times. "But I believe that those revelations pale in significance to the findings I bring before you now." He groped around on the podium for a moment, finally finding the control to bring up his first display.

"Here you see the double-helix that we are all familiar with," he explained as a strand of DNA slowly turned on the screen behind him. "While it varies depending on the species used for comparison, human DNA - a reconstruction of which you see on the screen behind me - is much more similar to other Earth-descended life forms than it is different. For example, we share roughly ninety-five percent commonality in our DNA with chimpanzees." A second strand of DNA appeared on the screen next to the first, with a watermark of a chimp behind it. To the untrained eye, the two strands were identical.

"Now, ladies and gentlemen," Larsen said, for the first time glancing up from his prepared notes, clearly excited, "I know that you expected me to ramble on about gene sequences and such. But there is no need once you've seen *this*."

The chimp DNA disappeared, and was replaced by the image of a new double helix. It was nearly twice as long as the human DNA strand, and had strange protrusions from the helix at regular intervals along its length. The audience made a collective gasp: Larsen's team had only just finished their analysis, and no one - not even Tiernan - had yet seen the results until now.

"Yes, ladies and gentlemen," Larsen told them, turning to look admiringly at the image. "This is something entirely new to our science! Nowhere in all the worlds we have surveyed have we seen anything like it. Some parts of it, we understand; others, such as these strange extensions-" he pointed to one of the protrusions, "-continue to baffle us. There is much controversy among those of us looking at the samples brought back by Lieutenant Sato. But there are two incontrovertible facts. First, that this gene sequence can encode vastly more information than our own DNA; and second, that it is not from any known species of life that humanity has ever encountered and sampled.

"While this is all still very preliminary," he went on, turning back to his stunned audience, "I feel compelled to point out that a majority of my colleagues are convinced that the species or sub-species that this sample came from was genetically engineered, that there is far too much data in the structure to have been encoded naturally, even over an extended period of evolution. Others believe differently. I myself am not yet decided on the matter. But we are all in agreement that it is of completely unknown origin."

"I don't bloody believe it," someone murmured.

I wish I could say that, Tiernan thought. Whether Sato had really found blue-skinned alien women from hell out in deep space or not, *something* was out there. "Thank you, Dr. Larsen," he told him, relieved that the haunting image of that alien DNA had been taken off the screen.

As Larsen shuffled off the stage, Tiernan turned to look directly at Sato. "Okay, son, it's your show."

Sato took his place at the podium, facing his audience. In his earlier life, he would have been terrified of briefing such an assembly of senior officers and civilians. But he had already come to know many of them fairly well over the last few weeks through an endless series of vidcom calls, and what he had experienced on the *Aurora* had forever changed his threshold of fear. His eye caught Steph sitting in the back row, again wearing her "killer red dress," as she liked to call it. He didn't acknowledge the wink she gave him, but her confidence warmed him nonetheless.

"Thank you, sir," Sato said, his strong voice carrying well without the need for artificial amplification. "Since most of you already know the background on what you're going to see - a comparison of the cloud formations on the alien artifact representing Keran with time-matched meteorological records sent back from the Keran government - I'll skip over the preliminaries and get to the bottom line." He pressed a button on the tiny remote he held, and the massive screen at the head of the room suddenly showed an image of a planet that looked much like Earth, with a set of time and date information at the bottom. "This is satellite data that was delivered to us this morning by courier from Keran," Sato explained. "Please note the date and time information, which is shown in Universal Standard to correspond with the times of the images I took while returning on *Aurora*." The view of the planet suddenly changed from that of a typical sphere, expanding to show a two-dimensional display of the entire planet, as if it had been converted to a wall map. Three red circles flashed on, illuminating some large cloud masses. "These three major storms are good points of reference for what we're about to see in this first sample."

He clicked the remote again, and that image shrank to half the screen, while another image of what looked like the same planet appeared, except that it was suspended on a metal ring in an image capture stand. Identical time and date information to what was on the first image appeared at the bottom. "This is the alien artifact that appears to represent Keran, taken at the same relative time." Another click, and the sphere was reformed to show a rectangular display of the entire planet's surface as Sato had done a moment before with the satellite imagery, with three red circles around major storm systems.

"These cloud formations look similar, but the question is, are they the same? I had the computer highlight any differences between them in bright red." Sato clicked the remote again. The two images came together and were merged. "As you can see, they appear to be the same. Closer analysis revealed, however, that the two images are not just similar, but are *identical.*" He paused. "This means that the alien artifact is showing not just some random representation of Keran, but is actually echoing an image of the planet in real-time, even from hundreds of light years away."

"That's impossible," someone blurted.

"To us, perhaps," Sato said. "But this isn't a fluke. I made a dozen different recordings over the four months of the journey back to Earth. Every single one of those recordings was a perfect match with the imagery from Keran."

"So what does this mean?" the Minister of Defense, Joshua Sabine, asked pointedly. "I've heard the arguments both ways about there being a Kreelan ship in Keran space somehow broadcasting to this...artifact. But how does it influence our strategy?"

"It means, Mr. Secretary," Tiernan pointed out, "that - aside from the implications such advanced technology has in general - the enemy has unparalleled reconnaissance and communications capabilities compared to our own forces. They'll know about anything that goes on in Keran space instantly, while we have to rely on couriers for inter-system communications. And, of course, if the Keran government doesn't allow us to preposition any forces in the system when the clock is about to run out, we'll have nothing in the way of reconnaissance to help us if the president orders us in." He tossed the pen he'd been idly twirling in his fingers onto the table. "We'll be going in completely blind."

"It's actually worse, admiral," Sato told him quietly, although his voice still carried easily through the hush that had settled on the room.

"How can it be worse?" Sabine growled.

"Sir," Sato went on, "it's something that we discovered this morning. I never thought to check for this myself, but Miss Guillaume," he nodded toward the back of the room toward Steph, "happened to be doing some video recording of the artifact, and had the idea of taking some very close-up macro shots. What she found prompted us to turn a high resolution microscope onto the artifact. Here are the results of some of the images we took."

With another click of the remote, a seaside city suddenly sprang into view. But it wasn't a typical landscape scene as taken from someone on the ground; it was as if it had been taken from the air. Oceangoing ships, vehicular traffic, even large groups of people could clearly be discerned in the video image. The scene shifted to what was clearly a military facility, with armored vehicles aligned next to vehicle sheds and rows of barracks nearby. It shifted again to show a major airport, with aerospace vehicles taking off and landing, shuttling people and cargo to low orbit.

"Dear mother of God," Sabine whispered. "Are you telling me that what we're seeing here is - was - really happening at the time these images were taken of the artifact?"

Sato nodded grimly. "Yes, sir. We haven't confirmed it directly, of course, because that would require another courier run to Keran for additional data. But based on our analysis this morning of both the meteorological and ocean wave data that we were able to compare with the artifact, we believe that what you are seeing here actually took place, and is not a random simulation of the activity on the planet." He paused. "And these images are really limited by the equipment we had available at the time. I believe that it would be theoretically possible to go to street level and see the individual people there as clearly as we see each other around the table here."

"Anything else to cheer us up with, Sato?" Tiernan sighed. He knew it wasn't the boy's fault, but this was all news that he definitely did not want to hear.

"Actually, yes, sir, there is some good news." He clicked the remote again, clearing the troubling close-ups of Keran from the screen. "As you know, I believe the artifact is a countdown timer for the invasion." Several heads around the table nodded. Very few had been inclined to believe his claim before, but he saw that much of the doubt about his story had faded quickly in the last half hour. "It is gradually changing what it shows over time, I believe morphing from a real-time image to some sort of artificial projection of what may happen." A recent view of the artifact showed the smoke from the northern continent swirling into the polar region, and a variety of ships orbiting, apparently in combat. "So, using what Miss Guillaume discovered this morning, we turned our attention to the ships we periodically see passing across the northern pole of the artifact, as well as to some of the surface areas that appear to have been attacked. It was very difficult in the short time we had to do the analysis this morning, so these results must be considered preliminary, but..."

He clicked again, and suddenly a rakish vessel, what could only have been a warship, swam into jittery focus. To those in the room who had knowledge of such things, it clearly was not of any human design. Where human warships, regardless of the builder, tended to be very utilitarian in nature, made up largely of basic shapes and sharp angles with a variety of antennas and weapons arrays poking out into space, this one looked almost like a supersized aerospace fighter aircraft. It fired what looked like a brace of missiles and followed up with a salvo of what appeared to be lasers at a target that was outside the field of view. "While we'll need more exact measurements," Sato said as his audience sat, transfixed by the scene, "we believe this particular ship to be roughly on a par in size with our heavy cruisers. It is nothing close to the size of the ships that attacked *Aurora*. And from what little we were able to tell this morning, reflected in what you see here, the weapons this ship is using appear to be roughly similar to those in general use by human warships."

"Has this information been turned over to my analysts for further study?" Vladimir Penkovsky, head of Terran Intelligence, asked pointedly.

Sato opened his mouth to respond, but was cut off by Vice Admiral Mary "Bunny" Richards, the Commander-in-Chief, Orbital Systems Command. Her command was responsible for all the orbital platforms like Africa Station, and she was at the top of Sato's current command chain. Sato had always wondered if anybody really ever called her Bunny. He knew that he certainly never would.

Eying Penkovsky with evident distaste, Admiral Richards told him in her heavily accented native British, "Lieutenant Sato and his team sent a report out this morning at oh-eight-forty, along with a request for support from TIA." TIA was Penkovsky's Terran Intelligence Agency.

"Listen, Joshua," Penkovsky told the Defense Minister, "we need better integration on the intelligence side of this. We've been kept at arm's length-"

"With all due respect, sir," Richards interjected. "TIA was invited from the very beginning to participate in the debriefing and on the analyses of *Aurora*, but you declined."

"Enough," the Defense Minister held up his hands. "Vlad, we'll take this up later off-line. On the one hand you're right: we do need better integration between operations and intelligence, particularly in light of these recent revelations." He nodded toward the screen, which now showed blurry images of what appeared to be some sort of assault boats disgorging from a larger vessel, probably an alien troop carrier, before they plunged toward the surface. "But let's count our blessings, people, what few of them we've got. I don't know if we can accept what we see here as valid - maybe the enemy is trying to deceive us - but at least we've got *something* to work with, and that's where we need to start." He looked at Sato. "Lieutenant, this is damn good work." Turning toward the back of the room, he nodded at Steph. "You, too, Miss Guillaume."

Steph smiled her thanks, grateful for the notice.

Sitting back in his chair, Sabine said, "Ladies and gentlemen, I'm going to be candid here: does anyone *not* believe that we have a real reason to be worried? Does anyone still think this is some sort of hoax, and if so, do you have any plausible story to back it up? I'm not looking for people to hit in the head, I just want to make sure we're not overlooking some other plausible explanation."

The faces around the table, along with the back-benchers, were uniformly grim. Those who had come into the presentation scoffing at the whole affair were now believers. They didn't even have to believe all of Sato's story: the evidence presented today was terrifying enough.

Sabine turned back to Sato. "How much time does Keran have left?"

Sato answered without hesitation. They had confirmed that the progression of the depiction of war southward across the artifact's surface was at a constant rate, and had refined his own original estimates. Unfortunately, the confirmed rate left them with less time than Sato had originally predicted. "Four hundred and eighty-three days from today, sir," he told him. "A little over sixteen months."

A lot of heads shook at that number, and Sato heard several groans and curses. No one in this room had really, truly believed it until then. But seeing an image of what was clearly an alien ship made it a lot more real than the word of an emotionally devastated midshipman-turned-lieutenant.

"All right," Sabine went on, "that's what we have to work with. Ladies and gentlemen, I can't emphasize enough how important it's going to be to pull what we can together as fast as possible. This is the president's number one priority. We're probably going to go through some rough changes in how we do things, so be flexible and remember what's at stake. Because if they can hit Keran, they can hit Earth. They proved that with how they sent *Aurora* back to us."

"Which brings up the question of why they even bothered to send you back," Penkovsky said, looking at Sato. "Why not just attack out of the blue and wipe us off the map? Why go to all this trouble of warning us?"

Sabine turned to look at Sato, too, as if the young lieutenant had all the answers.

"I believe," he said slowly, "that it is their sense of honor."

"Explain," Admiral Tiernan told him.

"I am only speculating, sir. But consider: only the members of the crew who fought back, or were in a group that collectively fought back, survived the original boarding attack. I believe the only exception was the engineers tasked with destroying the computer core, who apparently died fighting. From what Lieutenant Amundsen said, it sounded as if they forced the Kreelans to kill them before they could be stunned. But that is only a guess." He glanced at Steph, and saw her nod. It didn't matter how many times he'd thought or spoken of what happened in the arena, it was still impossible to talk about it without having to seize firm control of his emotions. "Then those of us who were herded into the arena faced off against warriors who were clearly chosen to be roughly equal to ourselves. We were given a choice of weapons, and they fought without the armor that they normally wore. Petty Officer Yao believed that it was a test of our character, and everything the aliens did seemed to be aimed at making the contest as equal as possible." He nodded toward the images on the screen, now showing the alien warship again. "The lottery was also clearly intended to choose one of us to send back, to bear witness to what happened. I believe that sending the *Aurora* back tells us that they are intentionally giving us a chance to prepare. I believe that they *want* us to put up a good fight." He shrugged. "It would have made my job much easier for them to have left the ship's sensor and navigational records intact, but perhaps that was all part of the test of our character, as well."

"What if we refuse to give them a fight?" Penkovsky mused. "What if they jump into Keran and are welcomed with open arms?"

"The people on the planet will be slaughtered," Sato said bluntly, "to the last man, woman, and child. Just like the Kreelans cut down everyone on *Aurora* who didn't fight back."

"You have no doubt of that?" Admiral Tiernan asked softly.

"None, sir," Sato told him, fists clenched at his sides. "I saw enough to convince me."

Tiernan nodded sadly. He had known Owen McClaren well, and his death and that of his crew hit him personally.

"All right, then, people," Sabine told them. "If the president can get us the money and the people, we've got a fleet to build and a war to prepare for. And we don't have much time..."

TWELVE

"So that's the best we can do?" President McKenna said quietly as she stood at the windows of her private office in the Presidential Complex, staring out over the water toward where the Statue of Liberty still stood. While the United States technically no longer existed, its constitutional values had evolved into the foundation for the Terran Government, and Lady Liberty was as much an icon of the planetary government as she had once been of the nation for which it had originally been created. But statues would not help defend Keran or the rest of the human sphere from the Kreelan Empire. "Forty-seven ships and two heavy ground divisions?"

"Yes, ma'am," Joshua Sabine told her, feeling ashamed that he had not been able to do better. But in the time they had been given, and with the incredibly stiff resistance the president had faced from Congress, he was amazed they had been able to accomplish that much. "That's what we'll be able to deploy in the expeditionary force, while maintaining roughly two-thirds of the fleet here. We've altered the refit cycle to have nearly one hundred percent readiness for a three-week window, long enough to find out what happens at Keran. We could provide a lot more ground troops if the Keran government would allow us to send them ahead of time, but two divisions is all we can embark at one time on the carriers without using civilian liners. And if we have to do that, there's no way we can deploy those troops in a combat environment. It's the same with the aerospace squadrons we'd wanted to send: there's simply no way to bring them in under combat conditions. So we settled for two interceptor squadrons carried on one of the fleet's support ships, along with enough logistics support for a month." He sighed in frustration. "But they won't be able to get into the fight unless we can get them down to the planet. And we can't do *that* unless we have permission from the government or, if the Kreelans do show up, control of the system so we can protect the support ships as they bring in the interceptors."

She turned to face him, and once again Sabine was stunned at how much of a toll the last year had taken on her. Her close-cropped black hair was now streaked with gray, and her forehead was creased with wrinkles from the enormous burden she had taken upon her shoulders: literally, the fate of humanity. A fate that so few still believed involved alien invaders from across the galaxy, even after the evidence the government had presented from the *Aurora* investigation.

But the president did believe it, and she had suffered for her perceived heresy at the hands of the press and from the Terran Congress. After the initial sensation of *Aurora's* return started to wear off, the public and the congressmen suddenly paid closer attention to exactly what the president was asking for, and it didn't take them long to start screaming bloody murder. President McKenna had enjoyed an extremely good working relationship with Congress, but the massive appropriations bill her staff had hammered together in an amazingly short time was met with shocked disbelief. The sale of war bonds, tax increases, possible federalization of key industries, and other measures brought a howl of indignation from the public and their elected representatives. The president had invited further attacks with an appeal for a vote to institute a draft that she sent to both houses. The resulting public uproar plunged her popularity into a tailspin. More than one critic had commented that had the Terran democratic institutions been based on a parliamentary system, McKenna would have been kicked out of office in a very one-sided vote of confidence.

On the diplomatic front, the story was equally bleak. The local diplomats were completely unsupportive, and the official government positions, delayed by weeks due to the communications time lag, were the same.

But there was a ray of hope. The one diplomat who took Hamilton Barca's entreaties seriously was Ambassador Laurent Navarre from the planet Avignon. Unlike most of the other ambassadors, Navarre was a former naval officer who had seen extensive combat during the St. Petersburg intervention, and he had taken a very keen interest in what had happened with the *Aurora*. After his initial meeting with Barca, he had taken the bold step of asking to speak directly with Sato. At Barca's request, the Navy had quickly provided a secure vidcom terminal, and Barca sat in Navarre's office while the French diplomat bombarded Sato - who at the time was still quarantined on *Aurora* - with very pointed questions. Impressed with the young man's responses, Navarre told Barca that not only would he recommend that his government support Earth's position, but that he would also recommend that Avignon and the other members of the Francophone Alliance offer to send military assistance to Keran. It was a huge diplomatic victory, particularly since the Francophone Alliance represented a major bloc of the human sphere. But it was the only such victory they had enjoyed.

Now, only six weeks were left before the invasion was to occur. A lot of people were becoming curious again as the day approached, drawing the populace away from the general apathy that had replaced the initial surge of reaction to *Aurora's* return. "Are they going to be ready in time?"

Sabine shrugged. "They'll be as ready as we can make them, Madam President," he told her. "Admiral Tiernan has been running them through a tough training cycle, trying to get the new ships and crews in shape. He's got a lot of challenges trying to pull everything together, but everyone's pushing as hard as they can. I think the ground forces are fine, as General Singh decided - wisely, I believe - to take two of our best divisions and tailor them for the deployment. So if we can get them on the ground, they'll be ready to go." He sighed. "Part of it is that we just don't know what we're going to be facing. For all we know, the Empire could throw a thousand ships at us in the first wave. Aside from the things we see from the crystal ball..." - that's what everyone had taken to calling the alien artifact showing Keran, which had almost completely transformed into a raging world at war - "...we have absolutely no intelligence information to go on."

"And the Keran government still hasn't budged?" McKenna asked.

"No, Madam President," Hamilton Barca sighed. "I've done everything I can think of, short of wringing bin Sultan's princely neck to get them to accept our help, even humanitarian assistance. They simply refuse to allow a Terran military presence in the system, even a single military vessel." It wasn't a surprise, of course: part of the reason for Keran's odd mix of Chinese and Arabic cultures was due to the last round of wars that were fought on Earth before the Diaspora. The old United States, together with India and Russia, had been heavily involved on the "opposite side." The inhabitants of Keran viewed the Terran Planetary Government - which was largely dominated by constituencies from the old United States, Russia, and India - with a great deal of circumspection, if not outright distrust.

"Then how the devil are we supposed to know if the invasion takes place?"

"That, at least, we have covered," Barca told her, nodding toward Vladimir Penkovsky.

"We've arranged the diplomatic courier shuttle schedule so that there are at least two courier ships in-system at any given time," Penkovsky explained, "with one in orbit and the other transiting in- or out-system. We've equipped all the courier ships with enhanced sensor packages that will augment their normal navigation and collision-avoidance systems to provide us with data on what is happening in local space and on the planet itself." He held up a hand to forestall the question he saw the president about to ask. "No, Madam President, none of the equipment is classified or in any way compromises the diplomatic integrity of the couriers in the unlikely event one of them should be examined. Everything is off-the-shelf and commercially available. The upgraded systems will not provide information as detailed as we could get from our military systems, but it will be close."

McKenna nodded, satisfied. The last thing she needed now was a major diplomatic incident with the Keran government. "What about the French?" she asked.

Barca smiled. When she said *French*, she meant the Francophone Alliance. Like virtually all the major nation-states since the formation of the Terran Planetary Government, the country once known as France still existed as an administrative entity. But in Terran Government circles, "France" referred to the group of worlds settled by refugees from France, Belgium, their former African colonies, and even some of the *Quebecois* from Canada, during the Diaspora. Unlike some of the other worlds that were settled during that period, they had benefitted from amazing luck in colonizing Avignon, La Seyne, and several other planets that were very compatible with humans and were rich in natural resources. Collectively they had become one of the major economic and military forces in the human sphere, and generally shared common interests with Earth. Fortunately, the Francophone Alliance also enjoyed very good relations with Keran that weren't tainted by unpleasantness from the past. "That's still our best news," Barca told her, "although it has its warts, too. The Alliance is preparing to deploy roughly one hundred warships to Keran, along with ten ground divisions. Ambassador Navarre indicated that the only real sticking point was the ground forces: the Keran Government is only going to allow them to deploy a single division planetside until or unless the enemy fleet actually materializes. The Kerans still don't think there's anything to worry about, and while they don't mind having a bunch of French warships in orbit, they don't want three full heavy corps of troops running amok on the streets."

"But the French don't have enough carriers to get their divisions deployed quickly from orbit," Sabine pointed out, incredulous. "Are they just going to hold the troops on starliners until the attack comes and then shuttle them down?" Barca nodded, shrugging. "Good, God," Sabine said, rolling his eyes, "they're going to be sitting ducks!"

"They don't have any choice," Barca pointed out. "Believe me, Navarre wasn't happy with the plan when he heard about it, either. But the Alliance approved it, so that's what they're going with."

"So which division are they allowing the French to land ahead of time?" the president asked.

"They're deploying the entire combat contingent of the Foreign Legion," Barca told her, "which is technically a division-plus. They're sending all twenty field infantry regiments, plus the Legion's independent armored brigade. Navarre said the decision is already raising hell with peacekeeping operations where they had to pull out some of the regiments, but they did it anyway."

Sabine grunted. "The Keran government would have been better off letting them deploy the other nine divisions and keep the legionnaires in orbit if they were worried about troops getting wild on the ground," he said. "On the other hand, they're a bunch of tough bastards. Good call. But they won't have any heavy artillery support outside of the armored brigade."

"So," the president asked, "what major problems do we have left, aside from the obvious ones."

"Command and control," Sabine said immediately. "We've been talking to the French about inter-operability, but we've gotten an ice-cold shoulder." The president gave him *the look*, the one where she seemed to promise that she'd rip the heart out of someone's chest if he or she hadn't been giving something their all. "Ma'am," Sabine said, leaning forward to emphasize his point, "we even offered to give them a set of our systems to look over and modify - no questions asked! - to be compatible with theirs so our ships and ground troops can communicate effectively. But they're so paranoid about their system security that they simply won't do it. They refused to even take the equipment and software that we offered them, even to just look at it."

"So when the attack comes and our ships jump in to assist," she asked him, a look of pained incredulity on her face, "they won't be able to communicate with the French fleet?"

"No, Madam President," Sabine told her grimly. "Aside from the normal basic communications that all ships - civilian or military - have, we'll have no way of integrating our battle management capabilities. The ships will be able to talk to each other with normal voice and video, but other than that both fleets will be fighting completely on their own..."

***

Aboard the recently commissioned destroyer *TNS Owen D. McClaren*, Lieutenant Ichiro Sato found himself far more worried about the survival of his own ship in the current fleet exercise than the strategic concerns guiding the president's cabinet discussion. What troubled him wasn't the complex targeting and maneuvering problems the exercise controllers were throwing at the ships. It was the ship's captain.

"*Goddammit, Sato!*" Commander Scott Morrison, the ship's captain, cursed, making half the bridge crew cringe. Glaring at his young tactical officer, he practically sneered, "I ordered you to fire on target Delta with the pulse cannon. Are you deaf or just incompetent?"

"Sir," Sato said, trying not to grit his teeth, "as I explained to you earlier, the pulse cannon has a thirty second recycle rate under optimal conditions." The pulse cannon was a highly modified laser that was mounted in the ship's keel. It could deliver a massive punch, but the entire ship had to be aligned on the target, and it took virtually all of the ship's energy reserves to fire. It was a powerful weapon, but had some serious tactical drawbacks. The *McClaren* was one of only two of the expeditionary force's ships that had been built with one. "You had already ordered a laser salvo against targets Alpha and Bravo, which depleted the energy buffers. Every time that happens, the recycle sequence for the pulse cannon resets-"

"Enough," Morrison snapped, waving his hand dismissively as he turned back to the primary bridge display. "The bottom line is you fucked up."

"Sir, I-"

"I said that's enough," the captain hissed. Getting out of his combat chair, which was strictly prohibited during exercises except for safety reasons, he stalked over to Sato's position. Pointing a finger in Sato's face, he went on, "The reason - the *only* reason - you are on this ship, mister, is because you managed to stuff your head up Admiral Tiernan's ass so far that you could look out his ears. All I ask from you, if it's not too much, is that you just sit there, keep your bloody mouth shut, and *do your fucking job!*" He paused, staring at Sato and clearly expecting the younger man to cave in. Tall but still gangly even in early middle age, Morrison normally towered over Sato. But now the captain's face, which could only be described as grossly ordinary, was a mere hand's breadth from Sato's nose. "Do I make myself clear?"

"Perfectly, captain," Sato replied stonily, his gaze unwavering, although his hands were digging into his armrests. He wasn't intimidated; he was disgusted and heartsick that such an awful man had been given command of one of the few ships humanity had to send against what Sato knew must be heading toward Keran even now. And it was an insult that someone like Morrison had been given command of the ship that bore Captain McClaren's name.

Sato had only come aboard two weeks earlier as the ship was finishing up her initial space trials, and had been immediately appalled by the state of the crew: sullen and quiet, the various departments of the ship in fierce competition to avoid the captain's ire. Morrison had effectively cowed all of the officers, including the exec, except for the chief engineer, Lieutenant Commander Vedette Pergolesi. But while Pergolesi stood as a human heat shield between the captain and the crewmen of the engineering department, the rest of the crew had to fend for themselves. After having their hides flayed a few times after he'd come aboard, even the senior chiefs stayed out of the path of the captain's vitriol. Most of them had seen his type before and kept their distance as much as possible. And that, as much as anything else, was devastating for the crew.

"We've just been hit by a brace of kinetics," the XO said in a matter-of-fact voice. While Morrison had been berating Sato, an enemy ship had fired the equivalent of giant shotgun shells at them. Since no one else on the bridge was about to interrupt his tirade to ask for maneuvering orders - or take the initiative to change the ship's course and avoid the incoming projectiles - the exercise computer declared five hits along the length of the hull.

"*Goddammit!*" Morrison cried disgustedly, stomping back to his command chair.

"And the captain has been declared a casualty because he wasn't in his combat chair," the XO added meekly, waiting for the spontaneous human combustion that he knew would result.

Morrison didn't disappoint him.

"Incoming from Commodore Santiago, sir," the communications rating announced in the middle of the captain's impressive stream of invective. Her voice was perfectly neutral, but Sato had no trouble identifying the underlying tone of vicious glee.

Morrison threw himself into his chair and snapped, "On my console." Sato knew that normally the captain took any calls from senior officers in private in his ready room adjacent to the bridge, but he couldn't get away with that in an exercise, especially since he'd just become a casualty for being out of his command chair. Even on the small console screen that was embedded in the chair, the entire bridge crew would be able to hear the admiral, even if they couldn't see his expression. All exercise communications were recorded for later analysis during the debriefing and lessons-learned discussions, and no one had any doubt that the recording of this particular discussion would make its way to the entire crew.

"Scott," Commodore Rafael Santiago, who commanded the flotilla to which *McClaren* was assigned, appeared on the vidcom and demanded, "what the devil is going on over there?"

"My apologies, sir," Morrison answered evenly. "We're having some difficulties adapting the pulse cannon to our tactics. It's playing hell with our energy buffer allocation, and our tactical officer lost the shot on target Charlie. I was trying to get that sorted out when the kinetic attack came in, but the XO failed to maneuver clear." He put a sympathetic but determined look on his face. "We've only had a couple weeks to hammer this crew together, commodore. We're not as tightly integrated yet as the other ships." *McClaren* was the only newly-launched ship in Santiago's flotilla; the other five ships had captains and crews that had served together for more than a year.

Santiago frowned. "I realize that, Scott," he sighed. "And training is where we're supposed to make our mistakes. Let's just make sure we all learn from them, because we won't get a second chance at this."

"Aye, aye, sir," Morrison replied, resolution evident in his voice. "We won't let you down."

"Good enough," Santiago said. "Carry on." The screen went blank.

***

Sato and some of the other junior officers from *McClaren* sat around the table at the back of Nightingale's, one of Africa Station's less reputable bars, enjoying their last bit of off-ship time before the expeditionary force prepared to deploy. While open twenty-four hours a day, the bar's schedule was really slaved to Universal Standard Time, which was now sixteen-hundred. Before the dinner hour the bar was fairly quiet and not too crowded, but business would pick up soon, with raucous music blaring over the bodies packed onto the dance floor and seated at the surrounding tables.

"We're fucked," Ensign Kayla Watanabe sighed. She was the ship's junior navigation officer, and had more than once been on the receiving end of a rebuke from her captain for things that weren't her fault. That didn't bother her so much; she could take the tongue lashings. What she couldn't take was the certain knowledge that their ship couldn't fight worth a damn.

Heads around the table nodded glumly. They had managed to do better during the rest of the exercise, but Sato attributed that to luck as much as anything else. Commodore Santiago had positioned *McClaren* in a support role during the following engagements, giving the other ships the lead in the flotilla's attacks while *McClaren* cleaned up the scraps. The ship had managed to survive, but the entire crew felt humiliated.

"What do you think, Sato?" Watanabe asked. "Are we going to get our asses reamed by the Kreelans?" In unison, the others turned to him, dejected, but eager to hear what he had to say.

It was odd, Sato thought, that here he was, again the youngest and least experienced officer on the ship, much as he had been on the *Aurora* as a midshipman. Yet, they were looking to him for an answer, for leadership. It was true that he outranked most of those around the table, but there was more to it than that. He was the only one aside from Pergolesi, the chief of engineering, who continued to stand up to the captain. Even during the shit-storm of their after-action review, when the captain had found fault with virtually every one of his officers, Sato had stood firm and said what needed to be said about his perceptions of the crew's performance - both the things they had done well, and those they hadn't - respectfully but firmly. *For the record, if nothing else,* he'd thought at the time. He had absorbed a lot of abuse from the captain after making contradictory observations on the actions of some of the other members of the bridge crew. It had been incredibly difficult to not spell out all the captain's mistakes, but he knew that wouldn't help. There was no way the commodore would replace Morrison at this late date unless he made some sort of flagrant violation, and the captain was too savvy for that. As with his conversation with the commodore during the exercise, he was an expert at taking just enough blame to make himself look responsible, while shoving the bulk of it off on the alleged inadequacies of his junior officers.

Sighing, Sato looked around the table at their expectant faces, the faces of people he'd only known for a couple weeks, but on whom his life would depend in the coming battle. He wished he had some good news for them, some way to give them some confidence. "Look," he told them, "I'll be honest and say that I don't think the expeditionary force is going to be nearly enough to stop them when they come, even if we had the best captain in the fleet. I don't think the Kreelans will be using ships like the ones that attacked *Aurora*, but they don't have to. Somehow they're going to level the playing field with us, but..." He shook his head. "I think Keran is going to be a much bigger version of the arena that my old crew fought and died in. I don't think they're going to let us win this battle."

"So all this is for nothing?" one of the others asked, disgusted. "We just go out there and get our asses kicked by an enemy we can't touch?"

"No," Sato replied forcefully. "That's not what I meant. I don't think we'll be able to save Keran from whatever the aliens plan to do. But I do think that they're going to give us a chance to show them what we're made of. I think if we fight hard and well, we'll buy humanity extra time to build its defenses. If we don't..." He shook his head. "If we don't meet their expectations, I believe they could wipe us from the universe without even trying."

"But what the hell do we do about Captain-fucking-Queeg?" someone asked.

"Nothing," Sato sighed in resignation. "The only thing we can do is our very best as individuals, and to try and work hard as a team. The captain's used to playing the department heads against each other, instead of having them work together." It was common knowledge that very few officers aboard a ship would ever qualify for command in what was a relatively small fleet. So the competition for top ratings on their first ship tour was critical: only the officers in the top one or two slots stood a chance at ever earning command wings. And the way most captains accomplished this winnowing of their junior officers was to pit them against each other, promoting those who wound up with the fewest marks against them. It was generally a divisive and corrosive way to run a ship, but only a few captains - such as Ichiro's old skipper, Owen McClaren - saw beyond it to cultivate a close sense of teamwork, basing officer evaluations primarily on how well they worked with one another. Almost all of McClaren's former junior officers qualified for command later in their careers, and Ichiro knew that the Navy was very shortly going to wish it had a great many more command qualified officers. "So," Ichiro went on, "we've *got* to do our best to work together. Forget all the career advancement garbage. That's not going to mean a thing if we get vaporized a few weeks from now."

Everyone agreed with that: what was the point of coming out in the top one or two position on your ratings when you were dead?

Sato picked up his glass and drained it, savoring the cold tea. Unlike the others, he didn't drink alcohol. "Okay, I've got to go." Standing up, he said, "I'll see you all back aboard tomorrow morning."

Watching Sato leave, Watanabe remarked, "Well, maybe when we go into combat the first time, the captain will forget to stay in his chair..."

***

Ichiro was covered in a fine sheen of sweat as he went through the various *katas* he had been taught, the movements to attack and defend with the *katana*. It had become an obsession, and the closest thing he had now to religion.

One of the first things he had done to fill up what little free time he had after being released from quarantine aboard the *Aurora* was to seek out a *sensei* to teach him how to use his grandfather's weapon. It was a difficult task for two reasons: he had no idea even where to look for someone with the right skills, and among those he found very few were really willing to offer what he truly wanted: a crash-course in how to kill with a sword. He wasn't interested in the finer points of swordsmanship, because he knew that he would never make a great, or probably even good, swordsman: that process took many years, and he only had a little over one year to learn what he could. The teachers he spoke to didn't understand that he didn't want to learn for sport or for some higher personal purpose. He wanted to learn how to kill.

Then one day a man appeared at the door of his cabin on Africa Station. When Sato opened the door, the man - of Japanese descent - bowed and then gestured for Sato to go with him. The man refused to say a word. Frustrated by the man's bizarre behavior, Sato was nonetheless curious and decided to follow him. The man took him to the station's sports complex, where they entered one of the many exercise rooms. It was empty except for two items: a pair of wooden swords, *bokken*, that lay in the center of the floor.

The man, who Sato judged to be in his late fifties, knelt gracefully on one side of the two *bokken*. Sato, shrugging, knelt opposite him. Giving in to ingrained habit from his childhood, he lowered himself to the floor in a deep bow, and the older man did the same. Then he handed Sato one of the *bokken*, and wordlessly began to teach him how to use it.

The scene repeated itself every day that Sato was on the station. Regardless of whether he was there early or late in the day, the old man magically appeared on his doorstep. Sato had tried everything he could think of to get some sort of information from him about who he was and what he was doing there - beyond the obvious of teaching Sato swordsmanship - but the old man calmly ignored him and simply got down to business as soon as they arrived at their designated workout room. Sato tried to find out who scheduled the room, but in every single case, it was listed as open. He tried finding out who the man was from the shuttle transit services, but they couldn't release passenger information, and even Steph couldn't dig her way to the bottom of it. It was maddening.

But aside from the strange circumstances, Sato could clearly see that the man - his silent *sensei* - knew what he was doing. The many hours they spent together were hard and challenging, and more than once Sato went back to his quarters sporting a number of welts where the *sensei* had underscored some of Sato's shortcomings. But that only made Sato want to train harder, because he knew that if his teacher had been a Kreelan wielding a real sword, Sato wouldn't just be bruised, he'd be dead.

After about eight months, they began to train with real *katanas*, but with their edges blunted. Sato knew that he didn't have the refinement or overall abilities of someone who had trained for years, but he now had confidence that he could fight. He knew that he would lose against a Kreelan warrior who had probably been trained since birth for combat, but he would never again be completely helpless as he had been in the arena aboard the Kreelan warship, seemingly so long ago.

Then, two weeks ago, his *sensei* suddenly stopped coming. Sato was worried that something had happened to the man - he still didn't even know his name - until a package arrived. It was a tube about fifty centimeters long and maybe fifteen in diameter. Carefully opening it, he was stunned at the contents: a *wakizashi*, the shorter companion sword that samurai warriors traditionally carried with the longer *katana*. But this wasn't just any *wakizashi*. It was the companion to his grandfather's sword.

Wrapped inside the tube was a brief handwritten note in flowing Japanese characters:

> *I regret the odd circumstances of our relationship, young Ichiro. But after your journalist friend sent word to Nagano of your adventures and mentioned your wish to learn the ways of the sword, your mother sent me. She swore me to silence, for she did not wish your father to find out for fear he might somehow learn what your mother had done. He is a most unworthy man, unlike his wife and son.*
>
> *She knew me through your grandfather, you see, who was an honored friend, and my* sensei *long ago. She wanted you to have this, your grandfather's* wakizashi, *when you completed the training I could give you. Your father had spitefully hidden it before you left home, but your mother found it again soon after, and kept it safe since then.*
>
> *You are a fine young man, Ichiro. Your mother is so very proud of you, as would be your honored grandfather.*
>
> *Rai Tomonaga*

It was a revelation for which Ichiro was totally unprepared. He simply sat in his quarters for most of that evening, staring at the note and the short sword that had come with it. Finally, he spent the next few hours - well into the night - composing a note to his mother, the first he had sent since he had left home.

Now, on his last free evening station-side, he had spent a full two hours practicing the moves Tomonaga had taught him when the door chime rang. Then he heard the door open. Only one person had his access code. Steph.

"Hey, kid," she called to him as she came in, the door automatically swishing closed behind her. She always called him that when they were alone, although she was only ten years older.

Steph leaned against the wall near the door, watching as Ichiro went through the remainder of a ballet of lethal moves with his grandfather's sword. Bare above the waist, the muscles of his upper body rippled as he slashed and thrust with the glittering weapon, and she marveled at how hard and chiseled his body had become. He hadn't exactly been in bad shape physically when she'd first met him on the *Aurora*, but he had totally transformed himself in the last year with the help of the mysterious Tomonaga-san. *Admit it, woman,* she chided herself, trying to look away but failing, *he's goddamn beautiful.*

After a few more moves, Ichiro sheathed the sword, making even that move graceful and deadly-looking. Holding the *katana* in both hands, he bowed his head to it, then carefully placed it on a small wooden stand that held the matched pair of swords.

"It's too bad the Navy didn't take you up on your suggestion to make close combat training and swordsmanship mandatory," she sighed. "Then they'd all be hunks like you."

Ichiro grinned at her as he toweled off the sweat. "Don't you wish," he quipped. "So, what's going on?"

She folded her arms at him and gave him a look that he knew from experience meant that he'd just said something incredibly stupid. "Gee, I don't know," she told him, stepping up to take the towel to rub down his back. "Maybe this'll be the last time I see you before you deploy, you moron." She paused, then added, "Although maybe I'll get to see you while you're on station at the rendezvous point."

Ichiro whipped around and took her wrists, not altogether gently. "What?" he exclaimed. "I thought you were staying back here to cover the president."

Steph's career had taken off into the stratosphere after her coverage of the *Aurora*, and she had been able to pick any assignment she'd wanted. She'd chosen a lead position on the press team that covered the president, and hadn't been disappointed by the massive battle that had been waged in the following months between the executive and legislative branches. While the fighting had only been waged in words and manipulation of governmental processes, it had been as fierce in its own way as men and women grappling on a battlefield.

"I know, Ichiro," she told him, reaching her hands up to touch his face, his own hands still wrapped around her wrists. "But I asked for an embed position in the expeditionary force. That's where the action's going to be, and I want to be in the middle of it."

"Stephanie," he nearly choked, looking as if he'd been sucker-punched, "you mustn't go. Please." He had never called her by her full name since she had told him she went by Steph.

She smiled up at him. "Trying to be Mister Chivalrous, are you?" she told him gently. "Listen, I know how to take care of myself." She moved closer, her nose almost touching his. "You don't have to worry about me."

"Most of us won't be coming back, Steph," he whispered, his dark almond eyes glittering. "Maybe none of us. I don't want...I don't want anything to happen to you."

"Nothing will," she whispered before bringing her lips to his. For just a moment, he didn't react. They had always been "just friends," never thinking that their relationship would ever be anything more. Then he returned her kiss, tentatively at first, and then with growing passion. When Steph felt his powerful arms wrap around her, drawing her body tight against his, a wave of heat rushed through her core. Suddenly, she wished that they'd done this a long time ago.

Without another word, Ichiro effortlessly picked her up and carried her to the bedroom.

THIRTEEN

Communications between ships, like everything else that was taken for granted in the normal universe, was impossible in hyperspace. But Tesh-Dar needed no machines to communicate with the warriors and shipmistresses of the fleet that now approached the end of the voyage to the human world of Keran. Distance and space were immaterial to the Bloodsong that linked her with the billions of her sisters and to the Empress. It was not the same as the spoken word, but Her will was clear. War was upon them.

Tesh-Dar thought back to the time before her fleet was launched, to the gathering of the warrior priestesses and mistresses of the guilds and castes on the Empress Moon. Orbiting above the Homeworld, the Empress Moon was the home of the Imperial City and dwelling place of the Empress, a physical monument to Her power. In the heart of the city lay the Great Tower, atop which was the throne room. Kilometers high in terms of human measure, the Great Tower was thousands of years beyond anything humans could build, yet it had been created by Kreelan hands untold centuries before. The throne room itself surpassed any human's imagination of magnificence: larger than all the palaces ever built by humankind and enclosed in a pyramidal ceiling of diamond-hard crystal, the room itself was a breathless work of art with giant frescoes and tapestries telling the great tale of the First Empress and the Unification.

This gathering was the first of its kind in many great cycles of the Empress Moon about the Homeworld, for this was one of the rare events that affected the entire race of *Kreela*. Upon the hundreds of steps to the great throne stood representatives of all the castes of Her Children, from the lowliest bearers of water to Tesh-Dar herself, greatest of the Empire's warriors. It was a trek the Empress made, from step to step, taking into account the needs of each and every caste, of all of Her Children from the lowliest to the mighty.

On this special day, She sat upon the throne as Her Children knelt before Her, Tesh-Dar foremost among them, kneeling upon the first step from the throne.

"My Children," the Empress began, Her voice carrying clearly across the great expanse of the throne room to the multitudes who knelt below, the crews and warriors of the ships that were about to go into battle against the humans, "today is a day that long shall be remembered in the Books of Time. For once again we have found a race worthy of our mettle, an alien species that in flesh is like us in many ways, but is yet soulless. Make their blood burn, My Children, in the fires of war. For if their blood sings to us, they may be saved. If it does not, then let them perish as animals without knowing the light or the love that awaits us among the Ancient Ones.

"You are led this day," the Empress went on, "by Tesh-Dar, high priestess of the Desh-Ka and a living legend of the sword. Thrill to the song of her blood in battle, My Children, and great honor shall be yours." She paused, and Tesh-Dar could feel a warm wind stir in her soul as the Empress said, "So has it been, so shall it forever be. Let the Challenge begin."

"In Thy name, let it be so," Tesh-Dar echoed along with the thousands below her.

Returning her thoughts to the present, Tesh-Dar watched the globe of the human world they sought in a twin of the energy capsule they had sent back with the Messenger. On and above the surface of the planet, fierce battles raged, a simulacrum of what was to begin only moments from now. The great priestess sat in her command chair, her talons scoring the metal of one of the armrests as she absently drummed her fingers on it. She had no idea what awaited them in the system, and her body tingled with eager anticipation at what they might find. Had her instincts been right, and the Messenger well-chosen? Did a war fleet await them, or would these *humans* succumb to utter obliteration because they refused to rise to battle?

She was not concerned about dying or even her entire fleet being destroyed, as long as it was lost in battle against a worthy adversary. For that would accomplish what she and her sisters lived and died for: to honor their Empress in battle. In the millennia-long interludes when they had no external enemies to fight, Her Children sought honor through combat in the multitude of arenas throughout the Empire, in ritual battles that were rarely fought to the death.

That was why this contest brought such a sense of excitement to Tesh-Dar and the warriors she led: this was not simply a ritual contest, but truly *war*. She could imagine no more terrible, no more glorious pursuit, and her blood raged with expectant fire.

Holding her breath in anticipation, she watched as the globe of the human world quickly began to darken...

***

What to do with the artifact had sparked a long and fierce debate throughout the Terran defense community, all the way up to the president. Some had wanted to keep it in Earth space, both to study and to use as an indicator of the progress of the battle in hopes that what would be reflected on the globe after the attack began would show what was really happening, and thus provide real-time intelligence. Others argued that it would make more sense for the expeditionary force to have the artifact for the very same reasons.

The decision had eventually wound up on the president's desk. She took less than thirty seconds to decide. "Send it with the fleet," she ordered as commander-in-chief. "If it provides any sort of warning, they'll need it a lot more than we will. It won't do us any good when it would take us a week and a half to get ships there. Assuming we had any more to send."

Once that had been determined, others raised concerns about whether it was a bomb. But after a great deal of discussion that essentially went nowhere, Admiral Tiernan decided that if it had been some sort of weapon, the Kreelans could have used it to good effect long before. He ordered that a special instrumentation enclosure be built aboard the flagship to record any emissions or changes in the artifact, and a close watch had been kept every moment since the fleet had jumped from Earth space.

The fleet had gathered at a point that was a two-hour hyperspace jump from Keran. That was as close as they felt they could come without alerting the colony or the French fleet in-system and creating a diplomatic mess. The Keran and French governments knew, of course, that the Terran expeditionary force had left Earth space, but as long as it stayed clear of the Keran system, no one was likely to complain too loudly.

Admiral Tiernan was now on the flag bridge of the heavy cruiser *Ticonderoga*. The flag bridge was a special compartment, separate from the ship's bridge, that had all the systems his staff needed to help him control the fleet's operations.

"What the hell?" someone yelped "Something's happening!"

Tiernan snapped his head up to look at the three-dimensional image of the alien orb that was being projected on one of the flag bridge view screens. The globe was quickly darkening, the scene of a world at war being swallowed by infinite black. Then it started to shrink. But it didn't appear to be just getting smaller. It looked more like it was moving away from them. Tiernan thought it was a trick of the view screen display, but wasn't sure.

"What's happening to it?" He asked one of the battery of scientists who had been monitoring the artifact.

"Admiral..." the lead scientist replied, then paused as he conferred with the others. "Sir, this is impossible..."

"Dammit, man, what's happening?"

"It's moving away from us, sir," the man said, shaking his head. In the view screen, the globe was now the relative size of a marble, and growing smaller by the second. "It can't be doing what the instruments are saying," he said, looking up at Tiernan with a helpless expression, "but it is. And it's accelerating-"

"Damn!" someone in the background shouted as a thunderous boom echoed from the instrumentation chamber.

"What was that?" *Ticonderoga's* captain interjected worriedly. "Did that thing explode?" The ship's executive officer was already moving a damage control party in. They weren't taking any chances on something that, even after all this time, was still a complete unknown.

"No..." the scientist said, shaken. "That was a sonic boom from within the chamber from displaced air. The globe just...vanished."

***

Amiral Jean-Claude Lefevre stood in a moment of tense quiet on the flag bridge of the heavy cruiser *Victorieuse,* the flagship of the *Alliance Française* fleet that had been deployed to Keran. Because of the prevailing political conditions, the deployment had been conducted under the guise of joint exercises with the Keran Navy, although everyone knew the cover explanation was a farce. Lefevre twisted his mouth into an ironic grin: any one of his five squadrons, with a total of one hundred and fifty-three naval vessels, was larger than the entire Keran fleet in terms of tonnage. And when one considered that most of the Keran ships were small corvettes with little real combat capability, the "joint" label became rather ludicrous. Nonetheless, the Alliance had taken the Terran information of an alien threat seriously, and Lefevre was trying to do the same.

Unfortunately, he was terribly frustrated by the total lack of intelligence information. His government believed the possibility of an alien attack was credible, as difficult as he himself found it to believe. But he had no idea of what size force he might be facing, where they might appear in the system, or even what their objective might be, other than - everyone assumed - occupation of Keran. And if any of the information he had received about the enemy's technical capabilities were true, his ships would be so grossly outclassed that the presence of his fleet - the largest assembled since the St. Petersburg war - would be little more than a token gesture of defiance.

The only concrete information he had was when the attack was to take place. The Terrans had some sort of device that they believed was a countdown timer, an artifact from these so-called "Kreelans." Terran military authorities provided Avignon's military attaché on Earth with a digital countdown timer that would approximate the time left, calibrated to the changes shown by the alien device. The time remaining on that digital timer was displayed on every bridge in the Alliance fleet, and he now watched it closely as it wound down to zero.

"Thirty seconds," his flag captain said quietly into the mounting tension on the flag bridge. All the ships of the fleet had been at general quarters for the last two hours, as no one was sure how accurate the timer might be. Lefevre's mouth compressed into a thin line as he stared at the flag bridge tactical display that showed the disposition of his ships. Without having any idea of what the enemy planned or was capable of, his tactical options were very limited. He didn't want to put his ships in low orbit, deep inside Keran's gravity well, because even with reactionless drives gravity was a source of drag on a ship's acceleration potential: ships farther away from the planet were subject to far less gravity influence and had a tactical advantage when maneuvering. But he also couldn't put his ships too far out from the planet, or they might not be able to respond rapidly in case the enemy was planning on an orbital bombardment rather than an assault on the surface with ground forces. Having no information about their intentions and capabilities was maddening.

So he had been forced to compromise. He had divided his fleet into five task forces and placed them around the planet in high orbit to cover the most important population centers on the surface. In low orbit were twenty-four civilian starliners, each carrying a heavy combat brigade and tended by dozens of shuttles that would get the troops down to the surface as quickly as possible if he received permission to deploy them. A flotilla of six destroyers was tasked with protecting the starliners, forming a protective globe around the formation of huge civilian vessels.

"Fifteen seconds," the flag captain breathed. Lefevre shot the man a look, more bemused than annoyed, and his flag captain rewarded him with a sheepish grin. None of them wanted to believe anything was going to happen, but the Alliance was deeply worried, or they would not have been willing to absorb the enormous cost of deploying this many ships here. Lefevre watched as the timer counted down: *three...two...one...*

"Zero," he said to himself. "*Capitaine* Monet," he said into a comms screen to the ship's captain who stood tensely on the ship's bridge, "there are no changes in sensor readings, I assume?"

"*Non, mon amiral*," he replied. "Nothing but merchant traffic coming into the normal inbound jump zones. Three ships in the last two hours."

Lefevre sighed. *All a wild goose chase*, he thought. *But it's just as well.* "Very well," he said. "We will remain at general quarters for another two hours, then resume our planned training-"

"*Amiral!*" the flag captain shouted, pointing at the flag bridge tactical display. The ships of the fleet were tied together in a data net, with the sensor readings and targeting data from each ship automatically distributed to the others to maximize situational awareness and coordinate their attacks. One of the task forces on the far side of the planet had picked up a set of bogies - unidentified contacts, presumed hostile - jumping in.

Lefevre looked up at the display and paled at what he saw. "*Oh, mon Dieu...*"

***

Aboard the two-person Terran *Hermes* class diplomatic courier ship *Alita*, pilot Amelia Cartwright was just settling down to a delicious dinner of reprocessed steak and potatoes from a foil packet when her copilot, Sid Dougherty, suddenly stiffened like he'd been hit with about ten thousand volts. They were on the modified courier run that had been established a number of weeks before, where at least one courier ship was in orbit and one was in transit at all times. *Alita* had just arrived the previous day, where she was supposed to remain for a week until their relief arrived.

"Sid?" she asked, then turned to see what he was staring at. On the monitor that had been installed a few weeks before as part of the ship's instrumentation upgrade, a wave of red icons had suddenly materialized roughly half a million kilometers from Keran. Inbound enemy ships.

"Shit!" she exclaimed, tossing her food onto the deck and strapping herself in. "Come on, Sid! Get on the departure checklist and let's get the hell out of here." They should be able to get underway in only a couple of minutes. She only hoped they had that long.

"Got it," Sid replied, tearing his eyes away from the screen. A tall, lanky Texan who always insisted on wearing a ridiculous-looking cowboy hat, she had never seen him rattled before. "Damn," he drawled as he quickly punched up the remaining pre-flight checks, "I just never believed this would happen. Look at all those bastards! There must be two hundred ships!"

"Keran control," Cartwright called over the planetary navigation network, "this is Terran diplomatic courier ship *Alita*, requesting emergency departure clearance, outbound vector radial three-five-one mark zero." The ship's computer was also sending the information in a more detailed format to its counterpart at Keran control, but it was longstanding tradition to establish positive human-to-human contact, as well.

"*Alita*, this is Keran control," a heavily accented but very pleasant voice replied immediately. "Please hold current position. Alliance fleet elements are on exercise in your sector, and have requested all vessels to remain clear. We will notify you immediately when we can grant departure clearance."

Sid glanced at her and shook his head. *No goddamn way*, he mouthed silently.

Cartwright paused for just a moment. In the fifteen years that she had been in the diplomatic courier service, she had never once disobeyed a controller. But this time she had no choice: her orders were very explicit, and they were signed by the Secretary of State himself. "Negative, Keran control," she said as Sid completed the last of the checklist items and gave her the thumbs-up that the ship was ready. She took the controls and poured power to the massive engines, breaking out of her assigned orbital position for open space. "My sincere apologies, but we have to depart immediately. Please inform the Alliance fleet that we're an outbound friendly. They have enough targets to worry about without wasting munitions on us."

She broke off the connection before the controller could reply. "Get me the ambassador," she told Sid.

"Already done," he told her, nodding to a secondary view screen on the console, where the face of a regal-looking older woman calmly looked out at them.

"Madam Ambassador," Cartwright said formally, "this is *Alita*. Be advised that a Kreelan fleet has - repeat, *has* - arrived in-system, and Alliance fleet units are maneuvering to engage. As you know, we have orders to jump out immediately. You should be receiving a download of all the data that we get until we jump, and if you have any last-minute information you want to send out with us, I request you transmit it immediately."

"Thank you, *Alita*," Ambassador Irina Pugachova replied. "Our final communiques are being uploaded as we speak, and I thank you for the sensor data. I have instructed our military attaché to provide it directly to the Keran military liaison. What is your assessment of the situation as it stands now?"

Cartwright tried not to cringe. "Ma'am...there are roughly two hundred enemy ships now in the system. I don't know how they stack up against what the Alliance has in terms of tonnage and weapons, but the Frenchies are going to have their hands full."

Ambassador Pugachova nodded gravely. She looked to the side briefly as someone spoke to her, then turned her attention back to Cartwright. "The invasion alert is being broadcast on the media. At least that did not take too long." She looked back at Cartwright. "Get to the fleet rendezvous as quickly as you can. Good luck and godspeed, pilot."

"Same to you, ma'am," Cartwright said. The ambassador's face disappeared as the screen went blank. The connection was closed.

"Five minutes to jump," Sid informed her as *Alita* fled toward open space. Fortunately, the vector Cartwright had chosen was largely free of Alliance ships, and the Kreelans were on the far side of the planet. She watched the sensor display as two of the Alliance task forces that were closest to the mass of Kreelan ships maneuvered, trying to optimize the geometry for deploying their weapons. Two of the other task forces were quickly accelerating around the planet to join the fray, while the last task force remained on station opposite the battle, probably in case the Kreelans tried to flank them with another inbound force.

In low orbit, the cloud of shuttles hovering around the starliners began to plunge toward the surface, desperately trying to ferry nine heavy divisions to the ground as quickly as possible.

"One minute," Sid said quietly, and Cartwright could hear the low thrum of the hyperdrive capacitors spooling up.

On the sensor screen, the nearest of the Alliance task forces had closed to within weapons range, and ships began to die. The sensor suite was not powerful enough to tell them anything about the weapons being employed, but icons representing both Alliance and Kreelan ships began to flare on the screen, then disappear.

Just before her ship jumped, Cartwright saw another cloud of red icons appear right on top of the lone Alliance task force guarding the far side of the planet.

***

Tesh-Dar's blood burned like fire as she felt the emotional surge from her sisters throughout the fleet as they began to engage the humans. Having no information on how many forces the humans may have gathered or how they might be deployed, she had settled on a simple strategy that was most likely to ensure rapid contact with at least some of the human ships, assuming there were any. While they knew a great deal about the humans after fully absorbing the information contained in the data of the primitive vessel on which the Messenger had come, there was much about these aliens that remained intriguing unknowns. She had divided the main attack fleet into two groups. The first, with about one hundred and fifty ships, would jump into the target system near the planet's two small moons to engage any forces there. The second formation of roughly fifty ships, including her flagship, would jump into low orbit.

She was not disappointed. The group bound for the moons in high orbit arrived first, and Tesh-Dar could feel in the Bloodsong the thrill of the warriors as they found human warships awaiting them. The fleet the humans had assembled was unimpressive, but would provide her warriors with an acceptable challenge. Tesh-Dar could only be pleased.

As her own group emerged in low orbit, she gasped with pleasant surprise: they had materialized right on top of a formation of human ships!

"Elai-Tura'an!" she called to the shipmistress, the warrior who was the rough equivalent in human terms to the ship's captain. "Send forth the boarding parties, then engage at will!"

"Yes, my priestess!" Elai-Tura'an responded instantly as she carried out Tesh-Dar's orders.

Throughout the ships of the second attack group, hundreds of warriors clad in what were to them primitive vacuum combat suits leaped from airlocks arranged along the ships' flanks, steering toward the human ships that were even now turning to meet them.

***

"Primary kinetics, *fire!*" *Capitaine de vaisseau* Pierre Monet, captain of the Alliance heavy cruiser *Victorieuse* ordered over the orchestrated chaos of the bridge. The ship was rocked down to her keel as a set of twenty rounds of two hundred millimeter armor-piercing shells was fired from the ship's five main gun turrets. While the current generation of lasers were generally more effective, kinetic weapons - not too far removed from the shells fired by wet navy ships centuries before - were far less expensive and could still be extremely lethal.

Just after the main guns fired, a low humming sound echoed through the ship, one of the smaller close-in defense lasers firing at incoming Kreelan projectiles.

Amiral Lefevre stood silently on the flag bridge, trying to make sense of the chaotic information on the tactical display. The task force to which *Victorieuse* was attached was involved in the equivalent of a knife fight with the second group of Kreelan ships that had jumped in. While this Kreelan force was only slightly bigger than his own task force, his formation had essentially lost any semblance of tactical integrity. The Alliance datalinks were still up, allowing their ships to coordinate their fire, but the targets were so close that the French ships were now in danger of committing fratricide.

"*Triomphante* reports she's being boarded!" one of the tactical officers shouted.

"*What?*" Lefevre demanded, incredulous. He had heard the report of the Kreelans boarding the Terran survey ship, but had dismissed the notion. It was a ridiculous concept in modern space warfare.

"Boarders, sir!" the officer repeated. "They report aliens in vacuum suits are aboard, attacking the crew."

"Sir," *Capitaine* Monet interrupted, worry lining his face as he looked out from the view screen on the flag bridge, "sensors are showing a cloud of objects directly in front of us, on a direct vector from one of the enemy ships."

Boarders, Lefevre thought again. *What kind of enemy are we fighting who would throw away their people in such a fashion?* But he didn't hesitate. "Fight your ship, captain."

Monet nodded, then ordered his weapons officer, "Put the forward batteries under manual control. Sweep those damn things from our path."

***

Li'ara-Zhurah floated through space with the dozens of other warriors of the attack group she led, trying to reach one of the many human ships that were maneuvering wildly in the fierce melee taking place around her. She hated the primitive vacuum suit she had to wear, but had fought a series of fierce challenges for the honor of wearing it, and would have done so again without a second thought. Her blood sang with the rapture and pain of her sisters who now fought and died in the battle raging above the human planet. Her hands clenched reflexively in anticipation as her chosen target, one of the larger human cruisers, swept toward her, belching fire at the attacking warships of the Imperial fleet.

Some of the warriors in her attack group suddenly cried out in shock and agony as rapid-fire laser bolts suddenly began to sweep through their formation. The ancient design of the vacuum suits incorporated reflective shielding, but even the comparatively small amount of energy it still allowed to bleed through was enough to severely burn or kill the warrior wearing it.

"*Attack!*" Li'ara-Zhurah cried as she fired her small maneuvering thrusters in hopes of throwing off the enemy's aim and getting that much closer to her target. "Move in!"

With a war cry from her surviving sisters, the group surged forward *en masse* toward the human warship that was now speeding directly toward them.

***

"They're inside minimum range!" the tactical officer exclaimed as the cloud of targets on the *Victorieuse's* tactical display passed inside the range rings of the close-in defense weapons. The weapons were primarily designed to stop missile and kinetic weapons, and had fared poorly against the alien attackers. The software that controlled the weapons' targeting wasn't expecting such slow moving targets, and while the small laser batteries had killed at least half of the aliens heading for the ship, that still left several dozen alive.

Capitaine Monet hit a button on his command console, opening a channel to the crew. "Prepare to repel boarders!" he barked, feeling mildly ridiculous saying those particular words, despite the potential severity of the situation. The Alliance Navy had no protocols for dealing with hostile boarders, and none of the ships carried marines who could mount an effective shipboard defense. In fact, the Alliance had no space marines at all: such a military force had been seen as unnecessary in the modern age. The only thing they had was a small armory containing light weapons that were used during inspection operations that had the potential to turn violent. Doing a quick calculation in his head, Monet ordered, "Every department is to send five men to the armory immediately to draw weapons! Defend the ship!"

Hearing Monet's orders, Lefevre immediately opened a fleet-wide broadcast. "All ships," he ordered, "be prepared to repel boarders. Repeat, be prepared to repel boarders."

Just then there was the sound of an explosion somewhere aft, followed by an alarm that one of the secured compartments was losing air.

"The hull has been breached," Monet hissed.

***

Matching velocity with the human ships that Li'ara-Zhurah and her warriors wanted to attack would have been virtually impossible without the inertial compensator that the builders had discovered far back in the Books of Time. It was on a level of technology comparable to what the humans possessed, so it was allowed by the priestess. Bulky and primitive compared to the energy bubbles used in the current day, the compensator was small enough to be fitted to a suit, and had originally been designed millennia before to allow boarding operations just such as this.

The human ship loomed before Li'ara-Zhurah, approaching faster than she would have thought possible. She could see its forward laser batteries still belching coherent light at her sisters; many had been lost, but many yet remained alive, their fury and bloodlust pounding in her own veins. The dull gray behemoth was nothing but angles and bulky protuberances, the muzzles of its larger weapons flashing with crimson brilliance as they fired. She knew that the ships of her fleet were absorbing a tremendous amount of damage while inflicting comparatively little to give her and her sisters the honor of taking the sword to the enemy. It was greater honor to the Empress to fight eye-to-eye with one's foe than to smash away at them with the guns of warships. Her Children would hardly shy away from such carnage, but their goal was a battle of being against being, not one fought by technology.

Holding her breath, Li'ara-Zhurah fired a magnetic grapple ahead of her, hoping that the hulls of the human ships were composed of ferrous alloys to which the grapple could adhere. *Yes!* she thought triumphantly as the grapple clung to the skin of the human ship as it sailed by, automatically triggering the inertial compensator. Suddenly, almost magically, Li'ara-Zhurah was traveling alongside the ship, her velocity relative to the vessel having been equalized by the compensator.

But there was a price to be paid. The device had to do something with the huge amount of energy it had just absorbed in matching her velocity to that of the ship, and it converted it all to heat. Li'ara-Zhurah cried out as her back was suddenly seared by the red-hot compensator just before it automatically separated from her suit and drifted off into space.

Gasping at the pain, she triggered the miniature winch that reeled her to where the grapple had attached itself to the vessel's metal skin. Once there, she activated the magnetic soles of her boots to anchor her feet to the alien hull. She looked around in wide-eyed wonder at the spectacle around her: ships everywhere, blasting away at one another with kinetic rounds and lasers; clouds of warriors maneuvering through space, trying to find their targets; and periodic eye-searing explosions as ships died. And it all took place in total, utter silence.

Bringing her mind back to the task at hand, she unwound a strip of putty-like material and stuck it onto the hull in a rough circle as big around as her arms spread wide. Walking awkwardly across the hull in her magnetic boots, she put some distance between herself and the putty-like material, then triggered it.

Rather than a conventional explosive, the boarding charges the warriors were using was a chemical compound much akin to thermite used by humans. Once ignited, it burned at a ferociously high temperature and could melt through virtually any metal that human technology could produce. Since the warriors would have no way of knowing if the part of the hull they landed on was merely a thin metal skin or armor an arm's length in thickness, primitive explosives might not be sufficient. But even the thickest metal could be penetrated with enough heat.

She watched as the boarding charge burst into brilliant flame, instantly melting the metal of the hull, which bubbled off into space. The flames sank into the ship's metal skin, eating it away with heat.

A moment later, the entire circle of the hull - plating, electrical conduits, piping - exploded outward from the air pressure in the compartment beneath as the boarding charge breached the interior wall. Two human figures, not wearing space suits, flew past her, ejected by explosive decompression. The flow of air stopped after a few moments.

Ignoring the pain from the burns on her back, Li'ara-Zhurah jumped through the breach, her sword held at the ready.

FOURTEEN

One of the enlisted sailors from engineering, *Second-maître* Emmanuelle Sabourin, led four other crewmen toward the nearest compartment that had been breached. They had been among the first to reach the armory, and had drawn two automatic shotguns and three sidearms, plus a pair of grenades. Sabourin had wanted all of her team to be armed with shotguns or rifles, but the armorer simply nodded over his shoulder at what he had available: three more shotguns, half a dozen assault rifles, and maybe a dozen pistols, plus a dozen grenades. That was it.

Disgusted, she'd taken the weapons the armorer had offered, along with a generous quantity of armor-piercing ammunition. That, at least, was not in short supply. She was actually surprised that the armorer was handing out armor-piercing rounds, as they could wreak havoc if they penetrated the inner walls of the ship and destroyed any of the underlying electrical systems or conduits. But he had told her it was on the captain's direct orders: he believed they would need it to fight the boarders. Unsettled by that bit of information, she led her team aft as another group arrived to pick over the meager weapons supply.

Unlike the other teams, Sabourin's team members were all wearing vacuum suits. While the ship had a plentiful supply of emergency "beach balls" that crewmen could quickly jump into in case of a loss of air pressure, there were only a small number of vacuum suits, which normally were used only for external repair work and the various odd jobs for which an EVA (Extra-Vehicular Activity) was required. There were only half a dozen or so, and they were all kept in engineering. When the chief engineer chose her, his senior enlisted rating, to lead the team from engineering to help repel the boarders, she and her companions grabbed the suits and put them on. The only problem was that they weren't designed for combat: she could puncture one with a screwdriver, and they only had basic communications gear. But it was more than the other teams had.

"This way," she said, turning right and pounding down an auxiliary stairway. The captain had locked all of the ship's elevators. Halfway down, the ship rocked to the side, throwing her off-balance. Losing her grip on the handrail, she chose to jump down the rest of the way rather than tumbling down the remaining steps. She landed on her feet and rolled, only to come face-to-face with an apparition the likes of which she had never seen before.

The Kreelan warrior bared her fangs and lunged forward, thrusting her sword at Sabourin's mid-section.

Caught totally off-guard, Sabourin instinctively swung her shotgun to deflect the alien's attack, the sword's tip barely missing her suit. But the movement put Sabourin off-balance, and she fell backward to the deck as the Kreelan raised her sword, preparing to bring it down in a savage double-handed strike.

But the alien warrior never got the chance. With a deafening blast, the other member of Sabourin's team with a shotgun blew the Kreelan back against the bulkhead. The alien slammed into the wall with a grunt of pain, but then got right back up again: her glossy black chest armor looked like someone had hit it with a fist hard enough to make a deep indentation, scraping the black coating off to reveal the gleaming raw metal beneath. But the shotgun's armor-piercing round hadn't gone through. The warrior was no doubt badly bruised, and may even have suffered some broken ribs, but otherwise was quite alive.

At least she was until Sabourin blew her unarmored head off with the shotgun. "*Salope*," she spat. *Bitch*.

"How did she get in here without a suit?" one of her teammates asked as he helped Sabourin get back on her feet, something that wasn't easy to do in the ship's artificial gravity while wearing the bulky suits. "There are no airlocks in this part of the ship."

"She made one," one of the others called from the nearby hatchway in the direction Sabourin had been leading them. "Look."

The hatch - which automatically closed any time general quarters was sounded - stood open. In the compartment beyond, which Sabourin knew had been breached, the Kreelan had attached some sort of thin membrane to the bulkhead around the hatch coaming that had been large enough for her to stand in. The membrane, however it was attached to the bulkhead (chemically bonded, Sabourin guessed), had formed a makeshift airlock, and the Kreelan must then have simply cut through the bulkhead to short out the hatch controls. With a quick blast of air that filled the bubble that now sealed her away from the vacuum in the compartment behind her, the alien could have then just stepped into the pressurized passageway, where she discarded her vacuum armor. Simple and effective.

Looking closer, Sabourin could see that the membrane was actually *two* membranes, with each one having a barely visible seam down the middle. Suddenly she understood: the outer membrane, which now was loosely draped against the bubble of the pressurized inner one, formed the first part of a double-airlock.

"*Merde*," she muttered.

"What is wrong?" one of the others asked.

"If more aliens enter that compartment," she nodded toward the hatchway and the improvised airlock, "through the hole that the first alien made in the hull, they can enter the bubble through the outer membrane, seal it, then enter the ship through the inner membrane without risking explosive decompression of the passageway on this side." She turned to look at her teammates, her angular face and dark brown eyes grim. "Anywhere they make one of these, they can easily gain access to the pressurized portions of the ship."

"But why?" one of the others asked. "If they just blow holes in the hull, they would eventually kill most of us. Would that not be easier?"

"Yes, it would," she said. The question bothered her, but she had no answer. She had to inform the captain. "Bridge," she called over her suit's comms system.

"Bridge," a communications technician answered immediately.

"This is *Second-maître* Sabourin on deck six at frame seventy-three," she reported. "We killed one of the boarders. But alert the other teams that the armor-piercing rounds from our shotguns will not penetrate their chest armor. Head shots only. Please also inform the captain that the boarders can create their own double airlocks. Wherever one of them makes a penetration, more aliens will be able to enter from the vacuum side without further decompression of the adjoining compartment."

There was a moment of silence, then she heard the captain's voice. "Sabourin," *Capitaine* Monet asked, "are you sure about the airlocks? We had assumed that one of the enemy's primary objectives would be to secure at least one of the ship's airlocks to allow them to get more warriors aboard faster. That is where we were going to concentrate our ship defense teams."

"*Oui, mon capitaine*," she told him grimly as she and the rest of her team began to back away from the hatch while bringing up their weapons, "I am sure these airlocks work. In fact, more aliens are trying to come through this one now..."

***

On the other side of the ship, Li'ara-Zhurah had finished fastening the airlock membrane to the bulkhead of the compartment she had entered. Aside from the two humans who had been blown out when she cut through the hull, the compartment had been empty. Behind her, four other warriors had managed to scramble through the hole and now stood by as she prepared the airlock. She waited for a moment more for the chemical matrix around the edges of the membrane to fuse with the metal of the bulkhead, and then - taking a wild guess - she hit the large green button of what she assumed was the control panel for the hatch. She was right: the hatch slid open, and after a small implosion of air that filled the inner bubble, she stepped through the hatch into the passageway beyond.

She could see in the strange yellow-tinged light that there were no humans about, and she signaled to the warriors behind her to follow. One by one, they entered the outer bubble, then the inner one. Some air was lost as they did so, but it was trivial for a ship this size.

As a second warrior joined her, Li'ara-Zhurah gratefully rid herself of the cumbersome vacuum suit, hissing with the pain as the suit snagged on her backplate and pressed it against her burned flesh. With a growl of anger, she tore the rest of the suit from her body, slashing at it with her black talons. At last free of the encumbrance, she felt like a warrior once again, and not like a piece of meat encased in a tin.

Once the other warriors of her group were through the airlock, they set off in search of the crew.

***

While more and more skirmishes broke out in the passageways of *Victorieuse*, Lefevre was desperately trying to extricate the fleet from what could easily turn into a colossal disaster. As the close-in slugging match with the Kreelan ships here in lower orbit intensified, Lefevre recalled the two squadrons that were streaming around the planet to engage the larger Kreelan force in high orbit. He ordered the remaining two squadrons, those that had the misfortune of being closest to the larger Kreelan group, to pull back. His goal was to try and achieve sufficient local superiority that he could smash the smaller Kreelan group *Victorieuse* and her sisters were fighting before facing off against the larger group of Kreelan ships.

Destroying the larger group or forcing them to withdraw, he knew, was little more than wishful thinking. While he had rough parity at the moment with the enemy here in low orbit, they had at least fifty more ships in the larger group near the moons than he had in his entire fleet. It appeared that the Kreelans were perfectly positioned to destroy the Alliance squadrons that were closest to the larger Kreelan force.

However, to his shock and surprise, they didn't. The Kreelans allowed the other Alliance squadrons to retreat back toward Lefevre's position near the planet. Some Kreelan ships pursued them, but only made harassing attacks, nothing more.

"What are they doing?" his flag captain asked.

Lefevre shook his head, completely confused. "I have no idea. Why do they not simply destroy our ships? They have overwhelming superiority."

The *Victorieuse* suddenly rocked with a hit, throwing both men off balance. They should have been in their combat chairs, but Lefevre had perversely always refused to sit in one. More alarms blared, signaling yet more damage to the ship, but Lefevre ignored them. That was *Capitaine* Monet's job.

"Are they simply toying with us?" he wondered aloud.

***

Tesh-Dar grunted with satisfaction at the humans' response. Realizing their tactical error, they were now trying to reconsolidate their forces. She would allow them to do as they wished - to a point. But only as it suited her. Much of this first battle was simply to study, to learn. Had this been an enemy that posed a true threat to the Empire, she would have clawed them from the skies in minutes, even with ships of a design as ancient as this.

But the humans were not a threat. They were an opportunity to glorify the Empress. They would die and this system would be taken into the Empire, yes, but she would allow them to fight on even ground. For the first time in several thousand cycles did the Children of the Empress have a worthy enemy, and she would take her time to blood her warriors properly and let the humans learn, as well. For the more they knew, the better they would fight.

She ordered that the formation in high orbit detach half its ships to follow the two closest human squadrons back toward the planet, harassing them without making many outright kills. Ships that could be crippled would be boarded, so her warriors could fight the humans face to face. But it was better for her purposes if the human ships were gathered in more closely together. She was sorely tempted to join the young ones in the bloodletting, but the time would soon come when the battle on the planet's surface would begin. Then she would indulge herself.

With that in mind, she had one of the warriors working a sensor console - Tesh-Dar was still amazed that their forebears had extended the Empire across the stars with the aid of such primitive devices - show her the progress of the human ships carrying troops to the surface. Clearly not designed for war, the odd assemblage of vessels were surrounded by a host of small shuttles that were equally ill-designed for ferrying troops and equipment quickly. It would take many trips for the small craft to carry all the humans aboard those ships down to the surface. And then it would no doubt take them some time to prepare their defenses.

It was just as well, Tesh-Dar thought as the guns of her command ship thundered. She was in no hurry.

***

Sabourin and her team stared at the handful of Kreelan warriors who had gathered in the compartment beyond the improvised airlock, and the Kreelans stared back.

But only for a moment.

"*Nique ta mere!*" Sabourin cursed at the Kreelans as she snatched one of the grenades from her utility pouch, mashed down on the activator and hurled it into the airlock bubble. "Take cover!" she cried before ducking behind the stairs.

One of her comrades made it to the safety of the stairs - the only real cover available - with her, but the remaining three never had a chance: three of the Kreelans threw some sort of weapons through the membrane. Like miniature buzz saws, the weapons whirred through the air and caught the three crewmen in mid-stride as they tried to dash out of the way. The weapons cut through the thick fabric of the vacuum suits as if it was made of rice paper, and did the same to the flesh and bone beneath. One crewman clutched at his chest before he fell to the deck; the second, who was hit in the neck, simply collapsed to the floor like a rag doll. Sabourin could see that he had been decapitated, just before his faceplate was covered in blood that still spewed from the carotid artery. The third weapon caught the last crewman in the back, severing his spine just below the shoulder blades. His screams of agony rang from the speakers in her helmet.

Then the grenade went off, and Sabourin held onto the metal skeleton of the stairs for dear life as the air in the passageway was explosively vented into space. The crewman who had managed to take shelter with her behind the stairs didn't have a firm hold and suddenly found himself carried out through the hatch into the adjoining compartment by the force of the explosive decompression. He would have been carried out into space except for the artificial gravity, which was still strong enough to hold him to the deck. But his good fortune was short lived as one of the surviving warriors leapt upon him, and they grappled with one another even as two more warriors clambered through the hole in the hull, dropping nimbly to the deck in spite of their bulky armored suits. Then another appeared to join them.

With tears of hate and anger clouding her eyes, Sabourin threw her second grenade into their midst.

***

Gritting her teeth in pain, Li'ara-Zhurah leaned against the bulkhead, waiting for a break in the weapons fire coming from the humans around the corner and down the passageway. She and her small band of warriors had already killed over a dozen members of the crew when they had run into this determined - and, for once, well-armed - group of defenders. They were proving a worthy challenge, and beyond the pain of the bullet wound in her left arm, her blood sang in blissful fury. She turned to look at one of her companion warriors, who knelt on the deck behind her, blood running from her mouth: one of the human projectile weapons had hammered against her chest armor and shattered several of her ribs, which in turn had punctured a lung. "You must rest, Ku'ira-Gol," she counseled the younger warrior. "This is merely the opening battle in a great war. You need not spend yourself in the first of it. Let the healers tend to you once we finish this. A host of humans yet await the attention of your sword and claws."

Looking up at Li'ara-Zhurah with eyes that bore the pain not of her body, but of her spirit, Ku'ira-Gol shook her head. "No, my sister," she said quietly. She had been a late arrival, and happened to discover the hole Li'ara-Zhurah had made in the hull, then followed her and the others here. "You speak with truth and wisdom, but my sword has not yet been blooded. Many combats did I fight in the arena for the honor to be here. I will not spend a moment in the company of a healer until I have spilled the blood of our enemy."

Li'ara-Zhurah understood completely. Not just the younger warrior's words, but the flame of her emotions, the melody of her Bloodsong. Ku'ira-Gol's answer she had expected, but honor demanded that Li'ara-Zhurah offer counsel as she had. "So has it been-" she whispered.

"-so shall it forever be," the others echoed in a simple timeless prayer to the Empress.

With one last look in Ku'ira-Gol's silver-flecked eyes, seeing that her face was now serene with the acceptance of what was soon to be, Li'ara-Zhurah nodded. "May you find a place among the Ancient Ones, my sister."

"In Her name," Ku'ira-Gol whispered just before she leapt out into the passageway to draw the humans' fire. She rolled nimbly to her feet before leaping into the air, hurling her last *shrekka* at one of the human animals.

The passageway was suddenly filled with the staccato roar of assault rifles as they poured fire into her. The bullets from the rifles, able to penetrate the Kreelan's armor, shattered Ku'ira-Gol's body even as her *shrekka* found its mark, severing the head of one of the defenders.

As Ku'ira-Gol's lifeless body fell to the deck, Li'ara-Zhurah and the four remaining warriors broke from cover and charged down the passageway, hurling their own *shrekkas*. They had not thrown them with the intent to kill, but to force the humans down, to give the warriors a few more precious seconds to get close enough to use their swords and claws. Baring their fangs and roaring with fury, they flung themselves into the group of half a dozen humans, blades flashing and claws tearing.

The humans put up a spirited fight, but it was all too brief. It had been clear to Li'ara-Zhurah from her first encounter with the humans aboard this vessel that even though they appeared to be soulless creatures, many of them had great courage and fighting spirit. But they were ill-trained and poorly equipped to engage properly in battle with Her Children. Perhaps their warriors who fought on the ground would prove more of a challenge. If she managed to survive the battle here in space, she would seek to find out.

Her sensitive nose filled with the unpleasant coppery scent from the human blood that now covered her like haphazardly splashed paint, she continued to lead the remaining warriors to her ultimate destination: the ship's bridge.

***

Alone now, the rest of her team dead, Sabourin was also cut off from the rest of the crew. There was no way she could enter the pressurized sections of the ship from here, for there was no airlock: having destroyed the one the Kreelans had made to the adjoining compartment where they had penetrated the hull, she had cut off her own escape route. Now, she had no choice but to head out through the hole the Kreelans had made in the ship's hull and try to find another one of their improvised airlocks, or one of the ship's main airlocks. She would settle for whichever was closer.

Clamping the shotgun to a utility sticky patch on her suit, she stepped into the compartment filled with the bodies of the Kreelans and the member of her team that she had killed with the grenade. She tried to console herself with the thought that there was no way she could have saved her fellow crewman, but another voice quietly reminded her that she hadn't even tried. She hadn't known him very well; she hadn't known any of the people on her short-lived team, as they had all been sent from different sections of engineering. She had killed him, and now she couldn't even remember his name. Kicking the mangled bodies of the Kreelans out of the way, she knelt by his lacerated suit for a moment, looking at his face. His expression was oddly peaceful, although his features were distorted from the swelling of his tissues as the fluids tried to turn to vapor in the pure vacuum of the compartment.

"I'm sorry," she said dully, squeezing his dead hand gently. Then she let go. There was nothing else to say.

Turning to the body of one of the warriors, she took the alien's sword. She had no training in how to use it, but it couldn't hurt to have such a weapon handy, especially since the shotgun didn't seem to do much to their armor. She slid the gleaming weapon into its scabbard, having wrenched it from the belt the alien wore, then attached it to another sticky patch on her suit. After a moment's consideration, she checked the rest of the warrior's belongings. Most of it she either could not figure out or could not use, but she found a small pouch that, when she squeezed it, suddenly popped out and expanded into one of the portable airlocks. *That could be useful*, she thought. Finding another warrior who still had hers, Sabourin took it and stuffed it into the utility pouch on her belt. She also found a wound-up strip of taffy-like material, packed together with a small electronic unit in a pouch. It dawned on her that this must be the explosive material that they had used to make the holes in the hull. She had no idea what she might do with it, but since it was small and no inconvenience, she stuffed that in her utility pouch, as well.

Looking at her suit's telltales in the head-up display on her visor, Sabourin saw that she only had an hour of air left. She had to find a way back into the pressurized parts of the ship.

Getting out onto the hull would be a bit tricky, only because the hole the Kreelans had made was in the "ceiling" of this compartment. And since the artificial gravity was still working, she couldn't just jump. Fortunately, this was one of the ship's many equipment storage areas, and after about fifteen minutes of grunting and heaving, interrupted frequently by either the vibration of the ship's kinetics firing or the compartment shuddering as *Victorieuse* took another hit, she had managed to push together enough pallets and other flotsam to build a platform high enough for her to reach the outside of the hull with her hands.

It took her a couple of minutes of frenzied scrabbling in the awkward suit, made worse by the shotgun and sword protruding at odd angles, but she finally made it. She rolled over on the outside of the hull, panting at the effort and holding on with a magnetized glove to keep from drifting away. The artificial gravity field actually stopped mid-way through the hull's thick skin, and it was a queasy sensation as she lifted herself through the hole to have part of her body still sensing gravity and the rest of it sensing weightlessness.

Looking out, the infinite blackness of space was lit with a cascade of fireworks as ships fired upon one other. While the engagement range for space combat was normally judged in thousands of kilometers, she could see at least two dozen ships - some of them very close aboard, *within hundreds of meters* - with her naked eye. Most were moving far slower than they normally would, either because of battle damage or just to hold formation with their wounded sisters. She saw a pair of ships, one clearly human, the other not, that had collided at some velocity slow enough that they had not been destroyed outright. She saw small shapes swarming over the human ship, and knew with bitter anguish exactly what they were. More boarders.

A shadow suddenly fell across her face, something breaking the glare of the system's star. Glancing to her left, she saw another Kreelan warrior floating through space, drifting directly toward her. With a growl, Sabourin ripped the shotgun from its sticky patch. While the weapon was not exactly optimized for space combat, its designers had at least ensured that the chemical composition of the propellant in the cartridges did not need oxygen to fire. The Kreelan was already reaching for one of the flying weapons attached to the outside of her armored suit, but Sabourin had no intention of letting the alien use it. Bracing the shotgun against the hull, holding it as if she were firing from the hip, Sabourin pulled the trigger.

The heavy shot caught the Kreelan warrior square in the chest. While the heavy shot didn't penetrate her armor, it gave proof to Newton's third law of motion: for every action, there is an equal and opposite reaction. The hit sent the warrior flying backward into space, tumbling head over heels.

Shaking with yet another surge of adrenalin, Sabourin managed to get back on her feet, locking the magnetic pads on her boots to the hull. Trying to ignore the distractions of the silent space battle going on around her, she first tried to spot any more Kreelan warriors on the hull or floating nearby. There were none that she could see. For a moment, she stood there, lungs heaving. Her orders had been clear before, if rather broad: repel the enemy and defend the ship. If her team's experience was any indication, the enemy must be gaining the upper hand, and she wasn't sure which way to go or what to do.

"Bridge," she called as she caught her breath.

There was a long pause, and she was about to call again when the same communications tech as before answered.

"Bridge," the tech said, somewhat breathlessly.

"This is Sabourin. I am outside the hull, roughly forty-five minutes of air remaining." She paused, not wanting to say what must be said. "I...I have lost the rest of my team. I need orders."

"Stand by."

The silence that followed was interminable. At one point Sabourin was nearly knocked to her knees by an explosion near the stern of the ship. The stars and the fireflies that were fighting and dying ships wheeled crazily around her before the ship gradually came back under control. But *Victorieuse* was clearly badly damaged. The ship was still in the fight - Sabourin could see the periodic flare from the muzzles of her kinetic guns and the emerald pulses from her lasers - but she suffered from a constant starboard yaw and downward pitch that the helmsman must be trying to control with thrusters. That meant the main engines had been very badly damaged, and no doubt the rest of the ship was faring no better. She gritted her teeth in frustration. There must be something more she could do.

"Sabourin," the captain's voice suddenly echoed in her earphones, "you must make for the main starboard airlock and do what you can to hold it against attack. We need to get off what is left of the crew, and the port side is controlled by the enemy."

"We are abandoning ship, sir?" she asked, mortified.

A long pause. "*Oui*," he answered heavily. "I was about to inform the *amiral* when you called. We have no choice."

He paused again, as if unsure what to say next. Her heart bled for him: while she did not know him very well personally, he had been a good and fair captain during her time aboard the ship. And to lose *Victorieuse* - the fleet flagship! - this way must have been horrible.

"Listen, Sabourin," he went on quietly, as if he did not want anyone else near him to hear, "aside from the officers' sidearms - which are useless - you have the only weapon left that can kill these beasts. All the other defense teams are gone. You *must* hold the starboard airlock. If you do not, the crew will be trapped in the ship and at the mercy of these creatures. We have no way of fighting our way past them."

"*Oui, mon capitaine*," she said grimly, already stalking across the hull to the starboard side. "I understand. And I will not fail you."

***

"We're losing the ship, *mon amiral*," *Capitaine* Monet reported to Lefevre even as screams - very close now - echoed through the blast doors that separated the flag and ship's bridges from the rest of the ship. The agony in his voice was no different - perhaps worse, if that were possible - than if his wife lay on an operating table in surgery, dying. "Engineering was under attack and no longer responds, and we have lost maneuvering control. While we still control the ship's weapons, fewer and fewer of the gun crews answer, and our fire has fallen to almost nothing. The aliens now control the port airlock, and we have lost contact with all the defense teams." He still had contact with Sabourin, but despite the young woman's determined vow, he held little hope that she alone could do what he had asked. He knew she would die trying, however, and he could ask no more of any of his crew. He took in a shuddering breath. "I recommend that we abandon ship."

As if to punctuate Monet's litany of doom, *Victorieuse* shuddered from another hit. Lefevre realized now that the fire from the Kreelan vessels was generally not intended to kill his ships, but to wound them enough that the boarding parties would have a better chance to attack. They were like pack animals, one tearing at the prey's legs to bring it down, while others pounced on its back or went for the throat. He found some solace in the knowledge that, once the threat of the boarders had been taken seriously, only three more ships had fallen victim to them by direct attack.

But for *Victorieuse* and a dozen or more other ships, it was too late.

His heart heavy, knowing the pain it was causing Monet to even suggest such a thing, he said, "Very well, *capitaine*." Turning to his flag captain, he said, "Signal *Jean Bart* to come alongside to take on survivors from the starboard side airlock; I will transfer my flag to her." He turned back to the ship's captain, but Monet was not looking at him.

Behind Lefevre, Monet had seen the port side blast door to the flag bridge suddenly slide open. At the threshold stood a small group of alien warriors. "*Get down!*" he screamed, tackling Lefevre to the deck as the keening of Kreelan flying weapons filled the flag bridge.

***

Li'ara-Zhurah once again found herself facing a determined group of humans, and her blood sang with the joy of battle. While they were pitifully armed with small handguns, the accuracy of the shots by one of the humans was making for a challenging fight. The human animal who had been facing the door that opened onto what must be part of the bridge had flung itself and another of its kind down behind a console, avoiding the volley of *shrekkas* that her warriors had hurled at the humans inside. But that same human had suddenly peeked above the console and fired his handgun twice, shooting two of her fellow warriors in the head and killing them instantly.

She looked at the three warriors who remained with her. All of them had sustained injuries of one sort or another, bearing witness to the ferocity of the humans, if not their skill. Truly, they were worthy opponents.

Gripping her last *shrekka*, she quickly peered around the hatch coaming, which was the only cover they had here in the corridor. Her other warriors crouched low to the deck, trying to stay out of sight of the sharpshooter.

She had stuck her head out just far enough to get a glimpse of the console where the two humans had hidden when the human again rose up and squeezed off a round. Had she been just a fraction of a second slower he would have killed her. As it was, she would have a handsome scar across her left cheek where the bullet grazed her. Assuming she survived.

***

Monet ducked back down behind the command console. He had surprised the Kreelans with his marksmanship, but he had certainly never expected to use his skills with a pistol, honed during his years of competition while attending university, to defend his ship. He keyed his wrist comm to the ship-wide annunciator circuit. "All hands, this is the captain," he said urgently. "Abandon ship. Repeat, abandon ship. Make way to the starboard side main airlock. Starboard side only. The port side airlock is controlled by the enemy." He paused for a moment. "Good luck and godspeed." Turning to *Amiral* Lefevre, who crouched next to him, his sidearm drawn and ready, Monet said, "It is time for you to leave, *mon amiral*. I will cover your withdrawal as best I can. Take the bridge crewmen through the starboard side path to the airlock."

"Monet..." Lefevre began, then stopped. There was no choice. He hated to leave him here in what could only be a last stand. But Lefevre had an entire fleet to worry about, and every moment counted now if he was to extricate the rest of his ships from certain disaster. "*Bonne chance, capitaine*," he said quietly, gripping Monet's shoulder.

Then, in a crouching run, he made his way forward to the main bridge, gathering the other crewman to him as he went. Only the senior officers had sidearms, and the guns were the only protection any of them had.

With one last look toward where Monet lay waiting for the Kreelans, Lefevre rendered him a salute. The captain returned it with a brave smile and a small wave of his hand.

Once the last member of the bridge crew had crept past him, staying low to keep out of the Kreelans' line of sight, Lefevre closed the blast door and locked it behind him as a volley of gunshots rang out on the other side.

***

While the *Victorieuse* was not a huge ship compared to some of the gigantic transports and starliners, the hull seemed to stretch for endless kilometers as Sabourin trudged step by exhausting step toward the starboard airlock. Walking in the suit required careful attention to first demagnetize one foot, set it, magnetize it, then demagnetize the other foot to repeat the process. It was dreadfully slow going, and while she was EVA qualified, almost all of her outside operations in a suit had been with a maneuvering pack. This was torture, and a river of sweat was running down her back and between her breasts, and from her forehead into her eyes where it burned like fire. That was perhaps the most frustrating thing, because she had to constantly look around and above for more Kreelan warriors trying to sneak up on her.

But no more had appeared by the time she reached the airlock. With her shotgun held at the ready - although she was not sure her magnetic boots would hold her to the hull against the weapon's recoil - she opened the outer hatch. It was empty. Stepping inside, she hit the controls to pressurize the lock. She was about to hit the button to open the inner door, then paused. It wouldn't do to have come all this way just to be shot by someone on the other side of the door, thinking she was a Kreelan. Of course, there could be Kreelans on the far side of the door, too.

Again holding her shotgun at the ready, she activated her suit's external microphone and punched the button for the airlock intercom. "This is *Second-maître* Sabourin in the airlock," she said. "Is anyone there?"

She nearly pulled the trigger of the shotgun as the door suddenly slid open, revealing what looked to be a couple dozen of her shipmates.

"*Merde!*" she exclaimed to the first of the people who stepped forward to greet her. "I almost blew your head off!" Then she recognized who it was and lowered the shotgun. "Um. Sir," she added sheepishly.

"You would have been quite right in doing so, petty officer," Lefevre told her warmly. "My apologies. Sabourin, isn't it?"

"*Oui, mon amiral*," she said, noting how haggard the admiral looked. He had gashes along the side of his face, and his uniform was in tatters.

The admiral glanced down at his uniform and nodded sadly. "We were ambushed by another group of boarders on the way here. We fought them off, but not before they killed another ten members of the crew." He had two bullets left for his sidearm. It had been a very close thing that any of them had gotten away. That and Sabourin's shotgun were all they had left. "*Jean Bart* is to dock any moment, petty officer," he told her. "I must ask you, as you have the only real weapon left among us, to do what you can to give the crew time to get off."

"This is all that is left of us?" she asked in a small voice.

The admiral nodded heavily. "I believe there are more - although not many - down below, barricaded in some of the engineering spaces. But there are boarding parties between them and us, and we have no weapons to try and fight our way through." While Lefevre knew that his first concern must be the fleet, if he had more weapons for his companions or a marine detachment on board he would have led them in an attempt to rescue the trapped members of the crew. But to do so unarmed was beyond hopeless. "We have closed the blast doors here in the main gangway, and I have used my override to lock them. But we know the enemy can open locked doors, do we not?"

Sabourin nodded grimly. She knew what he was going to ask before he asked it. "I will hold them off, sir," she said quietly.

He put a hand on her shoulder and squeezed tightly. She could barely feel it through the thick fabric of the suit. "I know you will," he told her proudly. "It should not be long now."

Raising her right arm, she saluted him, the gesture awkward in her suit, and he returned it. Then, looking past the crowd of worried faces, she asked him, "Sir, how many doors are there beyond this one that you were able to close and lock?"

"Two," he told her. "I doubt they will hold them long."

She pursed her lips, thinking. "*Amiral*, if you would, please open this door. I believe I have a plan that may buy us a bit more time."

***

Now at the tail of a group of a dozen warriors pursuing the remaining human survivors of the crew, Li'ara-Zhurah felt a quickening in her breast. The battle to take the bridge, while brief, had been exquisite. The lone human with a pistol had killed two of the other warriors when they had all attacked. Li'ara-Zhurah fought him in hand to hand combat to honor his skill. Such fighting clearly had not been his strength, but he still fought with spirit, and to her that mattered a great deal more. The outcome of that particular contest had never been in question. But when she finally rammed her outstretched fingers into the human's chest, her talons piercing his heart, it was with regret, for he had allowed Li'ara-Zhurah and the others to bring great glory to the Empress in the fight to overpower him.

And now, the battle to take the ship was almost over. She was exhausted and in great pain from her wounds, but her Bloodsong filled her spirit and merged with the infinite chorus of her sisters. No greater ecstasy had she ever known.

The warriors at the head of the group, senior to Li'ara-Zhurah in their order of the challenges fought for the honor to be in this first great battle, opened yet another door the humans had locked behind them. It was a crude if effective tactic to buy some time, but she did not know what they expected to accomplish: herded now to the ship's main starboard airlock, there was nowhere else for them to run.

She heard the warriors at the head of the group sing out with battle cries: the humans were before them! She let herself be swept along as the group surged forward, swords held high.

***

Sabourin stood alone in the passageway as the Kreelans forced open the door in front of her. Behind her, the last blast door in the main gangway stood open, with the terrified faces of the crew's survivors looking past her as they stood with their backs pressed up against the rear wall that held the airlock. She had confirmed through her suit radio that *Jean Bart*, one of *Victorieuse's* sister ships, was moving close aboard to extend a flexible dock. But they still needed just a few more precious minutes.

She held the shotgun at her side. She would use it at the last moment if she had to, but she was hoping that the Kreelans would not decide to send their flying weapons at her if she posed no direct threat. If they did and they killed her off first thing, her plan might not work so well. She grinned at her own morbid humor.

She had wondered if her presence, particularly while still wearing the suit (which was nearly out of air), would give the enemy pause. But it had the opposite effect: with a howl, they charged forward *en masse*, driven to a frenzy by the sight of the helpless crewmen behind her.

And so they never noticed the circle of putty-like material as they ran forward, at least until Sabourin pushed the single button on the electronic device that had been in the pouch with the putty strip. With a flash that seemed as bright as the sun, the boarding charge exploded into white-hot flame, burning the flesh of half the Kreelans still charging toward her.

As the aliens' battle cries turned to screams of agony, she flung herself out of the way, against the bulkhead with the open blast door leading to where her fellow crewmen waited, willing bait for her trap.

Kneeling down, Sabourin brought up her shotgun and began to fire into the mass of burning alien warriors.

***

Calling to the warriors ahead of her, trying to find out what had happened, Li'ara-Zhurah could get no answer. All she could see were silhouettes of warriors dancing amid white-hot flame, and her ears were deafened by shrieks of agony. The air was thick with the stench of burning meat, metal, and hair, and she instinctively backed up, away from the carnage ahead of her. Whatever had happened, her sense of honor did not dictate that she immolate herself.

Then she heard the booms of one of the human weapons, and caught site of the lone suited human, kneeling to the side of the open door. She was firing into her sisters, which to a warrior such as Li'ara-Zhurah was a mixed blessing in such a horrid situation: being killed by a weapon such as the human wielded would be no small blessing to those whose bodies were now burning like living torches.

But even had that thought not stayed her hand for a moment, she had no *shrekkas* left. The human was beyond her reach unless she wished to brave the fire.

Then it struck her what the fire truly was: one of the boarding charges. With widening eyes, she looked at the human in the suit again, still firing into the churning mass of her sisters, noting the crudely rigged tether that held the human to the bulkhead. And around the open hatchway that led to the airlock, where the other humans cowered, Li'ara-Zhurah saw the trace of one of their own portable airlocks. Transparent and hardly visible at this distance.

It was a trap.

"Oh, no," she breathed, backing up toward the next blast door. "Pull back, my sisters!" she screamed over the din. "*Pull back!*" Hissing in fear and rage, she grabbed two of the closest warriors and pulled them back with her to the bulkhead behind her. There was no telling how thick the hull was here, and so how long the charge would take to breach-

With a thunderous roar, a two meter diameter section of the deck dropped away, blasted into space by air pressure. With screams of surprise now blending with those of agony, the rest of the warriors who were still alive were sucked out the hole in the deck to their doom.

The two warriors she had just pulled back had failed to grab hold of anything, and both lost their footing and tumbled across the deck to disappear into the infinite void beyond. Li'ara-Zhurah had seized the bulkhead wall with one hand, gripping it so fiercely that her diamond-hard talons dug into the metal. With a supreme force of will, fighting against the pain of her eardrums bursting and the air being sucked out of her lungs, she pulled herself to the door controls and slammed her hand down on the various buttons until, to her great relief, the door began to close.

As it did, Li'ara-Zhurah caught a last glimpse of the human in the suit, who had acted as bait for the trap. The human gave her what appeared to be a salute: she held one arm straight out in front of her, the hand clenched in a fist, before she brought her other hand over onto the extended arm just above the elbow. Then she swung up her clenched fist as the door slammed shut.

***

"*Va te faire foutre,*" Sabourin gasped at the lone surviving warrior before she disappeared behind the closing blast door. *Go fuck yourself.*

All the other warriors were gone, swept down through the hole she had burned through the deck and the hull. Sabourin had hated to hurt the *Victorieuse* that way, but there was nothing for it.

Staggering to her feet, she undid the tether, still surprised that it had held when the hull gave way. Then she stumbled to the outer membrane, opening it only with great difficulty. The admiral and crew, while frightened when the air had exploded from the hull and snapped the inner membrane taut, had survived. Her plan had worked.

Her fingers were numb and her breathing was coming in quick gasps now: her suit was out of air. But if she didn't make it through the outer membrane, no one inside would be able to come get her. Glancing through to the airlock, she saw that *Amiral* Lefevre stood there, waiting for her. The other members of the crew had been ushered into the link to the *Jean Bart*, so they were safe, at least for the moment.

After what seemed like days, she finally sealed the outer membrane behind her. But she had strength for nothing more. Her hands reflexively going to her neck, she slumped to the floor, her vision darkening as her brain began to run out of oxygen.

She felt more than heard the *pop* of air as the inner membrane was opened, filling the outer bubble where she lay with air. Then someone undogged her helmet and pulled it off. Taking in huge lungfuls of air, she found Lefevre looking down at her with a warm smile on his battered face.

"Come along, Sabourin," he said kindly, shooing away the crewmen from the *Jean Bart* who had come to help. He lifted her to her feet, draping one of her arms over his shoulders as he gripped her tightly by the waist to help her to the other ship. "I think you have done enough for one day."

FIFTEEN

Admiral Tiernan stared grimly at the tactical data that the crew of *Alita* had brought from Keran. While the information was priceless, it was also dangerously out of date: even in the two hours that it had taken *Alita* to reach the rendezvous point, the battle could have been lost or won. Tiernan was a gambling man, a superb poker player, and he wouldn't have put much money on the Alliance fleet from the replay of the first few minutes of the battle. Even though their ships were good, and he knew the Alliance had many first-rate naval officers, it was clear from the information before him that they were also outnumbered two-to-one, and the French commander had placed himself at a tremendous disadvantage by splitting his forces. Had he kept his fleet intact in high orbit rather than distributing his squadrons around the planet, he would have been able to concentrate enough combat power to fight at even odds with the larger Kreelan task force, and would have been able to completely overwhelm the smaller one. Unless the French admiral had pulled a rabbit out of a hat, he was going to be feeding his squadrons piecemeal to the enemy. And that was assuming that any of them stood a chance in hell against the Kreelans' technology.

"How much longer?" he asked his flag captain as he continued to replay the opening sequence of the battle that *Alita* had recorded, trying to absorb every nuance that he could. This was the only intelligence information they had to work with, their only insights into Kreelan tactics. The decisions he made based on this information would likely decide the outcome of the battle.

"Three minutes and forty-seven seconds, admiral," Captain Hans Ostermann replied quietly, his own eyes fixed on the countdown to emergence that was displayed in every compartment of the ship, and in every ship in the fleet.

Tiernan nodded as he went back to his study of the display, carefully concealing his trepidation. He had allowed himself only five minutes to evaluate the data *Alita* had transmitted the instant she arrived at the rendezvous point. It was immediately clear to him that they had no time to lose if they were to stand any chance of helping the French. It already might very well be too late: four hours - the two hours *Alita* had taken to reach the rendezvous, and the two hours it would take the fleet to jump to Keran - was a lifetime in space combat.

His own plan called for splitting his forces, but not in quite the same way as the Alliance had. He had four assault carriers carrying the two heavy ground divisions. They were to jump in as close as they could to the planet, run like hell for low orbit to disembark their troops, and then jump back out to the safety of the rendezvous point. Tiernan had only detailed four destroyers to escort them on their inbound leg; he knew that he was taking a huge risk with that light of an escort, but he simply didn't have enough ships to go around.

He planned to commit the rest of his force - eight heavy cruisers, fourteen light cruisers, and sixteen destroyers - in two mutually supporting tactical squadrons. That decision had been easy. The more difficult one was how to use his fleet to best advantage. He only had two viable options: support the Alliance squadrons in high orbit that had begun to engage the larger Kreelan force, or link up with the single Alliance squadron that was facing a substantially smaller Kreelan force closer to the planet. Both options assumed that there would be enough Alliance ships left intact to matter, because his own fleet would not stand a chance against even half the Kreelan ships shown by *Alita's* data. His fear was that the Alliance squadrons that had been maneuvering to attack the larger Kreelan force might have already been defeated, since they would have been seriously outnumbered. But the sole Alliance squadron that had been engaged by the smaller Kreelan force was at least on fairly even terms, the unknowns of Kreelan technology notwithstanding.

Gambling is about numbers, luck, and guts, and Tiernan knew that you might have two of the three in any given hand. He knew the numbers from *Alita's* data, at least as of four hours ago, and knew that he and his crews had plenty of guts. The only question was how good their luck might be. He couldn't afford to take the long odds offered by the big fight going on in high orbit, even though a tactical victory there would likely kick the Kreelans out of the system. That left him with one option: his fleet would attack the smaller Kreelan force and pray that this Alliance squadron - and hopefully some of the others - had survived this long. Then they could regroup to take on the larger Kreelan force.

"Emergency jump protocols confirmed," the flag captain reported. If the fleet jumped in and the situation was untenable, Tiernan wasn't going to waste his fleet. They would immediately jump out again to the rendezvous point. And it wouldn't take two minutes for the hyperdrive engines to spool up as on the *Aurora*. That little safety interlock problem had been fixed.

"Stand by for transpace sequence," the ship's navigation computer announced to the crew. "Auto-lock engaged. Normal space emergence in five...four...three...two...one. Sequence initiated. Hyperspace Engines disengaged."

Tiernan suddenly found himself staring out at a scene straight from hell.

***

"Priestess!" called Tesh-Dar's First, Kumal-Utai. "More human ships have arrived!"

"Indeed?" Tesh-Dar replied, already feeling the change in tenor of the emotions of her young warriors on the ships around the planet. The Bloodsong had never rung with such fury and passion in her lifetime, and through every member of her race - to the Empress Herself - ran a thread of ecstasy not felt since millennia before. Fighting, killing, and dying in Her name: these were the things for which they all existed.

"Forty-six ships," Kumal-Utai reported. "Eight of them jumped in close to the planet and appear to be heading toward low orbit. The rest appeared near the remains of the human ships we fought upon emergence."

"Those eight must be transports carrying more warriors to defend the surface," Tesh-Dar mused. "Allow them to proceed unmolested. As for the newcomers," she said, her eyes surveying the flat-screen tactical display, "let us see the stuff of which they are made."

"Where do you wish our ship, my priestess?" Elai-Tura'an, the shipmistress, asked. Her blood burned for battle, but her mind understood the necessity of prudence. While Tesh-Dar would likely survive anything that happened to the ship, and Elai-Tura'an worried not about her own death, it would be...inconvenient for the fleet command ship to be destroyed.

The great priestess frowned momentarily. She sensed Elai-Tura'an's emotions, and felt much the same way. Tesh-Dar wanted to face the humans in a direct challenge, but it was not yet time. Instead, she would give the honor to the young ones. It was they, after all, who had fought so hard among the peers for the right to be here. "Assemble the remaining ships here in low orbit to bleed the newcomers. We shall take up a position at the trailing edge of the formation."

"Shall I call in additional ships from the high formation?" Kumal-Utai asked, indicating the larger force of ships that had remained near the orbit of the planet's moons.

Tesh-Dar shook her head. "No. Let the humans have the advantage here for now. Let our blood mingle with theirs."

***

"Christ!" Captain Morrison cried as *McClaren* suddenly materialized in normal space over Keran. The twisted and burning stern of a ship - it was impossible to tell if it was human or Kreelan - was hurtling directly for them, spewing air and flaming debris in its wake. "Hard aport, Z-vector minus fifty! All ahead flank!" he shouted at the navigator.

Like everyone else on the bridge, Ichiro Sato stared with unbelieving eyes as the tumbling wreck came closer, filling the bridge display. Had the *McClaren* been one of the larger cruisers, there was no way she would have been able to maneuver fast enough to avoid a collision. While Morrison was an imbecile when it came to leadership and tactics, he at least knew how to maneuver the ship. As it was, even with the navigator sending the ship into a sharp left downward turn and the destroyer accelerating like a greyhound, breaking out of their assigned position in the squadron formation, they barely escaped. Turning his eyes back to his targeting console, he saw that the wreckage cleared them by mere meters. But a near-collision was the least of their problems.

"Multiple contacts close aboard!" Sato called to the captain.

"Identify them, damn you!" Morrison bellowed as he looked at the tactical display, which was now filled with a cloud of yellow icons representing unidentified ships or the remains of ships. A few of them, then more and more, began to turn orange as the computer categorized them as wreckage that could potentially pose a navigation hazard. Sato felt his stomach lurch at what his display was showing: this side of the system was a charnel house of dead and dying ships. Flaming wreckage from at least fifty vessels was strewn through nearby space, and Sato could see what could only be hundreds, possibly thousands, of human - or Kreelan - bodies. His sensors indicated that some of them were in vacuum suits, blasting away at one another with small arms or grappling in zero-gee hand-to-hand combat.

"Trying, sir," Sato replied, "but we don't have the Alliance identification codes and the inter-ship datalink hasn't synchronized yet." That concerned Sato more than anything else. Like the ships of the Alliance fleet, the Terran ships had a datalink capability that - in theory - made the fleet one large virtual weapon. Only it still took time, even if just a few moments, to come up after a hyperspace jump. "We've got to identify the ships visually or by their emissions signatures."

"Well, *that's* not an Alliance ship!" the navigator exclaimed, pointing at the bridge screen. A ship that looked like a huge swept-wing fighter, dark gray with cyan runes painted on the bow, arced toward them from the port side. While it maneuvered smoothly, it had not come through the horrendous battle unscathed: its hull was covered with scorch marks and at least half a dozen ragged holes where kinetic weapons had found their mark.

"Primary kinetics," Sato called out, "hard lock!" The ship's targeting systems had painted the enemy ship and were tracking her. At this close range they could use almost any weapon, but the primary kinetics - the destroyer's main guns - were the best choice for this situation: they could do the most damage quickly.

"Stand by..." Morrison ordered before giving the navigator orders to twist *McClaren* hard to the right, unmasking all the ship's heavy weapons turrets, "Fire as she bears!"

Sato gave the computer firing authority, and it calculated the optimal firing point out to the twentieth decimal. The ship echoed with thunder as ten fifteen centimeter guns rippled off five rounds each in under two seconds.

"Clean hits!" Sato cried. None of the bridge crew needed the tactical display to tell them they'd hit their target: the bridge screen, now nearly filled with the image of the enemy ship, showed a cascade of explosions down her flank, blowing off the starboard wing and sending her spinning out of control.

There was a brief cheer on the bridge before Morrison called out, "Target, designate!" Using the command override on his console, he steered the crosshairs for the pulse cannon onto a distant Kreelan ship, silhouetted against the planet far below, that was roughly the size of a heavy cruiser. To him it appeared to be an easy target of opportunity. As the weapon was fixed along the *McClaren's* centerline, the ship altered course automatically to line up her bows with the target.

"Captain?" Sato asked, not believing what the captain was doing. "Captain, *no, wait-*"

"Firing!" Morrison said almost gleefully as he hit the *commit* button. The lights dimmed and the entire ship thrummed as the pulse gun fired, sending an extremely powerful beam of coherent emerald light streaking toward the target.

Unfortunately, when Morrison used the command override, locking Sato's station out of the weapon control cycle, he didn't realize that it would also bypass the additional target lock cues: he thought that as soon as the commit button was illuminated, the weapon was locked on target and ready to fire. The second half of his assumption - that it was ready to fire - was correct, but the targeting system hadn't established a hard lock on the enemy ship, and the *McClaren's* angular motion from the gentle turn hadn't completely stopped.

But an impending miss wasn't why Sato had tried to stop Morrison from firing. It was the Alliance starliner that was directly in the weapon's path, well beyond the Kreelan cruiser.

Expecting to see the enemy ship burst into a gigantic fireball, the navigator increased the bridge screen magnification so they could make a damage assessment. But the Kreelan warship had passed out of view. Now the only thing that was on the screen was an Alliance starliner and a host of shuttles.

"Oh, my God," someone whispered into the sudden stillness that took the bridge as the blast from the pulse cannon sheared off the drive section of the starliner, splitting the ship in two and sending the wreckage tumbling. Sparks cascaded from severed electrical conduits and streams of air bled from the compartments that were now suddenly exposed to hard vacuum. Hundreds of bodies, clearly visible with the high magnification of the screen, flew from the wreckage, arms and legs flailing as the blood of the hapless victims boiled in vacuum. Most of them were soldiers waiting to be ferried to the surface, and so they had no vacuum suits. Secondary explosions peppered the side of the ship where the civilian shuttles, still trying to get the rest of the troops down to the surface, were swatted like flies as the huge hull twisted out of control.

Sato looked away from the carnage, hating the man who now sat in the captain's chair. Morrison's jaw opened and closed like that of a fish as he fought to come to grips with what he'd just done. *That's one screwup he can't blame on the crew*, Sato thought bitterly.

But they clearly weren't out of it yet.

"*Incoming from starboard!*" Sato cried as he saw a volley of projectiles erupt from one of the dozen or more ships embroiled in a huge gunfight that had broken out to the right of *McClaren*. "Recommend coming to course-"

"Belay that!" Morrison shouted, throwing Sato a disgusted look. "I'll handle the ship." With a brief glance at the display, he said, "There's no way those rounds will hit us."

"But sir-"

"*You are relieved, mister!*" The captain screamed at the top of his lungs. The bridge suddenly became deathly quiet except for half a dozen tactical alarms clamoring for attention.

His face an iron mask, Sato unbuckled from his seat and came to attention. "Yes, *sir!*" he said before stepping away from his console.

"Bogdanova," Morrison snapped, "take over tactical."

Without a word, the young female ensign who normally manned communications unstrapped from her combat chair and rushed across the bridge. She had even less experience aboard than Sato, was terrified of the captain, and had very little time training on the tactical position. She looked up at Sato as she slipped into his still-warm combat chair, her eyes wide with barely-concealed terror.

"Get off my bridge, *lieutenant*," the captain ordered tersely.

Giving Bogdanova what he hoped was a reassuring squeeze on her shoulder, Sato turned to leave.

Morrison took another look at his own tactical display, and came to the sudden conclusion that the incoming enemy shells were getting uncomfortably close after all.

"Counter-battery fire, Bogdanova!" Morrison ordered.

Looking desperately at the tactical display, she replied in a hoarse voice, terrified as much by the captain as the incoming weapons, "We can't, sir."

"Goddammit, what do you mean?" he yelled frantically.

"Because, you fucking idiot," Sato told him, unafraid of the captain's ire with death looming so close, "our close-in defense weapons are all lasers, and you completely drained the energy buffers when you destroyed that starliner with the pulse cannon." Horrified realization dawned on Morrison's face. "That's right, captain," Sato told him quietly. "The lasers are useless until the energy buffers recharge. Congratulations. You've killed us all."

Two seconds later the enemy salvo hit.

***

"Admiral!" the flag communications officer suddenly shouted. "We've established contact with Admiral Lefevre aboard the *Jean Bart*."

"About bloody time," Tiernan said, relieved. His fleet had been in-system a full fifteen minutes, and had managed to clear the remaining Kreelan ships from the immediate area. Terran losses, surprisingly, had been very light: the only major casualty had been the destroyer *McClaren*. A part of him, a part he never would have admitted existed, was almost glad: he had seen *McClaren* kill the Alliance starliner. If the destroyer's captain had been alive, he would have been facing the court martial from hell, and Tiernan would have been standing ready with the noose to hang the bastard. But that unpleasantness, at least, was unnecessary: the destroyer's dead hulk was adrift among the other shattered hulls. But Tiernan wasn't looking forward to the formal apology he needed to render to the Alliance commander. "*Amiral* Lefevre," Tiernan said into the vidcom, "this is Admiral Patrick Tiernan of the Terran Navy. We are at your disposal, sir." The last words were hard for him to say, but he had direct orders from the president: unless he had reason to believe that his fleet was about to be defeated and had no choice but to withdraw, he was to place himself under the command of the senior Alliance officer.

The man who looked back at him from the vidcom smiled. Tiernan thought Lefevre looked like he'd been through an infantry battle: his face was a mess, and his uniform was in tatters. But the Alliance admiral's eyes were bright, and his expression showed no loss of determination.

Lefevre wasn't a quitter, Tiernan thought. *That's got to count for something.*

"*Amiral* Tiernan," Lefevre said, "you have no idea how welcome is the sight of your fleet. We had been told there was a chance of Terran support, but..." He gave a Gallic shrug.

"Sir..." Tiernan began, the next words sticking in his throat, "We have much to discuss, but first I wish to formally apologize for the destruction of one of your troopships by a destroyer under my command. I take full responsibility, and will ensure a thorough investigation-"

"*Amiral* Tiernan," Lefevre said quietly, holding up a hand, "this is a tragedy, there can be no doubt. But we are at war, and must first ensure that some of us, at least, survive to worry about such matters. Let it be enough for now that I accept your apology with the sincerity in which it was offered."

"Thank you, sir," Tiernan said, inwardly relieved. He had only met Lefevre once during a joint exercise the two navies had held several years ago. He had been favorably impressed with him then, and was more so now. He couldn't think of many Terran admirals who would have taken such a loss with the same equanimity. "What are your orders, admiral?"

"Our first objective must be to finish clearing the enemy from low orbit," Lefevre said decisively. "I believe that with your ships, we can now do that. Then, perhaps, we may consider our options against the force in high orbit." He paused, frowning. "But I must confess, *amiral*, that I do not understand the enemy's tactics or their overall objective."

"What do you mean, sir?" Tiernan asked.

"They had enough superiority to sweep us from the skies," Lefevre told him, his voice filled with a mixture of indignation and anger. "Their ships seem to be similar enough to ours, not nearly so powerful or advanced as the information provided us by your attaché indicated from your survey vessel's encounter. But..." he pursed his lips and shook his head. "They had a full two-to-one advantage over us, *amiral*, plus the advantage of surprise. They held the high ground with a superior force. They held every major tactical advantage. Yet...they simply threw it all away. *Pfft.* They fight with great ferocity and spirit, but it is as if we have been in a giant brawl, not a modern space battle. They have taken no more than a one-to-one ratio in any of our engagements, save the first surprise encounter, and seem to prefer to disable our ships rather than destroy them. They have not molested the deployment of our troops to the surface, when they have had plenty of opportunity to do so." He again shook his head. "Tell me, *amiral*, who would possibly turn away from such a target, especially when they must know that I would have to split away forces to defend the transports? Yet they did. It is as if they want those troops to land. But for what purpose, I cannot understand."

That gave Tiernan pause. He glanced at the flag tactical display and saw that his four carriers and their destroyer escorts were nearing the drop zones over Keran. And while there were no Kreelan ships in the immediate vicinity, there were plenty in higher orbit that could easily have made a play for the carriers, not to mention all the Alliance starliners that - even after the hours it had taken Tiernan's fleet to get here - had still not unloaded all their troops. In all that time, the only casualty among them had been the one *McClaren* had destroyed. He tried not to wince at the thought.

"And then there are the boarding parties," Lefevre said, his face darkening. "We did not take this information from your attaché seriously. Who would, in such an age as this? And we paid the price. We lost fifteen ships to those devils, including my flagship." He held fast his expression in front of the Terran admiral, but Lefevre inwardly shivered at the hell the compartments and passageways of *Victorieuse* had become after the Kreelan boarders had breached the hull.

"That, sir," Tiernan assured him, "I believe we are prepared to handle." He thought of Lieutenant Sato, who had suffered so much to give them the information that formed the core of the planning and preparation that had been put into action over the last year, and who now was as dead as the *McClaren*. He felt a deep sense of bitterness at the young man's loss. "Every ship in my task force has Marines aboard, along with a few other surprises for any would-be boarders. I don't think we have enough Marines for all of your ships, sir, but if you like, we have enough to at least put a full platoon aboard each of your cruisers to help provide some on-board defense." He hadn't brought extra Marines for the purpose of helping the Alliance ships, but he could thin out the companies aboard his cruisers by a couple of platoons without compromising the security of his own ships. It was clear from Lefevre's expression that he feared the boarders more than anything else. If giving up some Marines would boost the morale of the French fleet, then it was a small but worthwhile sacrifice on his part.

"Thank you, *amiral*," Lefevre said, his voice nearly cracking with relief. "You have no idea how much that would mean to my crews."

"It's the least we can do, sir," Tiernan told him. "If you'll have your flag captain coordinate with mine, we'll have our cutters start transferring the Marines immediately. And we'd also better see what we can do about integrating our maneuvering orders and fire control..."

Sixteen

There had been very few occasions in her career when Steph had questioned her sanity, but this was definitely one of them. Strapped into a sling chair aboard an assault boat deployed from the carrier *Subic Bay*, she felt like she was on the bobsled ride from hell as the boat plunged from the carrier's belly into Keran's atmosphere. She was one of half a dozen journalists embedded with the two heavy divisions Tiernan's fleet had brought along to shore up Keran's defenses, and was attached to the headquarters troop of the 7th Cavalry Regiment under the 1st Guards Armored Division. That division was an odd mix of American and Russian lineage, but together with its sister 31st Armored Division, which had its roots in the old Indian Army, they were the best-trained heavy divisions Earth could muster. The 7th Cav, as it was often known, was famous - or infamous, depending on one's point of view - as the last command of General George Armstrong Custer, who led the regiment to defeat and massacre in the Battle of the Little Bighorn. Traditionally it had the job of providing reconnaissance and security to its parent division. On the modern battlefield, the decision had been made many years before to convert it to a heavy armored brigade. The unit's traditional title had stuck, and it had also retained its reputation as one of the first units sent in to stir up trouble for the enemy.

True to form, the regiment would be the first on the ground on Keran, the lead element brought in by the assault boats that would then return to the carriers for a second load. And since they would be on the bleeding edge of the ground campaign - assuming the Kreelans landed - Steph had immediately decided that she wanted to be with them.

But now, as the assault boat screamed through the atmosphere, bouncing and jarring its occupants and cargo like it was flying through a tornado, she had to wonder just what the hell she had been thinking.

She also wondered about the fleet battle going on above. From the brief exchange she'd been able to have with the regimental commander before the boats deployed, the Terran fleet had jumped into the middle of a naval meat grinder that had already left dozens of burning hulks in its wake. No enemy ships had maneuvered to intercept the carriers as they raced from their in-bound jump points to the drop zones over Keran, for which everyone was thankful. But there were still plenty left that were hitting back at the Terran fleet and what ships were left of the French Alliance, and Steph felt herself uncharacteristically worried about Ichiro.

The thought of him gave her a momentary pause from her contemplations of falling through the atmosphere in the company of a bunch of suicidal cavalry troopers. What exactly did she feel for Ichiro? she asked herself. While the two of them had certainly become more than friends, could she say that she loved him? Even if she did - assuming that both of them survived this - what could they do about it? Ichiro had made it clear that he wanted to stay in the Navy, and the war would almost certainly mean extended service for everyone in the military, and possibly even a draft if the president could get it approved by Congress. Despite the series of events that had linked her fate to Ichiro's over the last year, her own career would no doubt take a separate road from his. Her being aboard this ship and not with the fleet above them was already proof enough of that. Looking beyond any love the two of them might share, even if she decided to settle down and start a family - a bridge she was not yet prepared to cross - did she want to be a Navy wife, with Ichiro off on deployment for months at a time?

She frowned inwardly, for she had no answers to those questions. But she cared enough about him that she felt they needed to have that conversation. If they mutually decided that they were better off as friends, fine. But she didn't want to pass up even a one in a thousand chance that they could be something more. He was as close as she'd ever come to finding someone who really cared about her, and she didn't want to throw it away.

While she was going into harm's way herself, she silently prayed for the Lord of All to keep him safe.

***

Lieutenant General Arjun Ray was furious. As the commander of the Terran Army's I Corps, the parent corps of the two armored divisions now plummeting toward the surface of Keran, Ray had been given the task of leading the ground portion of the battle. He was subordinate to Tiernan, who was in overall command of the expeditionary force, but once the admiral's carriers got Ray's troops to the surface he would largely be on his own. His greatest concern had been the threat of Kreelan attack against the carriers before his troops could even hit dirt. But soon after the boats had deployed for the surface he discovered that he had another battle to fight.

"My apologies, general," the brigadier of the Keran Defense Forces repeated sternly, and not sounding very apologetic at all, "but you have no clearance to land your troops. Our diplomatic service is already sending a démarche to the Terran embassy here to protest the presence of your fleet." He shook his head. "We will not allow, under any circumstances, Terran ground forces to land on Keran soil."

"My god, man, do you have any idea what is happening right over your heads?" Ray asked him, trying desperately to rein in his anger. "The Alliance Fleet has taken serious losses and may very well not be able to prevent the enemy from attempting a landing if they should choose to. If we don't get our troops on the ground now and consolidate our defenses, we may not get another chance. I'll speak to the Alliance commander and try to get him to convince you-"

"General," the brigadier rudely interrupted, enjoying the opportunity to tweak a superior officer from another planet's service, "the Alliance has no say in this matter. They are here simply for exercises with our own navy. We have received no reports of enemy activity-"

"*I can hear the bloody raid warning sirens going off in the background of your transmission, you idiot!*" Ray shouted, finally losing his temper. He had already been in contact with Ambassador Pugacheva of the Terran Embassy and so had some idea of the disarray the Keran government was in at the moment. But this was simply too much. Calmly dickering with this imbecile while strapped into a combat chair in an assault boat as it screamed toward the surface was simply beyond the patience of anyone but a saint. "Brigadier, let me make this clear to you," he said through gritted teeth. "I am landing my troops at the coordinates we sent you earlier, with the intention of taking up positions on the left flank of the Alliance Foreign Legion troops that have deployed on the outskirts of Foshan."

Foshan was the largest population center on the planet, although the planetary capital was a smaller city to the north. It was a bustling metropolis that had a nearly perfect balance between the Arabic and Chinese populations. The city center had an impressive skyline of high-rise office buildings sporting garish video banners, countered by the graceful spires of minarets from the many mosques that lined the downtown area. The city's main roads radiated from the downtown area like spokes of a wheel, serving a colorful hodgepodge of neighborhoods and shopping districts that were a mix of pagoda-style buildings and white- or tan-faced stone structures with intricate scrollwork that were typical of many of Earth's cities in what was once the Middle East.

Ray knew that three more French divisions would be deploying to Foshan, while the remaining five would be divided up among the three other largest population centers. It was scant coverage in terms of defending against a planetary assault, but it was all they had to work with. They would be leavened with men from the Keran paramilitary forces, but that was about all the support the off-world troops could expect. Like their navy, the Keran military had little actual combat capability, amounting to a total of three light infantry brigades and some antiquated aerospace defense systems.

"And let me make sure that you understand something," Ray continued. "You are dealing with the commander of two heavy armored divisions. If my troops or the assault boats transporting them are molested in any way by Keran forces," he growled as he leaned closer to the video pickup, "I will have those divisions blow you little fuckers to bits and grind what's left into fertilizer. Do I make myself clear, *brigadier?*"

The other man's darker skin - be it from Chinese or Arab descent, Ray could not have cared less - visibly paled. Beyond the insult, he must have immediately come to the conclusion that Ray wasn't bluffing. On that count, he would have been quite correct. "I will let my commander know that you intend to force a landing on our sovereign soil," he protested with as much indignation as he could muster, "and convey your threats against our forces. And I will lodge the strongest possible protest with your embassy, general!"

"Go right ahead, you little bastard," Ray spat dismissively as he killed the connection. "Just don't get in my way."

***

Lieutenant-Colonel Lev Stepanovich Grishin, commander of the *Première Régiment étranger de cavalerie*, or *1er REC*, of the Alliance *Légion étrangère* watched with professional interest as the Terran assault boats swept down to their drop sites to the south of his unit's position. He had briefly listened to the local Keran military liaison rant about the Terran "invasion" and orders he had for Grishin to fire on the boats before they landed. Making no attempt to conceal his contempt, Grishin kicked the fool out of his command vehicle and had him escorted out of the regiment's defense perimeter. He knew that not all Keran military officers were idiots, but there were enough in key positions to be causing trouble when they desperately needed to be pulling themselves together. The Legion operations staff had been keeping track of the hammering that the Alliance fleet had taken, and Grishin himself had given up a cheer when the Terran ships had appeared. While the Legion had been his home for nearly twenty years and he fully expected to die in uniform, he would prefer that he and his men not be wasted unnecessarily by incompetent bureaucrats.

"Have we made contact with them?" he asked his adjutant.

"Yes, sir," the man replied immediately. "We can only speak in the clear, *mon colonel*. The communications security systems are not compatible. Their commander is waiting to speak with you."

Nodding, Grishin spoke, his voice picked up by the tiny microphone embedded in his helmet. "Terran ground commander," he said, "this is *Lieutenant-Colonel* Grishin, commander of the First Cavalry Regiment of the Alliance Foreign Legion. To whom am I speaking, please?"

"*Bonjour*, colonel," came a gravelly voice that was unmistakably from the American South. While he appreciated the gesture, Grishin winced at the man's pronunciation of the traditional French greeting, hoping that the Terran officer would prefer to speak English. While his own French carried an unmistakable Russian accent, it was pure Parisian compared to this man's speech. "This is Colonel James Sparks, commanding the 7th Cavalry Regiment, 1st Guards Armored Division. We're going to be operating on your left flank, and I wanted to stop by and coordinate our lines and fire plans with you, if I may."

"Certainly, colonel," Grishin told him. "My command post is at-" he read off some coordinates, "-and I will be waiting for you."

"Thank you, colonel," Sparks said. "I'll be there in ten minutes. Sparks, out."

Grishin looked at his adjutant, who shrugged. "At least they will have tanks," his adjutant said. "That must count for something..."

Exactly ten minutes later, Grishin tried to keep the dismay from showing on his face as the Terran regimental commander dismounted from the wheeled reconnaissance vehicle that had pulled up in front of Grishin's mobile command post. Sparks looked as if he had walked off the set of an old - *very* old - American "western" movie. While he was dressed in the standard combat uniform of the Terran Army, the wiry man wore a cowboy-style black cavalry officer's hat replete with an insignia of crossed sabers and a gold acorn band, along with a matching bright yellow ascot showing from the vee of the neck of his combat tunic. And under his left arm, carried in a matte black leather shoulder holster, was the biggest handgun Grishin had ever seen. The huge weapon was nickel plated with contoured grips that he would have wagered a month's pay were made of mother-of-pearl.

But the most ridiculous thing, Grishin thought, aghast, was what the Terran wore on the heels of his boots: riding spurs, which made a *ching-ching-ching* sound as the Terran colonel strode purposefully toward him.

The man was simply outrageous.

"*Mon Dieu*," Grishin's adjutant whispered, desperately trying to hold his face rigid and not burst out laughing.

Grishin shared the sentiment right up until the moment that Sparks took off his sunglasses and tucked them in a pocket as he drew to within hand-shaking distance. While Grishin did not believe that the eyes told everything about a man, in some cases they could tell a great deal. And in this case, Sparks's piercing blue eyes and no-nonsense expression told him what he needed to know. A Hollywood dandy, this man might be. But Grishin suspected - and greatly hoped - that he was a formidable combat commander, as well.

Rendering a sharp salute, Grishin said formally, "On behalf of the men of the *1er Régiment étranger de cavalerie*, I welcome you, sir."

Sparks snapped a salute that was parade-ground perfect, then said, "Thank you, colonel. I appreciate the hospitality." As Grishin lowered his salute and shook the Terran colonel's extended hand, noting how strong the smaller man's grip was, Sparks went on, "But if it's all the same to you, I suggest we get down to business over a glass of whiskey." Like magic, he produced a small silver-plated flask and held it up with a devilish grin on his face.

Grishin could no longer help himself. Laughing, he gestured for Sparks to accompany him into the command post. "Come, colonel," he told Sparks. "If you have whiskey, there's no time to lose..."

***

Steph stood in the background, recording the coordination session and making verbal notes as she watched the two commanders and their small staffs huddle around the map display in Grishin's command vehicle. Of the two men, she wasn't sure which one was more unusual. Sparks was outwardly an extreme stereotype of the romantic cavalryman, but even in the short time she had been with his unit she had discovered that the men and women who served in his regiment would go to hell and back for him without a second thought. He was polite, thoughtful, and unquestionably loved the men and women who served under him as if they were family. But he could also be ruthless and absolutely merciless to those he found lacking in the will to do their best, or who in any way dishonored his regiment. And from hearing him speak, ruthless and merciless would be the lead traits of his personality that he planned to direct at the enemy.

Grishin, on the other hand, appeared to be what one might expect of a competent colonel in any army, with a very significant exception: of the twenty regiments of the *Légion étrangère*, he was the only regimental commander not seconded from one of the Alliance armies. One of those exceedingly rare individuals who had worked his way up the ranks from a lowly legionnaire to commander of a combat regiment, Grishin was a veteran of the St. Petersburg war. In fact, he had joined the Legion right after the armistice, and rumor had it that he was one of the few communists who had managed to escape the final destruction of the Red Army. But in the Legion, no one cared. His past - whatever it truly was - was left behind and gone. And if he was good enough to make it through the political battlefield that controlled Legion officer assignments, then maybe he would be a good match for the Kreelans, as well.

Turning her attention back to the discussion around the map table, she heard Sparks say, "Our biggest problem as I see it is intelligence. We have absolutely no idea what we may be up against, or which direction they'll be coming from."

"Surely, sir," said Grishin's adjutant, "they'll have to come from the south, over here." Foshan was situated in a forested area, with the western side of the city along the shore of one of Keran's freshwater seas. On the map, the adjutant indicated a large open area in the forest to the south. "That's the only decent nearby landing zone that's not in direct sight of our weapons here. There just aren't many other choices unless they want to drop right into the city, which..." He shrugged. "That would make no sense to me, but I do not know how they think."

"That is the problem," Grishin sighed. "We have no idea what they might do, what they could do. And what if they do drop directly into the city? Our tanks are made for fighting in the open. In the city they would be very vulnerable without more infantry support. And half of Foshan's streets are too narrow for our tanks, let alone yours." The Alliance-made wheeled light tanks that were used by the *1er REC* were not terribly dissimilar from vehicles used long in the past, for a very simple reason: the combination of mobility, lightness, and firepower was extremely effective for the types of low-tech opponents the Legion typically faced. The Terran heavy armor units, by contrast, were equipped with vehicles that weighed upward of one hundred metric tons and were marvels of every facet of human engineering. They were incredibly powerful, well-protected, and amazingly fast for something so heavy, but were totally out of their element in close-in street fighting.

"Yeah," Sparks agreed grimly. "We'd have to blow half the goddamn city down just to move through it. On the other hand, we're cavalry: if we have to dismount, every trooper in my regiment's got a rifle and he knows how to use it."

Grishin thought it would be ridiculous to use tank crews as infantry, but as far as he could tell, Sparks wasn't joking.

"Mobility has to be the key," Sparks said, finally. "It's the only thing we've got against so many unknowns. And the first thing I'd recommend," he went on, "would be to send a company of tanks forward - with some of your men, colonel, as guides - to this nice open patch your adjutant pointed out. That way if our friends do show up there, we can give them a warm welcome."

Thinking it over, Grishin nodded. It wouldn't cost them anything, since they had absolutely no idea what the enemy might do. If the Kreelans did try to land there, one of the 7th Cav's tank companies could give them a difficult time. "I agree, colonel," he told him. "I will detach one of my reconnaissance teams to you: they have been out to that area several times and know the route and commanding terrain well."

"Outstanding," Sparks told him. "My tanks will be outside your door here in thirty minutes. You'll know they're here when the ground starts shaking." He held out his hand. "Colonel, it's been a pleasure, and I'll definitely be in touch. But I need to get back to get the rest of my regiment squared away."

"My pleasure, sir," Grishin told him, meaning it, as he shook the Terran cavalryman's hand and they once again exchanged salutes. "We will be standing by."

On the brief trip back to the reconnaissance vehicle that had brought them over, Steph walked beside Sparks. The two staff officers who'd accompanied him were walking behind, already setting the colonel's orders into motion over the comm sets built into their uniform harnesses. She saw a look of unusual concern on his face. "Colonel," she asked quietly, "may I ask what you're thinking?"

He glanced over at her. "On or off the record?" he asked sharply.

That took her by surprise. One of the whole points of having journalists embedded with the forward units was that everything was "on the record" unless it might compromise the safety of friendly troops.

"Okay, colonel," she said guardedly as they reached the vehicle and she turned to face him. "Let's start with off the record."

Taking a look around them, with the city behind and the dense forest in front that led to the hills protecting the possible landing zone, he told her, "Unless I'm badly mistaken or the enemy really disappoints me, we may be in for the biggest defeat since Custer got his ass handed to him at the Little Big Horn."

"*What?*" Steph blurted. Sparks's comment was totally out of place from what she'd understood of his conversation with Grishin. "Why?"

"Listen, Miss Guillaume," he told her, beckoning her to the front of the vehicle and away from the droning of his staff officers as they continued issuing orders, "this is probably the first battle in modern history where at least one side - that would be us - knows virtually nothing about the enemy. *Nothing.* We don't know jack about their weapons, tactics, motivations, objectives: zippo. For Christ's sake, we don't even know what they look like aside from what that young boy Sato could tell us. And if you don't understand what your opponent wants, it's pretty damned hard to keep him - or her, in this case, I suppose - from getting it. And because we don't understand them, we can't take the initiative and force the battle on our terms: we can only make assumptions about what they want and try to prepare for it, react to what they do. But all our assumptions could be wrong. For all I know they might just start dropping nukes on the cities here and be done with it. Or what if they use a biological weapon? For the love of God, they attacked the French ships with boarding parties, just like Sato said they did to the *Aurora*. Who the devil would expect such a thing in this day and age? And the French paid the price for it from the reports I saw on the way down: they lost over a dozen ships just to that. And the enemy could do something as unexpected here that will throw us totally off-balance. We just don't know. And that just bothers the hell out of me." He dug his heel in the ground in a sign of frustration. "So we're all just guinea pigs right now, I guess," he sighed. "We just have to wait for them to show up at the party and take the lead."

Steph couldn't say that what Sparks said made her happy, but she understood his point well enough. "Well," she prompted, "how about what you think *on* the record?"

He looked at her, his blue eyes bright and his mouth set in a hard line. "*On* the record, if those alien witches come down here looking for trouble, the 7th Cav will be damned happy to oblige them."

SEVENTEEN

Having bled the humans in low orbit to her content, Tesh-Dar withdrew the remainder of her ships to the larger formation in orbit near the planet's moons. In part it was to give some rest to her crews; in part it was to see what the humans would do. Taking into account the losses each side had suffered, plus the recently arrived human ships, the two fleets had rough parity numerically. She was curious to see if the humans would try and take the initiative and attack her formation. Thus far, they had been content to consolidate their hold of lower orbit space and cover the vulnerable troop transports as they finally finished disgorging their cargoes of warriors and war machines. Tesh-Dar made no effort to intercept the huge ships as they broke from orbit for their jump points: killing them would offer no challenge. Her main interest now lay in the troops they had sent down to the surface.

In the meantime, she had sent some of her smaller warships to recover as many warriors as possible from the hulks adrift in the system, both from Imperial ships that had been destroyed and from human ships her warriors had boarded. Only two of the recovery ships had been molested when they probed overly close to the human formation, but they had escaped easily enough. She was happily surprised to see that so many of her warriors, particularly those who had boarded the human ships, had survived. She was especially relieved to see that Li'ara-Zhurah remained alive. A blood daughter of the Empress, she was a fine warrior who had well-proven her honor this day. Tesh-Dar had known Li'ara-Zhurah since she had arrived from the nursery world to enter training at Tesh-Dar's *kazha*, the school of the Way that focused on the teachings of the Desh-Ka. She had fought well against what was clearly a set of fine opponents on the human ship she had boarded. Tesh-Dar had been most pleased.

"My priestess," Li'ara-Zhurah asked, flexing her arm where the healers had repaired the bullet wound in her arm, "I would request the honor of the first wave to attack the surface."

Tesh-Dar turned to look at her. "Child, have you not had enough this day?" she asked gently. While she wanted to give her warriors every possible chance to prove themselves and bring honor to the Empress, she did not want to waste them needlessly. Despite the power of the Bloodsong and the primal need to fight that was ingrained in her people, she knew quite well the physical toll that combat exacted. And what Li'ara-Zhurah had survived this day had been brutal, even by Kreelan standards.

The younger warrior averted her eyes. "My apologies, priestess," she whispered, her voice quivering. "But my blood burns now as never before, even during the Challenge in the arena. I cannot see or think beyond it. It consumes me."

Tesh-Dar understood quite well. The Bloodsong, the spiritual bond that tied their race together and to the Empress, was normally like the sound of the sea washing upon the shore, a ceaseless background murmuring that every one of Her Children sensed since birth. In times of heightened passion, particularly during personal combat in the arena during one of the many Challenges that the warriors faced in life, the Bloodsong burned like holy fire. It could be harnessed and channelled by some, as if it were a source of spiritual adrenaline. To those like Tesh-Dar, who had a vastly greater understanding, the Bloodsong was far more: it was a spiritual river that bound the living even unto the spirits of the dead. It was through the Bloodsong that those such as she could even sense the Ancient Ones, the warriors of the spirit who had passed from life. For they, too, were bound to the Empress and Her will.

But this feeling of which Li'ara-Zhurah spoke was something more. It was the intensity of so many warriors engaged in life-and-death struggles in such a short time, triggering an emotional tidal wave surging through the Bloodsong that had begun to overwhelm some of the younger warriors. Not just here, but throughout the Empire, for the Bloodsong was universal. The effect of the emotional surge on Tesh-Dar had been profound, but as a priestess gifted with powers that even most of her disciples would not understand, she was easily able to control it. The younger ones would adapt in time, as well, for this war would likely go on for many cycles, but they would need help now that only the senior priestesses and clawless mistresses could provide. The healers who had studied the Books of Time recounting earlier encounters with other sentient species had told Tesh-Dar and the other priestesses that this would likely happen, and had prepared them to deal with it.

"Come to me, child," Tesh-Dar said gently as she stood up from her command chair. "Do not kneel," she said as Li'ara-Zhurah made to kneel down before her. "Stand. Try as best you can to clear your mind."

"I...cannot, my priestess," she said softly, her eyes fixed on the deck at her feet. "My thoughts tumble as if caught in a great storm, beyond my control."

"I understand," Tesh-Dar told her as she brought her hands up to rest on either side of Li'ara-Zhurah's face. The young warrior sighed at her touch, her body shivering involuntarily. Tesh-Dar closed her eyes and focused her concentration on the young woman's spirit, seeing it as a ghostly image, glowing brightly in her mind. Her spirit appeared to be caught in the center of a storm that made it flutter like a pennant snapping in a stiff wind. With the power of her own will, using her control of the Bloodsong, Tesh-Dar forced the storm to quiet, to be still. Her ears heard a shuddering sigh from Li'ara-Zhurah's lips, and her arms felt the caress of the young warrior's hands as the two of them stood locked in a spiritual embrace for but a moment that itself was timeless.

Looking deeper still into the young warrior's spirit in that infinite moment, Tesh-Dar discovered another reason for Li'ara-Zhurah's spiritual confusion: her time for breeding would again soon be upon her. Among their race, the need to mate was far more than a physiological condition, for it had its roots in an ancient curse of the spirit. As decreed by the First Empress many generations before, the clawless ones and those warriors with black talons had to mate every great cycle of the Empress Moon or they would die in terrible agony. Those like Tesh-Dar, who were born sterile, could only stand as silent witnesses to the continuity of their species, at least for the few centuries they had left. A part of Tesh-Dar deeply lamented that she could never bear children. But another part secretly rejoiced, for the act of consummation was not a pleasant affair: the males of their species, cursed along with the females by the First Empress so very long ago, now only existed as mindless tools for mating. And having done so once, they died in great pain, without even understanding what was happening to them, or why.

Pushing away those melancholy thoughts, she brought herself back to the pleasant warmth of the spiritual embrace she shared with Li'ara-Zhurah, letting it wash away the sense of despair that had momentarily taken hold of her heart.

And then it was done. Taking in a deep breath, Tesh-Dar opened her eyes and lowered her hands from the young woman's face, as Li'ara-Zhurah reluctantly released her light grip on Tesh-Dar's arms. The young warrior stood still for another moment, as if meditating, before opening her eyes. She met Tesh-Dar's gaze for a few beats of her heart, then lowered them in reverence.

"Thank you, my priestess," Li'ara-Zhurah breathed, the churning storm in her soul now stilled, Tesh-Dar's power echoing through her veins like the ripples of a great stone cast into a shallow pond.

"It is Her will," Tesh-Dar told her gently. "Go now. Eat and rest to restore your body. Then I will grant your wish." Turning to the display that showed the human deployments on the surface of the planet - at least what could be gleaned from the sensors of her ships in high orbit - she said, "You will accompany me in the attack on the planet."

***

Tiernan had no idea why the Kreelans had offered the humans a respite, their fleet now brooding in high orbit, but he and Lefevre had tried to put it to good use. The Terran fleet's Marines had been redistributed to provide some protection for the Alliance ships, and the Marines themselves had sorted out how to get at least a fire team aboard every single French ship, with a short platoon on each of the surviving cruisers. While Tiernan hesitated to use the example, the Terran Marines had been welcomed aboard the French ships like American troops must have been when they helped liberate France herself during the Second World War.

After dropping off the Marines, the cutters began to search through the scattered debris and hulks looking for any survivors. They found a few from some of the destroyed Alliance ships, but not very many.

The senior engineers of the two fleets had been working non-stop on trying to integrate the different data-link systems since the low-orbit battle had been decided. But that was a problem that could only be solved by the system designers working together: there were too many safeguards and security measures built into each system to allow any field expedient integration measures. So the admirals and captains had to rely on basic voice and video communications to relay orders and information to one another. It was a dangerous way to handle things in modern space combat, where the tactical situation could change completely in a matter of seconds, but they had no other choice.

On the ground, things were much the same. Tiernan had just spoken to General Ray, who reported that his divisions had deployed without incident (aside from the diplomatic démarche, which the ambassador was handling planetside), and were taking up defensive positions as best they could, given that they had no idea from where or how the Kreelans might attack. The Legion troops had been very accommodating, even before Lefevre issued their *Général de division* very explicit orders about coordinating with the Terrans.

As with their naval counterparts, the ground forces had been completely frustrated in trying to get the data-link systems to talk to one another. This was perhaps even more critical for the ground units because the Terran forces had heavy artillery and aerospace defense weapons that could be used to help support the neighboring Legion regiments, which themselves had few such weapons. Without effective integration of their combat data networks to share intelligence and targeting information, however, the overall effectiveness of employing the Terran heavy weapons outside of their own formations was going to be significantly degraded.

Tiernan, though, was most concerned about one thing: taking the initiative. Aside from the initial surprise his fleet had given them upon emergence, the Kreelans had largely enjoyed a free ride in how the battle had been fought. Now that the two opposing fleets had rough parity in numbers and tonnage, he and Lefevre intended to take the fight to the enemy.

The Kreelans, however, demonstrated an impeccable sense of timing.

"They're moving, sir!" the flag tactical officer reported, pointing to a sheaf of red icons that was separating away from the main body of the Kreelan fleet.

Tiernan held his breath. The temptation of some would have been to curse that the Kreelans had acted out of turn. But if they were splitting their forces, it might give him and Lefevre an opportunity to defeat them, concentrating their own massed squadrons against either smaller Kreelan force.

After a few minutes of watching the new trajectory traces on the tactical display, Tiernan cursed. It was clear where the Kreelan ships - sixty-seven of them, almost all of them cruiser-sized - were heading: directly for Keran.

***

"Fight them as you would, Amar-Marakh," Tesh-Dar said to the image of the senior shipmistress, a warrior priestess of the Ima'il-Kush order who remained with the formation in high orbit as she herself led the other ships in the first wave of the planetary assault. She knew that the shipmistresses had chafed somewhat at not being allowed to fight unfettered in the initial battles; Tesh-Dar was not unsympathetic, but it had been necessary at the time. But now, as the battle was about to open on the ground, she saw no reason to hold back anymore in the fighting that must erupt once more in space. The humans had proven themselves capable opponents, and would be treated as such. "We have bled them to learn what we would, and to give them the opportunity to do so, as well. Now challenge them to survive."

"Yes, my priestess," Amar-Marakh answered, clearly pleased. In the first battles, the ships had been used mainly to get the boarders close to their targets. Now they would be used to their fullest. "We are moving to engage now."

Tesh-Dar nodded. "In Her name, let it be so..."

***

"Admiral," Tiernan said, addressing Lefevre, "I believe our best choice would be to move to intercept the enemy ships heading toward the surface."

"I agree, *amiral*," Lefevre said at once over the vidcom. He, too, had seen the opportunity opened by the Kreelans splitting their forces. Attacking the group heading toward the planet was certainly the optimal choice: the human forces would have the advantage of being higher in the gravity well and a nearly three to one advantage in tonnage. Being able to intercept the enemy before they could land troops on the ground was simply icing on the cake. "I recommend that we-"

"Admiral," Tiernan's flag captain said tensely.

Tiernan told Lefevre, "Just a moment, admiral," and turned to see what was going on. His flag captain merely pointed at the tactical display, which now showed the larger Kreelan force reforming and starting to move. "Admiral Lefevre, are you seeing this?" Tiernan asked.

"*Oui*," Lefevre said gravely. "Shall we make a wager that they are headed our way?"

Tiernan snorted. "No takers here on that one, sir. You know bloody well they are." He didn't need the tactical computer's analysis for that. Taking a closer look at the trajectory for the enemy formation heading for the planet and doing some mental projections, he said, "So, do we go meet them head-to-head, or do we play a hand that's a bit riskier?"

Lefevre smiled. He had known Tiernan only this short time, but already had come to like the man. "Tell me what you have in mind, *amiral*."

***

Senior shipmistress Amar-Marakh hissed as she saw the human ships begin to deploy. Her reaction was not one of fear, but of annoyance. She had wanted to meet the human fleet head-on, but it was clear the humans had something else in mind. The great staggered wedges of their fleet were arrowing toward the planet, plunging downward with the clear intent of intercepting Tesh-Dar's force.

"I see them," came Tesh-Dar's voice, as if the great priestess had read Amar-Marakh's mind. "They come for us."

"We cannot intercept them before they reach you," Amar-Marakh warned. "They will have superiority."

Tesh-Dar shook her head. "They will not reach us," she reassured her senior shipmistress. "They are thinking in terms of their own vessels, not of ours. Be prepared for them when they realize their mistake and climb to engage you."

Amar-Marakh saluted and said only, "As you command, Tesh-Dar."

***

"We're missing something," Tiernan murmured to himself. The combined human fleet was speeding toward the planet on a course that would intercept the Kreelan ships now plunging down for what Tiernan believed could only be a planetary assault.

It was a perfect opportunity: the Kreelan ships would have to sail close to Keran to drop their troops. The human fleet would be in a perfect position to smash the enemy ships as they climbed up away from the planet, struggling against gravity. The combination of superior firepower and tactical positioning should let them pound the Kreelans into scrap, he had thought. Then the human fleet could deal with the larger enemy force still holding near Keran's moons.

It had been a good plan.

Except it wasn't going to work. With a sudden shock he realized why: the Kreelan ships were heading in too low. Tiernan had thought the streamlined nature of the enemy vessels was merely an alien aesthetic preference. Now he realized that they were streamlined for a specific reason: the aerodynamic shape, no doubt combined with more powerful electromagnetic shields and high-heat alloys so the ships could withstand the heat of reentry, would allow them to enter atmosphere and drop their troops without the need for assault boats. Not only that, but they'd likely be able to bring the main weapons of the ships to bear on ground targets, which put the human troops in extreme jeopardy.

"Get me Admiral Lefevre," he ordered the flag communications officer.

"*Oui, Amiral* Tiernan?" Lefevre answered immediately.

"They surprised us again," Tiernan told him. "Those ships are going to enter the atmosphere, possibly even land." Looking at the tactical plot, he shook his head. "I don't think we'll be able to catch them."

Lefevre frowned and spoke to someone off to the side. A moment later he said, "I agree with your assessment of their intentions, my friend," he said, "but not that we cannot catch them. If we depress our trajectory slightly and increase our speed, we should be able to give them a broadside at extreme range as we pass."

Ticonderoga's flag tactical officer, who was speaking at the same time with his counterpart on Lefevre's flag bridge aboard the *Jean Bart*, brought up a new set of navigation traces on the display. Tiernan saw that there was absolutely no margin for error. Even under the best of circumstances, it was likely that at least some of his ships were going to sustain damage from contact with the upper fringes of Keran's atmosphere. "That's cutting it awfully close, admiral," he said.

"It is, *amiral*," Lefevre replied grimly. "But if the Kreelans are able to use their ships to fire directly on our ground forces..." He shook his head: the troops on the planet would not stand a chance.

"Agreed, sir," Tiernan said, the decision made for lack of any better choices. "My navigation officer is uploading the new maneuvering orders to our ships. We'll await your signal to execute."

"Stand by," Lefevre told him as he waited for his own flag tactical officer to do the same. "Now, *amiral*."

Tiernan nodded to his tactical officer, who flashed the instructions to the rest of the fleet over the data-link. As one, the four dozen ships of Tiernan's force and the hundred-odd remaining ships of Lefevre's fleet accelerated and nosed down even further toward Keran.

Satisfied that the maneuver had been executed properly, Tiernan turned to his communications officer. "Get me General Ray immediately," he told him. "There's a lot of bad news headed his way."

***

"Sir, let me make sure I understand you properly," Ray said, fighting his disbelief. "They are bringing a force of cruisers and destroyers *into* the atmosphere?"

"That's right, general," Tiernan's image said from the vidcom. "There's no question of it at this point: they have sixty-seven ships inbound, and trajectory projections have a good third of them coming your way."

"Do we have any estimates of how many troops these ships might carry," Ray asked, looking helplessly at his operations and intelligence staff officers, who both had mortified expressions on their faces, "or what weapons they have to hit us with?"

"We don't know anything about troop capacity, general," Tiernan answered, "but the larger ships are roughly the size of the *Ticonderoga* here. If they really crammed warriors in like sardines, they might be able to fit a thousand or so in each ship over and above what we estimate for the crew complement. But that would be a damn tight squeeze. I'm figuring not more than a couple of divisions' worth, and they'll be spread out fairly thin based on the trajectories we're seeing.

"As for the weapons," Tiernan went on grimly, "that we have more information on based on the fighting we've been through up here. At a minimum, expect heavy rapid-fire kinetics in the twenty centimeter range and lasers that can kill destroyers. They have a variety of lighter weapons, but those are the ones to worry about."

Ray sat back at the admiral's understatement. Twenty centimeter shipboard kinetics were equivalent to heavy artillery on the ground, and the naval guns could spit out half a dozen rounds that size in a few seconds. Per tube. And cruisers mounted roughly a dozen such weapons. The lasers were as lethal: any laser that could burn through the hull of a destroyer, even at close range, would be more than a match for his tanks. And he had absolutely nothing that he could fight back with except his tanks in direct fire mode: all of his heavy aerospace defense weapons were intended to hit much smaller targets. He could - and would - fire them against ships in the atmosphere, but they would need incredible luck to get past their point defenses. Even if the weapons hit, they would cause little damage to a destroyer, let alone a cruiser. His real concern was the tanks: if he used them to attack the ships, they would become easy targets themselves. "This will make things a bit more exciting than we had planned, admiral," Ray deadpanned.

Managing a mirthless smile, Tiernan told him, "I know. Listen, Arun, we'll do everything we can to screw up their day as they ingress. But the geometry is against us and a lot of them are going to get through. They're going to have a big advantage in firepower, yes, but hopefully they won't be able to mass enough warriors anywhere to achieve local superiority over your troops."

It was Ray's turn to smile. Like a shark. "Even if they do achieve local superiority somewhere in our sector," he said, "that just gives my tanks more targets to shoot at."

***

Tesh-Dar watched as the human ships adjusted their trajectory. "More credit are they due," she murmured approvingly. The human leader was clearly taking a major risk: while she - or would it be a *he*, she wondered? - would temporarily be safe from the rest of Tesh-Dar's fleet, their ungainly ships could easily suffer damage, and possibly destruction, from the upper atmosphere. Their strategy, however, held merit: while they would not be able to force a decisive engagement with Tesh-Dar's ships, they would nonetheless have a single pass where they would be able to bring most, if not all, of their weapons to bear, but Tesh-Dar could not. Her ships would already be committed to reentry and would only be able to employ those weapons mounted on the upper hull.

Her shipmistress *humphed* appreciatively, flexing her fingers, her talons digging grooves into the palms of the armored gauntlets she wore.

"Courage, they lack not," Elai-Tura'an, the shipmistress of Tesh-Dar's flagship, said. "It seems we will have to pass through a rain of fire to reach the surface."

"A fitting way to begin the battle on the ground, is it not?" Tesh-Dar said as the ship began to roll and shudder as it kissed the outer fringes of Keran's atmosphere. "Alert the warriors that they may be prepared."

"In Her name," Elai-Tura'an said as she saluted, "it shall be so."

Turning her attention back to the tactical display, Tesh-Dar watched the rapidly approaching human ships, eagerly anticipating the coming clash.

EIGHTEEN

"Shit," Sparks cursed vehemently as he got off the vidcom with General Ray. The Terran ground forces commander had just held a remote conference with his division and brigade commanders. It had been brief and brutally to the point. "We've got incoming heavies, people," he told his staff, nodding toward the tactical display embedded in the forward wall of the command vehicle's tactical center. Traces of the Kreelan ships racing for the surface were being echoed from the *Ticonderoga*, and a good twenty of them were headed toward Foshan where the Terran divisions and some of their Alliance counterparts were deployed. "We need to get our vehicles under cover, pronto, and get the regiment ready for full EMCON on my command."

While the vehicles, particularly the tanks, provided a huge amount of firepower, they had one major tactical drawback: they were so large that they were extremely difficult to conceal. With the sensors carried by warships, the Kreelans would have no difficulty finding armored vehicles out in the open. And if they could find them, they could kill them.

As for going to full EMCON - emission control, or "radio silence" as it was once known - Sparks had argued during the vidcom with General Ray that it would be more advantageous to minimize the electromagnetic signature generated by the various data-link systems that networked the units together. Every single vehicle and soldier was networked to help provide a much greater sense of situational awareness of the battlefield and to coordinate their weapons use. It was a tremendous force multiplier, but it was also a major vulnerability if the enemy could use it to help pinpoint the locations of their units. Worse, many commanders had become so dependent on the rich battlefield detail provided by the networked warfare concept that if the network was lost, they would be, too. That was one of the reasons that Sparks routinely trained his men and women in how to fight under severely degraded network and communications conditions, to the point where his vehicle commanders knew how to use signal flags to communicate basic information and orders to one another. Most of Sparks's contemporaries thought he was insane, but no one could contest his results: his brigade was consistently at the top of the corps' combat readiness ratings.

In the end, General Ray had said, "Sparks, I agree there is a risk. But I feel the advantage we gain from the network outweighs the potential weakness."

And that, as the saying went, was that. Sparks wasn't happy about it, but he was a soldier who knew how to follow orders. But he was going to make sure his troopers were ready to take their data-links off the air if necessary.

"Sir," his operations officer asked, a puzzled expression on his face as he looked at the map display of the regiment's area, "where the devil do we have our people hide? We've got some forest cover to the front, for what little that might be worth. Other than that, the only place to find cover would be to drive into the buildings..." He tapered off, looking at Sparks's expression. "You don't really mean..."

"I do," Sparks said. "Get 'em moving, major. We've got about ten minutes before we're going to have Kreelan ships overhead. And make sure Grishin's gotten the word, too, would you?"

***

Staff Sergeant Patty Coyle couldn't keep herself from grinning. Part of her felt bad for what she was about to do, but the tanker in the soul of the petite blonde and blue-eyed woman - the absolute antithesis of what a tank commander might be expected to look like - was having a fucking orgasm. This was one of the things every tank commander dreamed of doing, but so few ever got a chance to do it. And here she was being ordered - *ordered!* - to.

Fuckin'-A, she thought as she called to her driver, "Okay, Mannie, back her up, a bit to the left."

Her driver, Corporal Manfred Holman, grunted in reply as he applied more power to the M-87 Wolfhound's tracks, slewing the hundred and twenty-five metric ton vehicle slightly, just as Coyle wanted.

"Perfect," Coyle told him as a crash, deafening even here inside the tank, rang out as the tank backed through the huge front glass window of a bakery. She watched through her cupola's vision displays as the massive hull crushed the displays of neatly arranged cookies, pastries and bread, then proceeded deeper into the shop to pulverize the tables and chairs. Above the din of shattering glass, plastic, and wood, she could hear the hysterical shouts of the shopkeeper and his wife, safe on the street outside.

She couldn't believe it when the operations officer had issued orders for all vehicle commanders to immediately find cover *inside nearby buildings.* The units had to pay for any damage they did to personal property if they deployed outside of their regular training areas. She was sure the Terran Government would pick up the tab for the huge mess the tanks were making, but the promise of a fat paycheck wouldn't have made the locals any happier as they watched the armored monsters drive into their shops and living rooms.

After getting the orders from regiment, Coyle had led her platoon down this street and found a three-story building whose first floor was tall enough to clear the tops of the turrets. Then she and the other tank commanders had gone in and asked - nicely at first, and then not so nicely - the occupants to clear out. Even with the raid sirens still wailing, most of the owners and quite a few patrons were still in the shops, living life as if nothing was different. That changed as soon as Coyle pulled out her sidearm and started shooting into the ceilings of the shops, finally getting her point across. A local cop had come running over to see what the fuss was, brandishing his pistol, but ran away even faster after Coyle's gunner, Sergeant Yuri Kirov, rotated the turret in his direction and pointed the main gun at him.

"Gotta hurry, guys," she said over the platoon push channel. She had a timer running in her cupola vision panel, counting down the minutes left until the enemy ships would be overhead, along with a miniature view of the tactical display showing their inbound tracks. "I'm coming around to check how you look." While her communications procedures reflected a less-than-military bearing in how she led her platoon, it was just one of her quirks. She put on the hard-core military façade when she absolutely had to, but otherwise she tossed it aside: it just got in her way. She'd been upbraided for what she called her own "girlishness" on more than one occasion, but nobody gave her too much grief: she was the most competent tank commander and platoon leader in the entire regiment. And the reason she was platoon leader right now rather than platoon sergeant was that her company was short a second lieutenant, and the company commander had trusted her to take her platoon and go raise hell. Besides, in a regiment commanded by a man who wore spurs and a cavalry officer's hat, and who used a cavalry saber as a pointer when he gave briefings, her own eccentricities hardly stood out.

Waiting until the sound of tinkling glass abated, she threw open the hatch and carefully crawled out onto the turret roof, crabbing along in the two feet of space between the turret and the building's ceiling, her gloves protecting her hands from the shards of glass and wood covering the top of her tank. Swinging down from the barrel to the steeply sloped front glacis plate of the hull, she dropped to the floor of the shop, debris crunching under her boots. A crowd of civilians started to close in on her, shouting and making gestures that she didn't need translated from Arabic and Chinese. She didn't want to hurt anybody, but she drew her sidearm and held it across her chest where they could all see it: it didn't shut them up, but they backed away quickly.

"Two minutes, sarge," her gunner said tensely.

"Roger," she replied as she ran out into the middle of the street. Turning around, she looked at her tank's position: it was fully concealed from overhead, with two more floors above it that hopefully would mask its heat signature. There wasn't even much debris on the sidewalk in front of the shop: most of it had imploded inward. She ran down the street, ignoring the passenger vehicles that still passed by, honking at her. *Fucking morons*, Coyle thought. *Why aren't they heading to shelter or something?*

She checked the positions for the other three tanks in her platoon, happily noting that they were all fully concealed in the building. The Kreelans wouldn't be able to see them unless they were standing right in front of them. *And if they did that*, she told herself, *my tanks'll blow the living shit out of them.*

"Sixty seconds!"

Coyle sprinted back to her tank, quickly clambering back up to the turret, which had *Chiquita* painted in a flamboyant script in black against the green and brown camouflage paint of the vehicle. Dropping neatly into the cupola, she told her platoon, "Okay, everybody, make sure you're buttoned up in case this building gets knocked down on top of us. The colonel would be really pissed if I lost anybody because they got hit on the head with a brick." She smiled as her quip drew some less-than-respectful responses from her platoon. But they instantly did as she had ordered. They were wired and ready.

Just before she dropped into the turret and closed the hatch, she thought she heard the boom of distant thunder.

***

"They are networked," shipmistress Elai-Tura'an informed Tesh-Dar, indicating the display of the land coming up to greet them. It was an unfamiliar term to her people, one that the builders had dug from the Books of Time as they built the ships and weapons to fight the humans. The *Kreela* of this age did not use such rudimentary technology, at least as any human would understand it. Tesh-Dar fully understood the concept, but it was for others to understand the details that made it work. Such technology was built into the ships of this ancient design, but - as with many of the electronic devices the builders had resurrected from those ages long past - the warriors had disdained to use them. Such things were from an age when nation-state warred against nation-state for dominance and resources, before the Unification and the founding of the First Empire. Since then, combat was waged as a means to glorify the Empress: it was a battle of spirit and will as much as force.

Thus had Tesh-Dar come to wage war against the humans face to face wherever possible, not to claw at them through layers of technology. She had allowed the human ships to use their data-links in the first encounter simply to give them an advantage, and because she did not yet have a feel for their skills. Many of their weapons she would allow as a challenge to her warriors, for if a human directed the weapon, it was still the human they fought. But she had no patience to fight the mindless calculations of machines. The humans had proven themselves worthy, and she decided that they did not need such devices in a battle that should be fought mainly with tooth and claw.

"Blind them as we return fire," Tesh-Dar ordered as her ship screamed downward through the atmosphere.

***

"Hell," Tiernan cursed as the *Ticonderoga* wallowed in the uppermost reaches of the atmosphere. Even the navigation computers were having a difficult time holding the ship and her sisters steady. His biggest concern now was whether the tactical computers would be able to take the atmospherics into account for the targeting calculations. Something else that they had never been designed to do.

"Thirty seconds!" the fleet tactical officer called out. On the tactical display, the two opposing forces were rushing at one another like out of control freight trains. The Kreelan ships were now thousands of meters below, well within the atmosphere. Some of their ships had broken off to head toward the smaller cities, but most were still arrowing directly for Foshan, head-on to the combined human fleet. "Hard target lock across the board, all weapons synchronized." The data-link systems and tactical computers aboard each ship in the Terran formation had formed a massive distributed processing network that had identified each Kreelan ship and assigned weapons from one or more Terran ships to fire on it. The same was happening in the Alliance fleet that flew to the Terran fleet's starboard side. Since the networks of the two fleets couldn't coordinate their targeting, Tiernan and Lefevre had minimized the potential overlap with a simple expedient: Tiernan took all the targets on their relative left, Lefevre took the ones on the right. The human ships would be shooting right down the Kreelans' throats as they passed below.

"Vampire! Vampire!" the tactical officer suddenly cried out: missiles had been launched from the enemy ships.

Tiernan whipped his head back to the tactical display in time to see a swarm of missiles fly from the Kreelan formation. While the human ships carried some missiles, in the age of laser defenses they were rarely used: their maneuverability and speed had never been able to keep up with laser technology, although missile designers kept trying. The only major exception were the torpedoes carried by the destroyers and some cruisers: they were large weapons that carried their own powerful drives and limited shielding. But a ship of a given tonnage could only carry a few, and even their ability to penetrate point defenses was far from guaranteed.

"Vector?" Tiernan snapped.

"They're all over the place, sir," the tactical officer replied, confused. "Some are heading this way, some to the surface. It looks like-"

His words were interrupted by a series of spectacular detonations that looked like a cascade of exploding balls of lightning that briefly overrode the brightness limits of the main displays on the ship.

"Jesus!" someone gasped.

"Were those nukes?" Tiernan shouted as he closed his eyes and turned his head away from the momentary brilliance of the display. The Terran fleet had no nuclear weapons, at the explicit orders of the president. He had argued mightily to have at least a few to use in space, but the president had been adamant, and so he had none. But that didn't mean the Kreelans couldn't use them.

"Negative, sir," the tactical officer replied, shaken, as the main flag bridge display faded to again show the perilously close surface - for ships that couldn't enter atmosphere - of Keran. "No indication of ionizing radiation from nuclear weapons. I don't know what those things were."

"I do," Tiernan growled, looking at the tactical display and the handful of icons that remained: just what *Ticonderoga* could see with her own sensors. "They knocked out the damned data-link. Do we still have weapons lock?"

"Only local, sir," the tactical officer reported, quickly coordinating with the tactical officer on the bridge. The *Ticonderoga* still held the targets that had been allocated to her and for which she had her own sensor lock-on. The targets she was to have engaged based on targeting by other ships in the Terran fleet were either gone from the display or were tagged in yellow: the fire control system could see the targets, but didn't have enough weapons available to service them. "The fleet firing solutions just went out the window."

"Do we have communications with the other ships?" Tiernan asked quickly. Only seconds were left before their opportunity would be lost.

"Laser voice and vidcom only, sir," the communications officer reported.

Tiernan held back a vicious curse. "Open a channel, fast," he ordered the fleet communications officer.

"Open sir," the woman replied immediately.

"All ships, this is admiral Tiernan," he said quickly as the countdown on the tactical display spun down to zero and the range rings of *Ticonderoga's* weapons intersected the lead Kreelan ships far below. "Local targeting mode, fire at will!"

He was instantly rewarded with an extended rumble from *Ticonderoga's* heavy weapons turrets on the bottom of the hull. They fired at full rate until they ran out of their basic load, which only took a dozen seconds. As the guns fell silent, the looming horizon of the planet rapidly rotated counterclockwise in the flag bridge display as the ship's captain immediately flipped *Ticonderoga* on her back to unmask the turrets on the top of the hull. As soon as the ship stabilized, those guns belched fire at the rapidly fleeing Kreelan targets. It was an outside chance, at best, that any of those rounds would catch the enemy ships. But in this situation Tiernan was not about to be stingy with his ammunition. *Ticonderoga* had plenty of that. Even now, the gun crews were moving the next loads of shells for their guns from the magazines as the captain brought the ship's bow up toward the reassuring blackness of space, the engines thundering with power to get her clear of the deadly atmosphere.

Tiernan silently watched the tactical display, willing the enemy ships to start falling prey to the human fleet's attack.

"*Inbound kinetics!*" the flag tactical officer suddenly shouted. The collision alarm sounded throughout the ship, and Tiernan and the rest of the crew braced for impact.

***

While the fire from the human ships had been far less deadly than it would have been with their data networks intact, more than a few of their rounds had found their mark. Several of them hit Tesh-Dar's ship, causing extensive damage to the engineering sections, and one of them penetrated the hull's armor to explode directly beneath the bridge. The resulting explosion had not been powerful enough to blow completely through the deck plating and vent the bridge to vacuum, but it had buckled the deck with such force that several of the heavy support frames had snapped. Tesh-Dar and several of the bridge crew had been slammed into the bulkheads by the force of the explosion: two of the bridge crew were dead, and three others injured. Tesh-Dar herself had been dazed momentarily.

Elai-Tura'an, the shipmistress, had been pinned to the deck by a thick support beam that weighed as much as ten warriors. Had she not been wearing her armor, she would have been killed instantly. As Tesh-Dar stumbled to her side, still dizzy from the impact and coughing from the dense and acrid smoke that now flooded the bridge, she could see that Elai-Tura'an was bleeding badly inside, with bright arterial blood streaming from her mouth.

Tesh-Dar gripped the lower edge of the beam with her hands, and with a roar of fury lifted it and tossed it aside with a horrendous crash. Kneeling by the woman's side, she placed a hand gently on her shoulder and said, "I will summon a healer."

"No," Elai-Tura'an replied, gripping Tesh-Dar's arm in a fierce grip as she looked into the priestess's eyes. "No...time. Must get me...to the navigation station." She spat out more blood from her pierced lungs, a mixed expression of pain and annoyance on her face. "Then get the warriors...off."

Nodding, Tesh-Dar picked her up and carried her to the navigation station, gently setting her down in what was left of the chair. The warrior who had been serving as navigator was one of those killed by the explosion below, her body and the upper part of the chair having been knocked aside by one of the flying support beams. Kneeling beside her, Tesh-Dar gripped Elai-Tura'an's arms in the way of warriors. "May you find Her light and love for eternity," she whispered.

"And may thy Way be long...and glorious, my priestess," Elai-Tura'an replied, bowing her head. "Now go. I will control the ship from here. Get all the others...away, before we are too low."

Turning her attention to the navigation panel, Elai-Tura'an took direct control of the mortally stricken ship as it continued to plunge toward the surface.

With one last look at her dying shipmistress, Tesh-Dar uttered a silent prayer for her soul to the Empress before she gathered the rest of the bridge crew and made her way quickly to the lower decks where her First had gathered the rest of the warriors. Li'ara-Zhurah awaited her, holding Tesh-Dar's other weapons, which the priestess quickly fastened to her armor. Li'ara-Zhurah offered the priestess a set of the special descent equipment the other warriors now wore, but the great warrior priestess refused: Tesh-Dar had no need of such things.

"As have Her Children for countless ages past," she told the gathered warriors, her voice booming over the howl of the air streaming past the ship's hull, "we go to battle with the enemy, face to face. Fight to honor Her, my children, and seek glory in battle and in death." She paused, looking over the hundreds of faces around her, taking in the Bloodsong that echoed from each of them, pulsing in her own veins. "So has it been-"

"-so shall it forever be," they echoed in a thunderous chorus.

Tesh-Dar nodded to Kamal-Utai, her First, who touched a control on the central console in the large ventral compartment the warriors now occupied. There was a momentary hissing of air as the pressure equalized with the outside atmosphere. Then the side panels of the compartment - large hatches, in reality - raised to the open air streaming by. Humans would have looked at instruments to tell them the altitude and speed of the ship, to know if it was going too high or low, or too fast. None of the warriors here needed such things: they knew such things by instinct.

"Go now," Tesh-Dar ordered above the shrieking airstream, and instantly the warriors began leaping from the ship, their arms and legs spread wide to control their fall.

Tesh-Dar waited until all but Kamal-Utai and Li'ara-Zhurah had gone, then she ushered them from the doomed ship before it flew too low for their descent equipment to function properly.

Satisfied that they were away safely, Tesh-Dar flexed her hands in anticipation, her great talons drawing blood from her palms. Then she leaped from the ship and was carried away by the roaring winds.

***

The grains of sand in the time-glass of shipmistress Elai-Tura'an's life were rapidly running out. With grim determination she kept her ship on course for its glorious ending. Making adjustments to compensate for the failing engines, she guided her last command to its destination.

With a smile on her lips, her heart enraptured by the glory it would bring to the Empress, she slammed her cruiser into the very center of the city of Foshan.

NINETEEN

Of the sixty-seven Kreelan ships that attacked Keran, fourteen suffered serious damage and six were destroyed outright from the humans' daring attack. Seven of those that had sustained damage would have to land, for they were in no shape to climb back into space with the other ships. And, of course, Tesh-Dar's ship had come to its own glorious end as it struck the human city.

The senior surviving shipmistress of the attack wave knew of Tesh-Dar's wishes regarding the humans, and observed over the shoulder of the warrior who served as the equivalent of a human tactical battle officer. While the human data-links had been effectively severed, there were still many human combat units that were broadcasting data, even though their companion units could no longer receive it.

Nodding to herself, the shipmistress designated targets for the tactical officer. "The humans at these locations," she said. "Destroy them."

With a brief flurry of her fingertips over the controls, the guns of the Kreelan ships fired as they flew over the human positions, then began the long climb through the atmosphere to reach open space. While most of their shells and lasers found their targets, the devastation seemed inconsequential after the spectacular detonation of Elai-Tura'an's cruiser.

***

One moment, Steph was sitting in the regimental command vehicle as Sparks barked orders to his battalion commanders over the vidcom after the strange Kreelan missiles took down the data-links. The next, she found herself lying on the floor of the vehicle, groggily looking up into Colonel Sparks's concerned and bloodied face. The command compartment was dark except for the red combat lights that shone dimly through swirling dust and acrid smoke. She thought it made Sparks look like Satan.

"Are you hurt, Miss Guillaume?" he said as if from very far away.

Steph's ears were ringing, the sound so loud she could hardly hear a thing. "No," she said, her tongue feeling like it was three sizes too big. She tasted blood. "At least...I don't think so." As she came to, she took stock of her body: aside from some scrapes and bruises, plus a big knot on the back of her head, she couldn't feel anything wrong. "What happened?"

Sparks nodded and helped her to her feet. "The Kreelan ships hit us as they passed over, and one of the bastards crashed right into the middle of the city." He had already been outside and seen the huge mushroom cloud rising from Foshan's center. It hadn't been a nuclear explosion - there was no trace of ionizing radiation on the command vehicle's sensors - but with a ship that must have massed on the order of a hundred thousand metric tons, with power cores that could propel it through space, it didn't have to be a nuclear weapon. The energy release of something like that hitting the surface, even at a comparatively low velocity, combined with the engine cores breaching would still be measured in hundreds of kilotons of explosive power. "Foshan has pretty much been wiped out," he told her grimly. He felt a terrible rending in his heart at the civilians who must have been killed, the people he and his regiment had been sent to try and save.

But at the same time he was indescribably relieved that his men and women had been deployed on the outskirts of the city. Most of the blast had been absorbed by the buildings between the crash site and here, although the command vehicle had still been tossed around like a toy, and the building they had hidden in had largely collapsed on top of them. Ironically, that had provided some incidental protection from the salvoes the other Kreelan ships had fired at them when they passed overhead. Built on the chassis of the M-87 Wolfhound tank, the command vehicle had been hammered hard, but had managed to protect its occupants from serious harm. "We've also lost contact with everyone, including division and corps, which definitely isn't good news."

"So what do you plan to do?" she asked, taking a drink of water from her canteen.

Sparks looked at her with fire in his eyes, glinting in the red combat lighting. "As soon as I can reestablish contact with at least some of my units and figure out where the hell the enemy is, I plan to attack."

"Sir," the driver called back to him as he struggled out of the cramped forward compartment. "This bitch is history. Oh," he said, embarrassed as he noticed Steph. "Sorry, ma'am," he mumbled.

"I've heard the term before, corporal," she reassured him with a tired smile.

"Uh, yes, ma'am. Anyway, sir," he went on, "the left track is busted and we've got half a dozen faults on the drive panel. Without the guys in the repair track working on this tub for a day, after they haul us out of this rubble, we're stuck. So if we need to go anywhere, we're gonna have to walk."

"Had our horse shot out from under us, have we?" Sparks said, already gathering up his personal combat gear. "Hadley," he called to the vehicle commander, "grab one of the extra rifles and give Miss Guillaume a crash-course in how to use it, then give her a combat harness and ammo. No grenades. You've got five minutes."

"But, colonel," Steph protested, "as a journalist, I can't carry a weapon. I'm legally a noncombatant."

Strapping the belt that held his cavalry saber to his waist, Sparks told her, "Not anymore, Miss Guillaume. Do you think for an instant that the Kreelans are going to give a damn about your legal status? They just nose-dived a starship into the center of the biggest city on the planet. That tells me a lot about their articles of war." He drew the massive pistol from its holster under his left arm and checked that the magazine was full. "I don't expect you to be a trooper, but you need to be able to help defend yourself." Turning to his ops officer, he said, "Do we have contact with *anybody* yet?"

"Yes, sir," the woman told him. "Colonel Grishin just came up on the tac-com." They had just had time to lay a tactical communications line between the 7th Cavalry and *1er REC* command posts before the Kreelans attacked. By a small miracle it hadn't been affected by the weapons the Kreelans had fired or the cruiser's explosion. "He says they have incoming enemy paratroops." She paused, a glint of fear in her eye as she heard a terrified shriek in the background. "They're coming in right on top of his positions."

***

The scream had come from one of the crewmen of Grishin's vehicle, who had been bodily wrenched from the rear hatch by what looked like an alien version of what was known as a "cat o' nine tails," a multi-tailed whip. One moment the man was telling Grishin there were alien paratroopers falling on top of them, the next he was gone. Grishin was sure that he had heard the hapless man's skull and legs shatter against the metal hatch coaming, even with the protection of his helmet and leg armor.

Beyond his broken body, which had landed in the dirt a few meters from the vehicle, stood a huge alien warrior that made a mockery out of the verbal descriptions and artist's renderings the Terran military attaché had provided the Alliance. With a snap of her arm the whip's barbed tendrils detached from the dead legionnaire as if they were alive, and her demonic eyes were fixed on him as she bared her ivory fangs and snapped the whip back, preparing for another attack.

"*Go, go, go!*" Grishin shouted through the intercom to his driver, reflexively pushing himself deeper into his seat to get away from the ferocious-looking warrior. The driver didn't need any encouragement: the command vehicle suddenly roared out of the pit the engineers had dug for it, snapping the thin tac-com cable that had connected Grishin with the Terran regimental commander. In any normal battle, being dug-in would have given their vehicle some cover and concealment from an approaching enemy. But when the enemy was literally landing right on top of you, the only thing the pit was good for was a grave.

The command vehicle shared the same wheeled chassis as the light tanks of the *1er REC's* combat squadrons, but had no turret and no main gun. One of the legionnaires was manning the vehicle's only weapon, the modern-day equivalent of a machinegun on a flexi-mount on the vehicle's roof, and was firing rounds non-stop at the warriors that were now landing all around them.

"Conserve your ammunition, you fool!" the vehicle commander shouted at him. But the legionnaire continued to hold down the trigger. The weapon's barrel was red hot.

Suddenly the firing ceased, and Grishin was relieved that the gunner had come to his senses. If he had kept firing that way, they would be out of ammunition in a matter of a few minutes, if that.

"*Putain!*" the vehicle commander swore, and Grishin looked up to see the legionnaire gunner slide back into the vehicle. Headless.

Focus, Grishin told himself as he fought back a wave of nausea. It wasn't the headless legionnaire that bothered him, for he had seen that and much worse in his career in the *Légion*. It had been the enormous enemy warrior about to snare him with that hellish whip. *Let the crew fight the immediate battle. You've got a regiment to worry about. You're their leader: so lead!*

That thought brought him back to his senses. Unfortunately, he had no communications right now with anyone: all types of radio communications were out, and the *Légion* did not have the funding for the latest vehicle-to-vehicle laser communications.

That left the old fashioned method. "Turn around," he ordered the driver. To this point, they had been barreling down the road that led toward the rear of the regiment's deployment area, and then to the Terran regiment, if any of them had survived the crazy cavalryman's idea of stuffing their huge tanks into buildings. He could see the mushroom cloud over Foshan through one of the vehicle's armored viewports, the orange and black writhing as if it were a living thing. All around it, the city was burning fiercely, and it was difficult for him to imagine the devastation. He wished Sparks and his troops good luck. But now he had to make some luck of his own. He needed to get back to his regiment.

"Sir?" the driver asked, his voice shaking. While they had all been told that aliens might come, none of them had really believed it. And none of them had been truly prepared for the sight of thousands of alien warriors dropping from the sky.

"Turn us around, *soldat*," Grishin ordered. "Without radio, I must make direct contact with our units. I've got to at least get to the squadron commanders."

The driver made no move to respond to Grishin's order.

"Tomaszewski," the vehicle commander said in a low voice over the intercom, "turn us around or I'll blow your fucking head off."

"*Oui, sergent*," the driver replied shakily, slowing the six-wheeled vehicle around enough to turn it without tipping them over.

Pulling the gunner's headless body out of the way, the vehicle commander took his place at the gun on the roof, hiking up his chest armor to try and protect his neck as they headed back toward the rest of their besieged regiment.

***

Tesh-Dar and the other warriors had been badly buffeted by the explosion as the cruiser hit the human city. But like many of the human warriors, they had received some protection as the buildings around the city absorbed much of the blast wave. A number of the warriors had lost control and crashed, with some of them no doubt killed. But the majority from her ship, nearly eight hundred, had survived. Around them, thousands of other warriors dropped by the other ships plummeted toward the human city and its defenders.

As they fell rapidly toward the ground, Tesh-Dar saw that they were almost perfectly positioned against one of the groups of human warriors. Almost all of this group were in large, boxy vehicles that were clearly heavily armed. Her blood thrilled with the challenge, for it would be difficult to kill the humans in vehicles such as these. She did not need to look around her to know that her warriors felt the same way, for their emotions sang from their very blood. But she looked anyway, turning to see Li'ara-Zhurah and Kamal-Utai flying beside her, their fangs bared in excitement.

Then it was time for the warriors to deploy their wings. Similar to a human-designed parafoil, they were actually much more akin to a natural wing: mounted to the warrior's back, with the wing supported by a thin but strong framework much like the bones of a bat's wing, it provided exceptional maneuverability.

While expressions of amazement and disbelief at Tesh-Dar's abilities were nothing new to her since she had become high priestess of the Desh-Ka order, she took some bemused enjoyment from the astonished looks on the faces of her warriors as they deployed their wings and she did not. Yet she continued to fly alongside them as if she did. The powers that she had inherited as part of the acceptance of the ways of the Desh-Ka were not infinite, and were nothing compared to the power of the Empress. But controlling her body above the earth was one of the gifts she had received, as was walking through solid objects. She herself did not understand how such things were possible, only that they were.

By now the humans had seen them swooping down upon their positions and began to fire projectile weapons. A number of warriors fell, stricken, while others fired back with weapons akin to those the humans were using. Tesh-Dar preferred close combat, but in this type of attack she would not have let her warriors be exposed at extended ranges to human weapons without being able to fight back. Challenge, she sought; wanton slaughter of her warriors, she did not.

Easing ahead of the other warriors, she arrowed toward a group of vehicles near the center of the area occupied by larger groups of spread-out vehicles. Touching down lightly near one of the vehicles, her sandals leaving no mark upon the dusty ground, she uncoiled her *grakh'ta*, the seven-barbed whip, from her belt.

A human momentarily stared at her open-mouthed from a hatch in the rear of the vehicle, then he turned away to say something in what was, to Tesh-Dar, one of their incomprehensible languages to someone inside. Baring her fangs, she snapped the *grakh'ta* behind her, then whipped it forward. It was a terribly difficult weapon to handle with precision, but Tesh-Dar had many, many cycles of practice and was expert in its use. The whip cracked as the seven barbed tips reached into the vehicle, wrapping themselves around the hapless human. With a titanic heave, she yanked the alien's body from the vehicle with such force that it smashed its head and legs to splinters against the armored interior.

As she snapped the whip again to clear the barbs from the human's flesh, her heightened senses warned her that danger was near. With a leap to one side that no human who witnessed it would have ever believed, she easily dodged the projectiles fired by the primitive weapon mounted on the vehicle. She watched as the vehicle suddenly burst from the hole the humans had dug for it - why they would do such a thing, she could not guess - to head quickly down the road, the human on top still firing madly at her warriors, and missing most of them. One of the warriors finally tired of him and took his head with a *shrekka*.

With her blood roaring a symphony in her spiritual ears, Tesh-Dar coiled her *grakh'ta* and set off toward one of the other vehicles, seeking new prey.

***

Grishin stood in one of the hatches, accepting the risk to his neck in exchange for the ability to see more clearly as the command vehicle swept around a bend in the road that passed by the positions of the *1er Escadron de combat*, the regiment's first tank squadron.

"*Merde...*" the vehicle commander cursed just before he started firing the top-mounted gun. There was certainly no shortage of targets.

Grishin looked on in horror as Kreelan warriors clad in black armor swarmed over the wheeled tanks of the *1er Escadron* like black ants. A few of the vehicles had made it out of their firing pits and were trying to keep the warriors at a distance while blasting away at them. Some vehicles had not, and Grishin saw a warrior atop a buttoned up tank stab her sword right through the armored commander's hatch. As she pulled the blade out of the metal, he saw that it was slick with blood.

Impossible, he thought. *No metal blade could cut through steel alloy armor like that!* Granted, it was not nearly so thick as the armor that protected the heavy Terran tanks, but it was simply not possible.

But it was. Other warriors did the same thing, stabbing their weapons through the armor of the driver's and gunner's hatches. Then one of them affixed some sort of bomb to the rear of the vehicle, and the warriors leaped clear as the light tank was consumed by what looked like a massive electrical discharge that left behind a smoldering, charred wreck.

"*Putain!*" the vehicle commander hissed, using one of his favorite curses. He dropped into the vehicle, his right arm hanging by a thread of flesh: most of the muscle and the bone had been cut through halfway above the elbow. "One of those bitches hit me with one of those flying things," he gasped, his face already turning pale from shock.

"Help me," Grishin ordered the last legionnaire left in the rear compartment, who had been firing his rifle at the enemy through one of the vehicle's gun ports. Unlike his Terran counterpart, Sparks, Grishin had his main staff officers in different vehicles, which was both a blessing and a curse. A blessing because if one of them was hit, the entire command staff would not be wiped out, and the most senior surviving officer could take over. A curse because without communications, he had no idea if any of them were even still alive to help get the regiment out of this disaster.

Grishin grabbed the sergeant around his chest, ignoring the blood cascading over his arms as he did so. The other legionnaire grabbed his legs, and together they moved him onto one of the combat seats along the side of the compartment.

"Do what you can for him," Grishin ordered before standing up through the roof hatch and manning the machinegun. He managed to clear some of the warriors off of the top of one of the tanks as it backed out of its firing pit, and he signaled for the commander to join on him. Two other tanks also joined up, and they quickly formed an echelon left, with the three tanks in a staggered line that gave all of them clear fields of fire into the bulk of the rampaging aliens, with Grishin's vehicle following close behind them.

Past their shock now, the legionnaires manning the three tanks began to give a good accounting of themselves as they poured machinegun fire into the groups of warriors attacking other tanks that hadn't had a chance to get out of their firing pits. The tank crews fired antipersonnel rounds, carrying thousands of needle-like flechettes, from their main guns, literally blasting the Kreelans from the backs of some of the tanks in clouds of bloody flesh and shrapnel.

Surely the enemy must be about to break, Grishin told himself as they killed Kreelans by the dozens, even as the warriors charged the tanks with swords raised high and war cries on their lips.

But they didn't break: the alien warriors kept on coming.

While the Kreelans had held the upper hand in the beginning, Grishin's legionnaires were now giving as good as they had gotten. But the enemy did not die easily, nor were they slaughtered without cost. As his formation swept along the rear of each of his companies, rallying the survivors, the enemy warriors fought even harder. They hurled themselves at his tanks, sometimes singly, sometimes in groups, but all as suicidal maniacs, and he could hear their fierce war cries through the chattering of the machineguns and the booming of the tanks' main guns.

When they made it to the rear of the last company, the *5ème Escadron*, and rallied what was left of it, Grishin was momentarily struck by despair. Of the roughly forty-eight tanks of the four tank squadrons, plus the various other vehicles that made up the regiment, he now only had half a dozen tanks and a handful of the other vehicles, most of which were as lightly armed as his command vehicle. Suicidal maniacs the Kreelans may have been, but they had effectively gutted his unit. And there were still hundreds left alive behind him.

From here, on the far right edge of his regiment's assigned area of responsibility, he should have been able to see the positions of the *2ème Régiment étranger de parachutistes*, the famous *2ème REP*, next to them. He had heard that the paratroops' commander had been livid at having to deploy his unit as regular infantry in prepared trenches, but those were his orders and he had carried them out. Now Grishin could see nothing of the famous elite unit, only a massive swarm of alien warriors. Looking through his field scope at the ferocious close combat there, he could think of no way to help them: the legionnaires were locked in bitter hand to hand fighting, and he could not use his tanks to good effect without killing his fellow legionnaires.

After a moment he realized that the point was moot: the paratroopers, while clearly fighting valiantly, were also being completely overwhelmed. Their part of the battle was already over.

"*Mon colonel,*" the vehicle commander said thickly through the painkillers that the attending legionnaire had pumped into his system after applying a tourniquet and self-sealing bandages. "Behind us."

Grishin turned to look behind them, and was shocked to see a line of Kreelan warriors standing there, clearly waiting for him and his men. There really was nowhere for him to run, not that he was inclined to. The road that had been the baseline for the regiment's deployment had relatively open ground to the front for a few hundred meters, but then swiftly turned into dense woods that would be difficult, if not impossible, for his tanks to traverse. To the rear was another hundred or so meters edged by a steep drainage culvert. He would have liked to deploy his regiment on the other side of that defensive feature - on the "inside" toward Foshan, rather than on the "outside" where he was now - but that had been forbidden by the Keran government because of the high-value property in this area. Grishin suddenly wished he had done what Sparks had, and driven his tanks right into the houses and business buildings there, the local government be damned. But it was too late for that.

Besides, while his motivations were different, he was no less a warrior than the alien creatures he now confronted. And while his personal courage had wavered for a moment after they had appeared, he was no longer afraid.

He knew that there was only one option left: to try and break through to link up with the Terran tank regiment, if it still survived. Against so many warriors, the legionnaires stood little chance of survival. Grishin smiled to himself. He had always wished that he could die in a modern-day Battle of Camarón, where centuries before a small band of legionnaires had held off an army of nearly two thousand men in a battle that had become legend. He had never thought this wish would come true. So few ever had.

Signaling his tank commanders to wheel right and come line-abreast facing the Kreelan warriors who stood patiently waiting for them, Grishin rendered his men a sharp salute, which they returned. Legionnaires, to the last.

"*Camarón!*" Grishin bellowed as the survivors of the *1er REC* charged the enemy line, guns thundering.

***

Tesh-Dar had quickly become bored with digging the humans out of their strange vehicles. Leaving Kamal-Utai and Li'ara-Zhurah to lead the warriors who had jumped from their doomed ship, for they could not keep up with her, Tesh-Dar raced along the human lines at an inhuman speed, far faster than any human being had ever run. She had seen in her mind's eye a nearby group of human warriors that had no vehicles, and went to meet them.

As she did, a group of warriors from one of the other ships was dropping onto that part of the human line, and the humans fired their projectile weapons at them. While the warriors preferred their swords and claws, they had no hesitation in unslinging their own projectile weapons and firing back. Tesh-Dar was proud to see that they were far more accurate than the humans, with nearly every round finding its target.

With a final great leap, her heart pounding with anticipation, she landed next to the strange trench they had dug for themselves and unleashed her *grakh'ta* whip.

***

Soldat 1e Classe Roland Mills had joined the *Légion étrangère* for the same reason countless others had over the centuries: he was an adventurer and soldier of fortune. Aside from his rugged good looks and muscular build, he was unlike the romantic stereotype of the legionnaire: he wasn't trying to escape his past or avoid pursuit by any authorities. In fact, he came from a very respectable English family back on Earth, and had never committed a crime. While he would have lightly scoffed at anyone who thought him a scholar, he was nonetheless quite well-educated. By all accounts, he would have made an excellent barrister and family man, except for one tiny quirk: he was a hopeless adrenaline junky. He had immersed himself in virtually every extreme and nearly-suicidal endeavor he could find, but eventually they came to bore him.

Then one day, he happened to see a news broadcast that played a bit about the Alliance *Légion étrangère*, and came to see it - unrealistically - as a nearly non-stop thrill-ride. Over his family's vehement protestations, he signed up two days later at the recruiting center in Paris.

Nearly eighteen months later, despite having had to adjust his perception of reality of what the Legion really was, he had come to really enjoy it. Learning French had been a snap for him, as had the other basic skills he had been taught.

In the end, he had gotten what he had hoped for: he was selected for the elite *2ème REP* and was given jump training (although he already knew how to jump and paraglide). He had loved every minute of it.

When he found the Alliance was deploying every one of the Legion's combat regiments to Keran to protect it against a possible (if far-fetched) alien threat, he had been elated. He had never seen combat, and was hoping that this would be his chance.

Now, however, elation wasn't the emotion he felt. It was gut-wrenching fear melded with the determination to survive as alien starships thundered overhead, dropping hundreds - thousands - of alien paratroops right on top of the regiment's lines. He had been looking for the ultimate thrill, and he was afraid that he might have found it.

"Fire!" his squad leader shouted, echoing the orders passed along the line of the entire regiment as the aliens flew down on their version of paragliders. Over a thousand legionnaires fired their rifles and automatic weapons nearly straight up at their swarming attackers. A handful of aliens, then dozens, began to fall from the sky, dead and wounded.

But the enemy proved to be far from helpless, even as they glided toward the ground. They had their own rifles, and with inhuman accuracy began to kill legionnaires. Some also dropped what looked like hand grenades where legionnaires had bunched together. But when they detonated they released an enormous electrical flux like lightning, turning everything - flesh, metal, and anything else - in a radius of four meters into smoldering carbon.

Easily outnumbered two to one, the legionnaires did what they had done since Camarón: they stood their ground, fought, and died.

Roland Mills, however, wasn't ready to die yet. He was terrified, but this was what he had joined the Legion for, after all: the opportunity to participate in unrestricted mayhem. Combat was the ultimate adrenaline rush.

Taking aim at the nearest cloud of warriors bearing down on their lines, he opened fire, emptying an entire magazine into their formation and taking grim satisfaction at seeing six of them plummet to the ground, out of control.

"Mills, *down!*" one of the other legionnaires in his squad shouted. Mills dropped to the bottom of the trench as a warrior swept down behind him. Three of his squad mates blasted the thing to bits with their rifles, spattering Mills with bloody gore.

Suddenly, over the unbelievable din of men and aliens shouting and screaming and the non-stop firing of rifles by both sides, he distinctly heard a strange *whip-crack!* from just beyond the parapet around the trench. Mills looked up just in time to see what looked like a set of thin, barbed tentacles snap over the top of the parapet to wrap themselves around one of his fellow legionnaires. The man screamed in fear and agony as the metal barbs pierced his flesh and the whip-like tails of whatever the thing was encircled his limbs and torso.

Ignoring the chaos around him, Mills leaped to his feet, drawing his combat knife in the same motion, intending to cut the man free of this thing that attacked him.

But in the blink of an eye and with a howl of terror the legionnaire was bodily snapped over the top of the parapet, as if he were a small fish that a fisherman had snatched from the water.

Trying to erase the image of the man's terrified expression from his mind, Mills ducked in time to avoid having his head taken off by a Kreelan warrior's sword. Marveling for just an instant the he was facing an alien, he lunged forward, blocking her sword arm with his left fist as he drove his knife into her gut below her armored breast plate.

The warrior screamed in pain, but was far from mortally stricken. She slashed at him with the claws of her free hand, tearing the cloth camouflage cover from his back armor. Kneeing her in the groin to throw her off-balance, he pulled his knife from her belly and rammed it up under her throat, the knife's tip burying itself in her brain.

Whip-crack!

Another legionnaire shrieked as he was seized by the devilish weapon and heaved by some unseen force from the trench.

But this time Mills had seen something he had not the first time: he saw where the tendrils had come from over the parapet. Pausing only for a moment to pick up a rifle and shoot a warrior in the back of the head, he threw a hand grenade over the parapet in the direction the legionnaire had disappeared.

***

Tesh-Dar bared her fangs in a sort of primal ecstasy that she had not felt since the Change, since the day she was accepted as a priestess into the order of the Desh-Ka. Having trained for combat since birth, she was finally experiencing war in its true form, without any of the rules that governed the challenges in the arena. Great would be the glory she brought to the Empress.

While her warriors occupied the humans in the trench, she allowed herself a minor indulgence. She knew that she should not be standing in the open as she was, focused on her prey. But it was an entertainment that she would allow herself. For now. With the whips wrapped around her next victim, she gripped the *grakh'ta* with both mighty hands and threw her entire body into the motion of snapping the whip back, reeling in the hapless human warrior. The human came flying out of the trench, arcing through the air toward her. As the creature drew to arm's length, her left hand snapped to her short sword in a move no human being could match. Twirling aside as her victim flew by, the sword sang from the sheath at her waist and neatly decapitated the human without the blade touching the tendril of the *grakh'ta* that was wrapped about its neck. She flicked the blade with her wrist, ridding it of most of the human's blood before she replaced the sword in its sheath.

She was just snapping her weapon free of the body when she sensed the small object sailing toward her. Abandoning the *grakh'ta*, she leaped clear as the grenade went off, shredding both the whip and the legionnaire's body. Had she not been a warrior priestess with her heightened senses, she would have been killed.

With her blood singing glory to her Empress, Tesh-Dar leaped into the trench to find the one who had come close to killing her, to honor him with death.

***

Mills's world had become a snarling orgy of stabbing, hacking, kicking, and grappling with the alien warriors. Few rifle shots rang out now, as the enemy was in so tightly among the legionnaires that a bullet was as likely to kill a friend as a foe. Besides, the enemy was simply too close: at one point, while Mills was fighting one alien, he suddenly realized that he had his back pressed up against another alien who was doing her best to strangle a legionnaire. Suddenly, all four of them were blown into a struggling heap as a grenade went off nearby. Mills was the only one to get to his feet alive.

In addition to his knife, which was by now soaked with blood and had a blade that was nicked in a dozen places, he held a Kreelan sword. He had never received training in how to use any edged weapons but his knife and bayonet, but he had nonetheless put it to good use. About as long as his arm and slightly curved, the sword had proved to be an excellent weapon in trench fighting.

A Kreelan warrior suddenly came staggering backward toward him, two legionnaires clutching at her arms, and he stabbed the alien in the back of the neck with the sword.

"*Down!*" he yelled at his two newfound companions as he saw another legionnaire, badly wounded, hurl himself into the midst of at least half a dozen warriors who had cornered two more legionnaires and were hacking them to death. Mills had seen that the man clutched a grenade in each hand, and the resulting explosions sent bits of bodies, shredded clothing, and twisted body armor for fifteen meters in every direction.

As he got back to his feet, helping up his compatriots, he saw something that made his skin crawl. Looking down the trench toward the end of the regiment's line, perhaps twenty meters away, was what looked like nothing so much as a living threshing machine. But it wasn't a machine. It was an alien warrior. She was huge compared to the others, and bigger than Mills, who stood a full two meters tall and weighed in at one hundred kilos of solid muscle. In one hand she had a short sword, and both it and the claws of her other hand were soaked with blood.

Eyes wide with disbelief, he watched as a legionnaire emptied an entire magazine from his rifle into her chest. But it was as if the bullets simply passed through her; he could even see the spray of dirt they kicked up from the trench wall behind her.

The warrior strode right up to the legionnaire and with what Mills thought must be a look of contempt stabbed her claws into his chest, right through his torso armor. Screaming in agony, blood spraying from his lips, she lifted him from his feet and tossed him from the trench as if he weighed no more than a piece of paper.

Suddenly, he realized what had been behind the whip-like weapon that had snatched some of the legionnaires from the trench earlier. It had been her.

The other Kreelan warriors moved aside as she passed, rendering what appeared to be some sort of salute. Killing every single legionnaire who stood before her with flashing steel or outstretched claws, she finally came to a stop directly in front of him, her strange cat's-eyes blazing, her entire body spattered with human blood.

As if it were some sort of signal, the rest of the Kreelan warriors in the trench eased away from their human opponents. The exhausted legionnaires - all too few of them now - used the unexpected respite to catch their breath, wondering just what was happening.

"What does she want, Mills?" one of the legionnaires next to him whispered, afraid to break the spell that had suddenly fallen over them all.

The warrior herself answered, but not with words. Raising her right arm, she pointed at Mills. Then she handed her weapons to one of the other warriors, who took them for safekeeping.

"I think," Mills said slowly, "she wants a bloody duel. But why me?" He wasn't the biggest or toughest man in the regiment, or the best close-in fighter. On the other hand, he was probably the biggest and toughest who was still standing. Of the regiment's roughly thirteen hundred men, he guessed that maybe a hundred, if that, were still alive.

"We'll fight with you," the legionnaire said. Mills didn't remember his name, as he was from one of the other companies.

"No," Mills told him, dropping his own weapons. "Let's see where this leads."

"But-"

"Quiet," one of the others, a *sergent*, ordered. "Mills, do what you need to do."

You always wanted the ultimate thrill, Mills chided himself. *Well, it looks like you finally found it.*

***

Tesh-Dar knew the one before her had thrown the grenade that had come close - in a very relative sense - to killing her earlier. She had never seen him, did not recognize him by scent, and had not seen him with her second sight. But among the gifts she had was the ability to sense some of the threads of time and action, cause and effect, that were woven together into the river of destiny. She could not read the future and predict where that river might lead. However, she could sometimes see a murky vision of the past that she had not witnessed through her other senses, a place where the river had once flowed. She could not see the river's trace for others, only for those events directly tied to herself.

And so it was that she now stood before this human. She had not had any idea what he would look like, or how fiercely he would fight. She only knew that he was the one she sought.

Around her, the other warriors gave the surviving humans some respite. Few were left now, but they had fought well and with great honor. Many of Her Children had died at their hands, and Tesh-Dar mourned their deaths deeply; not that they had died and were no longer with her, but that they could never again glorify the Empress in battle. For Tesh-Dar's people, death - honorably won - was the completion, the fulfillment, of life in Her eyes, and meant an eternal place in the afterlife among the Ancient Ones.

She pointed to the crude steps leading from the trench to flat ground above and led the human there. What motivated these creatures to burrow like sand-worms she did not know or care to understand. All she knew was that it would hardly serve as an impromptu arena.

***

Mills followed the huge warrior out of the trench and onto the ground behind it, his feet leaving small clouds of dust as he walked. He happened to see the alien's feet, shod in sandals, and noticed that she left no tracks at all. Nothing. A chill ran down his spine, wondering if she was some sort of supernatural creature. Perversely, that thought gave him even more of a high. He wasn't afraid, he was completely "juiced" as some of his friends might have said.

Behind him, a silent and altogether unnatural procession followed: the hundreds of Kreelan warriors and the comparative handful of surviving legionnaires, mixed together. The latter did not exactly seem to be prisoners, for the Kreelans did not seem to care if they came along or not, or if they kept their weapons, as long as they did not use them (the few who had were quickly butchered). But the legionnaires went anyway, for they had no idea what else to do, and few wanted to risk trying to take their leave of the Kreelans. As word spread that Mills would be facing off against the big warrior, all of them wanted to see the spectacle as much as the Kreelans apparently did.

The warriors formed a large circle around Mills and his opponent. The legionnaires, somewhat emboldened now by the mere fact of their continued survival, pressed up close behind the warriors who formed the inner edge of the circle so they could see.

Mills stood about two paces from the warrior, who kept her eyes locked on his. He had no idea what to do to get this particular ball rolling, so he simply waited for her to make the first move.

***

It was time. The human clearly had no idea what to expect or what to do, which was understandable, as he was not of the Way. He had no way of knowing that this challenge, defined by what may have been nothing more than a lucky throw of a grenade, would determine not only his fate, but that of his fellow animals, as well. She would not show him leniency, but she would show him fairness. She would use none of her special powers, for that would be no challenge in such a match, and would bring the Empress no glory. Even her claws, she would not use, for the human had none. She would not give the match away, for she knew that she could hardly lose, but she would measure him by his determination and will to survive.

Assuming one of many choices of combat stances, she opened the challenge with a restrained open-handed strike against the human animal.

***

Mills shook his head to clear his brain as he got to his feet, his ears ringing from the blow the alien had just landed on him. He knew intellectually that it had been little more than an open-handed slap, but it came at him like lightning and felt like a freight train had slammed into the side of his head.

"Get the *salope*, Mills!" one of the legionnaires suddenly yelled, tossing any remaining caution about the warriors surrounding them to the wind. His shout of encouragement led to a groundswell of others, and in but a moment every single legionnaire was shouting for him.

It was what he needed. He didn't expect to win against this alien killing machine, but he would do his best to make her remember the men of the *2ème REP.*

He raised his hands to protect his face, elbows held in tight to his sides, and moved closer to her. One of her arms shot out, but he was ready this time. He managed to grab hold of her arm and pull her slightly off-balance. As she grabbed for him with her other hand - *Damn those claws!* he thought, cursing - he pulled her in even closer and suddenly slammed his forehead into her chin.

With a surprised grunt she roughly shoved him away, and he couldn't escape the feeling that she had simply allowed him to get away with it. He had seen some of the things she could do, and he could hardly accept that his skills were a match for hers. But he didn't care. He moved in again quickly, leaving himself largely open to attack as he concentrated on his own offense.

***

While the human was no match for her skills, he was clearly determined, and continued to come after her no matter how many times she batted him away or threw him to the ground. His face was bruised and bleeding now, and he wheezed when he breathed. The knuckles of his hands were bloodied - with both her blood and his own - and no doubt some of his bones were broken.

But the human doggedly continued to attack her, even as he approached complete exhaustion. At one point they were locked in an embrace after he had moved in close to her, sustaining a rain of blows to get close enough to try and throw her to the ground. She had actually found herself holding him up for a moment as he clung to her, panting for breath. Sensing he had regained enough energy to at least stay on his feet, she released him, sending him back with another set of blows to the head that again knocked him to the ground.

The humans intermingled with her warriors - a strange phenomenon that she would never have expected - shouted their encouragement in gibberish, and she had to credit them with spirited support. Soulless creatures they might be, beyond Her love and light, but she could not fault their warrior spirit. Truly, she thought, the Empire had found a worthy race to bring honor to the Empress in battle.

She let the human continue to batter himself senseless against her, until at last, finally, he simply had not the strength to rise again. But even then, exhausted and beaten, he still struggled to rise, to fight.

"Enough," she murmured to herself, bringing the ritual challenge to an end.

***

"*Kazh*," the big warrior said softly.

At least that's what Mills thought she might have said - whatever it meant - over the ringing in his head and the sound of his own gasping for air. The legionnaires continued to shout their encouragement, their voices hoarse and frayed from yelling so long. Lying face down in the dirt, his body was totally, utterly exhausted. Every muscle quivered, and he could hardly move at all. He was bruised everywhere, and he knew that at least a few bones must be broken, mostly in his hands where they had hit the Kreelan's jaw, which was as hard as steel plate. Blood was running into both his eyes from cuts on his forehead from where she had hit him or her claws had lightly cut him, and he had dozens of other cuts everywhere that wasn't covered by his body armor. But he knew those cuts were merely incidental: she had clearly not used her claws as weapons, or he would have been dead in the first few seconds of the fight.

"Fuck," he gasped through lips that looked like crushed tomatoes, streaming blood down his chin. He didn't have to poke his tongue along his gums to know that he'd lost a few teeth: one he'd accidentally swallowed right after the Kreelan's fist had knocked it loose; the rest he'd managed to spit out.

He tried to get up, but simply couldn't. Finally, he gave up and simply lay there. There was nothing more he could do.

Suddenly, he felt a hand grip his arm and turn him over. It was the warrior. He offered up a bloody smile, knowing that she, too, had her own set of cuts and bruises, and he was the proud culprit. At this point he didn't care if she had gone easy and let him have some mercy hits against her. He'd managed to bloody her up a bit, and that was all that mattered.

The legionnaires fell silent as they waited for the axe, literally, to fall on Mills.

Much to their surprise - and his - it didn't. The big Kreelan merely nodded her head, then reached out with her hands to snip off a bit of his hair - no mean feat, considering that it was barely a finger's breadth in length. This she tucked into a small black leather pouch on her belt.

Then, standing up, she said something in her language loud enough for all the gathered warriors to hear. They all said something back in unison, and hammered their left fists against their right breasts.

With that, the huge warrior turned and walked away. The other warriors quietly followed after her, leaving eighty-seven very confused but infinitely relieved Legion paratroopers behind.

TWENTY

After the connection to Grishin had broken, Steph followed Sparks as he led the staff and crew of his command vehicle through the rubble of the building and out into the street. While many of the buildings looked fairly intact, most of them had suffered at least superficial damage from the blast when the cruiser had crashed, and there wasn't a single unbroken pane of glass in sight. The air was still heavy with smoke and dust from the shells the Kreelan ships had fired at his command vehicle and the other vehicles that made up the regiment's field headquarters. But the other vehicles had not been quite so lucky as his: the other three command vehicles of the headquarters company were smoldering wrecks. She looked up as what looked like snow started falling around them, carried by the artificial wind generated by the firestorm that was consuming the inner part of the city.

"Ash," Sparks said in a low voice, answering her unasked question as his eyes warily scanned the street. There had still been a lot of civilians out in the open when the Kreelans struck, despite the best efforts of Sparks and the other members of the company to convince the locals to find some sort of shelter. Sparks himself had been the last one under cover, staying until the very last second in the street to try and convince even a single civilian to get to safety. But all they were concerned about was the damage his vehicles were causing.

The air was filled with the cries and wails of the injured and the bereaved. Bodies were strewn haphazardly along the sidewalks, mostly victims of the Kreelan guns that had targeted the command vehicles. Others were victims of the titanic blast that had torn out the heart of the city, but they were far enough away here that most of those casualties were from flying debris. Still others were curled on the street or wandering, helpless, their hands covering their eyes from the pain of being flash-blinded.

Steph captured it all on video, as always making voice notes. But she noticed that her voice held an uncharacteristic flutter: she had never seen devastation on this scale, and the shock of it had deeply unsettled her. She momentarily focused the view on an Arab-descended woman near the center of the street, next to a car that she must have been in before the attack. She was sitting on the rough cobblestones, cradling a young girl - perhaps four years old - in her lap. Steph didn't know Arabic, but she didn't need to: the woman was shrieking with the anguish only a mother can truly know. From the amount of blood on the child's body, it was clear to Steph that the young girl was dead.

Steph had seen anguish and horror before, but never quite like this. Suddenly, it was too much. Dropping the rifle she now carried, she fell to her knees and vomited.

"Come on, miss," Sergeant Hadley, now her personal bodyguard, told her as he gently took hold of her arm to help her up. "We've got to keep moving."

Nodding, wiping the foulness from her mouth with one hand as she picked up the rifle with the other, Steph got to her feet. On unsteady legs, she let Hadley help her along to keep up with the colonel's pace.

"First Battalion shouldn't be more than half a block from here," the operations officer was saying. "We ought to be seeing tanks popping out of buildings all over the place."

"I'm not so sure, major," Sparks said as he checked the corner of a cross street, peering around the corner to make sure there weren't any enemy waiting for them. "I think the damn Kreelans pounded everything that was-"

"*You!*"

All of them turned at the sound of the voice. A middle-aged man, bloodied and dressed only in torn rags that once must have been nice clothes of the style the Chinese wore here, stood in the street holding a young man, what was left of him, in his arms.

"It was *you!*" the man cried. "This is your doing!" Then he yelled at them in Chinese, then in Arabic. Other survivors, up and down the street, took notice of the commotion. "*They* came because of *you*," the man went on, moving slowly toward them with his grisly burden. "My son died because of *you!*"

More people were gathering now, their faces ugly as they muttered in a mixture of Arabic and Chinese.

"Shit," Steph heard Hadley whisper. "Get behind me." Without asking questions, she slid behind him, noticing that while he wasn't pointing his rifle at anyone, he wasn't exactly pointing it away, either.

"The aliens were coming anyway," Sparks told the man calmly. Raising his voice so the crowd could hear him, he said, "The aliens have been planning this attack for over a year. We came to help protect you. We-"

"*No!*" The man screamed as he staggered closer with his son's limp form. "Your ship found them and led them to us," he cried. "A *Terran* ship gave away our world to them. You played us for pawns as your kind always has. Then you came with your weapons of war to fight them on our world. *Our world!*"

By now, the crowd had grown to well over a hundred people, with more coming to see what was going on.

"Listen, mister," Sparks tried one last time, frustration clearly evident in his voice. "We've got to reach my tanks before the enemy gets here-"

"*You* are the enemy!" the man cried, and the crowd's murmuring grew to an angry growl.

Steph noticed through her video pickup that people were picking up bricks, broken cobblestones, even big shards of glass. She was holding her rifle with a white-knuckled grip. She had fired a weapon before, but had never actually shot at anyone. And she sure as hell didn't want to shoot any of these poor people.

As the crowd began to close in, a new noise rose above their jeering: screaming. It wasn't the wailing of those who had lost their loved ones, or those who were in agony: it was a scream of fear, echoing from a multitude of voices.

Suddenly a handful of people rounded a corner about a hundred meters down the street in the direction of the city's burning center. All young men, they were running flat out toward where the crowd now surrounded Sparks and his troops. Then a torrent of people, not able to run quite as fast, surged around the corner, all of them screaming in terror. There were hundreds of them, then thousands, a river of terrified people that quickly filled the street.

Sparks knew what was coming. Walking up to the man who led the crowd surrounding them, he grabbed him by the arms and leaned over the man's dead son until their noses nearly touched. "The aliens are coming. Now. Let us go so we can fight them or you're going to all die right here."

The man didn't move, but simply stared at Sparks with accusatory eyes.

But the others crowded around them got the message. Even those who didn't understand English knew that something terrible was behind the crush of people stampeding toward them. Dropping their bricks and bits of glass, they turned to run.

"Get inside!" Sparks ordered as he let go of the man and dashed to the side of the street, kicking down the still-standing door of a shop. The others followed him.

Inside, Steph looked at the man who suddenly stood alone in the street, still holding his son. Then, in the blink of an eye, he was gone, shoved to the ground and trampled by thousands of screaming people.

Somewhere farther down the street, in the direction the mob was headed, a tank's main gun fired.

***

"Fuck," Coyle said as she wiped the blood from her lip. The unexpected shock wave that preceded the shells that hit her platoon's position had slammed her head against the commander's miniature control console. Its edges were padded, but even that didn't help when your lips were rammed into it full-force. "Status!" she barked.

"Green," Sergeant Yuri Kirov, her gunner, replied. "Weapons are up and ready."

"We can move," Mannie, the driver, told her, "but I've got two caution lights on the right-hand drive. Shouldn't be a problem unless you want to go flying cross-country."

"Let's just see if we can dig ourselves out of this shit," she told him. She had tried opening the hatch, but couldn't: it was blocked by rubble. Shifting views from her cupola sensors to the gunner's sight, then to the driver's sensors, it was clear that her Wolfhound was completely buried by the building they were in. "Mannie..." she paused. She wasn't sure if it would be smarter to try and move out of the rubble slowly to minimize the risk of damaging the tracks and the other equipment on the outside of the hull, or just gun it and get it over with. Normally, she would have gone slowly, but if there were Kreelans around, she'd be a sitting duck until the turret was clear. "Shit. Mannie, we're going to have to risk throwing a track. If there are bad guys out there, I don't want them to shoot the crap out of us while we're being all careful-like getting out of this dump."

"Roger that," he said, squirming a bit deeper into his seat as he gripped the controls. "Hang on to your hats, boys and girls," he warned as he gently goosed the Wolfhound's accelerator. Less experienced drivers might have just stomped on it, which Mannie knew would have most likely made a spectacular display of spinning the tracks and spewing debris everywhere, while not moving them a whit. Driving a heavy armored vehicle really well required more finesse than most people realized. He felt the meter-wide tracks pull tight, just to the point where the big tank lurched. Then at just the right moment he goosed the accelerator, sending a hundred and twenty-five tons of fighting steel through what was left of the building, scattering bits of brick and glass everywhere into the street beyond.

"Jesus!" Coyle cried as the vision displays showed what was ahead of them: the street was filled with people.

"Oh, fuck," Mannie whispered, slamming on the Wolfhound's brakes, rocking the huge vehicle to a hard stop. "God help me..."

"Take it easy," Coyle said, her voice brittle. "It's my responsibility, Mannie," she whispered as the close-in display showed her the bodies that had been crushed under her tank's tracks. There must have been at least half a dozen. If she listened closely, which she desperately tried not to, she could hear the screaming from at least one person whose legs were pinned under them. "Listen, I'll go out and help-"

"Stay put," Yuri, the gunner, said quietly. "Look at them all. They're running."

"You'd run, too, if somebody had just run over a bunch of your friends with a tank, you bastard!" Mannie shouted at him, tears in his eyes.

"No, Mannie," Yuri said. "They're not running from *us*; they're running from *them*." He hit the controls that echoed his gunsight display to the driver and commander stations. In the magnified view, it was clear that something far more horrible than their tank was stalking the people outside. For the first time, they saw the real-life version of the artist's renderings they had all laughed at during the pre-drop briefings, thinking the female warrior aliens had been a great joke.

But the lewd versions that a lot of the troops had come up with weren't so funny as Coyle and her crewmen watched a line of alien warriors moving along behind a group of two or three hundred people that had been streaming past the building, cutting down any that came within reach with swords and claws.

"Shit," Coyle cursed. "Mannie, move forward slowly. We've got to clear this building and get into a firing position away from those people." Firing the main gun over the heads of the fleeing civilians was out of the question: the overpressure near the muzzle of the barrel when the gun fired was so high that it would kill anyone inside half a dozen meters.

"No!" Mannie shouted, horrified. "I can't. There are more people in front of us!" The crowd had largely run past by now, but there were still dead and wounded lying in the street, most of them casualties of the Kreelan attack against the tanks.

"Mannie, if we don't move, we're going to get our asses kicked!" Coyle shouted at him. "*Move forward slowly, corporal!*"

"Okay," Mannie whispered, taking his foot off the brake and gingerly applying pressure to the accelerator. The tank's massive twin electric motors, powered by an equally huge bank of fuel cells deep in its armored belly, smoothly turned the drive sprockets and put the Wolfhound in motion again.

"Mannie," Coyle said more gently, "adjust the vertical gain on your forward display so you don't see what's down on the street. Just keep us from hitting the buildings, okay?"

"Roger," he managed, doing as she had told him. It wouldn't matter, because the images of the crushed bodies were burned into his brain.

"Shit," Yuri said, keeping the turret aligned in the direction of the warriors. "They see us." A number of the Kreelans looked straight at them and cried out to the others. But they kept coming after the civilians, driving them like cattle right toward the tank that now sat idling uncertainly in the middle of the street.

"They'd have to be blind not to," Coyle said as she scanned all around them in her vision display to make sure nothing took them by surprise. Aside from the still-rising fireball at the city center, all she could see were screaming people being pursued by the line of Kreelans. "Dammit, we're not going to have enough clearance from the civvies for the main gun. Yuri, use the coax."

"I don't have a clear shot," he told her, praying that she wouldn't order him to fire, anyway. In his digital gunsight, human heads bobbed in the sight picture as people ran past: if he fired, he would accidentally decapitate at least a few.

"Crap," Coyle snarled as she tried to bring her own weapon to bear. A three-barreled gatling gun that fired twenty millimeter shells at over a thousand rounds per minute, it was mounted high enough that it cleared the heads of the fleeing civilians in her own remote gunsight display. There was only one problem: it was jammed and wouldn't move. "It must be jimmied with rubble."

"Grenades!" Yuri warned as he saw some of the Kreelans, whose attention was now fixed on the tank, detach some sort of weapon from their belts that could only be some sort of anti-tank grenade. The weapons glowed with electric fire, and he definitely didn't like the look of them.

Coyle had no choice: risk killing some of the civilians or have the Kreelans attack her vehicle. "Close-in mortar," she warned, "danger close." She lifted up a clear cover over a small red button and jammed it with her finger. Her sight display switched to a computer-generated overhead view of what was around the vehicle. Clearly displayed were yellow-colored dots - unidentified, possible targets - representing the Kreelan warriors, and she quickly drew a box around them with her finger.

In the roof of the massive turret was one of the vehicle's close-in defense weapons: a small mortar that could fire one or more forty millimeter smart grenades. It could rotate and adjust the distance the projectiles would fire, covering the area she had marked on her display.

She hit the glowing "Fire" button on the weapon control panel, and the mortar pumped out eight rounds in two seconds with precisely controlled spurts of highly compressed air. The weapon couldn't reach more than a hundred meters, but that was more than enough for what Coyle needed.

The line of Kreelan warriors suddenly disintegrated as the small but potent mortar rounds exploded among them at waist height, with a shrapnel pattern that expanded horizontally like an opening fan. It was none too soon: a few more seconds and they would have been within throwing range for their grenades. As it was, they were close enough that some of the shrapnel pinged off of *Chiquita's* heavy armor

Amazingly, none of the civilians were injured, the bodies of the Kreelans having absorbed nearly all of the shrapnel.

The civilians safely past, Yuri opened up with the coaxial gun, another twenty millimeter cannon. The tank was suddenly filled with the weapon's growl as it spewed shells into the few surviving Kreelans, who were still dazed by the mortar explosions. The alien bodies exploded under Yuri's withering fire, and in a few seconds there were no targets left to shoot at.

"Sergeant Coyle?" a voice suddenly crackled over her headset. "Can you hear me?"

Breathing a huge sigh of relief that at least one of her platoon's other tanks was alive, she said, "I never thought I'd be happy to hear your voice, Gomez, but we're damned glad to see ya." In her cupola display, she watched as Gomez's tank moved to one side of hers, keeping its turret pointed in the opposite direction from where Coyle's turret was aimed, covering their collective backs. She looked at her console, her suspicion confirmed: the tanks only had communications in line-of-sight mode by laser. The Kreelans must have done something to mess up any radio frequency communications.

"Any word on the other two tracks?" she asked, wondering about the other two tanks in her platoon.

There was a slight pause. "They both bought it," Gomez said somberly. "Ivanova's tank took what must've been a twenty centimeter round from one of those enemy cruisers right on the turret mount. She didn't stand a chance. I don't know what happened to Inoue, but his track was a burning wreck. No survivors."

"Fuck," Coyle hissed, leaning her head against the coaming of the commander's hatch. "Any word from company or higher?"

"Zilch," Gomez said somberly. "We just dug our way out of that crap we were buried in, so you'd have had a better chance than us to hear anything. Only thing working is the fucking lasers, and all the whiskers on our left side got scraped off when we dug out of the building. So we can only talk and hear on the right side."

"Okay," Coyle said as she popped the hatch. She needed to try and free up her gatling gun. "Take up position in echelon left," she said, which would put Gomez's tank to her left so the other vehicle's communications lasers would be able to network with hers, "and let's move back toward the battalion CP to see if we can find anybody else. Surely there must be someone else left alive in this clusterfuck."

"Oh, shit," Yuri whispered as he scanned back and forth with the turret to cover their portion of the street and what lay beyond. "We've got company. And lots of it."

Coyle looked up from hammering at the gatling gun's mount to see what must have been hundreds, if not more, Kreelan warriors come striding around a corner a few hundred meters down the cross street from the intersection where the tanks now sat.

The warriors paused momentarily as they caught sight of the pair of tanks. Then they broke into a run straight toward the two human vehicles, and Coyle's skin crawled as the Kreelans howled their bloodlust.

Hammering one last desperate time at a bent pin that was all that was keeping the gatling gun's mount from moving freely, she grunted in satisfaction as the weapon suddenly slewed around on its mount, centering itself. Coyle dropped back into her seat, the hatch hissing shut behind her. "Jesus," she said in wonder as she looked at the display. "They must not have a fucking clue what they're attacking." The Kreelans were running headlong toward them like a bunch of primitives who had never seen an armored vehicle. "Fine by me," she muttered. "Dumbass alien bitches in the open," she called out her own version of the target type. "Load flechette, area fire."

"Up!" Yuri instantly replied, having already selected the round he knew she'd want.

"Fire!"

The tank rocked back as its twenty centimeter cannon - the same size as those fitted on the Terran heavy cruisers, but not as powerful or fast-loading - fired with a gout of flame. Propelled by a powerful binary liquid propellant that was injected into the breech and ignited, the flechette round wasn't simply a gigantic equivalent of a shotgun round. Much like the close-in defense weapon that could cover an area designated by the tank's commander, the flechette round could cover a larger or smaller area, as necessary. After he'd loaded it, Yuri had swiped his thumb across the line of Kreelan warriors shown in his display, designating the entire mass as a target. The tank's computers did the rest.

As the round sped downrange, miniature explosive charges inside detonated at precise intervals, spreading the thousands of flechettes into a broad horizontal pattern to cover most of the Kreelan line.

The results were horrific. Fully the first three ranks of alien warriors were cut to ribbons in a spray of bloody mist by the finger-length razor-sharp projectiles. Their breast armor was strong, but not strong enough to stand up to flechettes moving at three thousand meters per second. Coyle, as happy as she was to give the enemy a pounding, was sickened at the sight. The street was instantly awash in blood and bits of bodies. While she had fired flechette rounds at the ranges for training, of course, she had never actually used one on live targets. With the exception of a few of the senior officers and NCOs who had served during the St. Petersburg war, none of the soldiers of the Terran units had actually seen combat before this. Despite years of training, it was a rude awakening.

"Oh, God," Yuri said in nauseated wonder.

"That should slow them down..." Coyle said with a shaking voice as she clamped down on her own urgent desire to vomit.

But the alien warriors didn't slow down. If anything, the massacre of their front ranks sent them into even more of a frenzy. Coyle couldn't be sure, but it didn't seem like rage, either: it was like they were all having some sort of alien orgasm. But they weren't stupid: the mass of warriors instantly broke up into groups. Most of them headed for the cover of the surrounding buildings, while a couple of groups continued toward the tanks, running fast and weaving to make harder targets.

As Yuri tried to blast them with his coaxial weapon, Coyle ordered the driver, "Mannie, turn us around and head down the street toward where the battalion CP was. Gomez, echelon left." She needed to get the tanks away from the buildings the Kreelans were swarming into: if they could clamber through the rubble to this side of the buildings, they'd be in great positions to hit her tanks from above with whatever weapons they might have for the job. While the gatling guns on the roof could nail them on the upper floors, the main guns couldn't elevate that far.

Then again, they didn't necessarily have to.

"Target, building," Coyle snapped to Yuri as she moved the pipper on her command console over the nearest building the Kreelans had headed for, showing Yuri the target she wanted serviced. "HE-Thermo."

There was a brief whine as the turret's primary magazine whirred, bringing up the type of round she wanted, then a solid *thunk* as the autoloader rammed it into the breech. A second later, the gun now aligned to the target, Yuri barked, "Up!"

"Fire!"

Chiquita's main gun roared, sending the high-explosive thermobaric round into the already heavily damaged building across the street. Unlike a regular high-explosive round that exploded in much the same fashion, if with more effect, than its progenitor TNT centuries before, the HE-thermobaric rounds used a variety of chemical and metallic compounds, detonated in a precise fashion, to greatly enhance the weapon's explosive blast. They weren't useful in every situation or against every target, but in this case it was just what the doctor ordered: the round streaked through a window to hit the back wall of the room within, and the resulting fiery blast and shock wave blew out the entire front wall. A moment later, the roof sagged and what was left of the three-story building suddenly collapsed into a heap of flaming debris. She didn't see any bodies, but Coyle knew that if any of the enemy were in there, they wouldn't be a problem anymore.

"Punch it, Mannie," she said, keeping a close eye on her displays as the big tank rumbled down the street, with Gomez's alongside. She needed to find the rest of the battalion. Because as powerful as her tanks were, stuck here in the close confines of the city, it was only a matter of time before the Kreelans killed them.

***

"Colonel, this is suicide," the operations officer argued quietly. He kept his voice down because he didn't want to embarrass Sparks in front of the others.

Holed up in the shop they'd sought refuge in, the others looked out the remains of the front window, watching the terrified mob. They had barricaded the door to keep the river of people from flooding into their safe haven, but most of the civilians weren't interested in finding a hideout: they were simply trying to flee.

Momentarily ignoring the major, Sparks finally caught a glimpse of what had caused the panic outside: a mass of alien warriors, looking just like Sato had described them, were driving them down the street like cattle. But instead of using prods, the aliens were using swords and other weapons. The Kreelans didn't seem to be intent on massacring the civilians; it was more like they were simply trying to get them out of the way. Even at that, they were still killing dozens every second, hacking their way through the people at the rear of the mob who were penned in by the crush of people in front of them.

He didn't have any illusions about their own chances of survival: while he couldn't see them clearly, there must have been hundreds of warriors, and he only had half a dozen soldiers and a journalist. He knew at least some of his tanks had survived, because he could hear the piercing *crack* of their main guns and the rumbling purr of their gatling guns somewhere in the distance. But he couldn't see a way to reach them without being swallowed up by the mob. And the only way out of the shop was through the front: there was no back exit.

Even if there was a back way out, Sparks would not have taken it. This had gone beyond something that could be dealt with through application of the appropriate tactics and sufficient firepower. For him, it had become a question of honor. "Major," he said, loud enough that everyone could hear him, "when you first came to my regiment and I asked you what you thought your primary job was, you told me it was to help me manage the deployment of my regiment. Do you remember what I told you?"

"Yes, sir, I do," the major replied as everyone's head turned to watch them.

"What was it I said, major?"

"You said, sir," the operations officer managed, automatically bringing himself to attention, "that the first job of every member of the regiment was to kill the enemy."

"That would be correct, major," Sparks growled, turning to him with smoldering eyes. "*To kill the enemy.* That is what we do. *There,* major," he shouted, pointing to the rapidly approaching Kreelans, "is the enemy! If you think for one damned minute," he went on, lowering his voice slightly, "that I am going to simply stand here while those *things* butcher more civilians, you are badly mistaken. If we die, so be it. Nobody joins the 7th Cavalry because they want to live forever. Do you understand me, major?"

"*Garry Owen,* sir," the major said, saluting. The 7th Cav had been known as the *Garry Owen* regiment, the name taken from the Irish drinking song *Garryowen.* The tune had been a favorite of the regiment's most famous commander, General George Armstrong Custer, and *Garryowen* was made the regiment's official song. Since then, the term "Garry Owen" had come to mean a combination of *yes* and *can-do* underscored with the sort of determination that only those who are willing to risk their lives every day in the line of duty can truly understand. It was at once a very small thing, and at the same time a very important thing to those who served in the regiment.

"Good," Sparks said, dismissing the man with his eyes. "Listen up," he said to the rest of them. "This isn't going to be fancy or pretty. As soon as the enemy line reaches us and we have a clear shot down their flank, open fire with everything you've got. Hadley, you've got the best throwing arm: take whatever grenades we have and let fly. Everyone keep shooting until we run out of targets or ammo. Miss Guillaume," he said, turning to her, "this isn't something I can order or force you to do. But in the interests of what is no doubt a very slim chance of your own survival, it would behoove you to use your weapon to good effect."

Gulping, Steph nodded. "Yes, colonel," she said, her voice shaking. Her insides felt like everything had turned to jelly, and she felt like her stomach, bladder, and bowels were all ready to let go at the same time.

"Fix bayonets," Sparks growled as he pulled his own from his combat webbing and attached it to the muzzle of his rifle. The others immediately did the same, although Hadley had to help Steph attach hers, taking the bayonet from the standard combat webbing he'd given her when they abandoned the command vehicle.

She stared at the black blade, the silvery edge of the weapon reflecting the many colors of the people who were still streaming by. But they were getting to the end now, and the screams of fear were being replaced by cries of agony from those who were being cut down by the Kreelans. She thought she might be able to shoot one of the aliens, but to stab one with a bayonet? "Jesus," she breathed.

"Stick next to me," Hadley told her as he moved her behind a counter made of thick wood. After placing a handful of grenades on the floor by his feet, he put his rifle on top of the counter, pointing toward the window. "Remember, the rifle's going to kick some, so don't let it surprise you." He double-checked that her weapon was set for single-shot fire and not automatic: he didn't want her to accidentally spray bullets around the shop and hit the others. "Take your time and remember to breathe."

"Okay," she said in a small voice, trying desperately to rally her confidence. "God, I have to pee," she muttered to herself, then suddenly giggled as she realized that she was still recording everything. *I'd better win the Pulitzer for this one,* she thought giddily.

Sparks and the others had also taken cover where they could find it, some behind the counter, Sparks and the major kneeling on either side of the window. Luckily, the shop was big enough that they could all shoot through the front window without getting in each other's line of fire.

"Stand by," Sparks warned as he peered around the edge of the window, holding his rifle to his chest. The Kreelan line wasn't perfectly straight, of course, but it was close enough. "Steady..." he brought his own rifle up, making sure the muzzle would not protrude into the street. "*Open fire!*"

Half a dozen assault rifles chattered in unison, slamming hundreds of rounds into the flank of the Kreelan line, completely surprising the enemy warriors. Their chest armor saved some of them, but unlike the shotguns that the Alliance sailors had used against the Kreelan boarders, the Terran assault rifles - especially at point-blank range - had a lot more penetrating power.

"Down!" Sparks screamed as he saw a number of the Kreelans throwing something. Everyone ducked but a soldier who hadn't heard over the deafening rifle fire: she suddenly staggered back, a miniature flying buzz-saw having cut right through her combat helmet to embed itself in her brain. With a twitch, she pitched backward, dead.

Sparks and the major resumed firing, and the others joined in, popping up to fire a few rounds, then ducking down as more of the flying weapons sailed through the front window.

Hadley grabbed a grenade and hurled it through the window like a hail Mary pass, then dropped back down to snatch up another one. There was no need to look for a good target: the Kreelans were bunching up out in front of the shop. It didn't matter where he threw the grenades, because he just couldn't miss. The explosions rocked the shop and shook dust and plaster loose from the ceiling to rain down on them.

Steph was holding her rifle in front of her, pointed out the window, but still hadn't fired a single shot. She was staring wide-eyed at the frenzied action, watching it as if she were doing a slow-motion review of her own recording. The Kreelans, throwing any sort of tactics or caution to the wind, trying to rush the window. The cavalrymen, faces locked in expressions of grim determination, pouring rifle fire into the enemy. Two more of the soldiers being killed by the flying weapons, one of them decapitated, the other falling to the floor with one embedded in his chest. Hadley next to her, screaming epithets at the enemy as he bobbed up and down like a lethal jack-in-the-box, hurling grenades into the enemy's midst. The smoke from the rifles - acrid and foul-smelling, mixed with the coppery tang of blood and the dryness of plaster dust - that wreathed the soldiers. Colonel Sparks, his rifle's magazine having run dry, thrusting his bayonet into the neck of an alien warrior who had managed to leap through the window, falling on top of her, driving the bayonet's tip into the wood floor as the alien thrashed and clawed at him. And the terrible, terrible snarling of the enemy warriors, their fangs gleaming as they howled in some terrible ecstasy while they crashed in wave upon wave against the humans' defensive position.

All this she saw in what could only have been a few seconds before another warrior flung herself through the window to land right in front of Steph, the Kreelan's sword raised high and fangs bared in a killing rage. Time was suspended for a moment as Steph realized that there was no one else to help her: Hadley was down behind the counter, reloading his own rifle. Sparks, spattered with blood, was shouting something at her, even as he was trying to pull his bayonet from the Kreelan he had just killed. The others seemed not to have noticed that there was an enemy warrior in their midst as they frantically fired at the endless stream of warriors trying to climb through the window.

Steph tried to scream, but nothing came out: her body was completely paralyzed. She saw the gleaming blade of the sword - so beautiful! - swinging toward her neck, and in that moment she knew that she was going to die.

But before the blade could touch her flesh, the Kreelan warrior unexpectedly flew backward, still in slow motion, and Steph imagined a look of surprise and perhaps even disappointment on her alien features. There was a single round hole in her chest armor, right between her well-proportioned breasts, the black of the armor around the hole now a star of shiny metal.

With no small surprise, Steph saw the swirl of smoke streaming from the muzzle of her own rifle; she had not seen the muzzle flash as the round fired. Perhaps she had her eyes closed, an infinitely long time as she blinked. She felt her right index finger, curled around the trigger and holding it tight. With a conscious effort, she managed to let go: Hadley had told her that the rifle wouldn't fire again until she let up on the trigger.

For the first time in her life, she had killed another creature larger than a fly. A sentient being. An enemy of the human race. A being intent on killing her. She wasn't sure whether she wanted to celebrate or puke. But as her perception of time again sped up as the Kreelan warrior's body fell lifeless to the floor, she realized she didn't have time for either. With newfound determination, she raised the rifle to her shoulder and fired again. And again.

***

"What the fuck?" Coyle yelped as a huge stream of people came tearing around a street corner halfway up the block, heading straight toward them. Unlike the first group they had encountered, which had been a few hundred, this was a gigantic mob that filled the entire street. She heard screaming above the low whine of the tank's motors, accompanied by a frenzied volley of weapons fire. She could tell that the firing was from Terran assault rifles from their distinct staccato sound.

Standing up in the cupola so she could see better, she didn't have to tell Mannie to stop the tank. But he hit the brakes so hard that her chest slammed into the metal hatch coaming. Her body armor kept her from being bruised, but it was hard enough to almost knock the wind out of her. Mannie was still shaken by running over the people when they broke free of the building they'd used for cover, and she'd heard him vomit three times. But she didn't have anyone to relieve him.

They had passed by the First Battalion commander's position, and found his command track burned to a crisp with two gigantic holes punched through the armor. Of their own company commander there was no trace, nor had any of the other company commanders survived. Or if they were still alive, they hadn't been able to dig themselves out of the rubble. So Coyle had kept searching.

One tank from another company had joined them, but so far that was it for their entire battalion. It was clear that they had gotten the full treatment from the Kreelan ships as they passed overhead. Coyle couldn't be sure, but she suspected that they must have homed in on anything using a combat data-link, because the command tracks had received special attention. But you didn't have to be a genius to find a tank, she thought, disgusted.

Some tanks had survived the barrage, only to be killed by something else. She had found nearly half a dozen in the street that looked like they'd been incinerated. The sight made her very uneasy: while the streets here were quite wide, this being a newer upscale district, the tanks were still extremely vulnerable to attack by any Kreelans holed up in the buildings they passed.

The only good news was that she'd run into a platoon of infantry that had somehow survived. They were part of the mechanized infantry company that was task-organized to her battalion. Their infantry combat vehicle had been hit by the enemy ships, but had only been disabled. So they went looking for other survivors - and the enemy - on foot.

They soon found that the rest of their company hadn't been so lucky: every other vehicle in the company had been destroyed.

While the platoon was commanded by a second lieutenant, she knew that he was straight out of school and had zero leadership experience. She'd called him and his platoon sergeant - who also outranked her - up on top of her tank and told them quietly but bluntly that she wasn't going to obey any orders that she thought were stupid and would endanger her tanks needlessly, and if the boy had any sense he would listen to what she told him and do it.

Much to her surprise, the lieutenant had agreed. With a wry smile and no small amount of sarcastic wit, he turned to his platoon sergeant and said, "So, is this one of those leadership training opportunities you were telling me about?"

The three of them had a good chuckle at that, and after a brief discussion the lieutenant set about putting Coyle's "suggestions" into action, deploying his squads ahead, behind, and to either side of the tanks to help protect them from bomb-throwing alien wenches that the tankers might not see or be able to react to in time. Coyle was incredibly relieved.

Now, with the screaming horde of civilians flooding toward them, the infantry hurried to get out of the way, flattening themselves against the walls on either side of the street. A few of them - *Idiots!* Coyle cursed - tried to get in front of the mob and wave them to a stop. But at the last moment they all managed to dodge out of the way of the speeding human freight train.

The people surged around her tank, which was at the front of the modified three-tank wedge they had been moving in, and then suddenly started climbing on top of it, clearly with the intention of trying to get into its protective armored shell.

"Oh, no, you don't," Coyle cried as a man did an amazing set of acrobatics up the front glacis plate, over the gun, and onto the top of the turret, reaching for her hatch. She hit the panic bar, dropping her seat down inside the turret and slamming the hatch closed, barely missing the man's fingers. She hoped Gomez and the other tank crew had buttoned up or they were going to have an interesting time.

"What do we do?" Mannie croaked, terrified that she was going to tell him to move forward through this mass of people.

"Sit tight, Mannie," she told him. "Yuri," she said to her gunner, "watch for those bitches coming along behind them." Based on their first encounter with the Kreelans driving the civilians along, she figured there must be a ton of them behind this mob.

After a few minutes, though, the stream of people started to taper off, with no sign of the enemy behind them. The civilians on top of her tank, having decided that she wasn't going to invite them inside, had hopped off and followed their fellow scared-shitless citizens down the street.

"Okay, Mannie," she said, popping the hatch and sticking her head back out into the smoke-filled air again, "let's move it." The firing she'd heard earlier had tapered off drastically, then suddenly stopped. "And let's hurry..."

***

Only Sparks, Hadley, and - by some miracle - Steph were still alive. Two Kreelans had reached around the edge of the window and hauled the operations major off his feet: wielding his combat knife, he disappeared in a frenzied mob of tearing claws and slashing swords. Hadley lobbed his last grenade into the scrum of Kreelan warriors tearing at the fallen officer. The two other cavalry troopers had been killed by warriors who had managed to get in through the window, much like the one Steph had killed, and been quicker with their swords than the other cavalrymen had been with their rifles.

"Out!" Hadley cried: he was completely out of ammunition, even what he had gathered up from the other fallen soldiers. Steph was out, too: while she had been shooting non-stop, she had shared her spare magazines with Hadley, and had since then been crouching on the floor behind the cover of the counter, feeling like a coward. No longer worrying about the threat from the flying weapons, which the Kreelans had only used at first, he moved around the counter, holding his rifle now as the base of his bayonet.

"Out!" Sparks called, throwing down his empty rifle as half a dozen warriors clambered through the window. He quickly drew the big pistol he carried and emptied the magazine into them, killing five outright before more warriors came through, forcing him back.

Without time to reload his pistol and unable to reach his rifle now, Sparks had only one card left to play. While it was centuries out of date, an anachronism in this age as he himself was, he drew his saber from the scabbard at his side after dropping the now-empty pistol on the floor.

While a sword was still used as part of Terran Ground Forces ceremonial dress, the weapon Sparks held in his hand wasn't made of the inexpensive low-grade and brittle metal of the ceremonial weapons: it was a faithful replica of the last saber ever issued to the United States Cavalry, the Model 1913 that was designed by a young Army lieutenant by the name of George S. Patton, Jr. Made with a strong and flexible steel blade, it had cost Sparks a small fortune and had always been his most prized possession. He had even paid for formal training on how to use it, both from the back of a horse and dismounted. But even in his wildest dreams he had never thought he would actually use it in battle. Yet here he was.

With a confident thrust, Sparks stabbed the nearest Kreelan, who was turned toward Hadley as he charged from behind the wooden counter. He drove the blade into her armpit where there was a gap in her armor, the weapon's tip going deep into her chest. With a cry of shock, she fell to the floor, dead.

The impact on the other warriors was instantaneous and totally unexpected: they stopped their attack. Had Steph not been peering over the top of the counter, no longer content to cower behind it as Hadley had told her to, she would not have believed it. The half dozen warriors who had already come through the window stepped back away from the two cavalrymen, their swords held in what Steph took to be defensive positions. The warriors outside, having seen Sparks draw his sword, immediately backed away from the window, clambering past their many dead sisters who were stacked up in front of the devastated shop.

Hadley, in what otherwise might have been a comical moment, stopped in mid-charge, his war-cry dying on his lips.

Sparks, after tugging his bloodied sword from the side of the fallen Kreelan, backed farther away from the aliens, unsure of what was going on. He watched with disbelieving eyes as the Kreelans inside the shop warily retreated, moving to join the others who now stood outside in what looked like a wide circle open to the storefront. A Kreelan warrior, bloodied and injured, stepped into the center of the circle. In what he recognized as what must be a universal gesture, she beckoned him forward toward her.

"I'll be damned," he breathed.

"What do we do, colonel?" Hadley asked him.

Sparks glanced at him, then said, "We go kill as many as we can before we die."

***

Shanur-Tikhan stood in the circle of the gathered warriors as the humans unblocked the door to their small redoubt, apparently a shop of some kind not unlike those found in the cities of her own people. She was senior among her gathered sisters, and although she was already grievously injured, she would not be denied the privilege of matching her sword against the human's. While the warriors of Her Children were versed in the ways of weapons of many kinds, the sword was the ultimate balance of physical form and spirit. That this human possessed one spoke well of him and his kind, even if he was a soulless animal whose blood did not sing.

She grunted in appreciation as the human bearing the sword emerged from the doorway, walking with dignity instead of clambering awkwardly through the smashed window. Two others, a male and a female, accompanied him. The male, unarmed, stooped next to a fallen warrior to pick up her sword before coming forward to join the male who appeared to be the senior of the two. Shanur-Tikhan and her sisters took no offense at his taking the sword, for it was unbound from the dead warrior's spirit. The female human merely stood by and watched, which Shanur-Tikhan found highly curious.

The two males approached her, the dominant without fear, his subordinate with some obvious trepidation. The former held his weapon confidently, while the latter did not. If they meant to fight her two on one, she would accept such a challenge. Her wounds were serious and would soon kill her if she did not seek out a healer, but that was inconsequential. All that mattered was the challenge.

Opening her arms wide, she invited them to make the first move.

***

"Hadley," Sparks asked quietly, "do you have a damn clue what to do with that thing?"

Gripping the alien sword tightly, Hadley answered, "No sir, I don't. But if I'm going to die, I'm not going to die without a weapon in my hands."

"Well-spoken, son," Sparks told him. "For what it's worth, you've been a helluva soldier."

"Thank you, sir," Hadley said, his throat tightening up. He had been with Sparks for two years, and had been given his share of ass-reamings by the colonel. But the man had never done anything, even dressing down a man or woman under his command, without the goal of making him or her a better soldier. And he had always treated his soldiers with respect. "It's been an honor, sir."

Nodding, Sparks said simply, "Shall we, soldier?"

"Garry Owen, sir!"

Together, the two cavalrymen attacked.

***

"You saw *what?*" Coyle exclaimed, unable to believe what she was hearing.

"You heard me, sarge," the lieutenant said. "It's the colonel and another soldier fighting one of the Kreelans with swords! And that reporter is there, too. Surrounded by a few hundred hostiles."

The lieutenant's infantrymen had been scouting ahead, peering around the corners to make sure Coyle's tanks didn't get ambushed. They'd been heading as fast as they could in the direction from which they'd heard the firing, but the "crunchies" - the infantry - couldn't go nearly as fast as her tanks, and she dared not leave them behind. The woman on point had come running back to the lieutenant, telling him what she'd seen. Unable to believe what she'd said, he had gone forward himself for a look. And now he was relating the same ridiculous tale to Coyle.

It was so bizarre that it had to be true.

"We've gotta do something, sarge," the lieutenant said earnestly.

And there sat the big, fat and ugly problem: what to do. She had plenty of firepower to blast the Kreelans to bits, but she wanted to rescue the survivors of the headquarters company if she could. If she came in, all guns blazing, there's no way she could keep them from being killed in the crossfire.

Calling up a map of the neighborhood, she had an idea. "Okay, el-tee," she told him, "here's what we do..."

***

Sparks was gasping for breath, and his right shoulder was burning like fire from holding and swinging the saber. It wasn't a heavy weapon, but he wasn't used to fighting with it, and his body was exhausted after the frenetic firefight they had just gone through. But he was nothing if not determined, and he ignored the pain, willing his wiry body to stay in the fight.

Hadley, beside him, wasn't in any better shape. While bigger and physically stronger, he had no training at all with a sword in his hand, and had suffered a brutal cut to his upper left arm. He could still swing the sword with his right, but the pain and loss of blood were telling.

Their opponent, Sparks realized, was drawing out the affair. Even gravely wounded, as she clearly was from the amount of blood seeping from beneath her armor, he knew that she probably could have killed both of them in the first few seconds. He merely gave thanks for her sense of fair play - or whatever it was - because it just gave him that many more opportunities to kill her.

Steph watched as the two men battled the Kreelan warrior, furious with herself that she was unable to help them. She could try picking up a sword and dive into the melee, but she figured she would last about five seconds. Instead, she focused on doing her very best to capture the battle. She had forgotten about the Pulitzer. This was about posterity, assuming any of them actually survived.

Suddenly, she became aware of something that was totally out of place in this shattered street, filled with hundreds of alien warriors watching an uneven battle of survival: music. It was an instrumental of a song she didn't immediately recognize that sounded like something someone might hear in an old-style Irish pub.

But the effect of the music on the two cavalrymen and the aliens alike was profound: the Kreelans turned to look down the street to see what this strange noise was, while Sparks and Hadley charged their opponent as if they had been shot full of adrenaline.

Then Steph saw the first of the tanks belonging to the 7th Cavalry Regiment round the corner up the street with the regiment's official tune, the *Garryowen*, booming from the lead tank's external speakers.

***

Coyle's plan was straightforward: she would take the tanks straight in to try and draw the enemy's attention - which was something tanks were very good at - while the young lieutenant took his infantry platoon down the next street as fast as he could to get in position behind the Kreelans. Her hope was that most or all of the Kreelans would head toward the tanks, giving the infantry a chance to grab the colonel and the others, literally behind the enemy's back.

The tanks made very little noise when they moved, as the electric motors were practically silent. The only thing one could hear from any more than a few yards away was the tracks. Even that, with vehicles maintained as well as those of the 7th Cav, was lost in the background noise of the burning city. And Coyle wanted to make something of a grand entrance that wasn't potentially lethal to the colonel and the others.

So she decided on something a bit unconventional. The colonel loved the damned *Garryowen*, the Irish drinking song that was the regiment's official air, and every vehicle had a copy of it that could be played at his whim. She knew that to Sparks - and most of the rest of the regiment, even if many wouldn't admit it - *Garryowen* was a battle hymn that took him back to the era he wished he had been born in. "And the stupid song gives me goosebumps, too," she confessed quietly to herself. She switched on the external public address system that was standard on all the regiment's vehicles and cranked up the volume.

Rounding the corner, she saw that her efforts had met with good effect: the bulk of the Kreelans were now standing there simply staring at her tank, while the colonel and the other soldier charged the enemy warrior facing them.

With *Chiquita* taking up position in the center of the street, the two other tanks moved up beside her. Taking up virtually the entire width of the street, the three tanks moved forward to meet the Kreelans.

***

Shanur-Tikhan was shocked at the sudden surge of strength and determination in the humans she fought as soon as the strange noise washed over them. Breaking contact for a precious moment by shoving them both away, she turned to see three large vehicles moving toward her warriors. Why their war machines made such a noise, she could not imagine, but the threat to her warriors was clear.

The challenge, then, was finished.

***

Steph looked on in horror as the warrior, wounded though she was, easily parried a slash from Hadley's sword and then, with a brutal attack with her own weapon, opened him up from his left hip to his right shoulder, the sword cutting right through his armor as if it were made of cloth. With a startled cry, he crumpled to the ground.

Sparks attacked the Kreelan with a series of savage thrusts with his saber, but on the last he slightly over-extended himself, and the Kreelan took full advantage. Knocking his sword aside, sending him off-balance as if he were sprawling forward, she pirouetted and brought down her sword, stabbing him through the back. The colonel gasped in agony as the sword's blade ran him all the way through, the bloodied tip hissing through the armor of his breast plate. As he fell to the ground, the warrior yanked the sword from his body and flicked the blood from it.

***

"*Fucking bitch!*" Coyle screamed as she saw the colonel go down. Like the other Kreelans, the one who had just stabbed him had turned to look at Coyle's tanks, and in the magnified view of her combat console it seemed like the Kreelan was looking right into Coyle's hate-filled eyes. Coyle hoped she was, because it was the last thing the warrior would ever see.

Making sure her aiming pipper was on the center of the warrior's body in the targeting display, Coyle pulled the trigger on the cupola-mounted gatling gun. The Kreelan warrior disappeared in a gout of bloody mist as a dozen twenty millimeter rounds blew her apart.

***

Steph ignored the chaos that erupted around her as the warriors charged the tanks en masse, sprinting across the hundred meters or so of open street to reach them. The tanks' gatling guns and coaxial guns fired continuously, and she heard the *pop-pop-pop* of the tanks' close-in defense weapons launching grenades, then the explosions that followed. And over it all, the horrible war cries of the Kreelans as they charged and died.

She ignored it all as she crawled over the blood-soaked ground to get to Hadley and Sparks. She reached Hadley first, and was amazed to see that he was still alive. Unconscious, but alive. Gingerly prying the severed plate of his chest armor apart, she saw a great deal of blood and the white gleam of bone in the deep gash over his rib cage, but the sword hadn't penetrated his vitals. If they could keep him from bleeding to death, she was sure he would live.

Then she low-crawled the few meters to where the colonel lay face-down in the street, a pool of blood beneath his body. Gently turning him over, she saw that he was still conscious. She saw his lips moving, but couldn't hear what he was trying to say over the din of the tanks firing and the Kreelans screaming.

Putting her ear to his lips, she heard him say, "Turn me...so I can see..."

Nodding, she pulled him around enough to where he could see the battle, his head cradled in her lap.

As they watched the carnage together, they were suddenly surrounded by infantrymen.

"Medic!" a young lieutenant cried as he knelt next to the colonel, who simply nodded to him, then returned his gaze to the undulating dance of death taking place farther down the street. A medic was instantly at the colonel's side, with two other soldiers tending to Hadley.

There was a sudden *boom*, then another, and again as the tanks' last-ditch close-in defenses triggered: explosive strips with embedded ball bearings that were attached in segments all around the hull.

Steph saw the Kreelans dying by the dozens as they continued their insane assault. And more died as the lieutenant ordered his infantrymen to add their own fire to the mayhem, taking the Kreelans from behind.

It was a massacre.

In the end, the Kreelans refused to yield, they refused to even attempt to retreat. They were killed to the last one. But the regiment paid a high price: two of the three tanks were hit with Kreelan grenades, destroying the vehicles and killing the crews. The only survivor was *Chiquita*, a large patch of its left flank blackened from the intense heat.

Driving through the abattoir that was all that was left of the Kreelans, Coyle's tank - blackened and smoking, the suspension and most of the lower hull covered with Kreelan blood and gore - pulled up close to where the medic was stabilizing Sparks, whose eyes had never left the vehicle that rumbled to a stop in front of him.

Climbing out of the cupola and gingerly making her way down the gore-spattered hull to the street, an exhausted Staff Sergeant Patty Coyle saluted her regimental commander.

"That was good work, trooper," Sparks said quietly through the haze of painkillers the medic had pumped into him. He was hurt badly, but the medic had told him that if they could find a decent hospital or get back to the fleet, he would fully recover.

Her face dirtied with soot and flecks of blood from a Kreelan who had come within arm's length of killing her during the fight, Coyle managed a grim smile. "Garry fucking Owen, sir."

That was all the colonel needed to hear.

TWENTY-ONE

"Lieutenant," a voice said. It was vaguely familiar, but muffled and distant, as if in a dream. The voice itself was pleasant, that of a young woman, but even voicing that single word, she seemed distraught for some reason. "Lieutenant, can you hear me?"

Blinking his eyes open, Ichiro Sato saw a pale blur hovering above him that gradually resolved itself into a face: Natalya Bogdanova. The last few seconds of what happened on the bridge flashed through his mind, when Morrison had relieved him of duty and replaced him with Bogdanova as the Kreelan shells were about to hit.

And hit they had: the last thing Sato could recall was flying across the bridge as explosions wracked the ship. He remembered very clearly the thought that your life was supposed to flash before your eyes before you died, and he had felt cheated that he hadn't been able to see his own life replayed before his body smashed into the bulkhead.

Looking up at Bogdanova, he could still hardly see her face: the bridge was shadowed in darkness, with only a few of the emergency lighting strips working, throwing a ghastly dim red glow through the smoke that swirled slowly in the compartment. But what he could see wasn't good: she had a deep gash across her left cheek, and her face was smudged with blood and darkened by the heavy, acrid smoke. Her cheeks were wet with tears, from pain or the emotional trauma of what the ship must have endured, he couldn't tell.

"Lieutenant," she said again, and now he could feel one of her hands cupping the back of his head, and the faint sense of wetness there. Blood. "Please say something," she whispered desperately.

"Bogdanova," he managed, breaking into a wet cough. His head began to throb. Aside from that and some heavy bruising, he seemed to be well enough. Making a few exploratory movements with his hands and feet, he discovered that nothing was broken.

Hearing her name had an immediate effect on the young ensign. "Thank God," she whispered, lowering her head down to his chest, a sobbing cry sticking in her throat.

"Boarders?" he asked immediately, the nightmare from over a year ago coming back to him in an instant.

"No," she reassured him. "No sign of boarders or anyone else. After we were hit, the fleet moved on toward the planet, and we were just left floating in high orbit. I think the Kreelans must think we're dead."

Levering himself up on his elbows, his eyes stinging from the smoke, he asked her, "Where is everyone?" He couldn't see very far in the haze and dim red lighting, but the bridge should have been bustling with activity, the captain helping the XO direct damage control efforts to make the ship at least spaceworthy, if not ready for combat.

"Only four of us made it," she told him as she helped him sit up. "You, Beale, Akimov, and myself. Everyone else on the bridge is dead."

That tore through his headache and chilled his heart. Out of a combat crew of nearly a dozen men and women on the bridge, all but four had been killed? "The captain?" he asked. Regardless of how much he hated Morrison, he was nonetheless a competent ship's master and would have a good idea of how to get *McClaren* underway again. Not hearing his badgering voice was somehow disheartening.

"Dead," Ensign Drew Beale spat as he came forward through the smoky shadows with Seaman First Class Nikolai Akimov to join them. "The fucking bastard."

"What about the XO and the chief engineer?" Sato asked, his mind rapidly shedding the remaining cobwebs from his close encounter with the bulkhead. "And how's the ship?"

"We don't know if anyone else made it," Bogdanova told him. "We have no communications at all, inside or outside of the ship. The bridge has been holding air well enough, but I heard some venting up forward after we were hit. All the controls and consoles are out." She looked around through the dim red haze at the panels that should be glowing with buttons and information. "But we've still got artificial gravity, so main engineering must still be at least partially on-line. We can't get the hatch open to get to the rest of the ship, though."

"We haven't heard anyone outside in the passageway, sir," Akimov offered tentatively. "No one has come to try and find us."

Sato thought for a moment, then got to his feet with their help. He was still a bit unsteady, but they had no time to lose. It suddenly occurred to him that they all should be wearing respirators, if not full vacuum suits. The smoke in the air would be at least mildly toxic. And if the bridge suddenly did decompress, the respirators would allow them to breathe, even in a full vacuum environment, although they would suffer from the bends as nitrogen bubbles formed in their blood. It was a bad choice between ways to die. "Get your respirators on," he ordered. Something else Morrison - and the XO, by following a bad example - had fallen down on was basic survival and damage control drills. Sato was surprised that the ship had managed to survive at all.

The others quickly moved to the emergency lockers located at strategic points around the bridge, pulling out the respirators and putting them on. Bogdanova handed one to Sato, and after he'd pulled it on handed him a flashlight. Sato was eerily reminded of the first moments aboard the *Aurora* after the alien ship had immobilized them, when the crew had been cast into utter darkness before the strange blue glow began. He involuntarily shuddered, a chill running down his spine as the ghosts of his old ship's crew brushed against his soul.

Trying hard to ignore the bodies strewn about the bridge, Sato told the other survivors, "First, we need to get out of here and find out who else is left, and see what sort of shape the ship is in."

"But we can't open the hatch," Bogdanova said quietly.

"Yes, we can," Sato told her as he knelt down next to the small access panel, much like Yao Ming had done on the *Aurora* after the Kreelans had attacked. Sato had spent a great deal of time studying the *McClaren's* schematics after he had come aboard, and he had learned the trick that Yao Ming had used on their old ship. The mechanism was exactly the same, and he did it the same way Yao had. "I'll just crack the hatch first, in case the other side has been depressurized."

Turning the manual handle, an awkward process at best, the hatch began to slide open. Aside from a very slight hiss of pressure equalizing, it looked like the passageway was still holding atmosphere. Sato cranked it open the rest of the way.

Unlike the bridge, the passageway that led to the rest of the ship was fully illuminated by the emergency strips. Putting away the flashlight for the moment, Sato led the others aft and down. His first goal was main damage control, to see if the XO was still alive. Then on to engineering to find Lieutenant Commander Pergolesi.

It took nearly half an hour to reach the hatch for main damage control. Along the way they found over a dozen sailors still alive. After making sure that they all knew how to open the hatches manually, Sato sent half of them forward to find any other members of the crew who might still be trapped.

When he cracked open the hatch to damage control, he was instantly rewarded with a roar of air being sucked out of the passageway into the compartment on the other side of the hatch.

"It's been breached!" he shouted as he frantically cranked the hatch shut again. He knew there would be no survivors: none of the crewmen in the breached compartment would have had a chance to get into one of the inflatable emergency balls. And even if they had, they would have run out of air by now. With a heavy heart, he again led the others aft toward engineering.

Not long afterward, they turned down yet another passageway.

"Halt!"

Sato, leading the others, froze instantly. He couldn't see anyone else in the passageway.

"Identify!" the voice barked.

"Lieutenant Sato, tactical officer. You're a Marine, I take it?"

Suddenly a man dressed in a specially designed armored vacuum suit stepped into view. The suit was entirely off-white, a perfect match with the ship's interior. While he certainly wasn't invisible, he blended in quite well, and would have been difficult to spot for anyone who wasn't paying close attention or was moving fast.

"Gunnery Sergeant Ruiz, sir," the man answered through his external speakers as he lowered his rifle and made his faceplate transparent so Sato could see him. "Kinda glad to see you, sir," he allowed as several other Marines magically appeared behind him. They all looked huge and menacing in their combat armor.

"The feeling's mutual, gunny," Sato said earnestly, "believe me. How many of your men made it?"

"All of 'em, sir," Ruiz answered as if to say, *Of course they're all still here.* "I got eight here, including me, and the rest are still at their battle stations throughout the ship. Tanner almost caught a Kreelan shell, but he and his team made it okay."

"You've got comms with all of them?" Sato asked, incredulous.

"Yes, sir," Ruiz told him. "Just voice and vidcom over induction, none of the data-link stuff. The radio signals are for shit. But we don't need that to kick alien ass," he went on, gesturing with his enormous weapon, a recoilless rifle that was designed specifically for space combat.

For the first time since this disaster began, Sato managed a smile. The Marine combat suits not only had radio, which was currently useless, but also had the ability to send signals through the metal of the ship from induction sensors in the palms of the armored gauntlets, the soles of their shoes, and even a pickup sensor that could be attached to the ship with a simple magnetic clip. In testing during the hasty development of the suits, they had found that radio was often unreliable in the hull of a ship, so the Marines - ever inventive - had come up with an alternative. Just in case.

Looking down at the young Navy lieutenant, Gunnery Sergeant Pablo Ruiz couldn't help but feel a sense of admiration for him. That was something the big gunnery sergeant - or "gunny," as the rank was known - would say about very few of the Navy officers he'd met in his sixteen years as a Marine.

***

Formerly of the United States Marine Corps, or USMC, Ruiz was a plank owner - among the very first members - of the recently formed Terran Marine Corps. The USMC had been the last amphibious force to be maintained by any of the former nations under what was now the Terran Planetary Government. Through disuse and the virtual elimination of war on Earth after the final series of conflicts that would have destroyed Mankind had it not been for the advent of interstellar travel, the Marine Corps had been left with no real purpose, and had been reduced to little more than a curious anachronism, a pale reflection of bygone years. In truth, it had been retained not for any military function in the post-Diaspora world - for that, the Terran Planetary Ground Forces was the premier arm of the service - but because so many people who still lived in the former United States steadfastly refused to let go of it as a tradition. During one phase of this long twilight of its history, the Corps was even funded by donations from private citizens.

So the Marines had stubbornly lingered on, an institution with warrior traditions that had no more wars to fight.

In the aftermath of the *Aurora* incident, however, President McKenna had other ideas. Based on the analysis of Sato's information, it was clear that the ships of the fleet she was building would need a force of trained soldiers aboard to defend against Kreelan boarding attempts. Such soldiers should also be able to take the fight right back to the enemy. They would also have to become accustomed to serving aboard ships, rather than just being carried by them. Longer-term plans, assuming the Kreelan threat actually materialized, even envisioned divisions of troops traveling with the fleet for planetary assaults.

The Terran Ground Forces commander, General Jaswant Singh, naturally felt that this was a function of his arm of the service. Admiral Tiernan, Chief of the Naval Staff, was not so sure. While he and Singh got along well and generally saw eye to eye, he had a hard time believing that soldiers brought up in the Ground Forces could quickly be transplanted into this new role.

As it happened, Tiernan's youngest brother was a colonel in the USMC, and had been at a briefing where some of the fleet plans were being discussed, the topic of "fleet infantry" among them. Two weeks later, he had called his older brother, the admiral, and invited - begged might have been a more accurate, if somewhat demeaning, term - him to come to Quantico to see a demonstration. While Tiernan was loathe to do anything that might smack of nepotism, his brother had made a very convincing argument, and Tiernan had finally given in.

When he arrived at Quantico, he was taken to a large hanger that had once been used to house USMC aircraft, a facet of their force that they had long since lost. Inside, he found that the industrious Marines had put together a life-size mockup of the main sections of one of the candidate destroyer designs, almost entirely from scrounged materials. Tiernan cautiously followed the eager Marines inside for a quick tour. Four stories tall and two hundred feet long, it lacked all the details a real ship would have, but it didn't need them. The twisting passageways, stairs, elevators, and hatches were what mattered, for these formed the "terrain" on which the battle would be fought. Video cameras had been placed at key locations throughout the ship to monitor the action during the demonstration battle. After the tour of the mock ship's interior, they led Tiernan to the improvised control room inside a ramshackle trailer that squatted next to the mockup.

Tiernan's brother explained the demonstration engagement: a platoon of Marines would simulate the Kreelans as closely as they could, based on Sato's information. Inside the mockup, a number of Marines played the role of "helpless" sailors, while a platoon in armored suits, led by one Gunnery Sergeant Pablo Ruiz, defended the ship. The suits worn by the defenders were simple mockups of combat vacuum suits the Marines had designed after several intense brainstorming sessions. While the mockups were rough around the edges, Tiernan had to admit to himself that - if made a reality - such suits would be quite lethal.

The Marines showed him the computer that would keep score, and Tiernan's brother swore that it was as accurate and fair as they could make it. In fact, they had programmed in a level of bias against the defending Marines.

Having been in the military for four decades, Tiernan had seen violence exercised across a wide spectrum, and did not expect to be surprised by a group of what he thought of as little more than highly innovative military enthusiasts. But by the time the simulated attack was over, he had to redefine his concept of "violence," at least as it pertained to close-quarters combat. The defending Marines suffered heavy casualties, but they stopped the simulated Kreelan attack, which was quite spirited, right in its tracks. More importantly, they were able to protect the crew and the ship's vital compartments, which would have allowed a real ship to stay in the fight with the rest of the fleet.

The combat armor, which Ruiz had helped design, was a key ingredient in the success of the first exercise. But even in the second exercise, which Tiernan's brother ran with the defending Marines only wearing standard body armor, the Marines were still able to hold the ship. They suffered far more casualties, and some of the simulated crewmen were also killed, but the determined Kreelan attackers were again defeated.

After a review of the two "battles," Tiernan was ferried out to one of the handful of ships that the Terran Navy still maintained just for the Marines, showing him how the Marines were more than just soldiers carried by ships. They were truly adapted to shipboard life and coexistence with the Navy in a Corps tradition that literally spanned centuries, back to the time of tall-masted sailing ships.

The admiral was sold. Selling the idea to the defense minister through the uproar caused by General Singh wasn't nearly as easy. In fact, the Marines had to stage a second demonstration for the minister himself. Over General Singh's very strenuous objections, the minister took the idea to the president, who after a brief pointed discussion with the minister and all the service chiefs, approved the proposal Tiernan and the Commandant of the Marine Corps had drawn up. She signed an executive order federalizing the United States Marine Corps and officially changing its name to the Terran Marine Corps. As its predecessor had been, the "new" Corps was nominally subordinate to the Navy.

Singh was furious that a "second bloody army" was being formed, but the president was adamant: the Army and the Aerospace Defense Force would mainly be responsible for planetary defense and provide follow-on combat forces, while the Corps would protect the fleet and eventually have responsibility for planetary assaults.

It had been many years in coming, but the Corps had a real mission again. And when the Terran ships sailed for Keran, every able-bodied Marine, save a training cadre at Quantico that was already flooded with volunteers, shipped out with the fleet.

***

Standing here now on the stricken *McClaren*, Ruiz realized how much they really owed to Lieutenant Ichiro Sato. He had unknowingly saved the entire Marine Corps. *Should make him an honorary Marine*, Ruiz thought to himself. "Orders, sir?" Ruiz asked.

"Engineering," Sato said immediately. "We need to sort out how badly the ship's damaged. And find Lieutenant Commander Pergolesi." He paused. "Both the captain and the XO are dead. Commander Pergolesi is next in line."

Ruiz's expression darkened. "I got some bad news for you, sir," he said, his low voice dropping even lower. "The chief engineer bought it when the ship got nailed. Broke her neck."

Sato closed his eyes, mentally damning their luck. He had been counting on Pergolesi not only to know how to put the ship back in order, if it was possible, but to take command. Because of the surviving officers...

"As I reckon it, lieutenant," Ruiz finished the thought for him, "that leaves you as the skipper."

"Right," Sato managed. For just a moment, he felt a crushing weight on his shoulders, and in that brief flicker of time, the only thing he wanted to do was to run and hide somewhere, to cower in a closet like a child. He wasn't prepared for this. *But who ever is?* he asked himself.

He suddenly felt a real weight on his shoulder, and opened his eyes to see the Marine gunny's hand there. The older man gave him a brief reassuring squeeze and said quietly, "We're with you, sir. What are your orders?"

"Thanks, gunny," Sato said, and the Marine nodded and stepped back with the others. "Right," the *McClaren's* new commanding officer said, shoving his insecurities into a tiny box in his mind and slamming the lid shut. He had a crew to save and a ship to get back into the fight. "The first thing we have to do is get to anyone else who's trapped and free them. Gunny, that's a job for your Marines, since they're already spread around the ship and you have communications. We'll show you how to get the hatches open manually, but you may have a tough time for compartments where the passageways are in vacuum."

"Naw," Ruiz said, "every compartment has those beach ball survival things. We'll just make sure everybody's in those, then open the hatch and take them to the main starboard airlock. The passageways are pressurized all the way back here."

Sato nodded. "Good. Next is engineering. Can you patch me through to one of your Marines there to talk to whoever's senior?"

"Sure thing," Ruiz said. After a few seconds of talking to the squad leader in engineering, Sato heard the sound of Chief Petty Officer Antoinette DeFusco.

"Lieutenant," she said from the speakers in Ruiz's suit, "you heard about Commander Pergolesi, right?"

"Yes, chief," Sato said. "What about the other officers?"

"They were in the forward engine room with the commander when we were hit, sir," the chief answered. Normally a blindingly perky woman, her voice now was ragged. "A shell punched clean through. Nobody made it."

"Damn," Sato whispered. Not only were the deaths of the officers and crew in the compartment a tragedy, but the forward engine room housed the jump drive. *McClaren* wouldn't be leaving the Keran system without a lot of time in space dock. And unless the battle had gone well, he doubted that was going to happen.

"How are the main drives?" he asked, wanting to cross his fingers.

"The mains are up, sir," she told him. "Everything aft of the forward engine room seems to be fine."

"Up forward is a mess," he told her. "We haven't been able to do a damage control survey yet, but I'm guessing about a third of the main compartments on the port side have been breached, with most of the passageways in vacuum on that side. Starboard's not so bad."

"Let me guess," DeFusco said, "you've got artificial gravity but nothing else?"

Sato and Ruiz looked at each other with expressions of amazement. "Good guess, chief," Sato told her. "How'd you know?"

"Because of that fucking pulse cannon, if you'll pardon my saying so, sir," she explained. "It takes up the central conduit that most of the primary circuits would normally use in this ship design. But they had to move them around to make room for that hog. So they decided to put the main buses for the artificial gravity in the starboard cable runs, and everything else in the port side. The ship should have had redundant circuits, but they dropped that to meet the commissioning schedule."

"Do we still have the pulse cannon?" Sato asked.

"Green as a Christmas tree, sir," she told him, "at least for one shot. After that, who knows? The main energy buffers are in forward engineering, too. They show green, but the way that thing drains them, I don't know."

"Okay, chief, listen," he told her quickly. "That means we've got propulsion and we've even got something to shoot with. We've got to get the other main systems - especially life support, navigation, and sensors - back up. Then communications and the other weapons if we can."

"We'd love to, sir, if we could just get out of here to get forward!"

Sato looked up at Ruiz.

"Consider it done, sir," he said gruffly before barking a string of orders to his Marines.

***

Six tension-filled hours later, Sato again stood on the bridge. The bodies of the crew had been laid out under shrouds in the upper galley, awaiting proper burial, assuming the survivors were able to stay alive themselves. The surviving engineers, with the help of the rest of the crew, worked themselves to exhaustion to patch the ship's systems back together. Two of them died when a hatch, weakened by an explosion in an adjacent compartment, gave way. But at last Chief DeFusco, scraped, bruised, and dirty, rasped that she thought they were ready to start bringing the main systems back up.

The bridge was still dark and the stench of the smoke persisted, despite the fans the Marines had hauled up from one of the damage control lockers to try and clear it. Using one of the hand-held induction communicators that the Marines had brought up from the armory, Sato said, "Okay, chief, let there be light."

The bridge lights suddenly flickered on, then quickly died.

"Wait one," the chief said after a flurry of curses. A few minutes later, she came back on. "Hold on to your shorts, lieutenant..."

The dim and gloomy darkness was peeled away as the standard lighting flickered on, then held. On the bridge, the computer displays at the various control stations lit up and began their self-diagnostic routines.

A tired but exuberant cheer went up throughout the ship. The *McClaren* was alive again.

***

Sitting in the captain's chair was an experience that Sato had only dreamed of. Even on the rare occasions when Captain Morrison had let him and the other junior officers con the ship, he had never let anyone sit in "his" chair. Now, for better or worse, the ship was Sato's.

Looking around the bridge, it was clear to him that the ship was still terribly wounded: several of the main consoles remained dark, with no one to man them. Only half the crew had survived, and it was no small miracle the ship hadn't been completely destroyed. Of those control stations that were lit and active, every single one had crimson warnings and tell-tales glaring, but there were far fewer than before. Glancing at the navigation display, which right now was based on passive sensors only, he could see the *McClaren's* long ballistic trajectory from where she had been hit, taking her out just beyond the orbit of Keran's moons. The ship had drifted perilously close to the Kreelan force in high orbit, shown on the tactical display as a cloud of red circles where the passive sensors believed their ships to be, but had been ignored as another dead hulk. Sato and the others on the bridge had watched as a much smaller Kreelan force had climbed out of the gravity well of the planet toward high orbit, even as another group split from the main force to head down toward Keran.

As for the human fleet, they were just visible on the far side of the planet, also trying to regain the orbital high ground after what must have been an uncomfortably close run to low altitude. Unless the sensors were off, there were far fewer human ships than when *McClaren* had originally jumped in. It was difficult to tell from what the passive sensors could make out, as they were not nearly as sensitive or accurate as the active sensors, but if he was guessing right, Admiral Tiernan and the Alliance admiral were maneuvering to engage the Kreelan force that was staying in high orbit. Sato couldn't be sure of the number of ships on each side, but he could tell that it was going to be close enough that even a single destroyer might be able to make a big difference. He had no intention of letting *McClaren* miss this fight.

Setting his fears and reservations aside, Sato tightened the straps, the ones that Captain Morrison had neglected to use, on the captain's combat chair. Opening a channel to the crew, he said, "This is Lieutenant..." Then he stopped himself. He was no longer simply a lieutenant of the Terran Navy. As fate had decreed, he was now the commander of a warship. "This is the captain," he told them. "As you know, while we have been able to repair much of the critical damage to the ship, we can't jump into hyperspace and return to the rendezvous point and the repair ships. And even if we could, I wouldn't: our fleet and that of the Alliance have taken heavy losses, and it looks like Admiral Tiernan," Sato assumed the admiral was still alive, "is leading an engagement against the enemy in high orbit. We are going to join in that attack." He paused, thinking about his ill-fated ship's few minutes in action before they were struck. "The enemy thought they killed our ship and that we are no longer a threat. I plan to prove them wrong. Remember our fallen shipmates, and do your best. That is all."

Switching off the ship-wide channel, he said to Bogdanova, whom he had moved to the navigator's position, "Stand by to maneuver." The ship was still on a ballistic trajectory, rotating slowly about its long axis.

"Standing by, sir," she answered. She was still afraid, but wasn't terrified as she had been under Morrison's lashing tongue. Like the others among the crew, she wanted payback from the enemy. More than that, she trusted Sato.

"Maneuvering thrusters," Sato ordered. "Bring her straight and level, helm, zero mark zero."

"Aye, aye, sir." Bogdanova touched the controls, at first with unsure fingers, but she quickly gained confidence as the ship began to respond to her commands.

For Sato, it was a very tense moment, because they hadn't been able to test any of the ship's systems for fear of drawing the enemy's attention before they were ready. But having repaired the primary kinetics - two of the main batteries were fully functional - along with a pair of medium lasers and the close-in defense lasers on the starboard side, the ship could at least mount a credible defense. And with the pulse cannon, if it were properly used, and a brace of torpedoes, she still packed an offensive punch, too. But the maneuvering systems and the main drives, despite Chief DeFusco's belief that everything was functional, were still an uncertainty in his mind.

"The ship is at zero mark zero, system relative," Bogdanova reported. She had stopped the ship's tumbling, and now had her level relative to Keran's orbital plane, pointing toward the system's star.

"Very good, helm," Sato said, nodding. "Let's see if we can't get back into the game. All ahead one quarter, course zero four six mark zero zero seven." He was hoping that by not using any active sensors and keeping his acceleration low, the enemy ships might not notice him for a while, allowing them to get closer. He had not tried to raise the fleet for fear of being discovered prematurely by their signal emissions.

"All ahead one quarter, aye." Bogdanova smoothly advanced the analog control handle, which looked much like a throttle might have in fighter aircraft centuries before, to the appropriate stop. The actual propulsion control system and the underlying calculations behind "one quarter" power and the other standard settings were far more complex than simply moving a handle, but the simpler interface was more efficient for the human part of the control loop. After a moment, Bogdanova reported, "Sir, engineering answers all ahead one quarter, and the ship is now on course zero four six mark zero zero seven."

Sato's tension began to quickly fade as the deep and steady thrum of the ship's drives continued without the slightest indication of trouble. He watched her icon on the tactical display as the *Owen D. McClaren* once again sailed into harm's way.

TWENTY-TWO

"We've got to withdraw whatever ground troops are left, admiral," Tiernan told Admiral Lefevre over the vidcom. "The Kreelans are sending what looks like another strike force down to the surface. After the mauling our troops took from the first Kreelan attack, there won't be much left of them after a second."

While the ships of the combined human fleet had suffered only minor damage from the Kreelan force that had assaulted the planet, both the Terran and Alliance ground troops had suffered heavy casualties. Citing the inhumanly accurate fire from the Kreelan ships and the fearless warriors, General Ray's last report over his tactical laser uplink had painted a grim picture of the situation before the fleet had lost communications with both him and the general commanding the Alliance ground forces. None of the ground forces had been heard from since, although direct observations from the telescopes and other sensors aboard the human ships left little doubt that their troops on the ground were fighting for their lives. And losing.

"I agree, *mon amiral*," Lefevre said. "Recovering your troops must be the priority, as we do not have enough combat-capable lift capacity to retrieve our own." Those words were a heavy burden on Lefevre's soul, for he had just condemned tens of thousands of men and women to death if the combined human fleet failed to win the battle in space.

Tiernan gently contradicted him. "I believe you may be mistaken, sir, based on the projected losses we're coming up with. Unless we're badly mistaken - and I wouldn't mind being wrong on this one - the corps we sent in has maybe a brigade left, if that. And if your units have suffered similar losses, the available carriers may be enough to lift out the survivors."

"*Mon Dieu*," Lefevre whispered. His own operations staff had come to similar conclusions, but he hadn't wanted to believe them. He still didn't. There had been ten Alliance divisions on the surface. To think that the survivors of both forces would now fit into six assault carriers was simply unthinkable. And this after only the first Kreelan assault wave.

"I've already dispatched our courier ship to the rendezvous point to bring back our carriers," Tiernan told him. The four Terran carriers had jumped out to a holding position that was far enough away that they were safe from attack, but close enough in case they needed to be recalled quickly. He just hoped they would be able to return quickly enough.

"I will do the same," Lefevre said. "But I am not willing to concede defeat."

"Nor am I, sir," Tiernan reassured him. "I believe that the enemy is giving us an opportunity in disguise," he went on, eyeing the second assault force - roughly a third of the enemy's ship strength - as they began to head toward Keran. The first wave, the one that the human fleet had met head-on in the upper reaches of Keran's atmosphere, had almost rejoined the main group in high orbit. "The timing will be tricky, but if we can engage the second wave as they come up from Keran, we should have at least a two to one advantage in firepower. Of course, that assumes that the remaining enemy ships are content to stay in high orbit."

Lefevre offered a Gallic shrug. "Something we can never count on, the enemy doing what we would like. Still, it is an opportunity we cannot reasonably pass up. My operations officer will coordinate for maneuvering orders, since we still have no data-link connectivity. Then we will see if we cannot teach our blue-skinned friends a thing or two about naval combat."

***

Aboard the *Alita*, Amelia Cartwright waited tensely as the ship's navigation computer counted down the remaining seconds to their emergence into normal space. While she certainly didn't mind helping the fleet by acting as their courier, she also was itching to do more than just ferry messages back and forth. But *Alita* wasn't built for combat. In any engagement, the best she could be was a target, albeit a fast one.

"Transpace sequence in three...two...one," the computer announced. "Transpace sequence complete." Suddenly the swirling nothingness of hyperspace displayed on the screen before her dissolved into pinpoints of light and the glowing orb of Keran.

"Shit," Sid, her copilot, whispered as the sensor display stabilized and began to paint the situation in the space around the planet, with the large cloud of blue icons facing off against the red. "The admiral's going to kick some ass."

Cartwright nodded, taking a look at the tactical display as she made sure that the ship had come through the jump in one piece. A Kreelan force had headed down to the planet, and it was clear that Tiernan was maneuvering to try and catch the Kreelans on the flip side as they climbed out of the gravity well after their attack. So far the Kreelans remaining in high orbit were staying put, but she knew that wouldn't last if they had any sense at all.

"Five seconds for the carriers," Sid reminded her as she maneuvered the ship, taking her well forward of the carriers' inbound jump point. She had taken *Alita* in first to scout the situation and have a warning prepared for the carriers in case they were jumping into a hot zone. At this point, they were safe.

"There they are," Cartwright told him, seeing the four blue icons representing the Terran carriers materialize right behind *Alita* on the tactical display. "*Guadalcanal*," she called over the vidcom, "it looks like you're clear for now. We'll proceed ahead of you to make sure there aren't any surprises waiting for you."

"Roger that, *Alita*," the lead carrier's captain said. "We appreciate the assist. I've got to contact Admiral Tiernan. *Guadalcanal*, out."

"You sure you want to do this?" Sid asked her quietly, looking at the swarm of ships ahead of them moving toward a massive clash.

She gave him a determined look. "We can't just run, Sid," she told him. "I know we're not in the Navy, but we've got the fastest ship in the system, and we've got to help if we can."

Sid only nodded and readjusted his cowboy hat as he squirmed a bit deeper in his seat.

With a tingle of fear running down her spine, Cartwright throttled up the engines and led the four assault carriers toward Keran.

***

"Dammit!" Tiernan cursed under his breath. "So," he growled at his flag communications officer, "you're telling me that we still have no communication with anyone on the ground?"

"Correct, sir," the commander replied, trying not to flinch. "We haven't been able to get any voice or vidcom signals from the surface. The only way we might be able to get through is a direct laser link, but it's going to have to be a very low orbit pass, and the ship will only have a few minutes over any given location before it passes over the horizon and out of range."

Tiernan wasn't angry at his officer, just at the damnable situation. Whatever weapon the Kreelans had used earlier that had knocked out much of the human fleet's communications capability had completely befuddled the communications experts on both the Alliance and the Terran ships. Absolutely nothing that used the radio frequency spectrum would work. Direct laser communications still worked for basic voice and vidcom, but not for the data-link systems, even though there seemed to be nothing wrong with any of the equipment and software.

Regaining communications with the ground forces was vital in order to get them to assembly areas where the assault boats from the carriers could retrieve them: Tiernan couldn't have the boats wandering across the planet looking for his people. The carriers had to be able to get in and out quickly, as Tiernan couldn't afford to detach even a single destroyer to protect them. Without radio communications, which could be broadcast to a wide area, the only way to talk to the troops on the ground would be by sending a ship in low and praying they could make contact over a laser link, which had an extremely narrow broadcast area.

"What about that courier ship?" his flag captain suggested. "The *Alita*, isn't she? She could haul ahead of the carriers, get in low, and try to regain contact with General Ray."

"It's a civilian ship," the flag operations officer protested. "They're not going to do that, and they shouldn't. They're not trained or equipped for it."

Tiernan looked at the tiny icon on the main display that represented a small ship and its two-person crew. "Do they have laser link capability?"

"All diplomatic courier ships have a basic laser link capability, sir," the communications officer said. "It's not military grade, but it's powerful enough. Some of the diplomatic missions they have to serve are in places with pretty rough environmental conditions, and they need communications that can get through, no matter what. And the tactical sensor package that was retrofitted on all the Keran couriers has an improved laser link detection capability, so if anyone on the ground is calling, they have a better chance of picking it up. Assuming they're in the path of the laser."

That decided it. "Get me *Alita's* captain," Tiernan said.

***

"Do you know who that was?" Sid asked, incredulous.

Cartwright threw him a sidelong glance. "Of course I do, Sid," she said, exasperated. He'd said the same thing five times in as many minutes after Admiral Tiernan had given her his "request." As if she would even think of saying no.

Alita was now streaking toward Keran under full acceleration, leaving the fat carriers far behind. Orbital insertion was going to be tricky, not just because of the courier ship's speed, but also because the second wave of Kreelan ships, the ones that Admiral Tiernan was going to pound on, were going to be a lot closer than she would like. Low orbit space was going to be awfully crowded for a while.

The admiral's communications officer had given them coordinates for where the Terran and Alliance troops had been landed, and Sid had programmed the ship's laser link system to broadcast over as wide an area as possible. They had already started an automated broadcast, just on the off chance that someone might pick it up before they entered low orbit: they had nothing to lose but a bit of power. Some might have thought their chances were about as good as finding a needle in a haystack, with the qualification that they were looking for the needle through a straw about as big around as a strand of spaghetti.

***

Amar-Marakh, the senior shipmistress of the Imperial ships around the human planet, nodded in approval as the human ships began to deploy against her second attack wave, even as the surviving ships of the first wave rejoined her. Her blood burned that she herself was not in the force heading toward the planet, for the engagement the humans were planning would be fierce and her heart cried out for battle. But that would yet come. For now, it was up to the shipmistresses and warriors of the second wave to bring glory to the Empress.

She knew the humans could not pass up an attack against the second wave, and that Her warships would be greatly outnumbered. She also knew that the animals would not have things all their own way. While the ships of the second wave would be dropping many more warriors to engage the surviving humans warriors on the surface, they would be keeping nearly a third in reserve to send against the human fleet as they closed to engage. The human ships had proven very vulnerable to boarding attacks, which perfectly suited the desires of Her Children.

Her heart beat rapidly as she watched the unfolding battle on her display, the Bloodsong of her sisters a thundering chorus in her veins.

***

Tiernan was proud of his crews as the Terran ships slid into position in the new formation he had worked out with *Amiral* Lefevre. Normally, the data-link systems also provided navigational orders, allowing the ships to closely coordinate their movements. With that information gone, each ship had to maneuver independently, and it would have been a challenge under the best of circumstances to form up over one hundred warships from two different navies, all under manual control. But his crews and those of the Alliance made it look like such feats were easy.

After more discussion with Admiral Lefevre, they had decided to put the Terran ships at the head of the formation as they engaged the Kreelans. The Alliance ships had already seen an exhausting fight, and some of them were running dangerously low on munitions. *Ticonderoga* herself was the point ship of the third echelon wedge, with a wedge of cruisers ahead, and a flotilla of destroyers leading the attack. The plan was for the destroyers to fire their torpedoes to help distract and, if they were lucky, break up the Kreelan formation, and then have the destroyers peel away to the flanks so that the heavier guns of the cruisers could hammer the enemy ships into scrap.

As Tiernan watched the red icons of the Kreelan second wave near Keran, he saw the solitary blue icon of the *Alita*, which was now sailing ahead of the Kreelan ships. He nodded in approval: the commander of the tiny ship had both brains and guts. Had she tried an orbit that brought her head to head or even flank-on to the Kreelans, they would no doubt destroy her. But sailing ahead of them, as crazy as it seemed, was also safest: unless the Kreelans showed some of the hideously advanced technology that Sato had reported, there was no way they would be able to catch her.

"Come on, Cartwright," Tiernan breathed. The only chance the ground forces might have of survival rested with Cartwright and her tiny ship. Otherwise, the troops on Keran wouldn't even realize a second attack was on its way, and the carriers would have come back for nothing.

TWENTY-THREE

Coyle was exhausted, but there was no stopping. The 7th Cavalry Regiment, which had started with just over three thousand men and women, had been reduced to a short battalion of a few hundred, including the survivors she had picked up from a few other units. The officers, all of whom had been in or near vehicles that were using the data-links targeted by the Kreelan ships, had been decimated: the senior officer - the *only* combat effective officer - was Lieutenant Krumholtz, the infantry lieutenant she had picked up early on. That would have made him the acting commander, but Sparks had made Coyle a brevet captain once the extent of the disaster for the ground forces had become clear, and she'd found herself in charge of the clusterfuck they were in. After that, Sparks had passed out and had remained unconscious. He was holding on, but only through sheer stubbornness: riding in the back of a civilian vehicle that had been abandoned and put into service as an ambulance, he was being tossed around in what had become an increasingly desperate effort to escape the killing ground of Foshan.

Chiquita, Coyle's tank, was one of only four in the entire regiment to have survived the battle to this point. Since the fight to save the colonel, she had found seven other tanks, but three of them had been destroyed by a small but determined pack of Kreelan warriors. Her unit's progress was slow, both because most of her troops had to move on foot, and because of the successive waves of civilian refugees that were boiling out of the wreckage of the city, usually driven along by more Kreelan warriors. Coyle felt compelled to try and give the civilians as much protection as she could, which further slowed her down and made her tanks easier targets for the Kreelans and their devilish grenades.

She would have headed out of the city where her tanks would have a much easier time keeping the enemy at bay, but she knew they had to link up with any other survivors of the division, if they could find them.

After a nightmarish drive farther into Foshan, where she found the smoking wreckage that had been the division command post, she realized that the division, and the corps as a whole, had effectively been wiped out.

She had picked up a few more troops from some of the division's other brigades, but only a handful. She had no doubt that there were other pockets of survivors - she could hear sporadic bursts of gunfire in other parts of the city - but she wasn't going to expend any more effort or lives trying to find them.

She was going to try and get her people out of the city.

"The corps is well and truly fucked," she told Lieutenant Krumholtz and the senior NCOs who had gathered in front of *Chiquita*. Coyle hated to risk stopping even for a few minutes, which would let the Kreelans who were hunting her tanks catch up, but she didn't have any choice. They needed to get a new game plan together. "We've got to turn around and head out of the city."

"We can't do that," Krumholtz argued. If anything, he was more tired than Coyle was, having had to slog along with his troops through the rubble and past shell-shocked civilians as the Terran column had slowly made its way deeper into the city. "If we can find General Ray, he'll be able to-"

"He's dead!" Coyle snapped. "Look at this, for Christ's sake," she said, sweeping her arm around them. The entire block where the division command post vehicles had been hidden had been pulverized, with every single building reduced to ashes and chunks of brick no bigger than her fist. The hammering her own platoon had received from the Kreelan ships had been a love tap by comparison. She knew that it was remotely possible that someone could still be alive in their vehicle, buried under the rubble. But there was no time to search. "The corps CP won't be any different. Face it, el-tee, we're on our own."

The younger officer was about to make a fiery retort when Yuri, her gunner, shouted from his open hatch in the turret, "Coyle! We've got a laser-link from the fleet!"

"Hot damn," she said as she jumped up on *Chiquita* to reach her cupola. Normally she would have been able to take the call through her helmet's radio, but with all radio communications knocked out she had to physically plug in a cable from the helmet.

"This is Sergeant...scratch that," she said hastily. "This is Captain Coyle of the 7th Cavalry Regiment. Go ahead, over."

"Coyle," a woman's voice said quickly, "This is the *Alita*. I only have about ninety seconds before we lose you. The good news is that carriers are inbound for extraction of Terran and Alliance troops, but you have to reach one of the landing zones. The closest one to you will be..." she read off some coordinates that turned out to be near their original combat positions. "You've got forty minutes until the assault boats land."

"Forty minutes?" Coyle cried. "There's no fucking way we can get back there in forty goddamn minutes!" It had taken over an hour to get this far, wading through the tide of civilian refugees and fighting off the pursuing Kreelans.

"There are two other zones at-" the woman read off more coordinates as if she hadn't heard Coyle's outburst. Neither of them was even close to Foshan. "Forty minutes. Pass the word. Be advised that there is also a second wave of Kreelan ships inbound. Expect them in..."

The signal suddenly broke off.

Yuri was looking at her with disbelieving eyes. Tearing off her helmet, Coyle looked up at the sky, which was still a witch's brew of smoke and ash from the burning city center. "Give us a *fucking break*, will you?" she yelled at any god or God who might be listening.

"What happened?" Krumholtz asked, following her gaze to the dirty gray smoke overhead.

"They've recalled the carriers and are bringing down the boats to extract us," she told him through gritted teeth, "but we've only got forty goddamn minutes to make it back to the landing zone, which is right fucking where we started from. And as if that weren't bad enough, more Kreelans are on the way." She slammed her helmet against the cupola in frustration, then stuck it back on her head. "Have your people ditch everything they don't need, lieutenant. They've got to be able to move fast. Drop everything: body armor, water, and anything else they won't need to survive for the next forty minutes, except for weapons and ammo. Put out a dozen guys up front who can move fast and be our eyes and ears so my tanks don't get bushwhacked. If there are Kreelans around a corner or sneaking around in buildings, I want to know before they start lobbing those fucking grenades of theirs."

"You won't leave us behind, Coyle, will you?" he asked uncertainly.

She looked at him hard. "You've got to keep up, lieutenant." Then, softening slightly, she said, "Listen, I'd have some of your guys ride on the tanks, but we've got to keep the turrets and engine decks clear if - when - we run into Kreelans. Otherwise we'll either kill your guys with the muzzle blast if we have to fire the main guns, or get killed waiting for you to clear off. Now get going. We don't have a second to waste."

"Garry Owen," he replied as he and his platoon sergeant dashed off, frantically shouting orders at the infantry. Many of them hadn't started the battle as infantry, but if you had your vehicle shot out from under you and you were left on foot with nothing but a rifle, infantry is what you became.

Normally Coyle would have asked the other tank commanders how they were doing on ammunition and taken some time to redistribute as best they could. She was down to ten rounds of main gun ammunition, all of them armor piercing rounds that were totally useless against infantry. Worse, the close-in defense mortar was out of ammo, and she only had a couple thousand rounds for the coaxial gun and her gatling gun: enough for maybe twenty seconds of continuous firing. But there was no time now. None at all.

"Frederickson," she said to one of the other tank commanders, "you'll ride shotgun with me up in the front. Have your tank cover the right side of the road and I'll take the left. Hoyt, Gagarin, you guys bring up the rear. We'll keep the bulk of the infantry between us, and I'll have the lieutenant run out a skirmish line of whoever he's got who can move fast to scout in front of us. For God's sake, don't run over anybody, but don't let the infantry guys slow you down, either. Keep 'em moving. If we fall behind schedule, we're gonna miss the bus, and I don't need to tell you what that means with more of those blue-skinned bitches about to fall out of the sky on us. Questions?" There were none. "Then let's haul ass."

***

Steph felt like she was in a surreal nightmare as she struggled to keep up with the tanks. The cavalry troopers had offered to let her ride with Colonel Sparks and Sergeant Hadley in the civilian van they'd picked up along the way, but she'd given up her spot for a trooper whose hip had been sliced open by one of the Kreelan flying weapons. There were others who were wounded, but they had to do their best to keep up. They realized that there was no surrender. So they walked, ran, and shuffled as best they could, troopers who were uninjured helping those who were.

She wasn't in the military, but she had seen the elephant, as the ancient saying went, and it had changed her life forever. Her vidcam was still recording every moment, and she even muttered notes now and again when she came across some new vision of horror. But she clutched her rifle to her shoulder, imitating the more experienced infantry soldiers around her, and watched every window and door on her side of the street. She had even killed a number of Kreelans that the other soldiers had missed: being a journalist had given her a lot of experience in noticing small things that others often didn't see. The infantry squad that she had arbitrarily become attached to had at first looked at her as a burden, but after she blew the first Kreelan out of a window as she rose unseen to throw a grenade, they had shown her more than a little respect.

But she was tired, so tired from what seemed like an endless battle. She was tired of trudging through these cursed streets, littered with abandoned cars, dead civilians, glass and rubble, only to reach a dead end, and then to have to turn around and run-walk back the way they had come. She was in decent physical shape, largely thanks to Ichiro's intense interest in fitness, and had been able to keep up so far. But she was winded from this agonizing running shuffle behind Coyle's armored behemoths, her eyes stinging from the smoke and grimy sweat, her tongue feeling like it was coated with dust. Her shoulders burned from holding the rifle, which was like a lead ingot in her hands, and she was constantly stumbling on rubble or other bits of debris. And bodies. So many bodies.

But she refused to stop. She would *not* stop.

***

Li'ara-Zhurah paused to catch her breath. Her body trembled, but not from exhaustion or pain: her heart and muscles fluttered from a sense of pure exhilaration, the likes of which she had never known. Leading a small group of warriors, she was hunting some of the massive human vehicles that were shepherding a group of human warriors through the city. Curiously, the humans had come some distance into what was left of the metropolis, but then had turned around and were retracing their steps.

She had been hunting them since shortly after her earlier encounter with a group of different armored vehicles, the smaller ones with wheels, when Tesh-Dar had gone her own way. The humans had fought bravely, and after their last charge a few had even escaped; Li'ara-Zhurah and her warriors could have hunted them down, but she had let them go so that other warriors might have the honor. She was yet young and sometimes impetuous, but was already wise enough to understand the dignity of sharing the honor of the kill with her sisters.

When that battle was over, Kamal-Utai had gone to rejoin Tesh-Dar on whatever mission the priestess had set for herself, leaving Li'ara-Zhurah to seek out new challenges. She had been drawn to the sound of heavy guns firing in the nearby fringe of the city, and had run toward what was clearly a savage battle, marked in her blood by the joyful chorus of Her Children as they fought and died. Other warriors had the same idea, and it had become a spirited race to see who might first reach the source of the excitement.

Li'ara-Zhurah had been bested by several warriors, but her disappointment at losing the foot race was brief: incautiously rounding a corner, focusing more on winning than surviving long enough to take the fight to the enemy, the warriors disappeared in a bone-shattering deluge of weapons fire from a huge armored vehicle, much larger than those they had faced earlier.

Pitching herself behind a sturdy brick wall, Li'ara-Zhurah waited until the vehicle stopped firing. It paused, as if the humans inside it knew she was there and were waiting for her to show herself. But after a while, with much shouting and noise, the vehicle and its accompanying human warriors moved on.

Once the humans had turned a corner down the street, Li'ara-Zhurah stepped carefully out of her hiding place, and stood dead-still as she looked upon a killing ground the likes of which she had never before seen. Some few hundreds of warriors, Children of the Empress, lay slain in the street, their bodies torn as if by a great *genoth*, a species of monstrous dragon that inhabited the wastelands of the Homeworld. She and the other warriors who had followed her walked gingerly through the remains of the slaughter, their sandals awash in blood. They knelt here and there to honor their sisters, and gave the last rites to the few who were badly injured and claimed death as their just reward. For even as the daggers of their sisters pierced still-beating hearts, those who were given the gift of death could hear the call of the Empress to their souls, beckoning them onward to kneel alongside the Ancient Ones, basking in the eternal light of Her love.

Once they had finished the rites, there was no question of what must be done. Splitting up into hunting packs, they followed the human behemoth and its attending warriors. Li'ara-Zhurah felt no grief or anger at the carnage the humans had wrought upon her sisters. She felt instead a suffusing joy and a burning desire to take the beast, not in revenge, but as a prize. As on the Homeworld in ancient times, when warriors killed the *genoth* and won great glory in Her name, so it would be for the warrior or warriors who defeated such a beast as the one they now pursued. It was a challenge from which only the most courageous and ferocious warrior would emerge victorious.

The large group of warriors that had originally dogged the humans had gradually been whittled down, as those who were too young, inexperienced, or simply unlucky were culled from the pursuing pack. The effect had been similar on the humans, Li'ara-Zhurah knew: while several more of the great war machines had joined the group of humans, some of them were destroyed, and only the true survivors were left.

While other warriors had earned their honor in destroying some of the machines, none had yet survived the attacks. More important, the beast she herself desired, the one that she had first seen, remained alive. Its commander was cunning and skilled, and her death would be a great victory. The more difficult the situation, the greater the challenge, and all the greater the glory in Her eyes and soul. Li'ara-Zhurah's spirit trembled on the threshold of a type of ecstasy that no human being had ever known.

The greatest challenge was to get close enough to use one of the grenades, although she would have much preferred to use her sword. But even the living metal of her blade was likely not a match for the vehicle's thick armor. So a grenade it would be. She only had one, and would not risk throwing it unless she was sure of her target.

Leading her group of half a dozen warriors down a parallel street, she darted into a building ahead of where the humans were. They were moving faster now, as if they had to get somewhere at a particular time, and Li'ara-Zhurah was growing concerned that her opportunity may not come. She was unafraid of death, but she did not want to sacrifice her body without bringing glory to Her name. For Li'ara-Zhurah, more even than her spiritual sisters, this was paramount, for she was born from Her very womb, a blood daughter of the Empress. She had never met her mother in the flesh since the day she had been born, but she did not need to: she knew the Empress in her heart, in the Bloodsong that filled her spirit.

She had just crept up to a shattered windowsill that allowed her to peer down the street unobserved when another group of warriors began their attack.

***

Coyle's ad-hoc task force had just entered a narrower street, trying to get around a glut of refugees that blocked their original path, when all hell broke loose.

"*Grenade!*" someone screamed as a glowing cyan ball arced through the air from an upstairs window of a building. It landed squarely in the middle of the engine deck of Coyle's tank and instantly began to glow white hot.

Before it could explode into a shower of blue lightning, one of the infantry troopers following behind the tank threw down his weapon and climbed up onto the vehicle. Grabbing the grenade, the soldier screamed in agony as it seared his hands, but he somehow managed to pry it off before leaping from the back of the tank. The weapon detonated while he was still in mid-air, incinerating his body in a wild cascade of lightning that scorched everyone and everything in a three meter radius. *Chiquita's* rear armor was blackened and even melted in a few spots, but the tank still survived.

As the soldier's charred body slammed into the ground, several dozen Kreelan warriors surged out of the buildings along the right hand side of the street, tearing into the mass of weary infantry.

While Coyle's soldiers were taken by surprise, they had been through this before and reacted instantly, blasting away at their enemies at point blank range as the Kreelans hurled their lethal throwing weapons and slashed and stabbed with their swords.

Steph was just taking aim at a warrior when she was viciously knocked to the ground. She struggled to turn over, but couldn't: a foot was planted in the middle of her back, pinning her to the ground on top of her rifle. She could turn her head just far enough to see the Kreelan, the blade of her sword glinting in the smoky light as she swung it down to take Steph's head from her neck.

The blade never touched her. The Kreelan's chest disappeared in a spray of crimson as three rounds from *Chiquita's* gatling gun blew her to pieces. With a passionate curse, Steph struggled to her feet through the muck that fell on top of her, all that remained of her would-be killer. She moved to the rear of Coyle's tank, trying to offer it some protection from another grenade attack while the nearby infantrymen grappled with the alien warriors and the gatling guns on the tanks growled.

Without warning one of the tanks in the rear was suddenly lit by a corona of lightning after it was hit by a Kreelan grenade. The crew never had a chance to get out. The vehicle exploded, knocking everyone - human and Kreelan alike - to the ground. The turret flipped up into the air like a toy before crashing down on top of a still-wrestling mob of humans and Kreelans.

Steph could see that the other tank to the rear was also in trouble: it had stopped in the street, just ahead of the one that now lay burning. The hatches suddenly flew open and the crewmen scrambled to escape. All three were cut down by a flurry of Kreelan flying weapons.

"*Keep moving, goddammit!*" Steph heard Coyle screaming above the raging chaos. Indeed, *Chiquita* hadn't stopped or even slowed down, and Steph suddenly turned and ran to catch up, shouting at her surviving squad mates to do the same.

* * *

The gatling gun mounted to the top of the turret had never been designed as a sniper weapon, but Coyle was doing the best she could. The Kreelans had become so closely enmeshed with her own people that she couldn't open fire without shooting her own troopers. She killed the Kreelan who was about to lop the head off the reporter woman, and managed to get a few more, but her tank's power had effectively been neutralized: she couldn't use her more powerful weapons without taking out half of what was left of her scraped-up battalion.

As if the enemy weren't bad enough, the clock was still ticking. Coyle could almost hear it in her brain, counting down the minutes until they would be marooned on this world. They couldn't afford to get bogged down. Missing their extraction would kill them as surely as a blade to the heart.

"*Keep moving, goddammit!*" she screamed at the troops behind her. "Mannie," she told the driver, "don't fucking stop for anything. Keep us moving or we're dead."

"Roger," he said shakily. "Garry Owen," he whispered, as if to himself. Coyle thought he was losing it. And she knew she wasn't far behind him.

Chiquita was leaving most of the troops behind: they were too fixated on trying to keep from being killed by the Kreelans among them to worry about dying if they missed the boats.

Coyle turned on the loudspeakers for her tank again, her voice booming out, "Break contact! Break contact!"

Her order was rewarded by a surge of soldiers trying to break away from the close quarters fight. The ones on the fringes of the mayhem were able to turn and run after Coyle's tank. But for many, there was simply no getting away from the Kreelans without killing them first. Most of the infantry soldiers were running desperately low on ammunition at this point, or were completely out, and the Kreelans had a decided advantage in any close-in combat: their swords were infinitely better than the bayonets and knives wielded by their human opponents, and their claws were as lethal as any edged weapon.

Out of the corner of her eye, Coyle saw another, smaller group of Kreelans break out of the cover of one of the buildings, just behind Frederickson's tank, which was driving alongside her. She twisted her gun around as Frederickson was, but the warriors were too close: she couldn't depress the barrels enough to shoot at them. "Shoot them!" she screamed, pointing, hoping that some of the infantry would take them down.

Instead, she heard a rapid popping sound as Frederickson panicked, ripple firing the last half dozen rounds from his tank's close-in defense mortar as a Kreelan ran up and slapped a glowing grenade on the lower side of his tank, behind the track.

"No you stupid fuck!" Coyle cried as she watched the small grenades arc away from Frederickson's tank. She could tell from the dispersal pattern that he must have tried to target not only the ones now hunting his tank, but the others in the street, as well. That would have been just dandy, Coyle thought bitterly, except that most of their own people were in the blast zone.

"Get down!" she shouted over the loudspeakers as she dropped down into the turret and slammed the hatch. "*Incoming!*"

***

Steph was firing her rifle steadily, killing any warriors who stood far enough away from the humans around them for her to feel confident in taking a shot.

Then she heard a strange popping sound. She knew all the weapons the tanks carried from interviewing some of the cavalry soldiers before they landed on Keran, and she had heard the tanks use this one already. It just took a moment to register what weapon it was. *The self-defense mortars*, she thought. It took one more second to realize that they were close-in weapons, and that she was probably in the blast radius and completely in the open.

She heard Coyle shouting something over her tank's speakers, but Steph couldn't hear and didn't care. She slapped the nearest soldiers on the shoulder to get their attention before sprinting up the narrow chasm between the left side of Coyle's tank and the nearest building, putting the tank's bulk between her and the mortar rounds. She tumbled to the ground as the rounds exploded at waist height behind her.

As she was trying to get back up, the tank next to Coyle's exploded.

***

The explosion of Frederickson's tank slammed Coyle's head against the inside hatch coaming. Had she not been wearing a helmet, her skull would have been fractured. As it was, she got off with little more than temporary deafness from the blast and a massive headache.

Chiquita's systems didn't even flicker, but that was no consolation to the tank's commander. Coyle bit back her tears and the surge of bile that rose to her throat as she saw the carnage in the street. Frederickson's grenades would have been bad enough, detonating in the midst of the melee to kill Kreelans and humans alike. But the explosion of his tank was worse: the Kreelan who planted the grenade had the uncanny luck to have stuck it right over one of the fuel cells. The resulting explosion blew out the right rear of the vehicle in a spectacular fireball that killed most of those who managed to survive the grenades.

Coyle was glad Frederickson was dead. Had the Kreelan grenade not cooked him inside his tank, she would have killed him herself. But the heart of Coyle's cold, bitter rage was the knowledge that she would now have to leave so many behind: not just the dead, but the wounded and those simply too exhausted to keep up. She simply couldn't protect them, and if they continued at a shuffling pace, they were all going to die.

Her driver had kept the tank moving at a pace that would just barely get them to the extraction zone on time, assuming they didn't hit any major obstacles. But the time for that was over.

As *Chiquita* turned the corner about fifty meters down the street, she said, "Stop the tank, Mannie." She popped the hatch and wearily stood up to face the pitifully few soldiers who had managed to survive and stay with her. Ironically, the civilian van that was packed with wounded, including Colonel Sparks and Sergeant Hadley, was still with her. The Kreelans were completely ignoring it, as if it weren't worthy of being attacked, and it had been just far enough away to avoid major damage from Frederickson's tank when it blew.

Coyle could still hear screaming from behind them, whether just the agony of the wounded, or from terror of more Kreelans, she didn't know. She didn't want to know.

"Get on," she croaked through the loudspeakers to the exhausted infantry catching their breath in the tank's shadow.

For a moment, none of them moved. She was about to repeat herself when the female newshound awkwardly slung her rifle and clambered up the left side and onto the top deck of the hull. Turning around, she gestured to the other soldiers around her to climb on, and did her best to help them up. In a minute or two, the survivors of the 7th Cavalry Regiment had crammed themselves on top of Coyle's tank, holding on to any handy protrusion on the hull and turret, hanging on to each other.

"Whatever you do," Coyle shouted at them, "don't let go. If you fall off, we're not stopping for you." She caught the eye of the reporter, leaning against the turret near Coyle's cupola. The woman nodded, one hand holding onto the turret basket that contained all of the crew's gear and spare parts. Her other hand clutched her rifle.

"Yuri," she said through her helmet intercom to the gunner as she slewed her gatling gun to point behind the tank, just over the heads of the infantry crouching on the engine deck, "watch our front. I'll keep an eye on the rear." Then, to the driver, she said, "Go, Mannie. Go as fast as you can. And don't stop for shit."

"We're just going to leave them?" he said, his voice colored as much with relief as with guilt.

"Do you want to go back there, Mannie?" she whispered into the microphone, hoping the infantry clustered around her wouldn't hear.

But of course, they did. Heads turned away, faces clouded with shame. More than a few cheeks were streaked with tears. They were leaving behind friends and comrades, in some cases lovers. But none of them, not one, wanted to go back. They heard what Coyle said, but pretended not to.

Without another word, Mannie started *Chiquita* moving, the quiet whine of the powerful motors lost in the squeaking and clanking of the battered tracks as the heavy vehicle picked up speed.

The last thing Coyle heard, as plain as if he were standing right beside her, was the voice of Lieutenant Krumholtz, who had been hit in the leg and hadn't been able to keep up. He was among those who were now being left behind.

"Goddamn, you, Coyle!" she heard him scream. "*God damn you!*"

TWENTY-FOUR

Tiernan's attention was fixed on the tactical display. For once, the combined human fleet had a clear tactical advantage, and he and Lefevre were determined to make the most of it. They outnumbered the Kreelan force by roughly two to one in ships and tonnage both, and the admirals planned to force a decisive engagement before the remaining Kreelan ships in high orbit could maneuver to interfere. So far those enemy ships had been content to stay where they were, but Tiernan knew that couldn't last forever.

The disposition of the two fleets also clearly favored the humans: instead of the head-on stone throwing contest they had against the first Kreelan assault force, the human fleet would first pass across the head of the second Kreelan formation as it clawed its way up from low orbit, "crossing the T" in old wet navy terms. The human ships would be able to bring all of their main batteries to bear, while the Kreelans would only be able to target the humans with their forward-facing weapons. After that, the plan was to reverse course behind the Kreelans and take them the same way from behind, raking the vulnerable sterns of the enemy ships. Neither admiral expected the plan to go off as planned, as reality always intervened, but it was a good place to start.

"All ships reporting assigned target lock," the flag communications officer reported.

On the display, the range rings of the *Ticonderoga's* guns converged on her assigned target as the wedges of human ships swept across the front of the Kreelan formation.

"All ships," Tiernan ordered, "fire as you bear!" Without the data-link and the networked targeting computers to optimize the fleet's firing solutions, Tiernan had to count on each ship firing when it came in optimal range as the formations passed by one another.

At the head of the formation, the destroyers loosed a volley of torpedoes, the missiles streaking toward the Kreelan formation, twisting and jinking madly to avoid anti-missile fire. Not waiting to see if any of them hit, the destroyers hauled to the side to get out of the way of the larger cruisers as they began to open fire.

"Incoming," the flag tactical officer announced, warning of rounds from Kreelan guns heading toward them. Then *Ticonderoga's* primary kinetic weapons thundered, sending several dozen projectiles in a closely-spaced pattern at her assigned target, one of the leading Kreelan cruisers. "Ships maneuvering," he added as the individual human ships adjusted their courses to try and avoid the Kreelan weapons fire. It was a difficult balance: the human ships needed to try and avoid the incoming enemy salvoes, but still had to stay in formation to maximize the volume of fire they could bring to bear on the Kreelan ships.

Tiernan gave a death's head grin as the tactical display showed the imbalance of fire between the two fleets: for every Kreelan round fired, at least three rounds were going back at them from his and Lefevre's ships.

Kreelan ships suddenly began to dart and weave, but the weight of fire from the human fleet was too great: even if a Kreelan ship dodged the rounds targeted against it, it almost inevitably ran into another stream of projectiles fired at another target. The first echelon of cruisers in the enemy formation suddenly disintegrated, with half of the warships destroyed outright and the other half either damaged or maneuvering so wildly that they were unable to effectively return fire. A number of other enemy ships also suffered damage, which slowed them down and forced them to change course to avoid the withering fire pouring from the human fleet.

A cheer went up through the *Ticonderoga* from everyone who could see one of the tactical displays, and Tiernan felt a tingle run up his spine and gooseflesh pop up on his arms. *Eat that, damn you*, he thought savagely.

"Continue firing!" he ordered as *Ticonderoga* shuddered from a single hit. Alarms went off on the ship's bridge, but they were quickly silenced.

"Enemy is changing course," the tactical officer warned. The enemy formation had swung to the left and accelerated slightly, trying to close the range with the human fleet and at the same time unmask their aft batteries so they could bring more of their weapons into play against the human ships.

This was the part that Tiernan had been dreading. Without networked tactical control of the ships and the inability to broadcast orders to the entire fleet at once (as opposed to direct laser-links to individual ships), any large-scale maneuvering was impossible without the formation falling apart. If they tried to maneuver and keep the Kreelans at a distance, he knew they could pound them to hell and back. But only if the fleet maintained its integrity. If it lost that, if the individual flotillas that formed the wedges of the formation fell out to be left on their own, they could be destroyed.

"Admiral Lefevre," he said, "I recommend we hold course until the designated maneuver point. If we maintain integrity, we maintain our advantage in weight of fire, even if the enemy closes with us."

"If they get close enough," Lefevre warned, "they will try to attack with boarders."

"Let them try," Tiernan said.

**

Waiting in high orbit with the rest of the Kreelan fleet, Amar-Marakh watched as the second assault wave was savaged by the humans. She bowed her head in acknowledgement of the humans' ferocity and basic skills in naval combat. Had this been a true fight for the Empire's survival, she would never have committed ships - even as primitive ones as these - to battle this way. But this was not a life or death duel for the Empire. It was a great Challenge, a contest of wills and warrior spirit that Amar-Marakh knew would last for generations. Even being here, at this first great battle, was an honor that would be marked forever in the Books of Time.

The senior shipmistress of the second wave had been killed in the first volley fired by the human fleet, along with many of her sisters. Most of the ships would likely not survive, but enough would come within range to send forth their warriors to wreak havoc on the human ships in the preferred way. They had dropped most of their warriors on the planet's surface near the surviving human warriors, but still had several thousand in reserve.

She turned her attention to a curiosity that she had noticed a short time before: six large human ships that were far from the main human fleet and sailing directly toward the planet. She could not be sure at this range, but she suspected they were transports sent to retrieve the remaining human warriors on the surface.

Closing her eyes to help her concentrate, she listened more intently to the Bloodsong coursing through her, striving to hear the individual threads of some of those who fought on the surface, particularly that of Tesh-Dar. The great priestess's song was no challenge to find, and Amar-Marakh focused on the melody of fire and blood, seeking to divine her will.

After a moment, she opened her eyes, withdrawing her attention from the raging torrent of emotions that welled up from the warriors on the surface of the planet, mingling with the tidal wave of pain and ecstasy of the second wave now being mauled by the human ships.

The will of the Desh-Ka priestess was clear: the human warriors should not be allowed to leave.

With a few words to her equivalent of a flag tactical officer, Amar-Marakh sent four swift warships, about the size of human destroyers, in pursuit of the ungainly transports.

***

"Skipper," Ensign Bogdanova said, motioning toward the tactical display on the *McClaren's* bridge, "those ships..."

"I see them," Sato said, noting her use of the term "skipper." No one had ever used the term with Morrison, because he had never earned the crew's respect, only their fear and loathing. It was a small thing on the surface, only a single word, but it warmed Sato and helped him find the confidence to get beyond his insecurities as the ship's captain-by-default. There was so much he didn't know, so much that could get them killed. But he didn't have a choice. None of them did.

On the display, they watched as four Kreelan ships broke off and headed on what looked like an intercept course for six ships - presumably human - that had jumped in a short while before in two groups, and were now heading toward Keran. It was impossible to tell what they were from the passive sensors, but the emissions signatures from their engines indicated that the ships must be big. The devil of it was that *McClaren* was probably the only ship that could intervene: the raging battle now underway between the human fleet and the second Kreelan assault group had moved on toward the other side of, and farther away from, the planet. It would be a long stretch for any of Admiral Tiernan's ships to reach the six ships - carriers, he guessed - in time to help them.

As for the situation with his own vessel, *McClaren* had managed to sail past the Kreelan formation in high orbit unscathed. While the Kreelans hadn't been maneuvering, their natural movement along the orbital plane had carried them farther away as *McClaren* crept behind them. He had no idea if they simply hadn't noticed, or if they decided that a lone destroyer wasn't worth worrying about. If the latter, he hoped to prove them wrong.

"Helm," he said to Bogdanova, "plot an intercept course at your best speed to bring us up behind those four Kreelan ships. Communications," he said to Petty Officer Third Class Stephen Jaworski, a repair technician who was manning the communications console, "see if you can get a laser-link to one of the newcomers. Let's see who they are."

"I've been trying, sir," he said uncertainly, "but it's hard to get a directional lock for the laser at this range using just the passive sensors." He continued to peer at his instruments, and after several more moments exclaimed, "Got it! The signature on the laser says it's *Guadalcanal*, sir. Hard link established. But only voice right now. The link's really weak."

"*Guadalcanal*," Sato said immediately, "this is the destroyer *McClaren*. You've got four Kreelan ships headed your way. We are in pursuit."

"*McClaren*," a voice responded, badly distorted, "understood. We see them."

"Do you have an update on the situation?" Sato asked. "We've been out of communications for quite a while."

"The fleet is engaged with a smaller Kreelan force now. But the ground troops have taken extremely heavy casualties. We've been ordered to extract the survivors, but it's going to be hellishly tight. The boats are already away to the extraction zones. We've got a single orbit to pick them up, then we've got orders to pull out."

The news struck Sato in the gut. *Steph*, he thought. "Do you have any details on the ground forces?" he asked, not sure he wanted to hear the answer.

"*Ticonderoga* reported that they lost contact with General Ray soon after the first assault wave hit the planet," *Guadalcanal's* captain replied. "A diplomatic courier was able to make contact with a number of units on the ground, but nothing higher than company level. They think they can lift out the survivors - ours and the Alliance troops - with our carriers and the two that the French have. Assuming those Kreelan ships don't get us first."

Sato exchanged looks with the others around the bridge. If what *Guadalcanal* said was true, they had collectively lost the equivalent of nine out of twelve divisions, maybe more.

"They won't," Sato promised. "Bring them home. We'll cover you."

"Roger, *McClaren*. Good hunting. *Guadalcanal*, out."

In the tactical display, *McClaren* was cutting across space toward the four red circles representing the enemy ships pursuing the carriers, but he began to doubt they'd be able to engage them in time. They needed to close the range faster, and get the enemy's attention, maybe drawing one or more of them off the pursuit. The carriers had defensive weapons roughly equivalent to a destroyer, but were far larger and less maneuverable. The two French carriers were forming up with *Guadalcanal* and her sisters. They might be able to defend themselves from two, maybe three of the Kreelan ships, but not all four. "Bogdanova," he said, "all ahead flank. Bring our sensors to active status. Let's let the enemy know we're here."

***

Just like the warriors on the ground, the Kreelan ships refused to yield. Outnumbered, outgunned, and facing an opponent who held all the cards, Tiernan thought, they still came on.

Half a dozen ships in the human fleet had been destroyed thus far, and another two dozen damaged. It was a heavy price to pay, but Tiernan believed they had gotten a good deal on the butcher's bill: fully half of the Kreelan ships had been destroyed, and all the rest had been damaged.

But the human fleet wasn't out of the woods yet: the Kreelan ships were sailing straight into the human fleet's formation, with ranges so close now that his cruisers could no longer fire their primary kinetic weapons without fear of damage to themselves when the rounds hit the enemy ships. And some of his ships had to maneuver out of the way of Kreelans that were clearly trying to ram.

The Kreelan ships didn't seem to care: they continued to fire their kinetics with total abandon, and both sides slashed at each other with heavy lasers. The beams of coherent light vaporized armor and hull plating, venting the crew spaces beyond to vacuum, or seared off sensor arrays or engine mounts, sometimes sending a ship into an uncontrolled tumble.

"Sir!" the flag tactical officer called. "Multiple new contacts - hundreds, at least - across the sector. Designating as probable boarding parties."

"All ships," Tiernan ordered, "prepare to repel boarders!"

On the vidcom display, Admiral Lefevre aboard the *Jean Bart* pressed his lips into a thin line. Outside of the view of the camera, his hands clenched so tightly the knuckles bled white.

Tiernan had hoped that his own ships would bear the brunt of any boarding attacks, but the reality of the battle had determined otherwise. The cloud of targets, which had by now grown to several thousand tiny icons on the tactical display, blowing through his formation like dandelion seeds, was dispersed along the port side of the fleet. Many of the Alliance ships would again be on the receiving end of boarding attacks, although they had new weapons on board that would help even the odds: Terran Marines.

"Have the First Destroyer Flotilla redeploy here," he told the flag tactical officer, drawing a line on the tactical display along the flank of the Alliance warships that were in the heaviest part of the cloud of targets, "to give the Alliance ships some close-in protection."

Nodding, the tactical officer relayed the order to the communications officer, who ensured that the orders got to the commander of the destroyer flotilla.

Less than thirty seconds later, six Terran Fleet destroyers wove quickly through the formation to take up station between the Alliance cruisers and the rapidly approaching cloud of attackers.

"Engage," Tiernan ordered quietly.

Every Terran ship had been fitted with a set of weapons that were not dissimilar from the close-in defense weapons fitted to the Wolfhound tanks. They were large-bore mortars with a short barrel that could be aimed like most other shipboard weapons, and fired an explosive shell filled with thousands of needle-like flechettes. The mortars had a short range, but they were simple, reliable, and devastating against space suits, armored or not.

"Firing mortars," the tactical officer reported.

Seconds later, the crews of the Terran fleet began to hear a very distinct *crump* echo through the hulls of their ships as the mortars began to fire at the incoming clouds of Kreelan warriors.

***

Amar-Marakh, the senior shipmistress of the Kreelan fleet, gasped at the sudden turmoil in the Bloodsong as hundreds of warriors were wiped away, almost in an instant. The anticipation in the thread of the melodies sung by the warriors trying to board the human ships changed to shock and then fierce rage.

A challenge - even a great one, the pursuit of which would almost certainly lead to death - was to be sought to bring glory to the Empress. But to have the warriors slaughtered in such a fashion as this was not a challenge; it was a waste of precious blood. That, she could not tolerate.

"Deploy the fleet," she ordered tersely to her First. "We attack."

***

"Admiral," the tactical officer warned, "the Kreelan force in high orbit is moving."

Tiernan glanced up at the display, seeing the red icons of the other Kreelan ships heading on a course that would no doubt lead them into the fray. "Dammit," he cursed.

"It was inevitable, *amiral*," Lefevre told him from the vidcom. "We will only have a few minutes until we must break contact with our current opponents to try and regroup."

"*If* we can break contact, sir," Tiernan said as *Ticonderoga* rocked from another hit. "I think we're going to have to kill every last ship in this formation. They're not going to break contact, and we can't put our sterns to them and let them shoot us in the fantail."

"Then let us destroy them with all haste," Lefevre told him. "Engage with kinetics, danger close, *amiral*."

"Aye, aye, sir," Tiernan replied. Then, turning to his flag officer, "Pass the word: all ships are to engage with everything they have, including primary kinetics. Danger close. We *must* finish off these enemy ships!"

Less than one minute after Lefevre had given the order, every gun in the human fleet opened up on the two dozen remaining Kreelan warships. Four human ships died when their targets, only a few hundred meters away, exploded, taking the human ships with them.

But ten minutes after the order had been given, ten minutes that seemed like an eternal orgy of heavy weapons fire to the crews, every Kreelan ship of the second assault wave had been reduced to a blasted hulk.

The human fleet swept onward, mortar rounds continuing to blast the warriors who still were desperately trying to board the fleeing ships. But the efforts of the Kreelans were in vain: not a single warrior made it through the devastating fire from the defense mortars.

The Marines aboard the ships, who had been anticipating their first chance to prove themselves, were terribly disappointed.

TWENTY-FIVE

Pursuing the huge metal *genoth*, the human vehicle that was in her mind akin to one of the great dragons that prowled the wastelands of the Homeworld, Li'ara-Zhurah had never run as quickly in her life. She was on the ragged edge of exhaustion, as were the four warriors who had accompanied her on this great hunt. But she ignored the leaden pain in her legs and the burning in her lungs, the frantic beating of her heart. That beast was her prize, and she would not be denied it.

After the earlier attack by a different group of warriors that she had watched, with dozens of them wading into the human warriors and their armored escorts, only the single vehicle - the one she wanted so badly - had escaped, its hull crowded with the human warriors who had managed to survive the devastating battle.

But then the machine had fled at great speed, the massive tracks bearing it over the mounds of rubble, small passenger vehicles, and bodies alike. It slowed down only when it was forced to make a turn, and the only time it turned was when a street ended or was choked with unarmed humans that were still streaming out of the devastated city.

Wishing that she had powers beyond imagining as did the great priestess, Tesh-Dar, or even a simple vehicle, Li'ara-Zhurah did the best she could with the natural powers of the body the Empress had given her by birth: she ran. She gave up trying to run a parallel course to the vehicle for fear of losing it should it make a turn along the way. Instead, she simply ran at what she considered a safe distance behind it, "safe" being a relative term. Several times the human warrior whose head poked out of the turret had fired at her with the devastating weapon mounted on top of the vehicle. Some of the humans riding along had also fired at her. But the vehicle was moving so quickly over so much debris that their aim was poor.

A few of the humans on top of the vehicle had fallen off in the course of the pursuit, but the vehicle did not slow down. Li'ara-Zhurah had not expected it to, for Her Children would not have done so in battle. She simply ignored the abandoned humans, leaving the other warriors to tend to them with their blades.

Li'ara-Zhurah shut out the complaints of her body by focusing on the vision of thrusting her blade through the heart of the human female who commanded the vehicle.

***

Coyle kept a wary eye on the small group of Kreelans who were hunting her tank. Her gut churned at their single-minded intensity, particularly that of the leader. She had tried to blast them to bits, of course, but after the first few shots had given up: even with her gatling gun's gyro-stabilization giving her a rock-solid sight picture, the Kreelans seemed to almost anticipate Coyle's shots, dodging out of the way. And with as little ammunition as she had left, she couldn't afford to waste it.

The infantry had taken pot shots at their pursuers, but with no more effect. Coyle had ordered them to conserve their ammunition.

"How much longer?" the reporter, Steph something-or-other, asked.

"About five minutes to reach the LZ," Coyle told her, checking her map display for the location of the landing zone, or LZ. "Then about five minutes more until the boats are supposed to land."

"What about all the Kreelans who were there before we left?" Steph asked.

Coyle shrugged. "Hope they went somewhere else. If we can't secure the drop zone, the boats aren't gonna land."

A few minutes later, *Chiquita* passed by the original hide positions used by Coyle's platoon. Then they passed by the last buildings on the outskirts of the city, heading toward the positions originally occupied by the Alliance Legion's 1st Cavalry Regiment, the *1er REC*.

"Jesus," Coyle whispered as *Chiquita* slowed to a halt.

Ahead of them were about a hundred men, legionnaires, who were the only living people as far as she could see. From her vantage point on top of the tank, she could see the positions that had been occupied by the wheeled tanks of the *1er REC*, as well as those next to it that had been dug out for the paratroopers, the *2ème REP*. It was a charnel house, with at least a couple thousand human and Kreelan bodies strewn about, along with the burned-out hulks of the armored regiment's tanks and other vehicles. The smoke from the wrecks wafted away over the nearby forest to join the greater black cloud streaming from the devastated city.

The legionnaires were sitting or laying down, clearly exhausted. One of them, a big man who looked like he'd been on the losing end of a fight with a bulldozer, rose unsteadily to his feet and staggered toward *Chiquita*.

Coyle tried to get out of the turret to go meet him, but suddenly just...couldn't. Her legs, her body, wouldn't respond. "Oh, fuck," she said as she leaned forward and vomited. Nothing came up, as she hadn't had anything to eat or drink for hours. She had been running on adrenaline and fear alone.

She felt a comforting hand on her shoulder, then someone hugging her.

"It's okay," she heard the reporter, Steph, say softly.

After the heaves passed, Steph and one of the other soldiers helped Coyle from the cupola, and she made her way through *Chiquita's* human passengers, finally reaching the ground on shaky legs. Despite the lack of any Kreelan warriors - even the ones who had been pursuing them out of the city - none of the infantry wanted to leave the perceived safety of the tank's menacing bulk.

Coyle tried not to sway too much as she walked to meet the approaching legionnaire. "*Bonjour,*" she said, using the only word she knew in French that wouldn't start a bar fight. "Staff Sergeant Patty Coyle, 7th Cavalry Regiment."

The man offered her a smile through his battered face, and extended a paw that was equally mauled, with raw, broken knuckles and at least a couple of broken fingers. His grip, though, was still strong, and he didn't even wince when she applied gentle pressure, not wanting to appear to be a wimpy female to him.

"Happy to see you, Sergeant Coyle," he said in an accent she recognized as British, although he had a bit of a lisp from several missing teeth. He sounded far too perky for someone in his condition, particularly in contrast to the exhausted men around him. Then she realized that he was probably so high on painkillers and other drugs that she could have hit his foot with a sledge hammer and he'd only ask her for more.

"She's a brevet captain," Steph corrected him from where she stood behind Coyle.

The legionnaire raised his eyebrows, or would have if his face had not been so swollen. "Outstanding!" he said, saluting. "*Soldat 1e Classe* Roland Mills and the remainder of the *Légion étrangère* - well, two regiments of it, in any case - at your service. If you might like to meet our commanding officer?"

Coyle returned the salute, then turned around to give Steph her best evil eye. The reporter shrugged unapologetically before following Coyle, uninvited, after Mills.

When they reached the small circle of legionnaires clustered around one who was lying on the ground, Coyle bit back more bile. Both of the man's legs were badly burned, as was his left arm.

"*Mon colonel*," Mills said, "this is brevet Captain Coyle of..." Mills turned to her, leaving the rest of the sentence hanging.

"Of the 7th Cavalry Regiment," Coyle said. "Our commander, Colonel Sparks, is still alive, but very badly injured."

"A common theme among the officers, it would seem," the man on the ground said, a humorless smile touching his lips. "I am *Lieutenant-Colonel* Grishin, commander of the *1er REC*. I am glad your colonel survived. A most interesting man." Peering up at Steph, he added, "And I see the lovely Miss Guillaume survived thus far, as well. I am happy this is so."

"Thank you, sir," Steph replied, not sure what else to say. So many others, trained to be soldiers, had died, and yet she had somehow survived. It didn't make any sense. Then again, this entire war didn't make any sense.

"Our colonel's in very bad shape, sir," Coyle said. "He was run through with a sword and has severe internal injuries. I just hope he can make it back to the fleet." She looked to the sky. "There are boats coming in to pick all of us up, your people, as well. They should be here very soon if they stayed on schedule."

Grishin frowned, almost as if he were disappointed. "We did not know. I had thought this would be our Camarón."

Coyle had no idea who or what Camarón was, but from his tone of voice it sounded like it was the Legion's equivalent of the Little Bighorn for the 7th Cav.

Before she could say anything else, Grishin asked her, "Coyle, I am placing you in command of my men. We have no officers remaining, and I am in no shape to command. Will you do that?"

She looked at the weary hard-faced men around her, then up at Mills, who nodded slightly. "Yes, sir. If they're willing to follow my orders."

"They will," he said with a hint of a smile. "They have not followed the orders of a woman before, but with you commanding the only functional armored vehicle here, they can hardly argue, yes? And Mills will make sure they do not misbehave."

The big legionnaire nodded gravely. Coyle noticed that the other men regarded him with obvious awe. He was an impressive-looking man who had clearly managed to take a savage beating and survived to tell about it, but the expressions on the faces of the others said that there was more to the story. She'd have to find out about it later, assuming any of them survived.

"Then we should get into defensive positions," Coyle said. "All your men are clustered in one spot."

"We have no need," one of the other legionnaires said pointedly through a heavy German accent. "We are safe."

"What do you mean?" Steph said hotly. "Nobody's safe here."

The legionnaire pointed to Mills. "He fought one of the aliens, a huge one. She let us go. The aliens went away, let us live."

"It's true," Mills said. "I know it sounds absurd, but that's what happened. They were slaughtering us, then this giant of a female warrior came and tagged me for a bit of fun." He gestured at his face. "I guess I entertained her well enough. Then after beating me into the bloody ground, she and all her vixen friends trotted off somewhere else. They didn't give us a second thought after that."

"Well, you may be safe," Coyle said, not sure she could buy a story like that, "but we sure as hell aren't. We've been hounded from the start, and there was a group of warriors hunting us all the way out of the city. They disappeared, but I can't believe they followed us all that way to just give up right at the end." She glanced worriedly behind her, noting with some relief that Yuri, as tired as he was, had the foresight to turn the turret around and was constantly scanning the approaches to their position. The infantry on the rear deck had hopped - and in some cases simply tumbled - to the ground as the main gun swept back and forth. "I don't think they're just going to let us walk away when the boats get here."

That's when she heard a sound like thunder: sonic booms from the boats as they made their approach.

"It's about fucking time," she whispered, relief suddenly flooding through her. *We can do this*, she told herself. *Just a few minutes.*

"Coyle," one of the infantrymen called to her. She turned and looked where he was pointing. More uniformed figures were coming down the road, running, shuffling, and staggering. There were hundreds of them. As they got closer, she could see that it was a mix of men and women from the rest of her parent 31st Armored Division and a sprinkling of Alliance troops. No vehicles. But maybe there would be a real officer who could take charge of this fuckup.

As it turned out, there was. One of the company commanders from a different brigade, someone she had never met before, was the ranking officer. After she briefly explained what she knew, he did exactly what she should have figured would happen: he officially put her in charge of securing the perimeter, using her tank and "her" infantry. In the meantime, he began to organize the rest of the survivors into groups to get onto the boats, and completely ignored the legionnaires.

Coyle had seen that most of the new arrivals had thrown down their weapons after they'd run out of ammunition, so they weren't even armed. She tried to get at least some of them to run over and grab weapons from the dead Legion paratroopers, but they refused. The captain ordered her to attend to her duties, although in not very polite terms.

Disgusted to the point she was sure she would shoot the man, she ordered the survivors of the 7th Cavalry to gather weapons and ammunition. And like the professionals they were, they obeyed. But if looks could kill, the nameless captain would have died a hundred deaths.

As the cavalrymen trotted toward the paratroopers' former positions to hunt for weapons, Mills said to his comrades, "Once the boats get here, our blue lady friends will be back, and the honeymoon, lads, will be over." Then, with a nod to Coyle, he led them after the Terran troops to pick up more ammunition for their own weapons. He had no illusions that their survival to this point had been anything more than a stay of execution, and thought the Terran captain was an incredibly ignorant ass for not making sure everyone was armed before the boats arrived.

Coyle was willing to put up with the garbage the captain from the other brigade had dished out to that point, but when he tried to move Sparks, Hadley, and the regiment's other injured soldiers out of the battered civilian van that had carried them out of Foshan and arrange them in the group with the other survivors of his own brigade, she rebelled.

"I am *ordering* you to get your colonel and the other wounded in the first boat," the captain told her. He had been forced to come over and deal with the situation directly after Coyle and the other 7th Cav troopers who hadn't gone with Mills had faced off against the enlisted men the captain had sent over to take Colonel Sparks and the others away.

"Excuse me, *sir*," she told the captain icily from her cupola, "but my colonel stays with his regiment. We'll load him and our other wounded when it's our turn to board. Whenever that may be."

"Are you disobeying a direct order, soldier?" the officer said, his soot-covered face reddening with anger.

Looking down on him from the height of the tank's turret, Coyle thought tiredly, *What a jackass.* "Yes, sir, I am. With all due respect."

"Sergeant!" the captain snapped to the senior NCO of the gaggle of soldiers he'd brought over to take the wounded and deal with any insubordination. "Place this woman under arrest and escort her to the boat."

"Yes, sir," the sergeant said, saluting smartly, a grin on his face.

The grin vanished as he turned and found himself staring down the muzzles of a dozen assault rifles. Looking up, he saw that Coyle's gatling gun was pointed straight at him.

"This is mutiny," the captain breathed. "Sergeant, take her!"

"Sir," the NCO said quietly, staring at the tense 7th Cav troopers, "we don't have any weapons. You ordered us to ditch them all when we ran out of the city."

The captain, his face turning a deep purple, turned back to Coyle. "I'll have you shot for this, soldier," he grated.

"You know, captain," she told him, "that would probably be a relief for me right now." Her finger was shaking over the controls of the gatling gun. Part of her really wanted to shoot him, just for being such a prick. But another part didn't want to waste the ammunition, because she knew they'd need it. Soon. "But I think it'd just be best if you and your crunchies just left us alone so we can save your asses when the Kreelans come after us. *Sir.*"

Without another word, the captain turned and stalked off, shouting orders at his troops, taking out his frustrations on them.

Meanwhile, the cavalry troopers and legionnaires worked quickly to pick up weapons and enough ammunition to try and defend the LZ. When they were finished, Coyle had about a hundred and twenty troops altogether, about the size of an infantry company. The survivors of the equivalent of two combat brigades.

Without bothering to consult the captain, she had her NCOs break the group down into ad-hoc squads that took up positions around the LZ, facing in the direction of the smoldering city.

"I wish we had more ammo," Yuri lamented as he redistributed the rounds between the tank's coaxial gun and Coyle's gatling gun, giving her most of it. "We're going to be nothing but a pissed-off pillbox pretty soon." They hadn't fired any more rounds from the main gun, so they still had ten left in the magazine. But the anti-tank rounds were useless for killing anything but other armored vehicles.

"We'll do what we can," she said, hearing the roar of the boats as they came in. She couldn't see them yet, as they were making a low approach over the forest behind them, trying to stay masked by the terrain as long as possible.

"There they are!" someone shouted, and everyone stood up and whooped with joy as the dark gray Navy assault boats came in to land in the open area in the rear of the position originally occupied by the *1er REC.*

Steph snorted. "We don't have enough people to fill up one of them," she said. "Why'd they send two?"

"Without comms," Coyle told her, shouting now over the deafening scream of the boats' engines, "they wouldn't have any idea how many survivors there might be. Better there's too much room than too little."

Steph nodded, shielding her eyes from the dust kicked up by the big assault boats. "Boat" was perhaps a misnomer, as the vessels now settling down on their massive landing struts massed roughly two thousand tons and were over half as long as a football field. Each could carry a full company of Wolfhound tanks or an entire battalion of mechanized infantry. Despite their size, they carried no armor or weapons, sacrificing those traits for more lift capacity.

As the ships settled low to the ground, the boats' engines throttled back to a muted howl. The main rear ramps began to descend and the side personnel doors opened, with ladders sliding from the hull to drop to the ground. The loadmasters came out to help get everyone aboard.

"Coyle!" she heard Yuri shout from the top of the turret. She turned and saw him pointing in the direction of the city.

As if they had simply appeared out of nowhere, hundreds of Kreelan warriors stood on the slight rise, just over a hundred meters away, between the landing zone and the outer edge of Foshan. In the center stood a huge warrior, her body and face an odd maroon color.

It took Coyle a moment to realize that it was blood. Human blood.

"*Open fire!*" she screamed as the shock of adrenaline once more hit her system and she bolted for *Chiquita*.

The infantry nearest to her, the only ones who had been able to hear her order, began to fire.

With the first shot the Kreelans - all but the huge warrior and two others - charged.

***

Tesh-Dar held back Li'ara-Zhurah and Kamai-Utal from the massed attack, not to deny them glory, but to have them learn and - in Li'ara-Zhurah's case - to rest for a moment. The young warrior had given glory enough to the Empress simply in the passion of her pursuit of the human machine and its wily crew, and the great priestess would not see her blood spent here. Not yet. The charging warriors knew that the vehicle was to be left to Li'ara-Zhurah, and they ignored it, concentrating on the other humans.

Seeing some of the humans she had let live after her own small Challenge earlier with the solitary human, she felt a surge of relief: they were fighting back. Tesh-Dar had not intended it this way, but she would have been bitterly disappointed had they used her earlier magnanimity as an excuse to simply watch as their fellow animals were butchered, thinking themselves safe. Had they done so, they all would have died by her own hand.

As it was, she reconsidered her original plan to not let any of the humans go. Her thoughts were driven not by pity, for she felt none, but by the knowledge that some of them had proven such worthy adversaries that they might be used another day to bring glory to the Empress. It was a small enough sacrifice for Tesh-Dar to make.

She watched the line of her warriors surging forward toward the humans, and made her decision: if any of the humans were able to fend off her warriors and make their escape in these ships, she would allow them to leave the surface. From there, fate would have to favor them.

One of the humans, however, she would not allow to leave: the one who commanded the armored vehicle. That one's life belonged to Li'ara-Zhurah.

The warriors howled past the great vehicle to attack the humans who sought to leave without first offering battle.

***

Yuri had dropped back down in the turret after alerting Coyle and was firing nonstop at the rapidly approaching mass of howling alien warriors.

"Where the fuck did they come from?" Coyle asked frantically as she trained the gatling gun around to fire at the enemy.

"I don't know!" he said, pausing momentarily as he swiveled the turret slightly to try and keep up with the Kreelan line. He'd fired hundreds of rounds already, but the damned warriors seemed a lot more nimble than before, half of them dodging out of his line of fire at the last instant. "It's like they bloody stood up right out of the ground!"

Coyle squeezed the trigger for the gatling gun, sending a spray of twenty millimeter rounds through a section of the Kreelan line. Half a dozen of them were cut down: it wasn't easy to avoid being hit by a weapon that fired a hundred rounds per second.

"Shit!" Yuri shouted. "They're too close! I can't hit them!"

The Kreelans swarmed past her tank and the defensive positions of the infantry, ignoring them completely as they headed straight toward the first assault boat.

"Jesus, they're going right for the first boat!" Coyle cried as she spun the gatling gun around. She watched in horror as the wave of Kreelans reached the ship. The loadmasters had gotten everyone aboard and had closed the side personnel doors. Now they were frantically trying to bring up the rear ramp, which took nearly twenty seconds to close.

It was halfway shut when the Kreelans got there, and Coyle watched in horrified wonder as the lead warriors suddenly turned into acrobats, with a pair of warriors instantly stooping down to act as a jumping platform for a third. They did it smoothly, as if they practiced such a move all the time. Several groups did this, and half a dozen warriors were vaulted over the top of the closing ramp to disappear inside.

Other warriors, again propelled by their sisters, tried to climb up the hull, using their talons to gain purchase in the metal. All of them failed except for one, a smaller warrior who steadily climbed all the way to the cockpit window and began to batter away at the clearsteel with a long dagger. Coyle had no idea if she'd be able to get through, but she wouldn't have traded positions with the pilots for anything. She'd already had more than her fair share of close encounters.

Around her the legionnaires and infantry from her regiment fired at the enemy, but many of them were now on the far side of the assault boat, protected by its hull.

Coyle decided that there was no point in just sticking around. She felt sorry for the poor slobs in the first boat who were no doubt being cut to ribbons - since most of the fools had no weapons - but she'd take whatever advantage she could. "*Run for it!*" she screamed over the loudspeakers. "Get to the other boat! Mannie, move toward the boat, but don't run anybody over!"

The squads of her ad-hoc command leaped from their positions and dashed for the second boat, which had already closed the rear ramp and was spooling up its engines. The loadmasters were closing the personnel doors, the ladder already retracting from the ground.

"Don't leave us, you fuckers!" Coyle shouted at them as she blasted a few more Kreelans with her gatling gun. In her mind she could hear Lieutenant Krumholtz's voice, begging the same of her. She brutally shoved the thought to the back of her mind.

Suddenly Mills was at the boat. The big legionnaire jumped up and caught the bottom rung of the ladder as it retracted, then managed to reach up and grab the loadmaster's ankle as the ladder slid into the hull. The loadmaster tried to shake him off until another legionnaire leaped up and grabbed onto Mills' legs, their combined weight pulling the loadmaster halfway out of the boat.

"Take us right up to the hatch, Mannie!" Coyle ordered her driver.

"Shit, look!" Yuri cried.

The other boat, carrying the bastard captain and his gaggle of survivors, was taking off, but only made it a few meters into the air before it began to wobble. The Kreelans on the ground surrounding it ran toward the forest, trying to avoid the heat of the hover engines. Coyle thought for a moment that the pilots were maneuvering intentionally to kill the enemy, until the boat yawed drunkenly and she could see the small cockpit above the forward clamshell doors. The Kreelan who had been there had fallen off, but the inside of the windshield was spattered with blood. Then one of the personnel hatches opened and people started flinging themselves out. The boat wasn't very high yet, but it was certainly high enough that jumping wasn't an option. The bodies hit the unyielding ground and lay still.

The boat hit the trees and paused for just a moment, almost as if it might gently rebound to drift back over the LZ. Then it suddenly tipped over and crashed to the ground, its lift and drive engines still roaring, setting the forest on fire.

Mannie swiveled *Chiquita* around and brought her rear engine deck right under the personnel hatch of the second boat where Mills and the other legionnaire still dangled. The legionnaire released his grip and rolled to the ground, dashing out of the tank's way, as Mills flailed his feet, finally gaining purchase on the vehicle's rear deck. Then he hauled the loadmaster out of the boat and hammered him once in the face with an already bloodied fist. The man crumpled to the hot armor plate, holding both hands to his face to stem the blood from his shattered nose before Mills grabbed him by the scruff of the neck and tossed him off the tank. Then Mills ordered two other legionnaires, weapons at the ready, up into the boat.

Coyle couldn't hear what he said to them over the growing roar of the boat's lift engines: the pilots were trying to take off, the loadmaster and the rest of them be damned. She could see it start to rise, the landing struts extending as the boat's lift engines went to full power.

Suddenly the boat stopped going up, then settled back down. Coyle looked at Mills, who grinned and put his index finger to his temple, his thumb raised in the air to mime a pistol.

"Get aboard!" she shouted through the loudspeakers at the others, who were now clustered around *Chiquita*.

The first ones up were the two injured colonels, who were handed up as carefully as was possible in such a ludicrous situation, followed quickly by the rest of the injured.

Mills kept order on the back deck of the tank when it came time for everyone else to board the boat, making sure nobody pushed or shoved to try and get aboard ahead of someone else. The couple who tried that were tossed off the tank to wait their turn at the end of the line.

"Mannie, Yuri," she said, "up and out. Get in the boat!"

"We're not leaving you," Yuri said stubbornly. Mannie said nothing, but he didn't open his hatch to get out.

"Goddammit, get out of the tank!" she yelled at them. "You can't do anything else here."

"Fuck off, Coyle," Yuri told her, turning around as she dropped back into the turret. Looking her in the eyes, he told her, "We've come this far together. When you're ready to leave, we'll go with you. Not before."

She didn't know whether to punch him or kiss him. In the end she settled for saying, "You're both dumb fucks, you know that? But I'm glad you're here."

Looking back out the cupola, she saw that Mills had almost everyone aboard and was gesturing at her to come. "Okay, you idiots, I think it's our turn to get on the bus. Let's-"

Suddenly the huge warrior was simply *there*, right on the tank's engine deck next to Mills, right in front of the open hatch to the assault boat.

His eyes wide with disbelief, Mills lunged at her, trying to knock her off the tank. She did something - Coyle wasn't sure what, because it happened so fast her eyes couldn't follow it - and Mills was down on the deck, lying very still.

"No!" Coyle screamed, as a legionnaire standing in the boat's hatchway fired a full magazine from his rifle into the alien apparition. The rounds simply passed through her to ricochet off the tank's armor.

Baring her fangs, the alien reached up with one arm and plucked the legionnaire who had fired on her from the boat, sinking her talons into his chest before hurling his body to the ground. Then she did something even more unexpected: she picked up Mills like a huge rag doll and handed him up to the disbelieving soldiers crowded into the hatchway.

Coyle didn't want to believe that she had seen the legionnaire's bullets pass right through the big warrior, and was tempted to try and blow her away with the gatling gun. But she would've hit the boat, and that wouldn't do. Not after all this.

The warrior stood there, looking at her, then pointed past the front of the tank. A lone warrior stood there, waiting. Coyle recognized her as the leader of the group that had been hunting *Chiquita* during the regiment's escape from the city.

With a sinking feeling, Coyle suddenly understood. "Yuri, Mannie," she said in a brittle voice, "get out of the tank and get on the boat. Now."

"But-"

"*Now*, boys," she told them. "There's no more time." With that, she took her helmet off and dropped it on the ground beside the tank. She wouldn't need it anymore.

Yuri and Mannie opened their hatches uncertainly, then climbed out on top of the tank. Seeing the hulking warrior at the rear, next to the hatch to the boat, they stopped.

"It's okay," Coyle shouted. "Ignore her. Get in the damned boat."

"What about you?"

"Don't worry about me. I'll be fine," she lied.

She almost had a good laugh at the looks on their faces as they sidestepped past the warrior, who studiously ignored them, her interest focused only on Coyle.

"Goodbye, guys," she whispered into the roar of the boat's idling lift engines as her crew climbed into the boat. Mills looked out at her from the hatch, and she nodded to him. She hadn't believed his tale before, about dueling with the big warrior, but she did now. He nodded back, his face grim, before he hit the button to close the hatch.

The last face she saw as the hatch slid shut was that of the reporter woman, Steph, whose cheeks were wet with tears. Coyle raised her hand in farewell.

With a sigh of resignation, she climbed down from the tank as the boat's lift engines spooled up again, sending up a storm of dust and debris. After a few seconds the landing struts parted company with the ground, and the ship began to climb quickly. She watched it go, flying low over the burning forest in the direction it had come. The pilots weren't taking any chances against Kreelan air defense weapons. *Good luck*, she thought.

Then she turned to face the warrior who apparently wanted her head for a prize. It was a small enough price to pay for the safety of the others, Coyle thought.

As the big warrior looked on, Coyle's opponent approached and handed Coyle a sword. Coyle looked at it, having to admire the beauty of the craftsmanship and thinking that the Kreelans could get rich by making jewelry if they could only get over their urge to kill everyone in sight.

With a shrug, she held the sword up in a salute, whipping it up so the grip was a hand's breadth from her chin, the sword's tip high in the air, then lowering it to her right side, pointing it off at a forty-five degree angle at the ground. It was parade-ground perfect, and she knew that Colonel Sparks would have been proud.

Holding the sword at the ready, her attention focused on the Kreelan as the warrior moved forward into the attack, Coyle never felt the ten centimeter-long sliver of hull plating that killed her as the first assault boat finally exploded, scouring the landing zone with flame and metal debris.

TWENTY-SIX

"We're in range, sir," Bogdanova said as the tactical display showed the range ring for the pulse cannon intersect the Kreelan ships that were gaining on the Terran and Alliance carriers.

"Chief," Sato called to Chief DeFusco in engineering, "I'm going to bring up the pulse cannon."

"Go ahead, skipper," she said. "The damn thing should fire. The only thing I'm really worried about is the structural damage we've taken. Running the ship at flank speed is starting to stress what's left of the keel ahead of the forward engineering spaces. I've checked the alignment of the central conduit where the pulse cannon is mounted, and it looks okay for now. But I can't guarantee that it'll hold when we start maneuvering."

"I'll keep it in mind, chief," Sato told her. Then, to the rest of the bridge crew, "Stand by to engage." They were trailing the enemy ships now, slowly gaining on them as they closed with the carriers. *It's going to be close,* Sato knew. With no one available to man the tactical station, he had to take care of the weapons himself. "Pulse cannon, target, designate," he announced. Aligning the targeting pipper of the pulse cannon with one of the enemy ships, the *McClaren* turned slightly to starboard. Unlike the ill-fated Captain Morrison, Sato waited until the ship had steadied and the targeting computer confirmed a hard target lock and that the ship was slaved to the targeting computer. "Firing."

As when Morrison had fired, the ship thrummed as the energy buffers dumped their stored power into the pulse cannon, drawing on every non-critical system in the ship to feed the hungry weapon. The lights again dimmed as the *McClaren* was joined for just an instant with the target ship.

Unlike when Morrison fired, Sato's shot hit the intended target right between the twin flares of its engines. Designed to pierce the armor of a cruiser's hull, the emerald beam instantly vaporized tons of metal in the enemy warship's vulnerable stern. The resulting explosion obliterated the entire propulsion section, sending what was left of the forward part of the ship tumbling end over end, spewing air, debris, and bodies as it quickly fell behind the other three warships.

"Stand by kinetics!" Sato warned. He wasn't firing to try and hit the other ships - although he wouldn't pass on a luck shot - but to try and distract them from the carriers, which were now running in low orbit, waiting to pick up the assault boats that were even now coming back from the surface. He prayed that Steph had somehow made it onto one of them.

They had only been able to repair two of the ship's primary kinetic weapons. The aft ventral turret was of no use in a trailing fight like this. But the forward dorsal battery, mounted on the "top" of the forward part of the hull, was tracking the enemy ships and was locked on for barrage fire. Sato had programmed it to fire a brace of projectiles in a box pattern that would hit the lead ship if it didn't maneuver out of the way.

"Firing!" he said as he hit the *commit* button. The ship echoed with thunder as the big cannon fired half a dozen rounds.

The hull suddenly made a screeching shudder, an undulating vibration that shook the entire ship and made Sato's blood run cold.

"Captain!" DeFusco suddenly shouted over the ship's intercom from engineering. "We're losing the keel! I've got structural warnings on every frame from forward engineering halfway to the bridge. If we don't reduce speed, we're going to lose her, and for the love of God don't fire the forward kinetic battery again!"

"Can we fire the pulse cannon?" he asked her, ignoring her warning to slow the ship. The weapon display indicated that the energy buffers were still cycling. Twenty seconds remained.

For a moment, DeFusco said nothing. "Sir," she said quietly, "the ship is going to break up if we don't slow down. Doing anything else is about as good as detonating a torpedo amidships."

"Answer the question, chief," Sato ordered her, eyeing the weapon status. Ten more seconds. None of the remaining enemy ships had reacted to the death of their sister vessel, and he already had the target reticle locked on the trailing warship.

"The cannon might work properly, sir," DeFusco said stiffly. "Should I pass the word to abandon ship?"

"Stand by to fire," Sato said, ignoring her. Bogdanova and the others glanced at him as if he were slightly mad. "Those carriers are helpless unless we even the odds for them," he said. "One of them is worth half a dozen ships like this. Or more. And they're the only way our surviving troops can get home." *And the only chance Steph might have, if she's still alive,* he thought without a trace of guilt.

The weapon display flashed green: the energy buffers had recharged.

"Firing," he said, again punching the *commit* button.

Again the emerald beam flared from the *McClaren's* bow, and again it took the next target directly in the stern. The pulse cannon hit one of the ship's engines, resulting in a massive fireball that sent the ship tumbling around all three axes. It hadn't suffered fatal damage, but it was enough to take her out of the fight, and that was all Sato cared about.

Another shudder wrenched at the hull, more violently this time, and alarms began to blare on the bridge.

"Hull breach!" one of the crewmen manning the life support section cried. "The main torpedo room is in vacuum. Containment alarm in tubes one, three and four!"

"Dammit," Sato hissed. He had been hoping to use the torpedoes to take out the other ships if the pulse cannon failed. But the hull had wrenched itself out of line enough, twisting such that some of the torpedo launch tubes themselves had become warped, and three of the big missiles had been ruptured in their tubes. "Can we jettison them?"

"Negative, sir," the crewman said. "I can't even get the outer doors open, for any of the tubes."

The hull suddenly shook so hard that Sato's head was flung down against his chest. His jaw slammed shut, his teeth biting deep into his tongue.

"Bridge!" DeFusco's panicked voice called. "We're losing everything ahead of frame fifty-eight! *Get the fuck out of there!*"

"All stop!" Sato ordered, blood streaming from his lips from where he'd bitten his tongue. Hitting the control to open a channel to the entire ship, he said, "Crew, this is the captain. Move aft beyond frame fifty-eight! *Now!*" With that, he unbuckled from his combat chair and began ushering the bridge crew down the passageway aft.

"Sir, look!" Bogdanova exclaimed as she turned to look one last time at the tactical display. The Kreelan ship that was the target for the kinetic rounds flashed three times and began to lose way, falling out of formation with her surviving sister ship.

Got her, Sato thought as he managed a blood-smeared grin. *There's only one left, now. The carriers can manage that much.*

As he turned to run after the others, he saw the remaining Kreelan warship change course. He bit off a curse as he realized what she was doing: going after the unarmed assault boats that were rising from the surface.

***

Steph sat silently by herself in the cavernous bay of the assault boat, her senses withdrawn from reality, insulated by the dull roar of the ship's engines as it rose through the atmosphere. It was eerie, seeing so much space for so few people. The boat she had ridden down to the planet with the men and women of the 7th Cav had been packed full of soldiers, weapons, and equipment. It seemed like a lifetime ago.

She held her video array in one hand, amazed that - like her - it had survived. She wasn't yet sure what she would do with the footage she had recorded. After reviewing the last few moments before the boat had taken off, watching Coyle wave goodbye as they abandoned her to the Kreelans, Steph had broken down and wept uncontrollably. So many had died. So very many. She realized that what she had recorded wasn't news, or a story that might lead her to a Pulitzer prize. It was the death of whatever precious innocence Mankind had left, stabbed through the heart by an alien sword.

"Some coffee, miss?"

Unwillingly breaking from her melancholy reverie, she looked up at the big legionnaire, Mills. He sat down next to her in the ridiculous sling chairs that hung on the walls around the bay, handing her the steaming cup. "Be warned, though," he said, a smile shining through his battered face, "I almost had to beat that fucking loadmaster again before he'd hand over his thermos, and I think the bastard pissed in it."

Despite herself, Steph had to grin at the big Brit-turned-legionnaire. She took a sip, and was glad for the warning. "Jesus," she sputtered as the incredibly strong brew hit her tongue, "I think this tub's entire crew pissed in it."

Mills laughed. "Compliments of our Colonel Grishin, by the way," he told her, nodding at the coffee. "Went out like a light, he did, right after ordering me to poison you with it. But he's a tough bugger. He'll make it."

Suddenly there was a stir up front, and several of the NCOs came back looking for Mills and Steph. While they weren't in charge by rank, they had both earned a special sort of respect from the others.

"We've got a laser link to *Guadalcanal*," one of them said. Steph recognized the name as one of the four carriers the Terran fleet had brought; the carrier the 7th Cav had originally deployed from had been the *Inchon*. "They say we've got trouble heading our way..."

***

"We've got to risk one more shot, chief," Sato told a disbelieving Chief DeFusco. "That Kreelan ship got wise and isn't going to bother with the carriers: it's going to pick off the assault boats coming up from the surface. We've got to stop it."

"With all due respect," she said, not sounding very respectful at all, "you're fucking crazy. Sir. The ship can't take it. If somebody so much as farts in the forward section, let alone fires the main guns, we lose the forward third of the ship. We can't fire the torpedoes because the hull's warped. We can't fire the pulse cannon for the same reason: the optical path is out of alignment and we'd blow ourselves up. Did I miss anything?"

Sato saw Ruiz, a giant in his armored suit, stiffen beside him at the chief's remarks. Sato waved him back. "I'm not asking you, chief," he said icily. "I'm ordering you. *Now.*"

"Fine," she snapped. "Just fucking fine. *Captain.* You might want to have everybody get into their beach balls before you try this stunt, because if the hull warps anymore aft of forward engineering, we're going to lose integrity and atmosphere here, too." She set up one of the engineering consoles to echo the tactical display. "You realize that you'll lose all the forward tactical sensors, too? What are we supposed to aim with?"

Sato ignored her as he quickly set in the targeting commands for the forward main gun. He was aiming for the Kreelan ship, but didn't really expect to hit her. What he really needed the guns for was to do just what the chief was afraid of: break the ship's back. Even with the engines stopped, he could feel a sickening twisting motion in the ship as the hull flexed around her devastated mid-section and weakened keel. To Bogdanova, who had taken over one of the other engineering consoles, he said, "Stand by to maneuver."

"*What?*" DeFusco gasped.

"No time to explain, chief," Sato told her. "Stand by...firing!"

The forward main kinetic battery fired a full volley. Then another. And a third. The magazine ran dry as a horrible screech of metal, more akin to a human screaming in agony, echoed through the ship as the forward third began to break away.

"Engines, aft one quarter," Sato ordered quickly. "Hard a-starboard."

"Aye, aye, sir," Bogdanova said uncertainly as she did as she was told.

Sato called up one of the external cameras and watched as *McClaren* literally tore herself in two. The forward section, nearly a third of the ship, had been pushed to starboard by the firing of the main forward battery, which was aimed to port. Sato's maneuvering order put even more stress on the fractured hull, bending the metal further until finally, with a terrible banging and tearing noise from the rending metal, the front section broke free.

"Rudder amidships!" Sato snapped at Bogdanova. The ship, of course, did not have an actual rudder, but it was yet another wet navy term that had carried over into space, a shorthand order to stop the turn.

"Aye, sir," she said, amazed that they were still alive. "Rudder amidships."

"Status?" Sato barked at DeFusco.

"I don't believe it," she said as she scanned the engineering tell-tales. There were plenty that were in the red, but most of them were for the now-gone forward part of the ship. "She's holding, sir. Slight loss of pressure in some of the compartments aft of frame fifty-eight, but nothing critical."

Sato nodded, then ordered, "All ahead flank. Make your course..." he eyed the tactical display, which was now blank. All of the primary sensor arrays were in the forward part of the ship. Activating one of the remaining external cameras he quickly found what he wanted: a circular storm formation over Keran to use as a reference point they could navigate by. In the middle of it was a tiny speck. The Kreelan warship. "Bring her fifteen degrees to port, ten degrees down," he ordered. "Then just keep the target centered in the screen."

McClaren accelerated like a greyhound, freed of nearly a third of her mass. Sato knew that the severely weakened hull would not long stand the strain, but she only had to last long enough to catch the Kreelan warship. Then Sato planned to use the only weapon he had left that could still be brought to bear: the *McClaren* herself.

***

"You've got a Kreelan warship on your tail," the tactical controller aboard *Guadalcanal* told the pilot of the assault boat over the laser link. Mills, Steph, and the ranking NCOs were plugged into the comms system to listen. "The destroyer *McClaren* tagged three others that were coming after us before the last one thought better of attacking the carriers. But now it looks like that last Kreelan ship is hunting the boats."

Steph leaned her head against the cold metal of the bulkhead near the cockpit where she was standing, relief washing over her as she ignored the danger she herself was in. *Ichiro was alive*, she thought, wanting to cry again. God, she wanted to hold him. She would have given anything to be in his arms right now.

"What should we do?" the pilot asked, trying to mask his fear. He knew the Kreelan ships could operate in atmosphere, so there was no point in trying to run for the surface. They also couldn't outrun the enemy ship in space. They didn't have any other options.

"Maintain course," *Guadalcanal* ordered. The boat's trajectory happened to be in the same direction the Kreelan ship was heading, which would help hold the range open as long as possible as this boat and the others caught up to the orbit of the carriers. If they could escape the Kreelan now closing in on them. "The maniac commanding *McClaren* lost the forward part of his ship, but he's pursuing the Kreelan, anyway."

That certainly doesn't sound like Captain Morrison, Steph thought with a sinking feeling, *at least from what Ichiro said about him.*

"How long before the Kreelan ship can fire on us?" the pilot asked.

A pause. "We estimate five minutes."

"What about *McClaren*? When can she engage?"

A longer pause. "She'd be able to attack by now if she still had her forward weapons," the controller finally answered. "It looks like they're going to try and ram."

Steph slumped down to the deck, wanting to vomit up the bitter coffee in her stomach as she imagined Ichiro's destroyer slamming into the Kreelan ship, both of them disappearing in an expanding cloud of white-hot plasma. "No," she whispered. "Please, God, no..."

***

The only reason *McClaren* survived as long as she did was that she was directly astern of the Kreelan ship, in her baffles as the wet navy sailors used to say. While the analogy was inexact, the same basic principles applied: almost every ship had reduced sensor effectiveness directly behind it due to interference caused by the drives. The stern was also usually the weakest area in terms of weapons that could be brought to bear, and it was also generally highly vulnerable.

In the case of the Kreelan ship, either they had nothing mounted in the stern to shoot with, or they hadn't seen *McClaren*. Sato couldn't credit the latter notion, and so he kept his fingers crossed that they didn't have any weapons that could be trained directly aft. On the other hand, maybe they wanted *McClaren* to come close so they could fling boarders at her. If they tried, they'd be in for a very unpleasant surprise.

"We've got two minutes, sir," Bogdanova said nervously. They were measuring their closure rate by having one of the Marines, perched in the wreckage at the front of the ship, take range readings to the Kreelan vessel at intervals with a laser rangefinder. Combining the distance readings and information from the ship's chronometer told them how fast they were approaching, and how long they had left before impact.

"Remember the plan," he told Ruiz, who only nodded in his armored suit. While the crew originally thought Sato was just going to make a suicide attack, he had a different idea. "We've got to hit hard enough to damage her drives so she can't pursue the boats. That's the main objective. If we manage to survive that, Ruiz will lead the Marines aboard to take out her weapons or - better yet - destroy her completely. We can't get away from her while her weapons are still functional, since all we have to fight back with is the aft ventral battery. She'll blow us to pieces if any of her weapons are intact." He looked at the others, then said, "Any questions?"

"What if they send boarders at *us?*" DeFusco asked pointedly.

"That's why I had all of you draw weapons," Sato said grimly, conscious of the weight of the assault rifle slung over his shoulder, and the *katana* hanging at his side. Miraculously, his quarters hadn't suffered any damage and he had been able to retrieve it. And the newly commissioned warships that had come on this expedition, unlike the *Aurora*, had well-stocked armories and weapons lockers in several key locations, not just a handful of weapons concentrated in one place. "The Marines have to take the enemy ship. We have to defend our own."

"Any more questions?" Sato asked. Heads shook all around. "Then let's do it."

***

Ruiz thought the idea the lieutenant - *captain,* he reminded himself - had come up with was bug-fuck crazy, but he had to admit the boy had style. And as far as dim-witted stunts that could get you killed went, it appealed to his inner nature. Perched here among the twisted beams and torn plating that was now the "bow" of the ship, watching the Kreelan ship's drives grow ever larger as the *McClaren* charged right up her ass, he didn't doubt that he'd be smashed into paste before he had a chance to shoot one of the aliens. He hoped otherwise, but he'd never been a Pollyanna optimist. He hated people like that.

In the meantime, it was an awesome view. The planet below was a gorgeous blue and brown ball that got bigger as he watched, studded with swirling white clouds in the halo of the atmosphere. The stars shone like a million tiny beacons, and even the Kreelan ship was in its own way beautiful, her flowing lines an elegant contrast to the pragmatic ugliness of her human counterpart. Ruiz hardly thought himself a renaissance man, but seeing a sight like this made him appreciate how someone might be captivated enough to become an artist and put scenes like this on canvas with a brush.

But he'd leave that to others. His art was killing, and his preferred brush was the recoilless heavy assault rifle he clutched in his right hand.

"Stand by," he told his Marines on the platoon channel as he watched their approach to the enemy ship. They were dispersed in the wreckage of *McClaren's* fore end on the side opposite where they hoped to smash into the Kreelan vessel. He had divided them up into eight combat teams of four Marines each, hoping they could reach the hull of the enemy ship quickly after impact, spread out, then plant explosive charges on her gun mounts and anything else that looked vital. And if the enemy wanted to come out and play, the Marines were more than ready to oblige.

Then he switched over to a secondary channel on the induction circuit that linked him back to engineering. "We're ready, sir," he reported. "Jesus, we're getting close." The Kreelan ship was growing at an alarming rate. Ruiz had spent plenty of time in open space, training both for assaults on other ships and to repel boarders. But this was a lot closer than they'd ever come in training, and the alien ship suddenly seemed a lot bigger than he'd thought it would be.

"Hang on, gunny," Sato's voice, tinny-sounding over the induction ciruit, said.

"Three hundred meters," one of his Marines reported from a check of his laser rangefinder. "One-fifty..."

"Oh, Christ!" Ruiz cursed as the *McClaren* slammed into the other ship with the force of thousands of tons of mass moving at nearly ten meters per second. There was no sound, of course, but he could feel the screeching of the hulls grinding together through his hands and feet as he clung desperately to a pair of girders that had once been part of the ship's central conduit.

He saw that somehow the navigator, Bogdanova, had yawed *McClaren* to starboard at the last second so they didn't run right up the Kreelan ship's stern, then reversed the yaw to slam into the target. None of his men flew off into space, so he figured they all managed to survive.

"*Go, go, go!*" Ruiz yelled to his Marines. He could see that a number of protruding girders from what was left of *McClaren's* bow had impaled the other ship through its thin armor. But there was no way to tell how long the unholy union would last. They had to get aboard the Kreelan ship fast and do as much damage as they could. Everything else was gravy.

"Heads-up, gunny!" one of his men shouted. "Here they come!"

Dark shapes had begun to emerge from what must have been one of the enemy ship's airlocks in the shadow of *McClaren's* battered hull. Ruiz knew then that the enemy must have seen *McClaren* coming all along. Knowing she was impotent after losing her forward section, the Kreelans had been waiting for the human ship to get close enough, probably figuring they were trying to ram. *Holy Christ*, he thought to himself. *They could have blown us out of space a hundred times, but pulled this shit, instead.*

"Take 'em!" Ruiz ordered, dropping any attempt to comprehend idiotic alien behavior as he brought up his rifle. The head-up display, or HUD, in his helmet was painting over two dozen targets in red, with his Marines highlighted in blue. He took aim at the nearest Kreelan and fired, watching as the projectile streaked toward its target.

A specialized weapon, the type of rifle the Marines were using had been rushed into production from a hurriedly fabricated prototype. In testing it had turned in an outstanding performance, and Ruiz wasn't disappointed now. Firing small rocket projectiles to minimize recoil that could send the Marines spinning out of control in space, the weapons packed a much bigger punch than the standard assault rifles carried by the Ground Forces troops. The projectiles didn't travel as fast as bullets, and so weren't as accurate over longer ranges against moving targets, but this range - less than a hundred meters - was right in the middle of their sweet spot.

He watched with satisfaction as his round hit his target square in the chest, the semi-armor piercing projectile punching through her suit's armor before exploding inside. The suit instantly puffed up from the pressure of the small detonation, the faceplate turning red with blood as the Kreelan's body was blown up from the inside. "Die, motherfucker!" he hissed.

"Ruiz!" Sato's tinny voice interrupted his concentration as he picked out another target, a Kreelan who had just shot one of his Marines. "You've got to get to the ship! She's starting to pull free!"

With a start, Ruiz snapped his head up to look at where the two ships were joined, and sure enough, the Kreelan was trying to pull away to port. "Fuck," he cursed to himself. "Yes, sir!" he told Sato. Switching to the platoon channel, he boomed, "Marines! *Follow me!*"

Coiling his legs beneath him, he leaped toward the upper hull of the struggling enemy ship, firing at any warriors he saw as he flew over them. Most of his Marines jumped after him, but he could see more than a handful of suits bearing the names of his men and women spinning away, lifeless, from the battle.

Without warning, he was surrounded by three or four warriors that in his eyes looked more like giant black spiders than humanoids. They had him by the arms and legs, pulling at him as if they were trying to draw and quarter him. One of them drew a sword - his eyes couldn't credit the sight - and was about to try and run him through when all four of the aliens suddenly exploded in a cascade of gore as a fusillade of recoilless rifle fire tore through them.

"Christ, gunny!" he heard one of his Marines said as two of them grabbed his arms and propelled him with their micro-thrusters to the Kreelan ship, while two more provided covering fire. "That was too fucking close."

Shaking free of his Marines as he settled close to the hull, annoyed with himself for letting the Kreelans surprise him more than anything else, Ruiz said, "Get those damn charges planted! We don't have time to fuck around!"

"Check," the team leader said, and they took off toward the stern of the ship, skimming over its surface like bloated dark gray birds.

Other Marines tried to break contact with the Kreelans and get to the enemy ship. Some made it, some didn't. Others were simply fighting for their lives as more Kreelans poured out of the ship's airlocks. Ruiz's targeting system was painting at least four dozen enemy targets swarming his people who were still pinned down in the wreckage of *McClaren's* bow.

"Oh, *shit!*" one of his female Marines cried out. "Gunny, the ship-"

Her signal broke off as the *McClaren* sheered away, stripping away a fifty meter long piece of hull plating from the Kreelan ship and venting the enemy vessel's guts to vacuum. Atmosphere exploded in icy clouds into space, carrying along several dozen of the ship's crew - none of them wearing vacuum suits - and other debris.

"Ground!" he ordered as he used his micro-thrusters to slam his suit down on the already-shifting hull of the enemy ship. "Latch on or you'll get left behind!" He activated the magnetic grips in the palms of his armored gloves and the soles of his boots, praying that the ship's skin had enough ferrous metal to hold onto. Luckily, it did.

The good news, such as it was, was that he had good communications with his men and women again. It was a small consolation as he watched the ship pull away from the *McClaren*, most of his Marines left tumbling in her wake. The few Marines left defending *McClaren* went down fighting under a swarm of enemy warriors. Ruiz wondered if Sato's luck had just run out.

"Gunny," one of the team leaders said after Ruiz had taken a head count of the dozen Marines who had made it across, "we don't have enough charges left to take out half the weapon mounts on this bitch. What are we gonna do?"

"Get in close and fuck with 'em," he said. Then he led them over the side of the hull and into the ship through the section ripped open by *McClaren* as she had pulled away.

TWENTY-SEVEN

Admiral Tiernan watched the tactical display with quiet admiration as the *McClaren* took down the three Kreelan warships that had gone after the carriers, then drove off - and pursued - the fourth. *Morrison*, he thought about the ship's captain, whom he'd had the displeasure of knowing from a previous command, *as much of an asshole as you are, I'll pin the Medal of Honor on you myself for pulling off that stunt.*

They hadn't even realized *McClaren* was still with them until the *Ticonderoga's* sensors picked up her drive signature not long after the destroyer had quietly sailed behind the Kreelan fleet. Tiernan had wanted to contact her, but had decided not to risk drawing any more attention to her than necessary after it became clear that she was headed after the Kreelans pursuing the incoming carriers. That would have been what Tiernan ordered Morrison to do, anyway. The admiral only hoped that the destroyer would be able to keep the last Kreelan ship from doing too much harm to the carriers or the boats that were now rising from the surface with whatever was left of the ground forces.

"Engagement range in two minutes, admiral," his flag captain reported quietly.

On the tactical display, the two opposing fleets raced toward one another and what Tiernan knew would be a final orgy of destruction that would decide the outcome of the battle for Keran. He knew he was taking a huge risk: he was under direct orders not to lose his fleet as a fighting force, but was counting on more than a little luck to favor him in this engagement. He knew that he might very well lose everything in the next few minutes. But as the old saying went, "who dares, wins." An entire planet and millions of people were at stake. Neither he nor *Amiral* Lefevre were about to abandon them.

His only real concern was the ammunition stocks of the Alliance ships. They didn't have much left, and they hadn't been able to take the time to jump out to rearm. So, once again, the Terran ships were in the lead, with *Ticonderoga* in the center of the third wedge that was arrowing for the enemy formation's heart.

"Nothing fancy," he had told the flag staff officers as he had quickly sketched out the maneuvering orders after the Kreelan fleet had begun to come down from high orbit to attack. "We sail through their formation doing as much damage as we can. All ships are to fire at will as soon as the enemy's in range. Then we'll see where we stand." *And how many of our ships are left.*

Turning to the vidcom, Tiernan said, "Good luck, admiral." They didn't expect the laser links to be stable in the upcoming storm of ships and weapons.

"You, as well, my friend," Lefevre told him. "It has been an honor."

"Indeed, it has, sir," Tiernan said as the leading waves of the two fleets collided in fire and rending steel.

***

Thousands of kilometers away, Ichiro Sato and the surviving crew of the *McClaren* were fighting an altogether different kind of battle, although one every bit as deadly. The Kreelan warship had managed to free herself from the *McClaren's* embrace and was still closing on the helpless shuttles that were now rising in a loose formation to loop around Keran to rendezvous with the carriers. Sato could only hope that Ruiz and his Marines would be able to stop her.

Like a returning nightmare, there were once more Kreelan warriors aboard Sato's ship. The Marines in what was left of the forward section fought tenaciously, but in the end were simply overwhelmed by superior numbers. None of the crew had actually seen one of the enemy before, and had never really expected to up close. Fear was written on their faces as they ran in teams to defend the key passageways leading aft. They didn't have to worry about defending the main airlocks, as those had been carried away with the forward section when it broke away from the ship. The only airlock left was the auxiliary located aft of engineering.

"How'll they get in, sir?" one of the women in Sato's team asked as he led them forward to defend the ship. He had left DeFusco in charge of maneuvering *McClaren*, with very simple orders: try to catch up with the Kreelan warship, and slam what was left of *McClaren* into her drives.

"I don't know," he told her truthfully. The Kreelan ships were nothing like the massive vessels the *Aurora* had encountered, and he had no idea what other surprises might be in store. "But they'll find a way. Listen," he said, turning to the dozen men and women on his team, "the enemy is tough and extremely well-trained. But they can be killed. We just have to try and-"

He was interrupted by an explosion as the hatch at the end of the passageway disintegrated into white-hot fragments that blew inward toward them. There was a sudden, brief, gust of air down the passageway, and Sato's ears popped with the change in pressure. Two similar explosions sounded from elsewhere in the forward part of the ship.

"Get ready!" he ordered, and the men and women with him took up positions on the floor and behind the hatch coaming, trying to make themselves into the smallest possible targets as they aimed their rifles at the still-smoking hatchway.

As the smoke cleared, Sato saw a pair of Kreelans worming their way into what looked like a set of transparent membranes, clearly some sort of airlock, at the end of the passageway.

"Hold your fire," he said, a tingle of fear creeping down his spine. He had assumed the Kreelans would use the same advanced technology they had when they boarded the *Aurora*. But this was nothing more than a simple, if effective, set of membranes that could certainly be pierced or torn by the human weapons.

"Sir?" one of the sailors asked, his finger tensing on the trigger of his assault rifle.

"If we fire and damage that thing they're coming through, we're dead," Sato told him as he got to his feet. "None of us have vacuum suits."

As if to punctuate his warning, they could hear the staccato firing of several assault rifles, followed by a hollow *whoomp* as a grenade went off in one of the other passageways. That was followed by the shriek of air venting into space, one of the sounds that spacefaring sailors feared as much as fire. The screams of the crewmen as they were blown out of the ship were muted by the intervening compartments, but tore through his heart nonetheless.

"Get back," he told the others as he turned and quickly led them back down the passageway as the Kreelans stripped out of their vacuum suits. Their eyes were fixed on the humans, but otherwise they were not yet prepared to attack. *They know the score, too,* Sato thought. "Let them come," he said. "Once they're out of their suits, we're on even ground."

"If you say so, sir," one of the enlisted men said dubiously as he followed Sato through the hatch, closing it behind him as more alien warriors made their way through the airlock.

***

Gunny Ruiz grimaced in pain as he blasted yet another Kreelan out of his path. He had been hit with one of the flying weapons the enemy used: one of the blades was embedded in the thick pectoral muscles of his chest.

His suit was leaking air, but he figured he'd have enough to finish the job before he asphyxiated.

He was down to only four Marines in the short time they'd been inside the Kreelan ship. The enemy warriors were beyond fanatical in their defense. They were completely outclassed by the Marines in their combat armor with their recoilless rifles, and still they were murderous opponents. Even after the Marines blew a compartment open to the vacuum of space, the female warriors - without suits - attacked them with swords and claws as they were blown out into space. Two of his people had died that way, their suits slashed open as the enemy went flying past.

The Marines had blasted their way through the hatchways of the ship as they moved aft as quickly as they could, trying to reach the ship's engine room. Ruiz had figured the bridge was probably much farther forward, and at the rate his people were being killed, they'd never make it. And they didn't have time. He knew the ship would be in range of the fleeing shuttles any moment now.

"Down, gunny!" one of his men shouted as a warrior wearing a combat suit hurled herself at Ruiz from around the bend in a passageway.

Ruiz dropped to the deck, but it was the wrong move: he landed right on the Kreelan weapon still embedded in his chest and drove it even deeper. He was momentarily paralyzed with agony as the Kreelan fell on top of him.

His Marines couldn't shoot for fear of hitting him, but he wasn't important. "Forget about me!" he ground out through the pain as he fought to roll over so he could fight the alien. "Find the goddamn engine room! No time left!"

The four other Marines paused only for a second before following their orders, blasting their way through the passageways leading aft.

Using his massive upper body strength, Ruiz managed to push himself up off the deck, the warrior still writhing on top of him, and flip over, slamming his right elbow as hard as he could into her midsection. The warrior's armor absorbed the blow, but it gave him what he really wanted: just a few extra centimeters of room. He rolled back in the opposite direction, careful to keep his chest and the protruding weapon clear of the deck, then leapt on top of her before she could regain her feet. He clung desperately to her armored gloves, which were made to allow her razor-sharp talons to show through the fingertips of the metal and fabric. Using his superior weight, he shoved her to the floor, howling in pain as the throwing weapon was again driven deeper into his chest, the tip burying itself in the bone of his sternum.

Ironically, the inhumanly sharp blades that were sticking out were equally effective against Kreelan armor, and he watched with satisfaction as they sliced through his opponent's armor as well as his own. The blades didn't penetrate deep, but far enough: he suddenly yanked himself backward, pulling the blades out of the alien's suit.

Air rushed from her suit, crystals of water forming as the moisture in the suit's air froze almost instantly. He pinned her to the deck until she stopped twitching.

As he struggled to get up, he found two more suited warriors waiting for him, swords drawn.

He was just bringing up his rifle when a churning wall of fire exploded through the passageway from the aft end of the ship, testimony to the handiwork of his Marines.

***

"You're clear," the controller on the *Guadalcanal* informed the assault boat pilots. "The enemy ship that was on your tail is losing way."

The pilots didn't need to hear it from the carrier, as the enemy warship had gotten close enough for them to track it on the boat's sensors. Both pilots breathed a heavy sigh of relief when they saw the ship's icon suddenly slow down, rapidly falling behind them.

"We're actually going to make it," the pilot murmured, holding his hand down to his side out of sight and crossing his fingers. "Tell the *McClaren* that we're good for the bar tab in any port," he told the controller on the carrier. On the sensor display, he saw the icons representing the other shuttles climbing toward the still-invisible carriers. By his count, all but two had made it.

"Nice thought, but it looks like there are going to be some empty chairs around the table," the controller told him, his voice tinged with regret. "The *McClaren* rammed the other ship, then they separated and it looks like her drives have failed. She's not going to make it."

Hearing the words of the controller, Steph sat bolt upright from where she had slumped down to the deck. "We have to go back," she told the pilots. "We have to go back to the *McClaren*."

Both pilots stared at her. "Are you crazy?" the boat's command pilot said. "You see that?" he said, pointing to a blue icon just at the edge of the boat's forward sensor display that had *Guadalcanal* marked under it. "That's our carrier. They're going to leave us behind if we aren't aboard in about ten minutes."

"The people on that ship saved our lives," she argued. "We can help them. This boat has plenty of room for the survivors-"

"There's no time!" the pilot told her. "I'm sorry," he said, his apology utterly sincere. "I appreciate their sacrifice and what they did to save us. I really do. But it won't help them if we mount a rescue only to have all of us get left behind." He glanced at the other faces looking into the cockpit hatch and listening, the few surviving NCOs of the Legion and the 7th Cavalry. "*Guadalcanal* and the other carriers have direct orders from Admiral Tiernan that they are not to wait for stragglers."

"Please," she said, turning to Mills for support. "I know it's a risk, but we've got to go back. Ichiro Sato is on that ship along with the rest of the crew. None of us would have had a chance at all in this fight if it weren't for him."

Sato's name had an immediate effect on everyone who could hear Steph's voice. He was the prophet who had brought warning of the coming invasion. As with most prophets, few had believed his prophecy, and most had scorned and ridiculed him. The haggard men and women on the assault boat, however, had become true believers after coming face to face with the Kreelan nightmare.

"I think we'll go back, then," Mills said casually. "Shouldn't leave a lad like that go to waste. What say you, *sergent chef?*" he asked the ranking Legion NCO standing next to him.

The man answered without hesitation. "*Oui.* We go back."

Nodding their heads in agreement, the other NCOs representing the 7th Cavalry gave their support.

"This isn't a fucking democracy," the pilot told them hotly. "I'm the commander of this boat, and we have orders to return to *Guadalcanal.* And that's what we're-"

He froze as Mills smoothly raised his assault rifle and pressed the muzzle against the pilot's helmet. "Look, mate," he said in a low voice, "the more you flap those gums of yours the less time we have to pick up those fellows on that ship back there. If you or your friend here," he glanced at the copilot, who was staring down the muzzle of a weapon held by one of the 7th Cav NCOs, "utter one more word before you turn this tub around, I'll blow your bloody fucking head off. And please don't make the mistake of thinking I won't pull the trigger."

The pilot's mouth worked for a moment, but in the end he decided that discretion was the better part of valor. With a helpless, angry look at his copilot, he turned back to the ship's controls and turned them around.

Steph watched the starfield turn beyond the ship's cockpit window, praying that Ichiro was still alive.

***

Aboard *McClaren*, a very one-sided battle raged in the passageways and compartments of the stricken ship. While the crew fought bravely, they weren't trained as Marines. And without Ruiz and the others in their armored vacuum suits, the Kreelan warriors held the advantage. The *McClaren's* crewmen were killing the aliens, but not fast enough, and too many of the defending sailors were dying in the process.

Sato's team had managed to hold off the advance of the Kreelans who were trying to come down the passageway his men and women were defending, but he was suspicious: they hadn't been trying as hard as he thought they might. His sailors had killed three or four as they tried to force themselves around a turn, but aside from occasionally peering out to see if the humans were still there, they were staying put.

From the sounds coming from other parts of the ship, the same was clearly not true. Sato had sent two men as runners to find the other teams and report what was happening; neither had returned. The bark of automatic weapons and the explosion of grenades echoed through the metal of the bulkheads and the deck, clear indications of savage fighting.

Then he heard something that was at once familiar, and totally unexpected: the distant mechanical *clank* of docking clamps.

"Jesus," one of the crewmen cried, "one of their ships has docked with us!"

"They couldn't," one of the others said. "The only airlock that's left is the auxiliary in the after engine room. They couldn't dock with it."

"They can do anything," Sato whispered, more to himself than to the others, as one of the Kreelans quickly peered around the corner, then darted back as she was met with another fusillade of rifle fire; Sato's team had already run out of grenades.

He felt a change in the tempo of the fighting in the other parts of the ship, mostly aft of where they were. "Engineering," he said. "They've broken through to engineering!" Turning to the senior rating, one of the ship's computer engineers, he said, "Take the team back to help DeFusco. If they take engineering..." He didn't bother finishing the sentence.

"Aye, aye, sir," she said. "But what about you? You're coming with us, aren't you?"

"No," he said, shaking his head as he stood up and handed her what was left of his ammunition. He dropped the empty rifle to the deck. "I'll buy you a little time."

"But..."

"Go on," he told her quietly. "Save our ship."

Tears brimming in her eyes, the sailor turned and led the others back down the passageway toward the thundering fight that was raging near the engineering section.

Sato drew his *katana*, then placed the lacquered scabbard carefully on the deck. It would be destroyed with the rest of the ship when the enemy overpowered the crew, but even in his final moments he would never dream of treating it with disrespect by thoughtlessly casting it aside.

The *katana* held confidently in his hands, he stepped forward into the passageway to face the warriors awaiting him.

***

The first men and women to board the *McClaren* were almost cut down by the skeleton crew in engineering who expected nothing other than a flood of enemy warriors - that they themselves had not yet seen in the flesh - to come streaming through the airlock. They stared in open-mouthed surprise and wonder at the ragged legionnaires and cavalrymen who quickly marched aboard.

"Heard you could use a bit of a hand," Mills told a female engineer, a petty officer, who looked to be in charge.

"Jesus," DeFusco said, shaking her head. "I just don't believe it."

"Let's get a move on, shall we? *Allez!*" Mills said, and the legionnaires began to move to the forward end of the engine room, their weapons ready, the cavalrymen right beside them. They didn't need anyone to steer them through the ship. They could clearly hear the sounds of the fighting going on, and did as many soldiers have done through history: they marched toward the sound of the guns.

"Get your people aboard," Steph said, gesturing toward the waiting airlock.

"I can't leave," DeFusco told her bluntly. "I won't leave the ship until we've got everyone back."

"Then get your people into the boat and wait by the airlock," Steph told her, knowing exactly how she felt. "We don't have much time. I'll stay with you in case the Kreelans poke their heads in here." She gestured with her rifle, and DeFusco could tell she must have used it plenty already. The woman's hands were nearly black with dirt and residue from firing the weapon's caseless cartridges, and the rest of her wasn't much better. She was a complete mess, and judging from the sunken look of her eyes must have been running on nothing but fumes.

"You're that reporter woman, aren't you?" DeFusco suddenly realized. "The one that Lieutenant...I mean, Captain Sato was, um..."

Steph offered her a tired smile. "You can say it," she said. "We were dating. But *captain*? And did he...did he make it?"

"Yes on both counts," DeFusco said, a look of concern shadowing her face as she hustled the remaining members of the engineering crew past her into the waiting boat, "at least when I saw him last, leading a team forward to defend the ship. A ship's captain. And a damn good one, at that."

***

Mills and the other soldiers didn't have far to go to find the enemy. While none of the men and women who now swarmed through the passageways out of engineering and into what was left of the forward part of the ship had any experience in shipboard fighting, it was close enough to urban combat - with which most of them did have experience - that they adapted quickly. They also had the advantages of surprise and weight of numbers.

As they reached the survivors of the crew's defense teams, which were now down to a handful of men and women, the soldiers sent them aft to the assault boat.

Then the legionnaires and cavalrymen began to mercilessly cut down the boarders, blasting them into bloody pulp through sheer weight of fire from their assault rifles.

***

Sato was ready. He was prepared to die and join the ghosts who still haunted his dreams from the *Aurora*, where part of his soul had been lost forever. He had no regrets, save that he had never told Steph how much he really loved her. He knew she would understand, and hoped with all his heart that she had survived the disaster that had befallen the troops on the ground. He would have given anything to be with her now, but he knew that wasn't his destiny.

Four warriors stood before him in the passageway, having left their bulky armored vacuum suits behind. Two stepped forward, their black armor and the silvery blades of their weapons gleaming, while the others held back.

Standing in a ready position, his legs spread forward and back and bent slightly, ready to spring, Sato held his sword in a two-handed grip, down low on his right, the blade's tip pointing diagonally toward the deck. He knew his skills could not compare to the warriors he faced, but he would go down fighting. His *sensei* had given him that much.

That was what he thought up until the moment that the warriors - all of them - knelt down before him.

***

Taylan-Murir was a well-seasoned warrior with skills and scars from the many Challenges fought during her life. Like all others who had come here, save the great priestess and the senior shipmistress of the fleet, she had fought many for the honor to face the Empire's latest enemy.

But *this* honor was entirely unexpected. As she and her three sisters came upon this particular group of human defenders, she sensed something in one of the animals.

They had come upon the Messenger.

She and her sisters would not have been able to explain how they knew this, for - as with many things for their ancient race - what once might have required thought and understanding or visible technology to achieve now simply *was*. He carried no mark, nor did she recognize his face, homely and pale as it was to her eyes. But Taylan-Murir knew that this human was the Messenger as surely as she knew her own name. So did her fellow warriors, and so, too, did every member of the fleet - indeed, her entire race - as her Bloodsong echoed her wonder and surprise. It was a great honor to be in the presence of a Messenger, and it was forbidden to bring one to harm. Indeed, it was unthinkable. Thus they had been careful to hold the humans at bay, but had not pressed their attack for fear of harming him.

This Messenger, she knew, was different from all others who had come before in her civilization's half-million year history: he held a sword and clearly understood how to use it, and to die by his hand would be a very great honor.

Trembling with pride, she and her sisters knelt before him, waiting for his blade to fall.

***

"No," Sato whispered as the Kreelans knelt on the deck, their heads bowed in respect as if he were a lord come to call. He knew this wasn't just a coincidence. It couldn't be.

While most might have felt relief at such a reprieve, Sato felt a burning anger that rose into a fiery rage. He wanted a chance to prove himself, to take himself back to the sands of the arena where his shipmates from the *Aurora* had fought and died. He wanted to avenge their ghosts. "Get up!" he shouted at them, not caring that they couldn't understand his words. "*Get on your feet and fight!*"

The four warriors made no move, but were still as statues carved from the deepest ebony.

Rushing forward to the first one, the one he took to be their leader, he grabbed her by the arm and hauled her to her feet. "Fight me, damn you!"

He slammed the guard of his sword into her chest, knocking her back a step, trying to force a reaction from her.

But she again sank to her knees, and never met his gaze.

With a roar of anger and frustration, he yanked her to her feet once more, and put the blade of his sword to her throat above her collar and its glittering pendants, the razor sharp blade drawing a line of blood. Grabbing her chin, he forced her face up to look at his, and for a moment their eyes met. He knew he couldn't read her body language and expressions, but he had no doubt of what he saw in those cat-like eyes that were at once totally alien, yet had a sense of captivating beauty: pure, utter ecstasy, as if she were enjoying a high from some alien drug.

He pressed the sword's blade harder against her neck, deepening the wound, her blood running over her collar and down her chest under the breast plate. "Fight me," he hissed once more.

She only sighed as she stood there, trembling not with fear, but with pleasure, her weapon held loosely at her side, here eyes locked on his.

Finally, Sato let her go. The warrior sank to her knees, and then bowed her head to the floor. He thought briefly about trying to provoke the others into attacking, but knew it would be fruitless.

He also considered simply killing them, slicing through their necks with his sword, just like he had practiced under his *sensei's* supervision, chopping cleanly through targets of tightly woven fiber wound around a bamboo pole. Tightening his grip on his *katana*, he raised it over his head, preparing to kill her.

But he couldn't do it. He wanted to kill her, wanted to kill every last one of her kind for what they had done, but not in cold blood. He felt his rage dissipate like an ebbing tide, and the strength went out of his arms. Lowering the sword to his side, he slumped to the deck on his knees in front of the warrior, dispirited, empty.

Apparently intrigued by his refusal to kill her, she lifted her head from the floor and again met his gaze.

"Are you Lieutenant Sato?" a voice with what could only be a British accent whispered from behind him, pronouncing his rank as *leftenant.*

With a surprised start, Sato turned around to see a large soldier peering carefully around the hatch coaming in the passageway behind him, aiming his assault rifle at the aliens. He hadn't heard anyone come up behind him.

"Yes," he said. "Who the devil are you?" That was when Sato noticed that there were no longer any sounds of fighting coming from the other parts of the ship.

"The cavalry, you might say, lieutenant," Mills told him. "*Soldat 1e Classe* Roland Mills of the *Légion étrangère*, at your service. Sent by one Miss Stephanie Guillaume. And might I ask, sir," he went on, "just what the devil is going on here?"

Sato turned to look back at the warriors, who had taken absolutely no notice of Mills or the other men who now spread out behind him, aiming half a dozen assault rifles at the Kreelans. Their leader, blood still seeping down her neck from the cut he had given her - seeing it now gave him an odd feeling of guilt, rather than the satisfaction he would have expected - still watched him with her strange feline eyes, almost as if she were afraid or sad to see him go.

"I...don't really know," Sato told him honestly as he struggled to his feet, suddenly overwhelmed by physical and emotional exhaustion. He felt Mills' powerful hand take him under the arm to help him up, the big soldier smoothly moving Sato behind him as the legionnaire kept the muzzle of his rifle pointed at the lead Kreelan's head.

Mills tensed to pull the trigger, but felt a hand on his arm, gently but insistently pushing his rifle down.

"Leave them," Sato said quietly. "Just leave them be."

Pausing only to recover the scabbard for his sword, Sato headed back toward engineering, Mills and another legionnaire covering his back. Just before he turned the corner in the passageway, Sato glanced back to see that the Kreelan, still on her knees, was staring after him.

***

As soon as she caught sight of him, Steph threw herself in Sato's arms, not giving a damn about military etiquette, protocol, or anything else. "Ichiro," was all she could say before their lips met. She kissed him hard, and he returned every bit of her passion, holding her off her feet in a tight embrace.

"Sorry to dampen the reunion," Mills said, exchanging a tired grin with his NCO, "but I think we'd best be off, lieutenant."

Reluctantly letting go of Steph, Ichiro nodded. "Is everyone aboard the boat?"

"Yes, sir," DeFusco answered, stepping forward to salute him.

He returned it with a smile. "Then let's get the hell out of here."

Following DeFusco and Steph, he and the two legionnaires stepped through the auxiliary airlock into the boat, and Sato watched with sad but relieved eyes as the hatch closed on his first, and probably his last, command.

***

Taylan-Murir and her three companions followed the Messenger and his escorts to where the humans had left, no doubt from a boat that had come to rescue him. She put a hand to her neck, feeling the sticky track of blood that had now stopped flowing, and shivered at the memory of looking into his face as he had held her at his mercy. Her fellow warriors were not jealous of her experience, for they had sensed it in their own veins: the *Kreela* were not all of one mind, but they were bound in spirit. And what one sensed, the emotions one felt, was a stream that fed the timeless river of the Bloodsong.

After pausing for a time where the humans had left the ship, they circulated through the other compartments that were not in vacuum, gathering up what few of their sisters who remained alive. They gave the last rites and ritual death to those who were too severely injured to leave the ship, for there were no healers here. They all had brought the Empress much honor this day, and their deeds would be duly recorded in the Books of Time.

Once they were finished, the warriors again donned their vacuum suits and left the ship, taking refuge in the nothingness of space high above the human-settled world. Staying together in a group, they awaited the imminent arrival of the second fleet they sensed that the Empress had sent forth to continue the conquest of this world.

*** *** ***

"Not that it's a big surprise, but we're not going to make it," the boat's pilot said in a matter-of-fact voice as he watched the chronometer that had been running, marking the time remaining until the carriers were to jump.

The copilot had been frantically trying to establish a laser link with the big ships, but so far hadn't had any luck. "There they are," he said as the carriers suddenly flashed onto the extreme edge of the boat's tactical display. "Okay, I've got a laser lock on *Guadalcanal*..."

The icons for the carriers suddenly disappeared from the screen.

"Oh, shit," the copilot hissed.

"What's wrong?" Sato asked him, leaning over his shoulder to see the display. As the ranking Terran Navy officer, he now found himself in command again, albeit of a much smaller vessel. After speaking with the legionnaires, he had checked on Colonel Grishin, but he was barely lucid. If they didn't get him to a sickbay soon, he would die. Colonel Sparks was worse, his pulse weak and erratic. He was bleeding badly internally, and while every soldier had basic first aid skills, none were medics: all of them had been killed during the running battle on the planet.

"The carriers jumped," the pilot told him bitterly. "We're stuck here."

The soldiers and the survivors of *McClaren* were disappointed, but not surprised. The soldiers had known the risks of trying for a rescue, and had taken them anyway. The crew of the *McClaren* was grateful for even a few more minutes beyond the reach of the enemy's swords and claws.

"Well, that's that, then," Mills said with a sigh.

"Not quite," Sato told him, looking out the window to starboard, where a deadly dance of fireflies was taking place in the near space between the planet and its moons: lasers and the flares of explosions as the human and Kreelan fleets collided.

TWENTY-EIGHT

Ticonderoga shuddered as she took another hit from an enemy kinetic weapon, and her hull screamed as an enemy laser raked her flank, vaporizing tons of hardened steel alloy in an instant.

Tiernan and the rest of the flag staff did the only thing they could: they held on tightly, strapped into their combat chairs, and prayed. There was no point in giving orders: all semblance of cohesion in the fleet had vanished as they had slammed headlong into the onrushing Kreelan warships. Half the laser links had been lost in the snarling chaos of the battle, and effective control was impossible.

The ships fought in a swirling pass-through engagement that was more like a massive dogfight from the long-ago Second World War than a fleet space engagement. But there had never been a fleet battle in space nearly as big as this, and the reality of it had thrown half a century of modern naval thinking out the window. Tiernan knew the Navy was going to have to start from square one on tactics and strategy, because this enemy simply didn't act human, for the most obvious of reasons.

Cruisers and destroyers on both sides hacked away at one another in a knife fight at ranges of hundreds of meters, using weapons that were designed for combat at hundreds or thousands of *kilometers*. Kinetic guns ripple-fired until their magazines were empty, sometimes sending an entire salvo into the hull of an enemy vessel as it flashed by on an opposing course. Lasers slashed across hull plating, vaporizing armor and often penetrating into the target ship's vitals, sending streams of air and doomed crew members into space. Ships of both sides that were gutted and dying tried to ram the nearest enemy. In a few cases, the ships survived the collision, with the crews fighting each other hand to hand.

"Once our ships pass through the enemy formation," Tiernan told his flag communications officer, "they're to jump out to the rendezvous point. We can't fight like this and hope to win without losing most of the fleet."

"Admiral!" the fleet tactical officer called out, "*Jean Bart* is losing way - she's falling behind!"

Tiernan looked down at the vidcom and punched the control to ring up *Amiral* Lefevre. There was a long pause before the system connected, the laser array having to search through the cyclone of wildly maneuvering ships to find the *Jean Bart.*

When Lefevre's image at last appeared on Tiernan's console, the Terran admiral suppressed a grimace at his Alliance counterpart's appearance. Lefevre's face was covered in blood from a deep gash that ran from above his left eye to his left ear, and there was also a line of blood from the corner of his mouth. His uniform was tattered and scorched. Behind him, the video monitor showed a scene of chaos and smoldering devastation on the *Jean Bart's* flag bridge.

"*Mon ami,*" Lefevre wheezed, a weak smile on his face, "I fear I will not have the opportunity to beat you at a game of poker. Our ship is nearly finished."

"Sir, if one of your ships is unable to reach you, I'll send a destroyer to take you and your crew off-"

"No, *amiral.* You must not risk any more ships." He paused, gathering his breath as the *Jean Bart* shook from another hit. "I am sure the fleet that is here now is not all the enemy has. They would not send everything to invade another system. They must have reserves. And if our two fleets are destroyed here, our homeworlds will not be able to defend themselves."

"I'm not sure it would matter, admiral," Tiernan told him. "The Kreelans don't seem to care about their losses. Fighting like this, they could take Earth with a fleet half this size."

"Which is why you must save every ship that you can," Lefevre emphasized. "The loss of Keran will be a terrible tragedy. But if we lose Earth or any of the other core worlds like La Seyne, we will lose the industrial capacity to defend ourselves-"

In the background of the vidcom, *Jean Bart* shook furiously as she took a full broadside from an enemy warship, the impact sending Lefevre sprawling from his combat chair.

The signal broke off.

Tiernan looked at his tactical officer, but didn't have to ask the question: the man's expression told him what he needed to know. *Jean Bart* and all aboard her were gone.

"Contact every Alliance ship you can reach in this mess," Tiernan ordered his communications officer, "and let them know that we're jumping out as soon as we're clear of this furball. I have no idea who may be senior after Lefevre, but if they have any sense at all they'll get the hell out of here."

Ticonderoga shuddered again, and more alarms sounded from the bridge.

***

Tesh-Dar stood in the burned-out clearing where so many warriors had been killed by the small human ship when it had crashed. It was an irony of war that the actions of a few of their fellow warriors, in reaching for glory for the Empress in attacking the crew of the vessel, accidentally took many of their sisters' lives. At this, she grieved, but not as a human would understand it: she did not lament the loss of their company in this life, for even in death were they bound to Her will, and Tesh-Dar could yet sense their spirits. She mourned their loss because they could no longer serve the Empress in the most glorious conflict the Empire had seen in millennia, in what Tesh-Dar had begun to think of as the Last War. The humans had proven themselves to be worthy enemies, and they would be given many cycles to bleed among the stars to see if one among them had blood that would sing.

Or so Tesh-Dar hoped. The knowledge that her race had only a few human centuries left before it would die out in a single generation was a heavy weight upon her soul. That all her species had accomplished in half a million human years of civilization, and all the more that had been done in the last hundred thousand since the founding of the Empire, would disappear into dust and ash in an uncaring cosmos was a fate she dared not contemplate. Her great fists clenched in anxiety at the thought, her ebony talons piercing the flesh of her palms, drawing blood.

Pushing away her fears for the future, Tesh-Dar turned her attention back to Li'ara-Zhurah. The young warrior had built a traditional funeral pyre for the human female who had commanded the metal *genoth*, just as the other warriors had built similar pyres for their fallen sisters. She gathered the wood from the nearby forest and stacked it precisely as custom demanded, often staggering in pain. She would not let other warriors help her, nor would she let the healers - who had been sent by the Empress from the Homeworld in an act of will, their bodies materializing here out of thin air - treat her injuries. The explosion of the human ship that had killed Li'ara-Zhurah's human opponent had nearly killed her, as well. A shard of metal, not unlike that which killed the human warrior, had stabbed through Li'ara-Zhurah's abdomen, and was still lodged there. Tesh-Dar sensed the great pain she was in, but was more concerned about her spiritual distress, the discord of her Bloodsong. It was more than mere disappointment at not being able to claim victory over the human after pursuing her so ardently. It was almost as if Li'ara-Zhurah had lost her *tresh*, one to whom she was bound for life as a young warrior. The death of one's tresh was one of the most traumatic events in the life of Her Children, a time of great mourning.

Again Tesh-Dar tore herself away from such melancholy thoughts. They were difficult to avoid, for while her race had conquered this part of the galaxy, spreading across the worlds of ten thousand suns, their Way - the spiritual path of their existence - was a difficult one.

She thought of the Messenger, and the curious twist of fate that had brought him here. Knowing that he was on the tiny human ship that now approached the still-raging battle in space, the warriors of the fleet knew that the craft was not to be molested. Tesh-Dar could not directly assist him in returning home, but the fleet would not interfere in any attempts to join with one of the other human vessels now fighting for their lives.

***

Li'ara-Zhurah set the last bundle of wood in place. She fell to her knees for a moment, the loss of blood from her wound taking its toll. She did not understand the depth of her sense of loss over this human animal. The mourning marks, where the skin of her face had turned black under her eyes, flowed as if she had shed tears of ink. It was how her race displayed inner pain, unlike the wetness she had seen streaming down the cheeks of some of the humans. Including this one.

Waving away the warriors who came to assist her, she struggled to her feet, willing her body to obey, controlling the pain with the discipline of many cycles spent training in harsh conditions.

Steadying herself, she reached out a hand to touch the face of the human woman who had sacrificed herself for the others, the cool flesh so alien to her touch, yet so achingly familiar. Perhaps the creature was an echo of her own soul, she thought. If so, then Li'ara-Zhurah had done well in honoring the Empress.

Reverently, she took a lock of the human's hair, cutting it cleanly with one of her talons. She carefully placed it in the leatherite pouch at her waist. It was traditionally used to carry trophies earned in combat, almost always a lock of hair. These strands of light colored hair, too, were a trophy, but one to remember and honor this human and those like her. They may not have souls that could sing to the Empress, but their warrior spirit was no less than that of Her Children.

Stepping back, she took the torch held out by one of the younger warriors. Walking slowly around the pyre, she set the wood alight. Then she moved away to the side, facing the rising flames, close enough that the heat nearly scorched her face.

She did not feel the priestess's arms fold around her as she collapsed into unconsciousness.

***

"You're out of your fucking mind, *sir!*" the pilot cried, looking at Sato with wide, disbelieving eyes. "I don't care if you monkeys stick a gun to my head again, but we are not flying into the middle of a goddamn fleet battle."

"If you want to get home, we have no choice," Sato told him, too tired to argue anymore. The fact of his own survival had come to feel like a millstone around his neck. "The enemy won't fire on us."

"How do you know?" Mills asked, his voice carrying no trace of argument, only curiosity.

"Because..." Sato struggled for words as he looked out the cockpit window, his eyes lost in the glare and flash of hundreds of ships trying to destroy one another. "Because for some reason I'm not to be touched." He looked at Mills. "They let me go from the *Aurora*, and somehow that made me special to them. I don't understand how or why. But those warriors on the *McClaren* recognized me somehow. They let us go because of it. And I'm convinced that they know I'm on this boat, and they won't do anything to harm us. Besides," he looked at the pilot, who was staring at him as if he were a rabid dog, frothing at the mouth, "we have no choice. Keran is lost, at least for now. If we want to leave, we've got to link up with one of the fleet's ships before they jump out. And that's going to be soon."

The fleet battle was still on the edge of the boat's sensor array, but Sato could tell that Admiral Tiernan had suffered heavy losses. He would have no choice but to jump out before the fleet was completely gutted. Sato knew that the Kreelans could sustain the loss of the fleet they had sent here, which he suspected had been "dumbed down" to the current level of human technology. Otherwise they probably could have destroyed the human fleet with just one of the gigantic ships that had met the *Aurora*.

"It's our only chance," Steph told the pilot. "I don't want to go back to Keran." She tightened her grip on Sato's hand as the sight of Coyle waving at her as the boat lifted off rose again in her mind, unbidden.

The pilot and copilot exchanged glances. "Fuck," the pilot said. "Why the hell not. It wouldn't be any more nuts than everything else that's happened today."

Ramming the boat's throttles to the stops, he turned and accelerated toward the cascade of explosions that marked the silent battle in space that was rapidly drawing to its conclusion.

***

Ticonderoga was streaming air from half a dozen hits that had penetrated her armor, but she was still making full speed as she burst out the far side of the Kreelan formation. There were other ships behind her, but not many: Tiernan had ordered several of his heavy cruisers, including his flagship, to turn and help a number of the Alliance ships that had run out of ready ammunition and were being mercilessly hammered by the Kreelans. He had lost two of his own cruisers, but saved nearly a dozen Alliance vessels. In the massive butcher's bill being rung up over Keran, he had to consider it a good trade.

The enemy was already turning to consolidate and regroup for another attack, but Tiernan had had enough. He knew it was time to fold. The war wasn't over, not by a long shot, but this battle certainly was.

"Stand by to jump," he said stonily as the *Ticonderoga* and two of her sister ships blasted a Kreelan destroyer that had pursued them out of the swirling engagement. Ahead of the flagship, most of the surviving ships had already jumped out. He had given them very explicit orders to jump as soon as they were clear. They would worry about regrouping at the rendezvous point.

"Sir," the flag communications officer suddenly called, "there's an assault boat calling in a mayday. They didn't make the rendezvous with their carrier."

"We can't risk stopping for them," Tiernan told him. The words tore at his heart, but he simply couldn't risk it. The fleet had already bled far too much.

"It's Lieutenant Sato on the line, sir," the communications officer told him in the sudden silence of the flag bridge, the guns and alarms now quiet, the bridge crew focused on the jump sequence.

Tiernan sucked in a breath through his teeth. He knew it was wrong to even consider wavering in his decision simply because it was Sato: he knew that the life of every other person aboard the boat was as precious.

But Sato was also a strategic asset. His knowledge and understanding of the enemy had been critical leading up to the battle, and his insights into them now might be even more so. On that basis, he convinced himself, and on that alone, could he justify one more risk to the *Ticonderoga* and her crew.

"Captain," he called over the vidcom to the ship's commander, who was busily engaged in monitoring the jump sequence, "suspend the jump. We need to pick up that assault boat."

The captain blinked at him, then said crisply, "Aye, aye, sir," before issuing maneuvering orders to get to the boat before the Kreelans had a chance to catch them.

As *Ticonderoga* sped forward, the remaining Terran and Alliance ships jumped out.

***

"I don't believe it," the pilot said, shaking his head in wonder. "*Ticonderoga's* on her way to pick us up." He looked back at Sato, who still stared out the viewscreen. "You know, sir, you might be considered lucky if you didn't seem to attract so much trouble."

Sato couldn't help but smile. He had forgotten the pilot's insubordination. He had forgotten everything but the enemy, and those who had died fighting them. More ghosts, but ones that now he could live with, that he could help avenge.

Steph stood next to him, her shoulder pressing against his side. He looked down and saw her smile, her grimy, soot-covered face the most beautiful thing in the universe at that moment.

Ticonderoga was only a few minutes away when the second Kreelan fleet arrived.

***

"Good, God!" someone exclaimed on the flag bridge as the tactical display suddenly filled with new yellow icons that immediately began to turn an ugly red.

"*Enemy close aboard!*" Tiernan heard the ship's tactical officer shout at her captain. In the flag bridge's main display, he could see half a dozen Kreelan warships - all clearly heavy cruisers like *Ticonderoga* - that had materialized within tens of meters of the flagship. Even in the swirling fight they had just been through, no ships had come that close. Every detail of the sleek Kreelan warships was clear without any magnification as they slid through space next to *Ticonderoga* like the predators they were.

"Stand by to fire!" the captain called out.

"Belay that!" Tiernan ordered on an impulse. The cruisers surrounding *Ticonderoga* were among what must have been at least another hundred warships that had just jumped in-system. And his flagship was right in the middle of the formation. "If they were going to fire, they would have already," he said, not quite believing his own words, but hoping they were true.

"The boat's approaching the starboard main airlock, sir," the tactical officer reported shakily, his eyes darting from ship to ship in the tactical display. There was utter and complete silence on the bridge and flag bridge. The only thing Tiernan could hear was the deep thrum of the ship's drives.

"Get them aboard," Tiernan ordered, "and then let's get the hell out of here."

***

"Come on, let's go!" Sato told the others as he ushered them forward through the airlock into the wounded cruiser. As soon as they had opened the hatch to the ship's main airlock - which opened directly to the passageway, since both ships were pressurized - smoke streamed into the boat, along with a dozen of the ship's crewmen who had been sent to help.

"These men need to get to sickbay immediately," Sato told the ship's surgeon and her brace of nurses and Marine medics. They quickly but carefully gathered up Sparks, Grishin, Hadley, and the others, lifting them onto stretchers and moving them quickly to sickbay.

"Lieutenant Sato?" one of the crewmen, an ensign, called. "The admiral wants to see you right away, sir."

Nodding, Sato told him, "As soon as my people are off this boat." He stood near the hatch, giving a pat on the back or a helping hand, whichever was most needed, to the soldiers and sailors who streamed past.

Steph stood next to him, clutching her rifle to her chest. Not for fear of anything on the *Ticonderoga*, but for fear of what could happen any moment: she and the others had seen the Kreelan warships jump in all around them, and she knew they would be boarding at any second. Sato had assured her it wouldn't happen, but - while she wanted to believe him - she wasn't about to hand her rifle to anyone. And even now, her battered and grimy video array was still recording.

"But sir," the ensign protested, "the admiral said *right away*."

"He can wait a couple minutes," Sato said as he hustled his charges off.

In three minutes, everyone was off the boat. After a quick check of the little ship's cavernous interior to make sure they hadn't left anyone behind, Sato grabbed Steph by the hand and dashed through the airlock into *Ticonderoga*. A crewman slapped the emergency disconnect control, and the airlock doors slammed shut. Then the docking collar was released, and the assault boat fell behind as the big cruiser pulled away.

Together, Sato and Steph ran after the ensign toward the flag bridge as *Ticonderoga* jumped to safety.

***

On Keran, watching as the healers tended to Li'ara-Zhurah's wounds, Tesh-Dar's mind was simultaneously tens of thousands of kilometers away, her second sight watching as the ships of the second fleet arrived. Her mind's eye saw the small vessel bearing the Messenger dock with one of the surviving human ships, sailing bravely under the many guns of her Imperial consorts, and he was borne to safety when the human ship jumped away.

She sighed in contentment, drawing her mind fully back to her body. She had decided she would take Li'ara-Zhurah back to the *kazha*, the school of the Way, where Tesh-Dar was headmistress. For there could the injury to her soul be mended.

Looking around her, she frowned at the devastation that the opening battle had wrought. The Children of the Empress would have much preferred personal combat without the use of such weapons as had been used this day, but the humans did not understand. Tesh-Dar knew that they would try and develop greater weapons, but hoped that someday they would see that it made little sense outside the arena of space: there, yes, let the great ships fight on. But on the ground, they would not be allowed to use much of what they had long taken for granted. She shrugged inwardly. They would learn. They had no choice.

"She is ready, my priestess," one of the healers told her, head bowed as she gestured toward Li'ara-Zhurah, who still lay unconscious.

Tesh-Dar bowed her head in thanks as she knelt and picked up Li'ara-Zhurah in her arms, an easy burden to her great body, but one that yet troubled her soul. With one last look at the human's funeral pyre, its flames rising high in the smoke-filled sky, Tesh-Dar closed her eyes as the power of the Empress surged through her, bending the laws of space and time to return the two of them to the Homeworld.

***

Aboard the *Ticonderoga*, now safely away in hyperspace, Admiral Tiernan turned at the sudden commotion at the entrance to the flag bridge.

"Lieutenant Sato, reporting as ordered, sir." Ichiro stood at rigid attention, holding a perfect salute for the admiral. Beside him stood Steph, still clutching her rifle.

"Lieutenant," Tiernan said, returning the younger man's salute. "Miss Guillaume." He was quiet for a moment as he looked at the two of them. Their uniforms (as an embed, Steph wore one, but without any rank) were filthy and torn, and their faces and hands were no better. "I take it that it was you who took *McClaren* up against those Kreelan ships that went after the carriers," he said to Sato.

"Yes, sir," Sato told him. "Captain Morrison was killed soon after...soon after he destroyed the Alliance troopship and we were hit. I was the senior surviving officer. I...did the best I could, sir, but...I lost my ship."

Tiernan saw the young officer's eyes mist over with a kind of grief that the admiral understood all too well. He saw Steph take Sato's hand and grip it tight.

"Son," Tiernan said, stepping closer and putting a hand on Sato's shoulder, "I lost a lot of ships today, and a lot of good men and women.

You may have lost your ship, but you saved the carriers and their crews, and the soldiers from the planet. That's not a bad day's work for any ship's captain." He offered Sato a proud smile. "You and your crew did a damned fine job, Ichiro. A *damned* fine job."

EPILOGUE

President McKenna sat in a room deep in the heart of the presidential complex. It was surprisingly small and unassuming, considering the importance of the conversations that took place around the oval table at its center.

With her sat Minister of Defense Joshua Sabine, Admiral Tiernan, General Singh, and Secretary of State Hamilton Barca. General Sharine Metz, commander of the Terran Aerospace Defense Force, was also present. Metz was still angry that her service had been unable to participate in the defense of Keran, but part of her couldn't help but be relieved after hearing of the losses the other services had suffered.

This was the first unofficial debriefing that had been called by the president upon the fleet's return. The summary of the battle that Tiernan delivered had been more than sobering.

"So, you lost a third of your ships, admiral," McKenna said, looking at the room's display screen and the brutal list of losses it showed in stark text.

"Yes, Madam President," Tiernan said tightly. He was ready for the axe to fall. While the inevitability of being relieved had eaten at him like acid, he knew there was far more at stake than just his career or his pride. Had he been in McKenna's shoes he would not have hesitated to cashier an officer who had lost a full third of his fleet. The president had given him very strict instructions that he was not to sacrifice his fleet as a fighting force, but that's essentially what he had done when he and Lefevre had decided to go after the Kreelan force in high orbit. He had been appalled at how many ships were missing when *Ticonderoga* arrived at the rendezvous point. He had taken a high stakes gamble and lost.

She fixed him with her gaze, and the others in the room suddenly found other things to look at. They knew what was coming, too.

But, as she had on other occasions, McKenna surprised them. "Under the circumstances, Admiral, you and your crews did an amazing job," she told him. "I would have expected you to have lost far more of the fleet. And had you been given the ships and resources we had originally planned on, I suspect the battle might have gone a bit more in our favor."

Tiernan blinked, taken completely off-balance. "Ma'am, I've already prepared my resignation and retirement papers," he said automatically, as if he hadn't heard a word she had just said. He had practiced this conversation so many times on the trip home that his brain simply hadn't caught up with the reality.

"I don't think that will be necessary, admiral," Sabine, his direct boss, told him with a smile. "The president and I are of one mind on this. The losses suffered by the expeditionary force were extremely heavy. No one can dispute that. But you - and General Ray's troops in the ground battle - carried out the spirit of the president's orders."

"You might have been able to preserve more of your ships had you pulled out of the system before the final engagement with the Kreelan fleet," McKenna told him, "but that would have left our relations with the Alliance in a shambles. I'll say this only in this room, and it is never to be repeated: as great a tragedy as losing Keran might be, it is one we could diplomatically and politically afford in terms of Earth's standing in the human sphere. But we could not afford to leave the Alliance fleet hanging. That would have been an unmitigated disaster in this situation. Admiral," she told him, "I want you to know that the sacrifice of your ships and crews, and the sacrifice of General Singh's troops, was not in vain."

As if on cue, the door opened quietly and one of her aides poked his head in.

"He's here, Madam President," he said.

"Show him in, please." McKenna watched her companions as they all looked toward the door, curiosity evident on their faces.

Ambassador Laurent Navarre of Avignon stepped into the room, and the others came to their feet in surprise. All but President McKenna, of course.

"Mr. Ambassador," Barca said, taking Navarre's hand, "what a pleasant surprise." With a slight but unmistakeable emphasis on the last word, he glanced over his shoulder at the president, who remained silent.

"Please, Hamilton," Navarre told him as he took the big man's hand and shook it, "you may blame me for the cloak and dagger antics. I specifically requested that President McKenna keep my presence here a secret, even from you."

"Especially from me, you mean," Barca told him with a smile as Navarre shook the hands of the others.

"Madam President," he said as he came to McKenna. She stood, and he took her hand and kissed it. "Always a great honor."

"The honor is all mine," she told him, smiling despite herself at the man's charm. *You can take the Frenchman out of France*, she thought, *but you can't take France out of the Frenchman.* "But I have to admit we're all curious about the - as you put it - 'cloak and dagger antics.'"

"Yes," he said heavily as he waited until she had regained her seat, then sat down with the others around the table. He glanced at the information on the wall display, but only briefly. What it showed came as no surprise to him. "I come unofficially as a representative of the Alliance," he told them. "I am here so soon because my government arranged for a series of couriers to relay news as quickly as possible. Very expensive, but in this case a bargain." He licked his lips, clearly upset about what he had to tell them. "Madam President, my friends, the Alliance is in a state of near-panic. As you know, the fleet led by *Amiral* Lefevre was the greater part of our space combat power, and the ground divisions that were lost on Keran were our best troops. The opposition in the parliaments of every planet of the Alliance is calling for a vote of confidence against the Alliance Prime Minister, saying that the current government has left the entire Alliance open to alien invasion."

"But the opposition parties were the strongest proponents of sending the fleet in the first place!" Tiernan blurted, looking at Barca, who was shaking his head, not in disbelief, but in disgust. The opposition's reaction came as no surprise to him.

"Too true, *amiral*," Navarre said, "but they are equally free to blame the current government for any disasters. And what happened to *Amiral* Lefevre's fleet and the ground forces can only be considered a disaster. The greatest defeat in a single battle, perhaps, since Napoleon's defeat at Waterloo."

"How many ships did you lose?" McKenna asked.

"Lefevre sailed with just over one hundred and fifty warships, including half a dozen resupply ships," he told her, the pain of Lefevre's loss clearly written on his face. "Only fifty-seven returned, most of them damaged. And all ten ground divisions were virtually wiped out, although the *Légion étrangère* suffered the worst: of the twenty combat regiments deployed to Keran, only a few hundred legionnaires survived."

"It wasn't just about the numbers," Tiernan interjected. "We did the right thing, making a stand there and not just letting the enemy walk in with their swords swinging. Even with the second fleet the Kreelans sent in at the end, if we had only had a few dozen more ships - and a better idea of what to expect before we went in - I think we might have been able to hold them off. Our two fleets worked extremely well together, even without tightly linked command and control."

"No one would agree with you more than me, *amiral*," Navarre reassured him. "And that, truly, brings us to why I am here." He looked at the faces around the room, his gaze finally settling on the president. "The Alliance Prime Minister would like to establish a new government, an interplanetary government that goes beyond the Francophone worlds, beyond the existing *Alliance Française.*"

"Earth constituencies would never agree to become part of the Alliance," Barca interjected, shaking his head. "No matter how much sense it may make. We went through hell years ago just to form the planetary government."

"You misunderstand, *mon ami*," Navarre corrected him gently. "What we propose is the formation of a completely new interplanetary government, a confederation of all humanity, if you will, based on the original principles of the Human Sphere Defense Agreement proposal. In the aftermath of Keran, all of the planetary prime ministers of the Alliance support this, although in secret - for now. We believe that if Earth and the *Alliance Française* formally unite, other planetary governments will follow suit." He paused. "Especially once word of the Keran disaster reaches all the governments. There is likely to be an interstellar panic, and we must avoid it as much as possible, and concentrate our efforts on building up our defenses."

"Ambassador," Tiernan interjected, "with all due respect, before the deployment to Keran we couldn't even get your government to accept or even consider - even though it was *gratis* - critical hardware and software that would have helped our fleets work together."

"I assure you," Navarre told him, "that situation no longer pertains, *mon amiral.* Let me put it to you plainly: both the planetary and Alliance governments - majority and opposition, both - are terrified. And with good reason. We stand no hope of defending ourselves unless we can rebuild our fleet, and quickly. And a unified government with Mankind's homeworld right now makes a great deal of political sense." He gave them an ironic grin. "Fear opens many doors that before were firmly shut."

"It's going to be a hard sell to the Terran Congress," Barca told her.

"No, it won't," the president said coldly. "I've assured every member of Congress who voted against the appropriations bills for the expeditionary force that I'll make sure every human being on this planet knows that they were against building the fleet that might have saved Keran and held the Kreelan menace at bay. I don't expect this lovely honeymoon to last long, but for now we can count on a great deal of support from Congress. Right now they're tripping over themselves to build out our original appropriations, more than tripling the size of the *original* fleet we wanted to build over the next three years. Assuming we have that long." She turned back to Navarre. "But there will be problems setting up a government such as you propose, the same ones that killed the Human Sphere Defense Agreement proposal."

"Namely," Barca said, "who runs the show, and how to keep the leadership position from becoming a political plum for the 'haves' in the eyes of the 'have-nots.'"

"We have a solution for that much of it, I believe," Navarre said. "We propose that the new government's leader - president or prime minister - should be nominated from Earth alone. Earth has the greatest industrial capacity of any single planet in the human sphere, and - despite the differences among the various planetary governments - it is a symbolic home to us all. This will not be a hard sell, as you say, in the current climate. The Alliance will need some concessions, of course, but on that point agreement has already been made." He turned to President McKenna and smiled. "Madam President, I believe you may be in for a promotion."

"Now that we've sorted out that minor detail," Tiernan said quietly, an uncharacteristically worried expression on his face, "we only have one other thing to worry about." The others turned to him with questioning looks. "Where - and when - are the Kreelans going to strike next?"

***

Colonel Sparks was still in a great deal of pain from his injuries, but it paled in comparison to the sorrow he had endured in the weeks before he was able to bull his way out of the hospital. He had spent the time writing letters, by hand with pen and paper, from dawn until dusk, to the kin of his dead soldiers. Two thousand seven hundred and twenty-three, all told. Most of the letters had been brief; some had not. All of them had been heartfelt. Sparks was in many ways a hard and difficult man, but his soldiers were his family, and he refused to rest until he had reached out and touched the family or loved ones, or in some cases simply a friend, of every man and woman who had died under his command. He had written letters for all of them. All but one.

Among all the 7th Cavalry troopers who had made their final stand on Keran, there was one to whom they all owed their very lives. Standing now at the front porch of an old-style farm house surrounded by acres of golden wheat, in what had once been the American state of Iowa, he knocked on the sturdy but time- and weather-worn front door. In the window next to the door hung a small flag with a white background and red trim around the edges. In the center was a single gold star.

Sparks wore his dress blues, which as fate would have it was of a design loosely based on the uniform worn by cavalrymen when horses were the standard mode of transportation. Today there were no spurs, no flamboyant cavalry officer's hat. But there was a sword, held reverently in his white-gloved hands.

With him stood Sergeant Hadley, also wearing his dress blue uniform, and Stephanie Guillaume in a trim black dress. She wasn't here as a journalist, over the vehement protestations of her editor, who went ballistic at her snubbing what he had claimed was a once-in-a-lifetime human interest story. Steph knew that this would hardly be the only opportunity for someone who wanted to follow a story like this: the war would be filled with countless opportunities to report on stories of personal tragedy. She was here purely out of respect for a woman she had known only a very brief time. And to give her thanks to someone she had never met.

After a moment, movement could be heard inside. The door opened, swinging inward on well-oiled hinges. A man in his early fifties, as sturdy and weather-worn as the door to the house, looked out at them through the screen door.

"Mr. Coyle?" Sparks said, trying to force his voice to be clear. But despite his best efforts, his throat had choked up on him.

The man blinked at the uniforms, and then said quietly, cocking his head toward the flag with the gold star hanging in the window, "The Army already notified us."

"I understand that, sir," Sparks told him. "I was Patty's commander. I was only released from the hospital today, or I would have come to deliver the news myself."

"Who is it, John?" said a woman's voice from deeper in the house. Her face appeared beside her husband, and Steph could barely hold back her tears. Like her husband, the woman was in her fifties, and time hadn't treated her kindly. But her face was unmistakably that of her daughter.

"I'm Colonel James Sparks, ma'am," Sparks said through the screen door. "Your daughter, Patty, was under my command when she...when she died." He bit his lip, trying to stave off his own tears. He had delivered the news of the deaths of his men and women to many other parents and loved ones, but for some reason this was different. "This is Sergeant Jason Hadley and Miss Stephanie Guillaume," he went on, introducing his companions. "We wanted to come by and pay our respects to you and your husband. The other soldiers of the regiment...well, they all wanted to come, but I figured it had best be just a few of us. I know this must be a terribly difficult time for you, but your daughter...your daughter was a very special woman. A very special soldier."

John Coyle just stood there staring at them, saying nothing.

Gently pushing past her husband, she opened the screen door. "I'm Elaine," she told him. "Please, colonel, do come in." As she led them in, passing by her husband, she told Sparks in a quiet voice that echoed her own pain, "I apologize for my husband, colonel. Patty was always his little girl, even after she joined the Army. And he...he hasn't been able to grieve for her. He's still in shock, and I worry about him. I don't know that he's really accepted that she's gone."

Inside the house, sitting in the living room, Mrs. Coyle offered them something to drink, but they all declined. She sat down beside her husband on a sofa that, like them, had seen better times than these.

"We already know she's dead," John Coyle said woodenly.

"I know that, sir," Sparks told him, holding his gaze steadily. "I didn't come here to tell you that she died. I simply wanted to tell you about how she lived. How she saved hundreds of her fellow soldiers. Had it not been for your daughter, not a single one of the soldiers of my regiment - including the three of us - would have made it home alive. Us and the survivors of two regiments of the Alliance Foreign Legion. She saved us all."

Elaine Coyle had her arm around her husband's shoulders, and she nodded appreciatively at what Sparks was saying. Her eyes misted over, but she had come to grips with Patty's death.

John Coyle simply stared at the coffee table.

"I realize that it's no consolation, but your daughter is being submitted for a Medal of Honor," Sparks went on. "Lord knows she earned it.

"But I have something more personal I wanted to give you to honor her memory." He held out the saber he had brought, an exact duplicate of the one he had fought with and lost on Keran. Every bit of the sword and its scabbard had been polished until it gleamed. "This is a cavalry saber, the very same as those last used by the horse soldiers of the 7th Cavalry Regiment centuries ago. Like me, it's an anachronism, but it's the most fitting thing an old cavalryman could think of to represent your daughter's spirit and determination."

Elaine smiled uncertainly as she made to take the weapon, but suddenly her husband reached out to grasp it, taking the scabbard in both hands. He held the sheathed sword in his lap and stared at it, running a hand along its glossy surface.

Then, for the first time since being told about his daughter's death, the tears came. Cradling the saber as if it were his little girl so many years ago, yet only yesterday, John Coyle wept with grief.

***

On La Seyne, Emmanuelle Sabourin saw the news about the formation of a new interplanetary government, the Confederation of Humanity, that would bring together the Alliance with Earth, and any other worlds that wanted to join for mutual protection against the Kreelan menace.

Sitting in a café on a side street in the capital city of Rouen, sipping at a cup of strong coffee, she watched the reaction of the people around her as the news was broadcast over the planetary web. Most, she saw, were happy about the news. It gave them some hope that humanity might have a chance against the aliens.

Of that, Sabourin was not so sure. She herself should not have been here, relaxing like a tourist. She should be dead with the rest of the crew of the *Jean Bart*. But in an ironic twist of fate, when *Amiral* Lefevre was distributing the Terran Marines among the Alliance ships, someone had miscounted and the team earmarked for one of the destroyers was short by two people. Sabourin had volunteered to go with them. Emotionally drained as she had been, she wasn't about to sit by and leave one of their ships with a weak ability to defend itself against the horrid boarders. As fate would have it, the destroyer - while damaged by enemy fire - had managed to survive the last frantic engagement and had jumped to safety.

What caught her eye in the news report was the proposal to formally merge the combat forces of all constituent planets into a unified Confederation military, including a navy, ground forces (which people had begun to talk about as a Territorial Army), an aerospace arm, and a marine force that would fight from the ships of the fleet as the Terran Marines had at Keran. As she herself had. The report said that the new Confederation Marine Corps (the name had not been officially blessed, as the new government did not technically exist) was in desperate need of any personnel with combat experience to help train the wave of volunteers that was flooding into military recruiting centers across Earth and the Alliance worlds.

Sabourin only considered the thought as long as it took her to finish her coffee. Then she picked up her satchel and headed down the street toward the naval headquarters building where she had been temporarily posted. Her new commander had told her in no uncertain terms that she could have whatever assignment she wanted. But she had been unable - unwilling, perhaps, was more accurate - to decide on what her next posting should be.

Until now.

***

Sergent Chef Roland Mills felt very conspicuous wearing the red ribbon of the *Légion d'honneur (Commandeur)* on his uniform as he strode off the Earth-orbit shuttle from Africa Station onto the tarmac at the newly renamed Confederation Marine Corps Headquarters at Quantico in what was once the United States. The *Légion d'honneur* was the highest award the Alliance had for gallantry in the face of the enemy, much as the Medal of Honor was for the Terran military forces. Precious few legionnaires had won it in recent history, and few of those had been awarded a class higher than *Chevalier*. The reason Mills felt self-conscious about it was that he really had no other decorations to speak of, other than a couple of deployment medals. The bright red ribbon blazed from the drab camouflage of his battle uniform.

He was among the advance party, led by Colonel Grishin, sent by the Legion to coordinate its incorporation as a regiment in the new Marine Corps. Mills knew that the bureaucratic battles fought to keep the Legion as a separate entity had been every bit as fierce in their own way as the Battle for Keran, as it was now known. But in the end the Legion's leadership had been given a simple choice: become part of the new Marine Corps and continue to fight as an elite unit, or be dismantled and absorbed into the new Territorial Army formations that were being formed for homeland defense on every planet that was planning to join the nascent Confederation Government.

Faced with such an ultimatum, and after suffering the near-total loss of every single existing combat regiment, they had chosen for the Legion to become part of the Corps.

Mills shook hands with the greeting party, a group of Marines who, like him and most of the other legionnaires present, were veterans of Keran. But the term "veteran" was relative: none of the Marines here had actually fought the enemy, while Mills and the other legionnaires had seen more than their fair share of combat against the Kreelans. The Marines - *the* other *Marines*, Mills corrected himself - were eager to make up for that shortcoming, and wanted to take advantage of the legionnaires' experience.

As with nearly everyone he had met who knew what had happened on Keran, the very first thing they wanted to hear about was the famous hand-to-hand battle Mills had fought against the huge Kreelan warrior.

Mills had always thought that telling the tale would get easier over time through sheer mindless repetition of his greatest adrenalin rush. But it hadn't. It had only gotten more difficult with every telling. He had never been one to have nightmares, but after returning home the warrior began to haunt his dreams. More often than not, he woke in a cold sweat, breathing as if he had run a marathon, with the memory of her snarling blue face and ivory fangs fading like an afterimage in his eyes. He was smart enough to know that he was suffering from post-traumatic stress, but he was too proud to seek counseling. He also knew that the Legion - and the

Corps - needed him and those like him who had survived, and there simply wasn't time to waste kibitzing with a head doctor. And he would lose any chance he might have to go back into combat. Of that, more than anything else, was he afraid.

As he began to tell his latest group of eager listeners of his exploits, he put his hands on his thighs under the table so no one could see how badly his tightly clenched fists were shaking.

***

Lieutenant Amelia Cartwright, now an officer of the Terran (soon to be Confederation) Navy, sat in the pilot's chair of the recently commissioned military courier *Nyx*. Her hands tensed on the controls as the navigation computer went through its litany of announcements prior to the ship's reemergence into normal space. This would be the sixth mission she had flown in as many weeks from a support ship that had been positioned roughly a day's jump from Keran: far enough to - hopefully - avoid detection by Kreelan ships in the system, yet close enough to minimize the travel time for the couriers.

The design of the *Nyx* and her sisters emphasized speed and maneuverability above all else, and they were being used to monitor what was happening to Keran. The news they brought back was increasingly grim.

Any hopes the human sphere had of retaking Keran any time soon, if ever, had quickly been dispelled after the first few reconnaissance missions had returned. Keran was being transformed with frightening rapidity. While the changes being made appeared to be compatible with human life, the fundamental features of the planet were being reshaped by alien hands. The atmosphere was being altered with a combination of compounds that gave it a slight magenta hue. On the ground, large areas of the planet's deserts were turning dark, as if they were being transformed into black seas whose composition eluded every attempt at analysis.

It was increasingly difficult to ascertain the fate of Keran's people, but everyone expected the worst. Every reconnaissance mission brought back fewer and fewer recordings of transmissions from the surface, and every single one of them was a cry of agonizing despair. The Kreelans were killing them. All of them. As best anyone had been able to piece together, the aliens herded groups of them into arenas built for the purpose, to fight and die exactly as the crew of *Aurora* had. Men, women, children: it made no difference. They were forced to fight, and if they didn't, they were simply killed. Humanity was now in a war for survival, and the loser would become extinct.

"Standby for transpace sequence," the navigation computer purred. Cartwright had programmed a very close emergence this time, using the data from her last jump to refine the coordinates. It would be right on the theoretical edge of where the planet's gravity well would pose a major danger during their reemergence.

As the computer counted down the last seconds, Cartwright wondered how many ships would be in-system this time. The average had been a hundred ships, about half of them cruisers and the rest destroyers. What no one had been able to figure out was how the Kreelans were managing to change the planet so quickly without having a huge number of ships hauling in the necessary materials and machinery. It was as if they were simply doing it by magic. And that wasn't possible. Was it?

"...three...two...one," the computer said. "Normal space emergence."

Hyperspace dissolved into a panorama of the deepest black, and where Keran should be was...

"Holy Mother of God," Sid - now a lieutenant, junior grade in the Navy - breathed beside her.

The surface of Keran, the outlines of its continents where land met the sea, had changed. The deserts that had been turning dark were now gone, replaced by plains of grass. The ship's telescope array hunted the unfamiliar landscape for the major cities. Even during the last mission, they had still been clearly visible, even as burned out scars in the landscape. Now...they were gone, erased as if they had never existed.

"Jesus," Cartwright whispered. "How is this possible?"

"I don't know," Sid told her, his eyes wide, frightened by the changes in the planet below. "And it looks like they have more ships."

The tactical display showed nearly two hundred ships in near-Keran space and around its moons. The ship's telescope array took images of them, as well. As with the planet's deserts earlier, both moons were being consumed by a sea of blackness, some unknown and unfathomable material that denied its secrets to human science.

"Just a suggestion," Sid told her tightly as *Nyx* sped ever closer to the planet and the warships sailing around it, "but wouldn't it be a good idea to jump out?"

"Not yet," she said, adjusting the ship's course minutely. "I want to get all the data we can. Are you picking up any signals?" On previous missions, they had always been able to contact someone on the surface.

Sid didn't answer her right away as he worked the ship's instruments. After a few precious minutes, he said, "Nothing. Not a goddamn thing."

They shared a glance, then looked back at the globe of the planet, now alien and forbidding. Cartwright's hands clenched as she fought to keep her emotions under control. She knew that there were most likely still survivors on the planet, fleeing or fighting for their lives. But during the last reconnaissance mission they had picked up *hundreds* of different transmitters, radio and laser-links. Now there was nothing but shattering silence. Survivors there might yet be, but the silence on the airwaves told how effective the Kreelans had been in hunting them down.

Nyx flew onward for another minute, then two, when half a dozen of the cruisers that were headed to intercept her were almost close enough to fire.

"Time to go, boss," Sid reminded her.

"Yeah, I guess so," Cartwright said grudgingly as she hauled the ship around in a tight chandelle turn.

Five long minutes later they reached their jump point, and *Nyx* disappeared into hyperspace.

***

Tesh-Dar stood upon the central dais of one of the arenas on this, the newest world to be claimed for the Empire. Reshaping this planet was a a reflection of the compulsion of her race to bend the universe to their will. It was not for want of more living space: the Empire was so vast that Tesh-Dar could have traveled most of her life in the swiftest of starships, and still not reached from one far frontier to the other. The Empire spanned ten thousand suns and even more planets. When there had been need of a world for a particular purpose, or in a particular place as suited the Empress, often as not the builders had simply created it. Such was the power of Her Children.

But her race lived and breathed for battle. And here on this planet, in this arena, the final battle was being fought, pathetic though it had become. A brace of her warriors, using only the weapons they had been born with, faced off against the last human survivors. They had been very adept at evading their hunters, but at last Tesh-Dar had called an end to the game. Great wheels were turning in the heart of the Empire, and this first great combat between humans and Her Children was to be brought to a final ending.

The humans before her were dirty and starving. A ten of males and half as many females were all that remained of the planet's original population. In the many matches Tesh-Dar had watched as the humans had been sacrificed to the demands of the Way of her people, she had seen many fight bravely; some had clearly cried for mercy, of which there was none; others stood with what she admired as a quiet dignity, refusing to fight, until they at last were painlessly put to death. None were tortured or forced to endure pain beyond what was experienced in battle in the arena. Tesh-Dar understood the concept of cruelty, but did not believe it applied to her people. Their Way was extraordinarily difficult, and death came all too easily. But pain was never inflicted needlessly, or as an end unto itself.

One by one, the humans fell to her warriors. But these humans, the last upon this planet, did not give up, and did not surrender. They fought to the last, and died with honor.

***

In the capital city on his home planet of Nagano, Commander Ichiro Sato ignored the veiled stares he received as he made his way along a crowded street that led to his childhood home. He wore his dress black uniform, which made him stand out even more among the dour salarymen in cheap suits and the women in colorful kimonos, eyes downcast, who streamed past him. Around his neck he wore the Terran Medal of Honor, the only one to be granted for the battle of Keran that wasn't posthumous. He hadn't known most of those who had received "The Medal," as it was often called. But his own decoration served to remind him of the one he had: Gunnery Sergeant Pablo Ruiz. Sato's recommendation to award Ruiz The Medal had been taken up-chain almost without comment, followed by Silver Stars for bravery in the face of the enemy for every man and woman of *McClaren's* Marine detachment. Ensign - now Lieutenant - Bogdanova and Senior Chief Petty Officer DeFusco also wore Silver Stars, and every single survivor of the *McClaren* had received at least a Bronze Star. They had all earned it. And more.

Walking beside him, Stephanie held an exquisitely wrapped gift. She and Sato had spent nearly an hour getting the wrapping just so. She had thought it a fun but ultimately wasteful use of time, until he explained how important the wrapping of a gift was in Nagano's culture, and that it was as important as the gift itself.

And the gift? Two fresh pineapples in a box. She had laughed at him when he had first suggested it, but he was completely serious. "Listen, I know you don't believe this," he had told her, "but this is perfect! She absolutely loves pineapple, and they're almost impossible to get on Nagano. My uncle managed to get some a few times - that's where she first tasted it - but he must have paid a fortune."

"She," of course, was his mother, whom he hadn't seen since he had left for the Terran Naval Academy. Steph had suggested some gorgeous jewelry, but he only shook his head. "She doesn't wear any." It was hard for Steph to conceive of any woman not wanting to wear jewelry, but she had let it ride and trusted Ichiro's advice. He hadn't steered her wrong yet.

A few weeks before, they had both been at the commissioning of the first of the new shipyards that were being built in Earth orbit, where the keels of a dozen new warships were being laid down in a fast-build program that would have the new ships undergoing their first space trials in three months. One of them, the heavy cruiser *Yura*, would be Ichiro's to command.

The ceremony had been held on Africa Station, which - like the other orbital transfer points - was being radically enlarged to accomodate more traffic. While most of the attention had been riveted on the massive yards and the ships that were even now beginning to take shape, Sato had spent a considerable part of the ceremony staring out at the hulk of the *Aurora*, which rode quietly at anchor in the original space dock. The Navy had decided that she would never sail again, and would eventually be broken up. Part of him would have exchanged his new heavy cruiser for the old *Aurora* in an instant; another part was horrified at the thought of ever again setting foot on her decks.

Despite the maudlin thoughts about his old ship amid the martial pomp of the commissioning ceremony for the shipyards, the gathering on Africa Station was also one of joy: to a great deal of well-wishing and cat-calling, he and Steph announced their engagement and plans to marry. After returning from Keran, they quickly came to the conclusion that they were meant for each other. With him in command of a warship and her helping the government get people behind the formation of the Confederation, their married life would be difficult, to say the least. But they were determined to make it work. They knew now that the universe was not a hospitable place, and it was an immense comfort just knowing that they had each other to love and hold onto.

They arrived at the drab apartment building and rode up the cramped elevator to the fifteenth floor. Everything here was clean, almost antiseptic in appearance. And quiet. Their footsteps echoed as they walked down the tiled hall until they reached a certain door.

Looking one last time at Steph, who only nodded, Ichiro pressed the illuminated button that would let the occupants know they had visitors.

After a brief moment, the door opened to reveal a middle-aged woman of Japanese descent, not so different in appearance from a million others in the city. Physically she was still in the prime of beauty for those of her age, her face showing few wrinkles and only faint traces of gray in her otherwise lush raven hair. But her expression and eyes were blank, her thoughts and emotions carefully concealed, a defense mechanism developed over a lifetime of emotional and physical abuse.

"Greetings, Mother," Ichiro said in Japanese, bowing his head.

For a moment, she said nothing, did nothing. She made no reaction at all. Then the veneer that had been her shield against the pain of her life, built up over decades, suddenly shattered and fell away.

In that moment, she did what no self-respecting Nagano woman, even one who had been widowed only a week before when her hated husband had died of a burst aneurysm, would ever have admitted to: she burst into tears and took her only son in her arms.

About the Author

Born in 1963, Michael Hicks grew up in the age of the Apollo program and spent his youth glued to the television watching the original Star Trek series and other science fiction movies, which continues to be a source of entertainment and inspiration. Having spent the majority of his life as a voracious reader, he has been heavily influenced by writers ranging from Robert Heinlein to Jerry Pournelle and Larry Niven, and David Weber to S.M. Stirling. Living in Maryland with his beautiful wife, two wonderful stepsons and two mischievous Siberian cats, he continues to work full-time while dreaming and writing.

Afterword

I would like to personally thank you for purchasing and reading this book. It was a labor of love for me to write over the course of four years, and I sincerely hope that you enjoyed reading it as much as I enjoyed writing it!

Please consider taking a little extra time to help others find this book by leaving feedback where you purchased it. Your opinion does truly matter, both to myself and to other readers.

If you have any questions, comments, or suggestions, please don't hesitate to contact me through my web site at www.kreelanwarrior.com.

- Michael R. Hicks

CPSIA information can be obtained at www.ICGtesting.com
Printed in the USA
BVOW041014180712

295563BV00001B/30/P